CHASING REVENGE

Don't miss any of Doc Ephraim Bates'
exciting comedic action thrillers

Chasing Black Ice
Chasing Revenge
Chasing Liberation

CHASING REVENGE

Boom!!...Killers.
SERIES BOOK #2

Doc Ephraim Bates

Golden Alley Press
Emmaus, Pennsylvania

Golden Alley Press
37 South 6th Street
Emmaus, Pennsylvania 18049

www.goldenalleypress.com

Golden Alley Press books may be purchased for educational, business, or sales promotional use. For information please contact the publisher.

Printed in the United States of America

Chasing Revenge: Boom!!...Killers. series book #2 / Doc Ephraim Bates.

This book contains an excerpt from the forthcoming book *Chasing Liberation* by Doc Ephraim Bates. This excerpt has been set for this edition only and may not reflect the final content of the forthcoming edition.

ISBN 978-0-9984429-0-7 print
ISBN 978-0-9984429-1-4 ebook

Back cover photograph of the author ©Starr Belle Photography

Cover design by Michael Sayre

10 9 8 7 6 5 4 3 2

It has been written that
"Into every life a little rain must fall,
but losing someone you love
is like a storm."

During the writing of this book,
I was saddened to have to say goodbye to my marvelous
proofreader and wonderful friend, Bill E. Payne. Bill was the
kind of guy that did not have a "best friend." If you were his
friend, you were his best friend. He did not have any sort of
pecking order or ranking system for those he loved. He gave
his utmost to everyone he cared about. Bill always looked out
for me, and now that he is gone I miss him dearly.
We all do.

So, it is with great pleasure that I dedicate
this book to Bill's memory and to all of the great people
that he affected in his amazing lifetime.

See ya 'round downtown, Bill E. Boy.

PROLOGUE

(A.K.A. WHAT YOU MISSED IN THE FIRST BOOK)

What if –

there was a discovery so great that it had the potential to stop wars and pestilence, disease and hunger?

What if –

the secret had been stolen by the best thief in the world and put on the open market for the entire planet to bid on?

And what if –

your trusted government tasked you with finding the thief and recovering the property, all the while lying to you, killing without prejudice, and preparing to abandon you as nothing more than a dead scapegoat?

Just over eighteen months ago, this was the scenario that found its way into the lives of government wetwork agents Kinley Devereaux and Harper Rowe, and United States DEA Agent Laurie Chase.

The government had sent Deveraux and Rowe to join Agent Chase in Mexico City to recover highly-classified materials that had been stolen by Tara Madison, a.k.a. Black Ice, the world's top international thief.

The trio had no idea what they had been sent to recover. They only knew that it had caused lies, deaths, and cover-ups from the highest ranks of the U.S. Government.

However, once the three had possession of the stolen merchandise, they realized what it was: an invention that could either advance mankind if used for good, or end mankind if used in the service of greed and power.

Rowe, Devereaux, and Chase knew that, for all the good the invention could someday do, they had to use it to destroy the menace of evil embodied in United States Secretary of Defense Paul Michaels.

The job got done, but the cost was immense.

A major U.S. political figure was assassinated, more lies were told, more blame was cast. In the end, the trio was scattered across the globe with Kinley Devereaux and Laurie Chase living underground and presumed dead, and Harper Rowe on the run from the country he once called home.

Still, somehow – hope survived.

Awkward

"David," she poked him. It was around 3:30 a.m.

He was a light sleeper and woke up amazingly aware and attentive.

"Can I ask you a question?" she asked.

"Can it wait till morning?" David whispered.

"We've been dating for almost three months," she continued, disregarding his request, "and I know you've told me that the second cell phone that you keep with you at all times is nothing more than a memento of a friend that you used to have, but–" and she stopped awkwardly for a moment.

"But?"

"Just not sure how comfortable I am with you having that."

David Pleasance scooched himself up in the bed that he and his girlfriend, Michelle Runkle, shared. "What?"

"Yeah, it makes me feel uncomfortable."

"My cell phone that I never use?"

"Yeah."

"I've let you check it at your leisure whenever you wanted to in the last few weeks. I'm not using it for anything. Just something that I keep on me. Kinda like that locket that you keep around your neck that reminds you of your mom."

"Yeah, I know, but–" She went silent.

"But?" David asked again.

"But other guys can't call me on my mother's locket."

"Michelle, I feel pretty confident that other guys aren't going to call me, either."

"It's just weird, is all."

"It's three-thirty in the morning, and you want to talk to me about a cell phone that I never get calls on. That's pretty stinkin' weird, too." Pleasance rolled over and away from her and pulled the covers up over his shoulder. "Get some sleep, baby. Tomorrow's a new day."

The couple stopped arguing and began to resume their slumber.

Pleasance had his back to Michelle. She reluctantly moved in behind him, assumed the spoon position, and fell asleep with her arms around him.

It may have been fifteen minutes, but then again, it could have been a few hours. She heard it first.

"David, your phone's ringing," she mumbled, half awake.

Pleasance heard it and answered it quickly. It was not his regular cell that was ringing – it was his second cell phone. The cell phone that just moments – or hours – ago Michelle had been making a fuss about. The cell phone that he said he never gets calls on.

He answered it so it would stop ringing, so Michelle would not have time to notice the difference between his regular cell phone ring and this odd new ring. To his credit, he had tried to set his second cell ringtone to one that was similar to his usual ringtone. And although it had been a long time since it last rang, he immediately recognized the difference.

Pleasance stealthily crawled out of bed.

"Kin?" he asked in a hushed yet excited whisper.

"I can assure you it's not Mother Theresa, David Pleasance."

"Yeah," Harper said. "I'm pretty sure she's dead."

2

I Need a Favor

"You able to talk?" Devereaux asked.

"Yeah, just give me a second," Harper said in a susurrated tone as he hurriedly made his way out of the bedroom, down the hall, and into the kitchen. "I'm good now."

"David Pleasance." Kinley said dryly. "Hmm, that has a nice peaceful, serene sound to it. So, what number alias is this one?"

"I don't know. I seem to change up identities about once every two to three weeks. Bounce around amongst seven or eight different ones. By the way, how did you know I was going by David Pleasance these days?"

"Same way I know that Michelle Runkle is your current house-mate. I keep tabs on you as much as I can."

"It's been eighteen months – give or take – since Mexico City. You've been spyin' on me for that long?"

"Not spying, just keeping tabs. In a way, you could say that I have been your guardian angel – only slightly more violent than your standard guardian angel. But, yeah, you definitely ain't kiddin' about moving around a lot. I've seen nomads trying to avoid a bench warrant that didn't move around as much as you do."

"Yeah, well, I guess it's a little bit easier for you, buddy. Everyone thinks you died up on that rooftop in Mexico City. I've still got people trying to track me down, and the majority of them coming from your United States Government."

"Hey, if you keep showing your face then they're going to know where you are."

"Make no mistake about it, Kin. I show my face not so that they will know where I am, but rather so I will know where they are."

"Oh, is that what your strategy is?"

"Precisely."

"That worries me."

"What? My strategy?"

"No. The fact that I agree with your technique. By the way, nice job on tidying up those last few loose ends from the situation in Mexico City. You saved me from having to take care of it."

"Think nothing of it," Harper tiptoed around the kitchen. "So, if you know where I am, as well as who I am, are you in Johannesburg, too?"

"I was up until Christmas Eve. I, too, have been keeping myself busy. Ya know what they say about idle hands and all that. I have been doing jobs here and there for whoever wants to bankroll me for their particular cause at that particular time."

"Is that working out all right for ya?"

"Eh, it keeps me in pop tarts and Underoos. Nothing spectacular. I see that you are still doing the occasional job yourself. Last week I saw you walk into a therapist's office there in Johannesburg, and then three hours after you walked back out of there I'm hearing on the radio that – lo and behold – someone in said therapist's office suddenly dropped dead of a massive heart attack. You haven't missed a beat since Mexico City."

"Missed? No. However, when it comes to tidying up the loose ends from Mexico City, there is one beat that I did miss," Harper admitted.

"You referring to Chase?"

"I am referring to Chase. Why? Did I miss something else?"

"Not that I'm aware of, but if ya did, it won't segue into what I was calling you about nearly as nice."

"Oh," Rowe said in disappointment, "you didn't call just to catch up?"

"Afraid not. Sorry."

"You say with all the sincerity of Dick Cheney reloading his hunting rifle."

"So – about that," Devereaux went on, "you couldn't find Chase to tidy her up, but I did."

"What? You killed Laurie Chase?"

"I did not say that I killed her. I am just saying that she is one of the reasons that I was calling you. As it turns out, she is the secondary reason I called."

"If she's secondary then what is the primary reason you've reached out to me?"

Devereaux paused, took a deep breath, and then said, "Um, I kinda, sorta–"

"Spit it out, stammering studly."

"I need a favor."

DEVEREAUX'S QUANDARY

Harper Rowe thought he heard some movement coming from his bedroom. Moving the phone away from his ear, he took a long, intent listen. He heard nothing. Still, he waited a bit longer until he heard Kinley's voice rattle through the cell phone.

"Still there, Harp?"

Satisfied that the coast was clear and that Michelle was still soundly asleep, Harper put the phone back up to his ear. "Still here. You were saying?"

"Ya know how sometimes you pour too much milk on your Raisin Bran, and then the flakes get unenjoyably soggy, and you wish you could un-pour some of that milk?"

"Eerily so, yes. Where ya goin' with this, Kin?"

"Like I said, I need a favor. It's a pretty big favor."

"How big?"

"Let's just say that this favor is going to do for favors what King Kong did for gorillas."

"Ah geez," Harper said in exasperation, "how much milk did you pour this time, Dev?"

"This is something that I am relatively sure I couldn't ask of anyone else I know, or, for that matter, anyone else that has ever existed in the history of man."

"Spill it, milkman."

"I need you to get to JNB. You have a 5 a.m. flight to London. There's a tic–"

"Judas Priest, dude. That's less than an hour and a half from now."

"It's okay. You don't need to pack. In fact, it's probably best if you don't," Devereaux said matter-of-factly.

"You really know–"

"Like I was saying," Kinley continued, "there's a ticket waiting for you at the counter under the name of 'David Pleasance'. The 5 a.m. direct to London. Keep your head down from the security cameras in there. Once you land in London, you'll deplane, and there will be someone there waiting for you. They'll have one of those VIP signs with your name on it – well, not your name, but David Pleasance's name – and they will usher you to a private jet that will fly you at Mach 4 to Atlanta, Georgia."

"Atlanta? For real?" Harper asked. "Geez, Kin, I can't help but wonder if you can actually hear me furrowing my brow on my end of the phone here. What is this favor you're getting ready to ask of me, chief?"

"I need you to come to Atlanta and get arrested."

Harper was silent. He was not even breathing heavily.

"Harp?"

"Shh. I need you to be quiet while I scroll through my Rolodex of the drastically inane to be sure there isn't someone else you can ask to do this 'favor' you want done."

"Well, while you're doing that, I guess this is probably as good a time as any to add the addendum that I need you to not break any laws in the process."

"Okay. Just okay," Harper whispered harshly, now completely irritated. "I'm pretty sure this is the part where I totally turn off my thought process and just let you tell me exactly what's going on here, Kinley. I swear on Oral Roberts' grave that if I didn't have to keep my voice down to keep my girlfriend from waking up and having me committed for still listening to your insanity, I'd be yelling the wax right out the other side of your ear."

"Remember the part of our conversation when I told you that I was doing jobs 'here and there'? And the part when I told you that I was in Johannesburg until a week ago?"

"Rings a bell, yes."

"I left Johannesburg to do a job just outside of Atlanta. Two nights ago I was doing just that: I was set up in the sixth floor of a downtown building, locked and loaded."

"So what went wrong?"

"I pulled the trigger and hit my target. Bang!!...assassin, baby. Done and done."

"And then someone started up the fan and took a crap?" Harper asked.

"Pretty much. I was getting ready to recoil my rifle, pack up, and hit the pavement, but I got spooked. Something made a ruckus behind me, and caused my normal steady self to lurch, which in turn sent my gun up against the side of the window, out of my hands, and down to the street below. What's even worse? When it landed, it fired again right into someone's car and set its stupid alarm off."

"Oh no."

"Yeah, that's pretty much what I said except that it started with a 'Sh' and ended with an 'it', and then I ran like a man on fire down to street level."

"Hang on a second, Kin. I made myself some tea to help wake me up. It's boiling and I need both hands to deal with this. Can't put you on speaker phone because, well, it's almost 4 a.m. here. Naturally, I don't want to miss any of this riveting story, so just hang tight."

Harper set the phone down, grabbed the old-fashioned tea kettle before it began to whistle, put a teabag in a cup, poured water over it, picked up the phone, and sat down on one of the stools that

Michelle had in her kitchen.

"Okay. I'm back."

"So I hit the sidewalk running, but I was too late. A crowd had already formed and the sirens of incoming cop cars told me it was time to wait and hide."

"Was your car close?"

"Yeah, so I sneaked away from the scene, got in my car, slid down in the seat and waited to see which cop from which precinct picked up my weapon and hauled it off."

"Well, it's nice to know that you're not above such second-grade tactics like slinking down in the seat of a car to hide from the cops."

"Well, dude. I saw what I needed to see."

"I'm sure ya did," Harper smiled as he took a sip from his cup of tea. "I'm also relatively sure that – reading in between the lines – I can see where my arrest comes into play – without breaking the law."

"You never let me down, kid."

"It's like that song says – I can get the punishment, but I just don't get to do the sin."

Devereaux let out a relieved chuckle. "I'll see you when that jet lands in about 17 hours."

"It'll be New Year's Eve. Don't think we'll have too much trouble getting me arrested."

SAYING GOODBYE

Harper walked back into the bedroom. He gently grabbed Michelle Runkle's shoulder and shook it.

"Hey, girlie."

"What?" she answered grumpily, without lifting her head from the pillow.

"I gotta go."

"Whatever," Michelle mumbled into her pillow.

"I mean, I'm going for good. I won't be back."

"Good, go," she said without rolling over.

"I'm going to make a water balloon and bust it over your head. You good with that? And then I'm going to steal all your silverware."

"Sounds good," Michelle said before drifting back to sleep.

And that was when Harper realized that he had been blessed with the one gift that all men pray for: an easy escape from a relationship.

He let go of Michelle's shoulder, went into the bathroom to brush his teeth, then collected the four things he had entered the relationship with – his wallet and the contents within, his passport, and two cell phones – and walked quietly out the front door.

He looked both ways before crossing the street, pulled up the collar on his shirt and headed off into the night.

Flight Plans

Harper hated to fly.

Not so much for the air travel, or the way it made his ears pop like a bag of microwavable popcorn when a plane hit 20,000 feet, but mostly because of the complete idiots that the TSA put in charge of airport security.

He made his way through the cattle chute just like everyone else.

"Take off your shoes and place them in the basket, sir," he was instructed.

"No. I don't think so."

"Sir," the TSA agent said sternly, "take your shoes off and place them in the basket."

"What? No Please?"

"Sir–"

"Aw, c'mon, dude, I really don't want to bend over like that. Especially when the guy behind me looks a little light in his own loafers. Maybe you should ask him to take *his* shoes off to make sure that he's actually in them."

"Please step out of line, sir."

"Geez, boss, can't you just wand me or something?"

The ATF officer grabbed Harper and pulled him out of the line.

"I'm being depressed," Rowe yelled. "Someone take a picture.

I'm being depressed." He did not resist the officer and went willingly out of the line.

"Put your hands up against the wall, sir," the ATF agent said as he relieved Harper of his two cell phones.

"Since we're getting ready to become a little too familiar with one another, by all means, call me David."

Rowe put his hands up against the wall. Looking to his right to see the ATF office, he noticed a lot of movement behind its half-opened blinds.

"Spread your legs, sir."

"Hey, pal, I'm gonna do you a favor–"

"I said spread your legs, sir!" The officer kicked Harper in the right ankle, causing his legs to shoot out.

The door of the ATF office opened up and an anonymous man stuck his head out. "Get that man back in line and put him on the plane."

"But, sir," the officer objected.

"Just do what you're told," Harper whispered under his breath.

"Just do what you're told, agent. Put him back in line and get him on the stupid plane."

Harper straightened himself up against the wall, turned to the ATF agent and said, "It's okay. I'm fine."

"I don't like it, but orders are orders. Get back in line."

"If I didn't respect what you do so much, I swear to Pete Moss, I'd punch you right in the face. So, instead," and Harper kicked the man in his shins. "I'm gonna go get back in line now."

Harper grabbed his two cell phones off the nearby table and made his way back to the line. Just then one of his cell phones rang.

He answered with a cheerful, "Hey, buddy, I knew you'd be calling."

"You stupid jerk! Do you know how many favors I had to call in for you just now?"

"I'm gonna go out on a limb and say 'A lot.' How did I do?"

"I knew getting back together with you was a stupid, stupid idea."

"Yeah, probably," Harper agreed, "but who's gonna help you get your gun back?" With that, he disconnected the call and got on the plane.

Packing Light

Just under twelve hours.

That is how long the flight from Johannesburg to London was.

At least Kinley was nice enough to buy Harper a first class ticket. For the first three hours of the flight he got exquisitely wasted on free champagne, talked it up with the flight staff and his fellow passengers as only he could, and commenced to fall asleep in the big comfortable seat he had been afforded for the flight. As he drifted pleasantly into unconsciousness he thought to himself how broken and turbulent the last year and a half of his life had been, and how peaceful he now felt as he winged his way to meet up with his best friend once again.

"Mr. Pleasance," the flight attendant said to him softly.

"Yeah," Harper said as he opened his eyes.

"We'll be landing at Heathrow in just a few minutes. I will need for you to put your seat in the upright position before we do."

"Oh," he said, somewhat disappointed. "I thought that was just for the coach people."

"Afraid not," she laughed.

"What time is it? Here in London."

"It's currently 2:37 p.m. GMT."

"Wow." Harper leaned over and looked out his window to see London's bright blue winter sky. He loved London and was sorry that he was just passing through this time. He looked down at the beautiful city as the plane descended. "That is some view," he said to no one in particular. Then, as requested, he moved his seat into the upright position to prepare for landing.

"Do you have someone there to get him as soon as he gets off the plane?"

"Yes, Kinley," Rob Perry said, a bit bothered and annoyed. "For the love of God, I gave the two of you safe haven after Mexico City last year, didn't I? I'm pretty sure I can do this."

"Yeah, but that was then and this is now. What have you done for me lately, chief?"

"This. I'm doing this for you right now. I got a guy at Heathrow ready to get him once he gets off the plane. He'll drive him to the jet that I have fueled and ready to go. That will fly him to you just outside of Hartsfield. What more do you want?"

"Who's your guy at Heathrow?"

"His name is Brian Holbrook. I have him on a two-way right now. Do you want me to hold my other phone up to this one so you can talk to him directly?"

"That seems unnecessary," Kinley said, seemingly oblivious to Rob Perry's irritation. "Your guy, Holbrook, he'll let you know when he's got Harper in the car and on his way to the jet, yes?"

"He has orders to check in once he has Harper in the car and on the way to the jet. Geez, Kinley, will you just calm down and let me do what you hired me to do? I mean, he's one guy getting off a plane and into a car. How much damage can he do?"

"Believe me, the guy is Clouseau-like with the damage he can do – given the chance."

The plane had been at a complete stop for almost a minute and a half when permission was given for its passengers to unbuckle and deplane. The flight attendant next to Harper's seat gestured for him to stand up and move toward the exit. It reminded the assassin of when he sat in a pew at the church he often attended and was silently instructed to go forward and take part in the communion ceremony.

Harper stood up and checked his pockets for the contents with which he boarded the plane.

Two cell phones. Check.

Passport. Check.

Wallet. Check.

Feeling confident that he had everything, Harper moved from his seat, up the aisle, and toward the designated exit.

"Happy New Year, Mr. Pleasance," the flight attendant said as Harper left the plane.

"You, too," Harper smiled back pleasantly at the woman.

Harper hated to fly, and walking down the exit tunnel from the plane was just another reason why. There were always thirty to forty people waiting to greet those that were walking out of the gate, but there was never anyone there to meet ol' Harper Rowe.

Or whoever he was when he got off a plane.

Just get herded like the rest of the cattle through customs, a quick check of my passport, and then out ya go, he thought.

For Harper, it was a lonely walk into an even bigger reminder that he was, truly, on his own. So when he walked out of the customs gate and into the open causeway of the airport and saw a strapping young man standing there with a sign with the name of David Pleasance on it, he smiled.

"I'm David Pleasance."

"Good afternoon, Mr. Pleasance. I'm Brian Holbrook. I have a car outside waiting for you once we get your luggage."

"Great news, Mr. Holbrook. I'm packing light today. Everything that I have is just what I have on me."

"Good enough, Mr. Pleasance. Let's get to the car then. Keep your head down."

Harper was quick to notice the complete lack of a British accent in Holbrook's speech. "You're an American; sounds like you have spent most of your formative years in northeastern Maryland."

"Yeah," Brian laughed, "how did you know that?"

"Ah, just a party trick I learned in college."

"I went to college. Never learned any tricks like that. Hey, we're this way, Mr. Pleasance." The lanky driver moved quickly through the crowd of Heathrow's main thoroughfare to a small hallway off to the right.

"I'm with you, Mr. Holbrook," Harper said, looking around at the airport's busy environment.

"Man, I have to tell you, I really love Heathrow. It's like they took the whole of London – the locals, the tourists, the food, the pace, the sights – as if someone took the entire city and folded it up nicely and neatly to put right into your pocket, ya know?"

"Just so you know, Mr. Pleasance, if your pockets are that big then I'm pretty sure that you're not going to fit in the car that I have outside for you."

Harper laughed. "So, how long from here to our destination?"

The duo walked through a door that was clearly marked "No Exit" and out into the bright London afternoon.

"This time of day on New Year's Eve afternoon, eh, it might take us a bit longer than normal. About forty-five minutes, give or take. No worries, though. The back of the car is stocked with a full bar, Blu-ray player, onboard computer with roaming Wi-Fi, and full cellular capability so you can talk to anyone that's anywhere on the planet – provided they have cellular service, as well."

"Can I sit up front and talk to you?"

Brian stopped short. "I'm sorry? What?"

"I don't really care about the rest of that stuff, man. I'm more of a people person. I can do the rest of that stuff whenever I want to. I'd much rather sit up front and take in the town, chat it up with you for a bit."

"Believe me, Mr. Pleasance, I'd love nothing more, but my insurance doesn't allow for me to carry people up front when I'm doing this sort of driving."

"Your insurance? Were you planning on having an accident or something on the way to our destination?"

"I find that accidents are rarely planned, Mr. Pleasance."

"Good point, my good man."

"This is us," Mr. Holbrook said as the two approached a black stretch limousine. Brian was quick to open the passenger's side back door. "Watch your head," he said as Harper climbed into the back seat. Holbrook shut the door to the expensive ride and made his way around to the driver's side and got in.

"Help yourself to whatever you want back there. You want me to put the privacy divider up?"

"Yeah, for now. I have to make a phone call, and I'm pretty sure that 93% of it is going to be about illegal things, so I think for your own best interest you should put the divider up. But, hey, before you do," and Harper made sure he had Brian's attention, "if I come banging on it like I'm the last floating survivor trying to get into Noah's Ark, you'll put it back down, right?"

"Absolutely, sir."

"Put 'er up then, Cap'n. I'll talk to you in ten."

As Holbrook put up the privacy divider, Harper pulled out the appropriate cell phone and dialed Kinley.

It rang twice before Kinley picked up.

"You in the car, Harper?"

"Alive and ridin'," Rowe replied.

"Could you do me a favor and just not give the driver a hard time, okay?"

"Hey, Kin, I wouldn't have given those Johannesburg airport jerkoffs a hard time if they hadn't started with me, okay? I mean, I was more than happy to stand in line, go through airport security, and get on the plane. Nevertheless, *mon frère*, they felt the need to make an example out of me – so I made an example out of them."

"Why?"

"I wanted to get one for the little guy. The guy that never has anyone stand up for him and say 'Enough is enough.' And that is what I did."

"Since when did you decide to give a crap about the little guy?"

"Since I was pulled out of line in the Johannesburg airport."

Knowing he was getting nowhere with this particular conversation, Kinley moved on to a more pertinent topic. "You on your way to the jet?"

"That I am."

"That guy bein' good to ya?"

"Best guy in the business, Kin. You're lucky I'm talking to you and not in the front seat talking to him."

"Yeah, I know. He was given specific instructions to not let that happen."

"Then be sure to leave him a big gratuity on the 'Let's rope Harper into something completely insane' tab."

"Do me a favor, Harp, will ya?"

"What's that?"

"Please shut your pie hole for the next minute and a half. Can we agree that you'll do that for me? Please?"

Harper breathed in deeply through his nostrils and exhaled heavily out of his mouth. He shook his head from side to side and then said, "What can I do for you, my buddy?"

"Enjoy your ride to the jet, get out of the car and onto the jet, ride the jet to Atlanta, and let me greet you as you deplane – before you do something really, really stupid again. Can you do that for me?"

"Well, since your plan is to get me arrested in the Deep South on New Year's Eve – of course, I'll behave. Why wouldn't I?"

And in the most serious of tones, Kinley Devereaux said, "You know I need you on this."

"You had me at 'I need you to come to Atlanta and get arrested.' Ya really did."

"Against my better judgment," Kinley laughed, "I'll see you in a few hours – in Atlanta."

LAURIE CHASE THESE DAYS

She knew she was a pawn.

Not all along, mind you, but once she met Kinley Devereaux and Harper Rowe, she knew that she had been played the whole time.

Laurie Chase had always been "God and Country" through and through. She had seen what the drug scene had done to her town and to her childhood and high school friends, so she took it upon herself to do something about the damage that had been done to them.

She joined the DEA to make a difference. She used to believe she could. She was in Mexico City with her DEA team to get one of the biggest drug dealers in the world, Tito del Fuento.

Sadly, it was he that got them. Not counting Laurie Chase, he got them all.

Before she could do anything about it, she had been given a new assignment by the U.S. Government, and that was to help two random hit men by the name of Kinley Devereaux and Harper Rowe find a thief that had stolen some crucial government documents. While on this mission, her eyes had been opened to what powerful men would do to get even more power.

She hated the duo of Kinley and Harper while she had to work with them. Then she grew to love them.

It's true what they say: the truth really does set you free. Kinley and Harper had redirected her attention for a bit, but once she had shaken herself free of everything, it was time to get back to work – and work was in Rio de Janeiro.

Rio – the home base of Tito del Fuento, Laurie Chase's enemy. So she went there and she watched him. Learned his movements. Learned his habits. Learned that when he left the country, whether it was business or pleasure, he took about one-third of his men with him.

Tito stays home – three hundred men to deal with. Tito goes on vacation, he travels light – one hundred men or less.

Why? Because Tito del Fuento was respected. Whoever it was that invited Tito to wherever it was that he was being invited to, he always brought his best guys, and he expected his host to have their best guys, as well.

Chase knew that trying to get Tito while he was on the move was not what she wanted to do. Besides, she didn't just want to get Tito del Fuento and his men. She wanted to bring down the entire show: the compounds, the fields, the workers, everything.

It was no secret that Colombia and Peru had a pretty good stranglehold on drug trafficking in South America, but Tito was getting ready to change that. He had struck up a deal with some businessmen in Dresden, Germany – the kind of businessmen that dealt in narcotics and weapons rather than stocks and bonds – and together they had put together a pretty good package that was going to bring a nice chunk of the European drug trade to Brazil. A big enough chunk to release Colombia and Peru's tight grasp on the neck of the whole dirty market, and all the while get del Fuento's cartel up there with the likes of the Medellin and the Knights Templar.

Tito and his best men would be gone for 48 hours on their trip to Dresden. Over the last eighteen months, this brigade had left the compound exactly three times, and each time Laurie had stealthily made her way onto the premises to learn all that she could in order to formulate a plan to bring del Fuento's empire to ruins. This particular trip that was taking Tito and his soldiers out of town would give Laurie the time she needed to start setting her plan in motion. The plan that would bring Tito del Fuento and his drug empire to the ground. The plan that would avenge the DEA team that he had murdered eighteen months ago. The plan that would bring revenge to Laurie Chase.

Still, she knew she was going to need help. She also knew she had a cell phone that Kinley Devereaux had given her some eighteen months ago.

"Thanks for stickin' with us through all of this," he had told her. "If ya ever need me or Harp – you can reach us on this. Don't ever let it out of your sight. If you do then don't ever call us on it."

She had never, ever let the phone out of her sight. Knowing full well that she had upheld this condition, Laurie had reached out to Kinley some two weeks ago, and Kinley, as promised, had reached back.

Soon she would be reunited with the duo she knew she could trust as far as she could throw them. Nevertheless, Kinley and Harper were the only two people in the world that Laurie Chase could call friends.

Soon it would be killing time for Laurie Chase.

THAT'S JUST CROOL

It had been a year and a half since Agent Jeb Crool had been handed the assignment of trying to find out who was behind the assassination of the former U.S. Secretary of Defense, Paul Michaels.

In his head, Jeb knew who it was. He just wanted to find the proof necessary to make it stand up in any court across the land. Checking all of the global imagery – both near and far – there seemed to be a dozen men that had their guns trained on Paul Michaels and the man he was speaking to when he got shot that day.

All of these wanna-be assassins had been rounded up – at least the ones that had survived. Most of them had turned themselves in, actually, just to get out of the way of the investigation. And none of them had fired a round that matched the trajectory of the bullet that had been the kill shot of Crool's former boss.

In fact, most of them had fessed up that Secretary of Defense Michaels had asked them there in the first place to kill the man with whom Michaels was going to be talking.

Jeb had looked over and over and over the evidence from the rooftops in Mexico City, the last place that Kinley Devereaux, Harper Rowe, and Laurie Chase had been – as best as he had known. The bodies had been gone over time and time again with a fine toothed comb. He was convinced that Kinley Devereaux and Laurie Chase were dead.

Having ruled them out, he moved the scope of his investigation increasingly broader. In the end, every last piece of evidence that he came up with led him right back to the same person: Harper Rowe.

But was Harper Rowe the victim or the vigilante?

And exactly what was it that the Secretary of Defense had never come clean to Jeb about in all of this? Most days, Crool knew he was chasing the right man. He just had no idea why.

Harper Rowe. He showed his face. He caused a scene. He lit a fuse that would never go off, but caused a global uproar.

Jeb had chased him, but this morning he was tired and not wanting any more of it. That was when his right-hand man, David Baldwin, burst into his office.

"Jeb! We are tracking him."

"Rowe?"

"Yes. We had a small hint of facial recognition in Johannesburg – twenty-four percent positive, and then we had another hit of facial recognition – forty percent positive, just a few minutes ago at Heathrow. We think he left the airport with someone and got into a car. A limo, sir. The time matches up for a flight that left Tambo Airport about 12 hours ago. Do you want me to get the data to your computer?"

For the first time in several months, Crool smiled.

"No. Don't send anything. Don't send anyone. That's what he wants, and I am getting way too tired of being this jock's dance partner. Do we have satellite imagery on him?"

"It's not precise as of right now, sir, but within the minute we expect to have him looped in."

"Good. Let's just watch him for a bit. I'm tired of him dictating our every move. Let's see where he goes and why he's going there.

I want to give him just enough rope to hang himself and then we will we go in and cut down his dead body."

"Sir?"

Jeb Crool looked up sleepily from his desk. "Did I stutter or stammer? Or did you just want to see your pay grade cut in half?"

"Got it, sir."

Best Friends Reunite at an Airport

She knew she was late, so she walked hurriedly through the entrance of the Václav Havel Airport. Her tardiness couldn't have been helped; she had to make sure she was not followed. Plus, the snow-covered streets out of Prague had made the normally 30-minute trek treacherous and very, very slow.

Even though she had been careful to not be followed, she still found herself still looking over her shoulder for most of the shuttle ride from her car to the terminal. Once inside the bustling airport, she pulled down the snow-dusted hood on her parka and shook her long brown hair free of the cumbersome collar. She kept her head down and did her best to blend into the bustling crowd as she made her way to the electronic board marked *příjezdy* to see if her friend's plane had, indeed, arrived on time. It had.

The woman pulled her cell phone out of her coat pocket and fumbled with it nervously before she hit the #2 speed dial. After just one ring on the other end she heard a familiar voice answer, "Hey, Eliska, where are you?"

"At front of airport," she said in very broken English, her distinct Czech accent coming through. "Sorry I am late. Did you find luggage bay?"

"I rarely, if ever, travel with luggage. It's too much of a pain in the *kád'*."

Eliska laughed nervously. "I understand."

"Hey, I see you. Stay right where you are. I'm about twenty-five meters from you."

Eliska began to look around excitedly.

"I'm to your left."

She looked to her left and immediately spotted her best friend. A few quick steps by both parties bridged the gap and brought them into a firm embrace.

"Oh, girlie, it is so good to see you, Eliska."

"Is good to see you, too."

She broke the embrace suddenly. "Oh, Ellie," which is what she usually called her best friend, Eliska Lukasik, since they had met five years ago, "you're shaking something awful. What is going on? And don't tell me that you are excited to see me. You called me and said it was urgent so I got on the first flight I could get out of Milan."

"You have good flight, yes?"

"Yes, Ellie, I had a good flight," she said somewhat frustrated. "Please tell me why you had me fly here, *dítě*."

Eliska began looking around nervously as the airport crowd hurried around her. "Need to go. We will catch shuttle to my car, and I tell you then. Too many people here," Ellie said. She glanced around once more before she turned toward the exit.

"Hey," she said as she grabbed her friend's arm and stopped her.

"Yes?" The look on her face was one part surprise and one part fear.

"It's going to be okay. Okay? I'm here now, and whatever this is about, we'll figure it out and get it right. I won't let anyone hurt you."

"Yes. Is why I called you." Ellie grabbed her hand.

"Hey, before we leave let me go to an ATM in the arrival hall so that I can get some Czech crowns. The airport *bureau de change* outlets here are a rip."

"I understand. Is good that you remember these things."

Just South of Atlanta

Harper was in the middle of his umpteenth fascinating dream of Minnie Driver when a familiar hand shook him awake. "Harp, it's never gonna happen. Time to wake up." Kinley grabbed his friend's left wrist.

Harper came up quickly out of his dream, felt held down, and started kicking and flailing about.

"Easy! Easy, Silver," Kinley laughed, cowering a bit.

"Holy crap!" exclaimed a confused Harper as he came to his senses and eyed his friend's new look. Kinley had let his typically short hair grow to the point that it now covered the collar on his button-down shirt. And his normal five o'clock shadow looked more like midnight, as it was a good six inches long. "Did you join a cult or something?"

Without answering, Kinley ratcheted his buddy up out of his seat and said, "Welcome home, dude. Ready to get to work?"

"I thought I was supposed to meet you on the ground. How'd you get on the plane?"

"Number one, it's a jet. And numbers two, three, and four, I paid for the jet. I paid for the crew. I get to board the jet when it lands. Anything else?"

"You have about one minute and forty-two seconds to get me to a Waffle House and get some food into me, or else I'm going to beat your face into a pulp."

"You're in luck. We're in Atlanta, home of the Waffle Houses – Huts – things." And when Kinley looked at his friend for some approval, he realized that Harper was already halfway asleep again. "I'll get us a cab."

A short time later Kinley repeated the same routine. "Harp," Kinley slapped his friend's face lightly. "Wake up, captain. We're here at the hotel."

"I'm all right, already. Judas Priest!"

Kinley recoiled and stood upright outside of the car. "Ya need some help getting up outta there?"

Harper grabbed the back of the seat in front of him and muttered, "I got this – I think." He pulled himself up out of the cab and onto his feet. "Are we here? Is this where I'm supposed to be? I kinda wanna breathe – can I?"

"Yeah, you're here," Kinley laughed. He patted his buddy on the back and leaned into the car. He handed the driver an extra hundred, gave him a wink and a smile, and as the cab pulled away Devereaux returned his attention to Harper. "You're right where you need to be, buddy. Just hang with me for about another three minutes, and you can crash for a few hours."

Harper shook his head from side to side trying to get back to a good cognitive state. "Where am I? This time yesterday I was – crap. Too tired to remember."

Kinley looked his friend up and down. "Well, give the old man a hug, will ya?"

"I don't feel like I have the strength to even hug my grandma right now."

"It's just jet lag, babe. I'll get you where you need to be, and then we can talk about our plans for tonight. You're still excited about getting arrested, right?"

"I will ask you this, and then I am going to go to sleep: how arrested do you need me to get? I am a wanted man, ya know. Even here in the Deep South I'm sure it won't take them too long to figure that out."

Kinley smiled. "It's all part of the plan. No need to worry, buddy, this will go off without a hitch." Devereaux took his partner up to the room he had already secured.

Three hours later Harper opened his eyes to a beautifully blurry luxury suite. He shook the cobwebs out of his head and rubbed his eyes sleepily. Kinley was across the room watching a college bowl game on the room's television.

"Who's winnin'?"

"Nobody. Tied up at 72 in the 6th overtime. Oddly enough, when the game ended in regulation the score was 24 to 24. Now it's like watching a tennis match – back and forth, back and forth, back and forth."

"What bowl game is this?"

"Does it matter? It's the John Smackle Faded Dungaree Bowl for all I know. Just something to watch until you finished off your beauty sleep."

"What time is it?" Harper asked as he pulled back the covers and sat upright on the side of the bed.

"It's 6:30, local time."

"Got anything to eat in this place? I'm kinda hungry."

"There's a Waffle House just ten minutes away," Kinley smiled.

Harper's eyes got big as he said, "That's what I like about you, Kin. You know just how to treat a dame."

"Indeed, and by the way, for the time being I'm ATF Agent Jeff Samples and you are Melvin Powell from Monroe, Louisiana." Kinley reached into his pants pocket, retrieved a driver's license and flipped it to Harper.

Harp snagged it out of the air with two fingers and looked it over. "Hmm, Monroe, Louisiana. Geez, where'd you get this picture from. I look like I'm 112 in this thing."

"Not important. Let's go get some grub and I'll tell you about my plan for tonight."

Gone Again

"What do you mean you lost him?" Crool screamed at Agent David Baldwin. "How do you lose an entire man?"

"We tracked him to an airfield just west of London. He got on a jet and disappeared."

"So what you're telling me is that you not only lost an entire man, but you lost an entire jet, too? I'll admit the guy is good, but he's not freakin' Houdini. We've got satellites. We've got radar. We've got the best technology that money can buy. So how is it that you lost an entire jet, Agent Baldwin?"

"Whoever was flying knew exactly how to fly to avoid being picked up by radar. We tracked them using satellite imagery flying out over the Atlantic, but they flew out of range for the satellite we were using, and before we could pick them up again we had lost them in regular air traffic."

"I'm guessing it's too much to hope that they submitted a flight plan, huh?"

"Nothing. I'm guessing they found the flight path of a commercial airliner and followed that as far as they could until they had to break out of it to get to their destination, making it virtually impossible for us to find them once they flew back into range of another satellite."

"What you're saying is that they flew low enough to avoid radar, and then they flew underneath another airplane to avoid being picked up by satellite?"

"Yes. They probably flew under more than one plane – bounced around a bit – but stayed close enough in line with any other aircraft to avoid being picked up by a satellite."

"Unbelievable," Jeb mumbled as he shook his head back and forth. "So you say that he left London and headed over the Atlantic?"

"Yes sir."

"He's coming back home."

"Sir?"

"Rowe. He's headed back to the States."

"Yeah, but he hasn't set foot on American soil since the Secretary was assassinated, and that's going on two years now."

"Well, no kidding, Agent Baldwin, but you can be good and sure that he isn't being this careful just to go get a good hotel rate in Tijuana."

"Why do you think he's coming back here?"

"How should I know?" Crool asked in a voice about an octave higher than his normal pitch. "He didn't exactly phone ahead his itinerary to me. But it's like they say, 'Every good criminal returns to the scene of his crime.' Maybe this is his return."

"Okay," Baldwin concurred, "well, what do you want us to do?"

"As far as I'm concerned, Rowe is here in the States, and until further notice that is exactly how we are going to act. Get his picture out to every bus station, train station, airport, post office, every news outlet, every gas station and police station in the country. He may be getting in here without too much fanfare, but we're going to make it harder than old molasses for him to get back out."

"And just like molasses it's going to be pretty sweet when we catch him," Baldwin said, trying to be funny.

Jeb looked at him blankly and said, "Just do what I told ya to do, and we'll be fine."

The Scene at the Restaurant

"What are you getting?" Harper asked as he looked over the laminated Waffle House menu. "It all looks so greasy and unhealthy. I want to order the entire menu."

"I was thinking about getting the sausage gravy and biscuits with some toast and OJ with a side order of scrapple and grits."

A bedraggled-looking waitress meandered her way up to the side of their booth. Her brown hair was pulled back into a bun to reveal a rather attractive face, but the crow's feet around her eyes played traitor to her youthful age of 28 years. "Happy New Year's Eve, gentlemen," she said, sounding like she had been awake since Christmas. "My name is Stacy, and I will be taking good care of you this evening. What can I get you to drink?"

"Orange juice," replied Kinley.

"Some unsweetened tea for me, sugar," Harper smiled.

"Orange juice and unsweetened tea," she confirmed without looking up from her order pad. "I'll have that right out for you in just a minute."

As she walked away from them Harper put his menu down on the table. "So what gives, Bill Gates? I don't hear from you for a year and a half, and then all of a sudden you call me because you dropped a rifle? What's so special about that gun anyway?"

"It's not the gun so much. It's the scope. I mean, heck, I use a different rifle for almost every job just so one job can never be linked with another, forensics being what it is these days."

"Okay, so what's so special about the scope you used for this gun as opposed to – let's say – a scope you used two weeks ago?"

"This scope was special. Not only did it have night vision, but it also had infrared. I had a weapons engineer from Seoul, South Korea make it for me. I paid seven grand for that thing."

"I can see why. With a scope like that you could–" Harper became immediately silent as he saw Stacy coming back to the table with their drink orders.

"Orange juice for you – and unsweetened tea for you, sugar," she smiled at Harper as she set the drinks down on the table. "And are we ready to order?"

 Kin looked across the table at Harper, "Are we?"

"Yes. Yes, we are. I will have the ham and cheese omelet with onions and green peppers and a side of the warm cinnamon apples."

"And for you, sir?"

"The sausage gravy and biscuits with some toast and OJ along with a side of scrapple and grits."

"All right, guys, I'll get that right up for y'all. Should be about twenty minutes."

As soon as she walked away, Harper picked right back up where he had left off. "–pick up targets at night even if they were indoors. What's the maximum thickness a wall can be, and this thing still accurately detect a target?"

"A standard wall: siding, brick, sheetrock and studs. If my target's inside some kind of bunker or stone building or cinder block structure then it's not too terribly accurate. Fortunately, here lately my targets have been in your standard structures. Best investment I ever made. Now it's sitting inside of police evidence locker at the APD Zone 5."

"APD Zone 5?"

"Stands for Atlanta Police Department Zone 5."

"Right on. Okay, so, what's the plan, Stan?"

"Well," Kinley took a second to look around and be sure that no one was eavesdropping before he continued in a hushed tone, "it's New Year's Eve, and the good law enforcement officers of this city – to protect those in and around this town – have sobriety checkpoints set up to nab any and all drunk drivers that may think it's a good idea to be drinkin' it up and then going for a little scooch."

"Right. Seems like a good idea."

"Well, I did some quick homework to find out which sobriety checkpoints correlate with which precinct houses. So I figured out where I would need you to get arrested so that you would go to APD Zone 5."

"So I go to the check point, the cop thinks I'm drunk – even though I'm not – I get taken back to Atlanta Police Department Zone 5, and then what? How am I supposed to get to the evidence locker to get your gun? And remind me again how I'm supposed to get nabbed at the checkpoint for drunkards when I'm not drunk?"

"Don't worry. I've got that and everything else taken care of."

Harper took a sip of his drink, set it back down on the table, and said, "You having taken care of things makes me worry like a hooker on judgment day."

"Never underestimate a man when he's been separated from his ridiculously expensive scope."

"Well, after young Stacy brings our grub back I'll expect you to fill me in on just how much you really do have this taken care of."

Stacy returned with their food. As they ate, they talked about various and sundry things until Kinley said it was time to discuss the night's plan.

"Before I forget, let me give you this, " and from his front shirt pocket Kinley produced a piece of hard white plastic about the size of the end of a cotton swab.

"Ah–" Harper said as he took it from him, "a com."

"Got that right, a com. I'm going to be in your ear the whole time. We have a small window to work with here, and we have to be sharp and precise."

"Okay, so exactly what is the plan here?"

"There's a liquor store a few blocks from here. That's our next stop. We're going to go there and get the stinkiest, foulest, most reprehensible-smelling liquor known to man and douse you in it."

"Tequila?"

"Tequila."

Harper's face soured as he whined, "C'mon, man, do we really have to do that? I mean, I hear that bourbon smells pretty bad, too."

"Once we douse you in tequila, you're going to drop me just up the street from the checkpoint so I can watch what's going on and know when to move."

"Oh, I can tell this plan is going to work already," Harper said sarcastically.

"It's going to work. Dude. We're in the Deep South. We are the hot knife that is cutting through their butter."

"For all intents and purposes, let's just say that I'm with you. We douse me and drop you, I go through the checkpoint and get arrested, taken back to APD 5 – now, how do I get to your gun?"

"You're not going to have to worry about that. I'm going to be the one getting my gun. After all, I'm the one that knows what it looks like."

Harper was starting to get frustrated. "What am I missing here?"

"Do you remember stink bombs? From high school?"

"I do."

"It kinda goes something like that."

"Still out in the cold here, dude."

Kinley slid a small envelope over to Harper.

"What's this?"

"What you are going to find in there is something that looks like a hearing aid and a rather large belt buckle."

"So no french fries?"

"Not this time. Just open it up."

Harper tore into the package like it was Christmas morning.

"Take it easy, Red Ryder."

"It looks like," and Harp fingered through the package, "a hearing aid and a rubbery belt buckle."

"How you never made it onto 'Who Wants To Be A Horse's Ass' is beyond me."

"So, what is it I'm supposed to do with these things?"

"It is going to go something like this." Kinley looked around from side to side to make sure that no one was listening before he began again. "Once you drop me off, you're going to go to that checkpoint reeking of booze. You're going to be wearing the belt buckle like you are the proudest son of Texas. You'll have the hearing aid on your right ear. Be sure to ask 'Huh? I didn't catch that last part' or whatever so the dumb cop doesn't try to take it off of you for some silly ass reason. You will get arrested, and you will not smart off to the cops. Still, once you are on the inside of the building, you have to put on your acting shoes and get them to let you go to the bathroom. You can do that, can't you?"

"I can make a cop think I have to pee. I'll do whatever it takes."

"Good, because once you are alone for a moment in the stall you will need to take the belt buckle and place it under the toilet and then take the hearing aid and stick it into the belt buckle. By the way, did I mention that the belt buckle is C-4?"

"It's just like Christmas at Grandma's house," Harper smiled.

"The detonator is synced up to a cell phone I have. Here's the next step in the process. Soon after they have you back to the house, I'm going to come in, flash the necessary ATF credentials and let whoever is at the front desk know that you are with me and I need to get you out of there ASAP."

"What time do you think this will be taking place?"

"Around ten or so. Depends how fast you can convince them that they need to take you in. I need to do this early. Hopefully, before all the real drunk fools are actually being brought in. Plus, the fewer the better when it comes to poppin' some C-4."

"Crowded house or not, man, this is still an extreme risk for me," Harper said as he stared at the rest of his breakfast for a moment, deep in thought. "You are asking me to get arrested – taken in and handcuffed – and if anyone from the government realizes who I am, they're going to throw me in a cell that is deeper than Canada. I might have someone check on me right around the time Madonna's grandkids get into office. Is this what you want me to do?"

"Yeah, it kinda is."

Harper stared at Kinley for several seconds.

"Just don't forget that you are in the situation that you are in because I told Paul Michaels that you and Agent Chase died up on that rooftop in Mexico City."

"C'mon, man," Kin said.

"Oh, is that your closing argument? The 'Come on, man' defense? Well, heck, in that case I am all in."

"I can't do this without you."

"I know."

"I just thought from one friend to another – you'd do this for me."

"Tell ya what, bud. You get the check, and I'll go get arrested."

"Yeah. Okay, that sounds decent," Kinley said agreeably.

GETTING ARRESTED

Despite Harper's protests, he and Kinley drove to a liquor store. Kinley went in and purchased a small bottle of tequila.

Returning to the car, he got in and said, "You ready for this?"

"Do it."

Kinley began sprinkling tequila all over his friend. When it took longer than Harper wanted it to, the assassin pushed his friend away.

"What?"

"You need a funnel or something? How long does it take to dump liquor on me?"

"I'm just trying to spread it around is all."

"For what? You think the cop is going to be sniffing my shirt sleeve? Just finish it up already."

For spite, Devereaux dumped the remaining contents of the bottle straight into his partner's crotch. "There. Maybe the cop will sniff that."

Harper looked at his friend incredulously. "You know, for a guy that is at the mercy of me getting arrested so that he can get his new toy back, you should be nicer."

"How 'bout this. You get arrested, we get my gun back, and I will take you on an all-expenses paid trip to Rio. Does that sound like a fair trade?"

"Really?"

"Yes. Really. I need to work on my tan anyway."

"So where am I dropping you?"

"Take a left out of here and go about three miles on this road. The checkpoint won't be too far. The cops around here are hungry to catch the early partiers, too, so they will have this thing up and running already."

Harper did as he was instructed. They drove in silence for a bit before he asked, "So if I'm getting arrested, and you are going to be coming to get me shortly after that, then what is going to happen to this car?"

"Once they haul you off, I'll trek down to the checkpoint, flash a badge and some ID, and tell them that I'm commandeering the vehicle. Turn in here," Devereaux instructed as he pointed to his right, "and drop me in this parking lot. The checkpoint is just up ahead."

"So, I have the com in my ear, I smell like a booze hound, I have the belt buckle and the hearing aid behind my ear. Guess I'm as ready as I'm gonna be. Any sage words of advice before I drop you here?"

"When they put the handcuffs on you be sure to tighten the muscles in your arms and wrist. Once they're on, relax your muscles and that will give you a little bit of wiggle room and the cuffs won't cut into you. Cops tend to make those things so tight that you'd think that they were arresting Houdini."

"Well, I have been known to do a few disappearing acts myself from time to time. Still, we're going to have to move fast because every second that I'm in there is another chance for them to find out who I am and put that whole place on lockdown."

"As soon as you get the explosives set, I'll be in. I don't think you will have too much trouble. I made your Melvin Powell background kinda sketchy and shady. That way when they get word that you are a government informant it will sync up to what they'll have seen in your past."

Harper pulled the car to a stop. "I guess this is where you get off," he said.

Devereaux got out of the vehicle and shut the door behind him. As he walked away he said, "Checking the com again. You reading me, partner?"

"Loud and clear," Harper replied as he pulled out of the parking lot and back onto the main road toward the sobriety checkpoint. "Heading toward my destination now."

"Just be cool, Harp. Get arrested without incident, keep your head down, plant the explosives, and we'll be in Rio for New Year's Day."

"Sounds good to me, man. I have nothing but bad memories of the greater Atlanta area. Remember about four years ago I was down here doing a job for your United States of America's government, and there was this backwoods cop named Jerry Daugherty who beat the holy type A right out of me? And for no good reason, either."

"I remember. Well, just put those memories to bed, boss. This is a new night and a new cause. Stay chill, Harp."

Harper saw the checkpoint. Roughly seven or eight cars sat between him and the Georgia State Police that were running the show. He could see that they were letting the clean ones go right on through. The people that seemed suspect were being directed into a shopping center parking lot to the right of the checkpoint. Harper checked his seatbelt, sniffed his clothes, and made sure he had his fake driver's license ready.

"Just a little bit before it's my turn," he said to Kinley.

"I'm about two hundred yards back. Walking the side of the road behind you. The cop is going to ask you if you've been drinking. Just tell him that you have. The way you smell he will probably ask you to get out of your vehicle and hand you off to another officer to do your field sobriety test. The original officer will take the car into the shopping center parking lot, and I'll pick it up from there. You will get arrested and taken to the Zone 5 house. Just remember that I'm with you the whole way," Kin reassured his friend.

"Looks like I'm up, chief," Rowe said as he pulled up to the officer that was standing to the left of his vehicle. Harper rolled down his window and greeted the cop with a cordial, "Evening, Officer. What's all of this mess?"

"Good evening, sir. This is a sobriety checkpoint. License and registration, please."

Harper was quick to hand the policeman his license before saying, "This is a rental so I am guessing the registration is in the glove box." Harper placed his hands on the steering wheel, palms up. "Here are my hands, Officer. I'm going to reach over–"

"Don't worry about it, sir. I smell the distinct odor of alcohol on your breath. Have you been drinking tonight, sir?"

"Oh, yeah. Absolutely. I mean, it's New Year's Eve. Who isn't drinking?"

"How much have you had to drink tonight, sir?"

"Oh, wait. Hold that thought, Officer," Harper said and pointed excitedly to the car radio. "It's the Bee Gees!" Harp reached down and turned the volume up and began to sing along loudly, "*Nobody gets too much Heaven no more, it's much harder to come by, I'm waiting in line.*" He turned to the policeman and yelled, "Sing along with me, Officer! *Nobody gets too much love–*"

"Sir, turn down your radio," the patrolman barked.

Harper did as he was told. "Not a Bee Gees fan, I take it?"

"I'll ask you again, sir, how much have you had to drink?"

"I don't know," Harper muttered, and he gave the officer a dopey look before he answered, "All of it?"

"And you thought it was a good idea to drive?"

"Well, I definitely couldn't've walked. I would have fallen right on my face."

"Please turn off your vehicle, sir, and step outside," the officer ordered.

"No problem, sir. I am easy like Sunday morning – the Richard Lionel song – cool like that." Harper shut the car off, unbuckled his seatbelt, and slowly opened the vehicle's door. "We're all good here, Officer," Rowe repeated again.

"I am going to turn you over to Officer Daugherty. He is going to give you a series of sobriety tests. In the interim I am going to take your vehicle over here in the parking lot. If you pass the tests, you will be able to come over and get your vehicle and drive home. Do you understand the parameters that I have set for you?"

"You did say Officer Daugherty, yes?"

"Yes, sir, I did."

"Officer Jerry Daugherty?"

"Oh, you've got to be kidding me," Harper heard Kinley sigh into his com, and Harper knew that Kinley was painfully recalling the scene from a few years ago when Harper had gotten into a scrape with this very officer.

In that incident, Harper had stopped in the middle of rush hour traffic to help a damsel in distress change a flat tire. The woman was in the third lane of I-75 and afraid to get out of her car, so he pulled his car up next to hers, thus blocking a second lane of traffic. Harper, being ever prepared, pulled out some orange cones and roadside flares to protect the area he was going to be in while he performed the tire change.

While he was doing his good deed, a policeman pulled up to the scene and arrested Harper for impeding traffic. The officer finished changing the woman's tire, saw her on her way, and drove Harper to the area's local precinct to finish his arrest of the good Samaritan. The officer's name was–

An officer stepped up and said, "Sir, I'm going to need you to come over here right now."

"Daugherty? Officer Jerry Daugherty, I assume?" Harper asked, smiling.

"Boy, I will beat you to your knees if you don't do as you're told, and I will drive home with a smile. Now get your ass over here!"

Harper got out of the car and said to the first officer, "The keys are in it. The brakes are a bit touchy so watch that. Otherwise, she drives like a dream."

"Driver!" Daugherty barked.

"Hey, my bad, Officer Daugherty. What do I need to do?" Rowe asked as he walked toward the patrolman.

"I need you to spread your legs and put your arms out to the side. I need to search you before we get started."

Harper obligingly did as instructed. The policeman started at Rowe's shoulders and patted down his arms, then his torso, down the right leg and then the left leg before he took an uppercut to Harper's crotch.

Harper doubled up in pain from the crotch shot.

"Looks like we're clean here," Officer Daugherty said. He grabbed Rowe and maneuvered him over to a white line that the officer had chalked out. "Walk this line – heel to toe – ten steps out then turn on your heels and nine steps back – heel to toe. Do you understand my instructions?"

"That doesn't seem to make a whole lot of sense – ten out and nine back – not only does it leave me one step short of where I started, but the algorithm in its simplest form is a prime number whose theorem is relegated to an inconclusive state."

Daugherty gave Harper a perplexed look. "Just walk the line, boy."

"Whatever you say," Harper said, still trying to catch his breath from the strike in his cash and prizes. He walked the ten steps along the white line to perfection, heel to toe. When he got to the end of his trek, he spun on his heels and squealed out a perfect-ly-pitched Michael Jackson "He he!" and heeled and toed it back to Officer Daugherty.

"How'd I do?"

Daugherty stood speechless.

"All right, all right," Harper put his hands up. "I give, Officer. I cheated a bit. That wasn't really a fair test to see how drunk I am. Honest to goodness, I used to be a guard at the Tomb of the Unknown Soldier. I could probably walk a straight line in my sleep. How's 'bout we do another one of those sobriety tests? Like the alphabet test or the stand on one foot and count to ten test? Or maybe you'd like to frisk me again just to make absolutely certain that I never have children."

Officer Daugherty took his nightstick out and pressed the end of it tightly underneath Harper Rowe's chin. "You screwin' with me, boy?"

"Enough screwin' around, Harp," Kinley said through the com. "Just let the guy arrest you already before he decides to circumcise you."

"I'm already circumcised, bud."

"I'm sorry. What did you say?" Daugherty asked.

About that time one of the many officers that were in and around the checkpoint strolled over. "Everything all right here, Officer Daugherty?"

"Peachy keen," Daugherty answered as he pulled his night stick away from Harper's chin.

"No," the assassin spoke up, "not even close. This officer is wanting to let me go back on my merry way when it is aromatically obvious that I am drunker than an otter during Halloween."

The two officers looked at each other confused. "What?"

"Who's a brother gotta blow to get a breathalyzer around here?" Harper said vociferously.

"The breathalyzers are back at the house."

Harper nodded toward the police cruiser. "Let's go back to the house then."

"Now we're talkin'," Daugherty said as he approached Harper.

"Put your hands behind your back. You're under arrest for suspicion of driving under the influence."

"Thank goodness," Kinley said with a breath of relief into Harper's ear.

14

ARRESTS, EXPLOSIONS, AND OTHER SHENANIGANS

"Hey, Officer Daugherty, you don't mind if I sing 'Swing Low Sweet Chariot' back here do ya? I just like to give every scene in my life a good soundtrack song so that it plays a little better on judgment day."

"Son, it don't matter to me if you sing 'Amazing Grace' or some 183 Blink song. I gotcha off the streets, and I'm gonna make sure you don't see the road again for a long, long time."

"I have to pee."

"Oh, don't you dare pee in my cruiser. You will not know the end of the word pain, boy."

"No, I'm serious. I really have to pee. Can you pull over?"

"Do I look like one of them mongoloid kids to you, boy? Do you really think I'm going to just pull over and let you out on a leash to take a leak?"

"You don't need to yell. I wasn't yelling in my request. I just need to go to the bathroom. I believe you mongoloids call it 'going number one'. But I'm asking respectfully."

"I'm about to pull this car over and beat the living crap out of you. Is that what you want, son?"

"For as bad as I have to go," Harper said flatly, "if I could do my business while you were beating the living crap out of me, yeah, I'm willing to trade off."

"Well, you're in luck," Officer Daugherty said. "We just arrived at the station. I'm going to turn you over to my brethren. I'm sure they will take real good care of you."

At that point the back door of the police cruiser opened up and two officers were there to remove Harper from the vehicle and escort him into the police squad room headquarters.

"Hey, take it easy, kids," Harper said as he was escorted into the station. "I'm like an antique – pretty to look at but hard to move."

"You should be happy," the first officer said. "Sometimes Daugherty doesn't even bring his prisoners in. Sometimes we find them, miraculously, in a shallow grave outside of town."

"Ah, don't give Officer Daugherty a hard time. He's in a marriage where his kids don't listen to him, and his mother-in-law treats him like a second-hand citizen. He's gotta get his rocks off somewhere."

The two officers took Harper back to a holding room. "Hang tight here for a few minutes. We'll take the cuffs off in a bit. We'll bring the breathalyzer in when we do."

"Well, don't wait too long. I have to pee."

Harper was left alone for a few minutes.

"Kin, are you still there?" Harp asked without moving his lips.

"Dude, I am, lit'rally, thirty seconds away. As soon as you plant the pudding I will be there to get you."

"I'm doing the best I can. I promise you."

"I know. I am hearing everything that you're saying."

An officer walked back into the holding area. "Are you talking to somebody?"

Harper looked up at the cop and said, "I am. I am talking to my cock. It's what I do when I have to pee really bad, and I'm not given that chance for whatever reason. You ain't mad at me, are ya, officer?"

"Man, I don't know," the officer looked around nervously, "I know they searched you before they brought you back here so ya must be clean. Go ahead and stand up. I'll take you to the john."

"Thank you, thank you, thank you."

"Still," the officer said hesitantly, "let me check you just the same."

"Absolutely," Harper obliged and assumed the position against the nearest wall.

The officer patted Harper down from head to toe, never taking notice of the hearing aid behind his right ear.

"You're clean. Let's go to the bathroom." He led Harper into the bathroom and pointed to a stall.

"Can you turn on some water or something?" Harp asked.

"Why?"

"I'm a nervous pee-body. If I know you are out here listening, I'm gonna get nervous. I won't be able to let loose. You get that, don't ya?"

The cop laughed out loud. "Oddly enough, I do."

"You know and I know that me taking a leak isn't going to affect my breathalyzer results. I really do have to go–"

Officer Jerry Daugherty suddenly walked in. "The kid ain't lyin'. He's been wanting to take a shot since he got into the back of my car. I patted him down. Dude's clean. He'll still breathe a solid three. I mean, Judas Priest, can't you smell the distillery from here?"

The cop pushed Harper into a stall.

"Officer Daugherty and I are right out here – running water." The officer looked at Daugherty and laughed, "So don't think about doing anything stupid."

Harper was not thinking about doing anything stupid. He grabbed the silly putty belt buckle and mashed it into a ball. He took the hearing aid device from behind his right ear and shoved it into the small ball of C-4 and placed it underneath the back of the potty.

"It's in place. You're a go, grasshopper," he whispered just loud enough for Kinley to hear, then said loudly, "I think I'm finished. Come get me."

"I'm on my way," Devereaux said just about the time Officer Daugherty kicked in the stall door.

"Hello, Princess."

Harper put his hands up. "I'm in the undoubtedly seated position, officer."

"Get up. Time for you to breathe."

Harper stood up and pulled up his trousers. "Yeah, I'm pretty excited to see how this goes, too."

The officers led Harper back to the holding cell and left.

A few minutes later a woman carrying a breathalyzer mechanism entered Harper's cell. "Hello, sir. My name is Amy McCormick. Feel free to ask me any questions during this process. What I need you to do is open your mouth so that I can inspect it for any foreign materials."

Harper sighed as he was anxious for Kinley to come through the front door at any point now.

"Ahhhhhh – la la la la – see anything?"

"Nope. Looks good to me. Now I just need you to put your mouth on the breathalyzer and breathe into it for three seconds."

"Has this thing even been decontaminated?"

"I assure you, sir, it is fine. Please just breathe into it."

"No," Harper objected. "I'm gonna need to see you swab it first. Some kind of sani-wipes or something. You people must have something like that around here, don't ya?" And Harper ducked his head down and whispered, "Where are you?"

"Red lights," Kin replied. "I'm almost there."

"Sir, we're done playing with you," McCormick said rather curtly. "Perform this breathalyzer right now, or we will lock you up until we deem it time to release you on your own recognizance, or we call your attorney. The choice is yours."

Harper lifted his head. "Sure. Let's do this." He put his mouth on the breathalyzer straw and blew like the big bad wolf. He was not surprised at all when the reading came up 0.0.

"Uh-oh", the assassin said with a straight face. "Looks like your machine is broken."

"The machine is fine," Officer McCormick re-assured him. "We just had it calibrated. How much have you had to drink tonight?"

"Like I told the officer. All of it. They all seemed relatively sure that I was over the limit. I smell ridiculously profound, wouldn't you say?"

"Yeah, I would say. I'll be right back."

Right at that moment Kinley burst through the front door of the precinct house, flashed his badge, and said, "Jeff Samples, ATF. You have one of my guys back there in your holding area."

"Gonna need something besides a badge and an attitude," the front desk officer said. She looked up from some paperwork and took a long look at the hirsute Devereaux. "Wow, you ATF guys don't really give two craps about your grooming habits, do ya?"

"I'm just coming off a two-month undercover assignment, officer. I was taking the long-awaited and well-deserved trip home when I got a call to stop by this place and pick up one of our guys that was picked up on suspicion of DUI. Apparently they want this joker back at headquarters and *now*. They said they think his cover might've been blown in the process of the arrest."

Devereaux pulled his wallet out and retrieved something from inside of it.

"Here," Kinley said, "call this number," and he handed the female officer a very official-looking business card. "You're going to get a recorded message. Just press six and a tired-sounding operator is going to come on the line – her name is Lucille, for the record – and ask for a verification code. That's when you will say 'ten-alpha-zebra-twelve' and you will be put through to my boss."

So, while the woman was dialing the number on the business card that Kinley had handed her, and was in the process of verifying that Jeff Samples really was who he said he was, Kinley hit the detonator button on a key fob in his hand. Instantaneously, the toilet that Harper had put the explosives under erupted into a shower of splintered porcelain, water, plastic, and metal.

The front desk officer instinctively jumped off her chair and under her desk in a panic. Kin moved stealthily toward the staircase that led down to the evidence room. Doing his best to look like a scared victim, he made his way down the stairs and locked eyes with the old man guarding the room.

"They're clearing the building!" he yelled. "Get up on outta here!"

"I haven't been given the go-ahead to leave my post," the old timer said.

Kinley flashed his fake credentials once again. "I'm with the ATF. Get on outta here! I'm right behind you. This place is under attack."

That was all the old dude needed to see and hear. He was out of his post and out of the building in less than thirty seconds, leaving Kinley alone to go through the evidence lockers and find his gun.

Harper had been hauled out of the precinct headquarters in handcuffs. He and two other perps were now standing at gunpoint in the police precinct parking lot.

"Is everybody out?" somebody yelled.

"Is Mortimer out? The evidence guard from downstairs?"

"I'm out," Mortimer hollered.

"Are the prisoners accounted for? God knows we don't need a lawsuit."

"Carol?"

"Right here, skipper," the front desk officer sounded off.

"Anyone sitting in the front room that we need to account for?"

"Oh gosh, there was a man from the ATF–"

"I'm right here," Devereaux said as he arrived on the scene from nowhere. "Jeff Samples, ATF. And this guy," Devereaux walked up to Harper and grabbed him sternly by the arm, "This guy needs to come with me. Can we get him out of the iron works, please? Last thing we need is to have his cover blown, if it isn't already." Devereaux looked back at the smoky precinct building, and then he looked at Carol. "Did you get the verification?"

"I was in the middle–"

"Look, it's not safe for this guy to be here. It's not safe for him, and it seems blatantly obvious that it's not safe for you guys either."

"What? You think somebody just blew up our building because of this jackass?"

"You tell me, officer. Does your house get lit up like this on a regular basis?"

"Can't say that it does."

"I've already called the AFD and paramedics. The government appreciates your fine work," Kinley said to whomever was listening. "Let's go, jack monkey!" he yelled into Harper's face.

One of the cops came over and took the cuffs off Harper's wrists.

"He's all yours, Samples, but we're gonna need you to stick around and give a statement. Or maybe come back in the morning."

"Not a problem. I'll swing by on my way home." Sirens were heard off in the distance and variable red, blue, and white emergency vehicle lights flashed as the vehicles approached the precinct.

"Appreciate ya," Devereaux said courteously.

Once the cuffs had been removed, Harper and Kin made their way away from the parking lot, got into the rental car and discreetly drove off.

Several minutes after the police precinct building had been cleared by the bomb squad, the officers walked back in to find a picture that had been faxed to them from the NSA.

A picture of a man to detain without question.

A picture of a man that was on the top of every federal agency's most-wanted list.

A picture of the man that they had detained at a sobriety checkpoint and had in their custody just moments earlier.

A picture of Harper Rowe.

Getaway

Barely two minutes out from APD Zone 5 precinct house, Harper confessed, "I gotta tell ya, Kin, I really didn't think that plan of yours was going to work in a million years. How did you get your gun and then get out of there so fast?"

"I ain't gonna lie to ya, bud. The lock on that evidence locker was apparently made out of cellophane. I was able to get through it in about thirty seconds. Once I did, I was still figuring on needing a good two to three minutes – tops – to find the gun itself, but no, not even," Kinley was smiling upon reflection. "My rifle was sitting right at the very front of the locker with a bunch of other stuff that was supposed to be put away in its proper place."

"Procrastinators of the world unite – tomorrow," Harper laughed.

"The gods were definitely smiling on us tonight."

"The God," Rowe corrected his friend.

"Fine. The God. Just keep your pants on there, Falwell. What I said is just an expression, ya know?"

"I know, but you know how a lot of people are easily offended by the term cu– , well, the "c" word, right?"

"Yes. I'm pretty confident that about 97% of all Americans are offended by that term."

"Well, I'm the same way when people say 'the gods were on

our side' or 'thank our lucky stars' and the like. Why do people think that there's some kind of board of gods for, lit'rally, every subject in the world: the weather gods, the traffic gods, the baseball gods. I'm much more comfortable with the concept of one God being in charge of everything as opposed to some committee of beings arguing like the U.S. Congress over what should be allowed and what shouldn't be allowed."

"Hey, Harp – dude – I'm with you on that a hundred and ten percent. I was just using a figure of speech. That's all."

Harper bit his lower lip as if he were trying to keep himself from saying anything else. If that was what he was endeavoring to do, it did not work.

"Okay. Okay – and I know I may be getting picky here – but that's another saying that I think is ridiculous: a hundred and ten percent."

"Oh boy. Here we go," Devereaux said, becoming somewhat irritated. "Please enlighten me, oh master of the English language."

"Hey, now, before you go getting all upset just hear me out, okay?"

"I suppose at this point it would be too much to suggest that we see what we can find on the radio, huh?"

Kinley had barely gotten the question out of his mouth before Harper was off on his rant. "It's common knowledge that most of the world's number systems are based on tens, hundreds, and thousands, right? I mean, you don't ever hear anyone saying 'Based on a scale of 1 to 14', do ya? No, you do not. It's always on a scale of 1 to 10. If you're taking a test, and you get all the questions right, then you get a hundred percent. If you are playing baseball, and you get a hit every time up to bat then you're batting a thousand. People might try to tell you that there are other standards like a five-star restaurant or a 12-step program or 36 inches in a yard or some crap like that, but all those are just random, made-up, lazy American numbers. Definitely not the standards that the rest of the world goes by. Once you start using numbers higher than ten, then you are entering one hundred as your standard of excellence. Once you start using numbers that are larger than one hundred, okay, then one thousand becomes the ultimate goal. Ergo, when someone says that they are giving a hundred and ten percent they're basically saying that they're giving eleven percent."

"I would just like to go on record as saying that you, Harper Rowe, are the only one who thinks like that."

"So I guess it's safe to say that you are disagreeing with me a hundred and ten percent then?"

"Let's just say on a scale of 1 to 10, you're batting a thousand."

Harper smirked at the comment.

"Not to mention that while you're slamming the U.S. for the fact that they use a different format for weights and measures, you should also keep in mind that the greater majority believe it's America's reluctance to switch over to the metric system that is keeping a one-world government and a global economy from taking over."

"Ya don't say?"

A global economy is just no good, Harper. Do you know what makes an economy rise and fall? The value of their currency. For instance, in the States our unit of money is the dollar, and the value of the dollar gains or loses when it is compared to other countries' currencies. The euro, the yen, the rupee, if all of these were to become extinct – which is exactly what would happen in a global economy – there would cease to be any sort of economic comparisons. In other words, it will be an economy that will never be able to grow. And if history has taught us anything, it's that when an economy ceases to grow, its nation soon collapses. So, if you've been paying attention then it's pretty easy to see why a global economy would fail miserably."

"I wouldn't want a global economy anyway because when I lived in D.C., and I was just two blocks away from my bank's main office, it would take forever to get those dopes to return my calls when I had an issue with my bank statement. I can only imagine the headaches that would arise if I had to deal with a main branch that was in Zurich or Brisbane."

"And then there's that," Kinley agreed.

"So, where's this rifle that we rescued from certain doom? I want to check it out."

"It's right there in the back seat, but why don't you wait until we get where we're going to check it out. There's not a whole–"

Before Devereaux could finish his sentence Harper was squeezing himself through the car's bucket seats. Once his torso and waist had cleared the front seats, he maneuvered his legs a little too quickly and ended up planting a knee into Kin's left shoulder.

"What the – daggonit, Harper."

"Hey, did you say that we were heading to Rio?"

"I did. I did, indeed. That is if your squirmin' around doesn't get us into a car wreck first, ya kooky little monkey."

"You sure you want to be seen with me? I'm a wanted man, ya know. I'm sure at some point your mother probably warned you about people like me. Then again, my mom was always telling me to stay away from you long-haired, hippie types, too." Harper reached out and ran his fingers through Kinley's long beard. "Hey, man, you got any birds in this nest?"

Kinley knocked Harper's hands away from his beard. "I'm thinking at some point you might ask me why we're heading to Rio."

"Come on, man. I haven't seen ya in over a year. Can't we just goof off for a few? All work and no play makes Jack a communist. Don't be a communist, Kin. Let's goof off and catch up for a bit."

"We're going to Rio to meet up with Laurie."

Harper was quiet for a moment. "Our Laurie? From the DEA? From Mexico City?"

"She's making a play to go after Tito del Fuento. She needs our help."

"Our help? Or your help?"

"Ya know, Harp, I really don't get the fascination you have with me and Laurie getting together like some kind of star-struck lovers. Just because she didn't shine on you doesn't mean that she and I have something going on. Stop being so childish. I love her, for sure, but it's more like the love a brother has for a sister. You get that?"

"I get that. You love her like a sister – if you're from West Virginia."

Too Crool for School

He dialed the phone number that was on the fax, his fingers trembling with equal parts excitement and panic.

A woman answered the line. He interrupted her before she could finish saying whatever it was that she was saying.

"My name is Officer Jerry Daugherty. I work for the Atlanta, Georgia, Police Department, and I'm calling in regards to the fax that was sent out about a wanted subject named Harper Rowe. It said to call this number and ask for an agent named Jeb Crool."

"My name is Jennifer VanSciver, Officer Daugherty. You have reached a hotline for the NSA. Please stay on the line, sir."

Daugherty held the line impatiently yet nervously. He had never had occasion to deal with, or even talk to, anyone from a government agency. In all of his years on the police force, the highest person on the chain of command that he had ever spoken to was the assistant chief of police of the Eastern Atlanta sector of the State of Georgia Police Department.

While he was on hold, Daugherty wondered if he should have called his superior before calling the number on the bottom of the fax. But with it being New Year's Eve, he thought it would be better to leave the bigwigs alone for the time being and handle things himself.

He drifted a bit before he finally heard a voice on the other end of the line.

"This is Agent Jeb Crool of the National Security Agency. With whom am I speaking?"

Daugherty paused nervously for a moment before saying, "This is Deputy Jerry Daugherty of the Atlanta Police Department."

"What do you have for me, Daugherty? Are you calling about the Harper Rowe fax that was sent out?"

"Yessir, that is exactly why I'm calling. We had your boy here earlier tonight. Was going by the name of Melvin Powell."

"Where is he now?"

"Eh, it's kinda sketchy as to where he is now, but I promise ya, Agent Crool, I've got all my people out finding him."

"Well, what happened, Daugherty? How is it that he came into your custody and then he got out of it?"

"It's like this. We had a sobriety checkpoint set up for tonight, for the New Year's Eve partiers that might get a little tanked and–"

"Yeah, yeah, yeah. Tell me about Harper Rowe. How does he fit into your story?"

"Like I was saying, we had a sobriety checkpoint set up, and your guy – he was calling himself Melvin Powell at the time – came driving right into it. Smelled like a drunken fag, admitted to having been drinking all day, so we arrested him and brought him back to the station."

"Let me get this straight," Crool asked incredulously, "you are telling me that this guy – Melvin Powell – just drove right into your sobriety point and let you arrest him?"

"Well, yessir. That's what we were doing at the time."

"Then what?"

Daugherty cleared his throat before he began again. "We arrested him, and we brought him back to the station. He was in the holding area and asked to go to the bathroom so we sent an officer with him to use the facilities."

"Really?"

"Like I said," and Daugherty was really starting to sweat now, "he was being very–"

"Fast forward, officer. How did he get away from you so that it has brought you to the point that you do not have him anymore, you saw my fax, decided it was a good idea to call me, and now you have all of your officers out looking for him?"

"Honestly, sir, we are still putting all the pieces together. There was an explosion, a guy named Samples showed up from the ATF and grabbed the Melvin – I mean, the Harper Rowe suspect."

"I'm sorry, what – What? Did you just say that there was an explosion?"

"Yes sir."

"As in a bomb?"

"Yes sir."

"Where?"

"In the bathroom."

"Your bathroom? Like the bathroom that your officers use? Or in the public restroom where anyone and everyone goes?"

"Yes sir, that one."

"Well, which one is it? Stop yankin' my chain, Daugherty!"

"The public one."

"The one that you let Rowe use?"

"Yes, sir."

Crool shook his head as he was trying to take in the Atlanta policeman's tale. "So you're telling me that you let our guy use the bathroom and in the next few minutes after that there was an explosion from that very same bathroom?"

"Yes sir."

"Okay, so then what happened?"

Daugherty wiped the sweat from his face with his shirt sleeve. "We evacuated the building like our protocol tells us to do."

"Was Rowe with you?"

"Absolutely."

"So when was it that he got away from you?" Jeb asked shortly.

"There was an agent from ATF named Jeff Samples. He showed up, had his credentials, and told us that Powell was his guy, and that we had to hand him over to him."

"Hang on," Crool barked as he put the phone down. He stuck his head out of his office door and hollered at David Baldwin, "Who's Jeff Samples from ATF?"

Baldwin started punching keys on his computer keyboard. "Jeff Samples from ATF is a cover name that some of our agents use, but it's a cover that has been retired. No one uses it anymore."

"Find me the agents that have ever used that cover, and you get me those names on my desk in the next ten minutes. Do you understand?"

"In ten minutes, sir."

"Hello? Is anyone still there?" Daugherty was asking on the other end of the phone.

Crool put the phone back to his ear and said, "I'm here. What did he look like? This Jeff Samples guy from the ATF?"

"Well, he kinda looked like Grizzly Adams. Long, disheveled, unkempt hair and a big bushy beard."

"And you thought that this was a guy that you should just hand over a prisoner to? Grizzly Adams?"

"Like I said, he had the credentials and all. I was way too worried about making sure that my people were out of the building and making sure they were okay. Honest to God, Agent Crool. I had no idea who I had on my hands until we just came back into the building."

"Duly noted, Daugherty. Do yourself a favor and pull your people back in. Send them back to their sobriety checkpoints and what not. If you had Harper Rowe that close to you and couldn't contain him, you won't get him now. Do me a favor and send any video footage you have from tonight, please. Send it to me on your secure server. Okay?"

"Consider it done, sir," and with that Daugherty hung up the phone.

That did not sound good, sir," Amy McCormick commented to Daugherty.

"Frankly, Amy, I think I'd rather attend a dental school for alligators than to have to talk to that guy again. I think that man could probably use some Xanax and a pint of whiskey to wash it down."

17

REASONS FOR RIO

Kinley and Harper rode in silence for a few brief moments before Harp started in again. Having climbed back in the front seat of the rental car, he asked, "So we're headed to one of your jets to take us to Rio to meet up with Chase?"

"Yeah, we'll be in the air in about twenty minutes."

"Well, when do we get to toast a Happy New Year to each other?"

"Probably somewhere over Cuba, dude."

"Seriously, why are we going to Rio?"

"You know how you and I have been playing hide and seek from the United States Government for the last year and a half?"

"Yeah."

"Well, Laurie has committed herself to staying off the grid, too. Thing is, while we have been doing our thing, she has baptized herself in the goal of bringing down Tito del Fuento and his whole cartel – bringing them down to their knees. Now she needs our help."

"You must be kidding me. What are you and I going to be able to lend to these proceedings?"

"And you must be kidding me," Kinley said harshly. "Apparently you must have forgotten about that little incident a year and a half ago. The one where our government felt its best move was to throw you and me like darts into a fully-emblazoned fireplace with no backup. Chase didn't have to have our backs. She could have very easily gone along with Secretary of Defense Paul Michaels, and she would have been a rock star back in the States, but she didn't. She put her faith in you and me. She was our only ally, our only friend. C'mon, man. We owe her this. I know I do."

"Calm down there, chooch. I didn't say I wasn't on board. I just asked you what kind of difference you and I are going to make on this whole setup."

"I don't even know what the plan is. I'm still waiting to hear from her on that one."

"Wait," Harper said as he tried adjusting his uncomfortably tight seat belt, "please don't tell me that Agent Chase asked you for a favor, and you just blindly agreed?"

"Like I said. We owe her."

"Look, dude, I have three rules that I live by. Number one: never believe a single word from someone that assures you that they never lie. Number two: never let anyone blindfold you. It rarely, if ever, ends well. And number three: never indiscriminately tell someone that you will do them a favor until you know what said favor is."

"Well, then I guess I just figured we could help her *indiscriminately* the same way she helped us." Kin paused for a moment before saying, "Those are good rules to live by though."

"So, tell me. Exactly what you do know about this whole thing? Are we going to assassinate this guy? Are we going to detain him and turn him over to the U.N.? Are we going for just del Fuento or are we going to try to take down his whole operation?"

"What she said is that she's been in Rio checking out del Fuento and his operation for the last year or so. She said that she had figured a way to take out his entire enterprise, but it was going to be very time sensitive, and that she was going to need us and maybe a few more, but not too many because it would increase our chances of being caught. That was pretty much all she said."

Harper was silent for a few moments as he let his mind process what Kinley had just told him. "Okay, okay. I gotta guy we can use. He can definitely help us out a bit."

"Oh, yeah?"

"I mean, we're probably going to get killed in the first thirty-eight seconds of the attack, but it's better than not attacking at all. Right?"

"Stop screwin' around, Harp. Do you really have a guy that might be able to help out?"

"Well, yeah," Harper looked out the window before beginning again. "You know my magic key card that gets me in and out of hotel rooms all over the world?"

"Yeah. How is that going to help us?"

"The dude that made it for me, he's a former Brazilian black ops guy, and now he's a weapons and arms dealer in Brazil. And he hails from the Rio area. And he owes me about thirty-eight favors. Although he'll tell you it's just twelve favors, he knows it's thirty-eight."

"Well, maybe you can help him even it up. See what he can do for us this go 'round, and you can hash out the rest later. What's his name?"

"His real name? I have no idea. I've just always called him 'Big James' because that's what he told me to call him. He and I have gone back and forth over the years doing favors for each other, but the topic of real names hasn't ever come up."

"We'll be up in the air and on our way to Rio in less than fifteen minutes. See if you can't get up with Big James once we are on our way."

"Roger that, Houston."

Plane Conversation

Within minutes, they arrived at a desolate airstrip and boarded a jet that was plenty big enough to fit Kinley, Harper, and the pilot. Within thirty seconds of the two assassins boarding, the plane was down the bumpy runway and into the air.

"So, you're doing okay? Moneywise?" Harper asked.

"Yeah, oddly enough, now that I'm dead I have never been in such high demand. Now that I'm not limiting jobs just to the U.S., I seem to have bidders from all over."

"Hopefully, none of them will hear about your little incident in Atlanta," Harper smiled.

"Which is exactly why I called you, old chap. Not only did I know you would help me without question, but I also knew you would keep a lid on this whole thing."

"Not a word, not a syllable." Harper looked around the small cabin. "I feel quite confident that there won't be an in-flight movie. Ya got anything to drink on this cruise missile with wings?"

"Hey, don't knock it. What it lacks in luxury it more than makes up for in power. This cruise missile, as you call it, is winging its way in record time to Rio. We'll be there in less than five hours. And yeah, under your seat you will find some soda."

Harper reached into a compartment under his seat to find a couple cans of soda. "Is this what we're going to be drinking to the New Year?"

"Nope. I have that under my seat," Kin laughed. "So you can't be doing too bad yourself. Upon my watching of you I have seen you do more than a few jobs."

"Eh," Harper shrugged, "most of my jobs lately have been for charity. Nothing against what you're doing, but I guess at the end of the day when it comes time for me to lay my head down on my pillow I'd rather have a clear conscience than a fat wallet."

"There's no law against having them both, ya know?"

"Anymore, Kin, it just seems the world is one big wastebasket, and we're the ones that have to empty it. If you want to know how screwed up people are, then just listen to this story. A woman is having an affair with this guy. She's just banging him; she's not even doing her old man. So it comes to pass that the woman gets pregnant by her lover. The lover is happier than the devil in a whorehouse. The plan is for the woman to leave her husband, and her and the lover to start a family of their own. Unfortunately, hubby gets wind of her plans to hit the road for whatever reason, and he sets in on his Mrs. with some fisticuffs, some roundhouse kicks, and a lead pipe.

"Thanks to the beating, the woman miscarries the child. The woman sends her lover some pictures of just how bad she's been beaten. Obviously this makes the lover irate, but the woman tells him that her husband still has no idea about the affair that the two of them are having and convinces the lover to keep things quiet.

"Well, a few weeks later the lover is checking his email, and lo and behold, there's an email from the woman with a picture of an ultrasound. The woman's pregnant again, but this time she's having twins. The lover and the woman once again conspire for the woman to leave her husband, start their own family, yada, yada and so on. Then somehow – just like the first time – the husband gets wind of the plan and beats the woman into submission and causes her to miscarry the set of twins."

"*Déjà vu* all over again?"

"Seems so. Well, by now, you can imagine how pissed the lover is. I mean, this woman's husband has not only beaten the woman our guy loves dearly, but he has, for all intents and purposes, killed off three of his would-be children. In a fit of rage our lover goes to where the husband works, waits for him to leave, and he shoots the guy twice in the chest with a .44 Magnum. Kills the husband dead as Kennedy.

"It doesn't take too long before the guy is picked up on a murder charge. So he tells the police about everything that has transpired over the last six months with him, the woman, and her husband. The cops do their due diligence to see if what the guy's saying is true and you'll never guess what they find out."

"What?"

"Turns out that everything the woman was saying to him was a complete and utter lie. She was never pregnant – not with the one child and not with the set of twins – and the pictures she sent him of her being beaten was just some makeup she used. By the time they figure all of this out, the woman is gone with the life insurance money from her dead husband, and our lovesick patsy is left holding the bag. A month or so later a jury of his peers finds him guilty of the husband's murder."

"Whoa, what a jip job," Kin commented in disbelief.

"No kidding," Harper agreed. "However, turns out that our patsy and I have a mutual acquaintance. This acquaintance gets me in touch with this guy's sister who, in turn, takes me to visit the guy in the slammer.

"He tells me about a place that he and the woman would always talk about running away to. It's a little fishing village called Westport, Ontario – right on Lake Rideau which is an offshoot of Lake Ontario.

He and his sister hire me to go to this town, find the woman, and deal with her in a fashion of my own choosing. Of course, they don't have any money because they spent it all on his defense attorneys to try to keep him out of jail, so I took the job with the condition that if ever in the future I might need a favor of some sort that they may be able to help me with, well, then we would call the slate clean."

"So was she there? Was the woman in Ontario?"

"That she was."

"And did you take out the trash?"

"Like only I know how."

"How'd ya do it?"

Harper popped the top on his can of soda and drank down half of it. "Sorry. Dry mouth. Must be from all that alcohol I drank earlier tonight."

"Alcohol does have that effect. Meanwhile, back at the farm–"

"Right. The farm. It's like I said before, Westport is just this little fishing village, so it's not like there is a bevy of nightlife spots to hang out in." Harper paused a moment before releasing an obnoxiously loud belch that lasted the better part of three seconds. "Whoa. Excuse me. That was a bit raucous, huh, buddy?"

"Excused."

"So I follow this woman to the one bar in town. It's a combination bar and dance club, but it's about the size of a Burger King. I'm guessing she's trying to drown her conscience because it's about ten o'clock local time, and she's already a fresh set of linens on the clothesline. It wasn't too hard for yours truly to strike up a conversation chock full of blatant flirtations. It was also fairly easy to make her understand how intoxicated she was. I ask her if she has to work in the morning, to which she replies that she is new in town and is still looking for employment.

"I tell her that I couldn't in good conscience let her drive in the condition that she's in. I volunteer to give her a ride home, and then she can call a cab in the morning to come back to get her car."

"Wait. You couldn't in good conscience let her potentially get killed on the drive home even though you're planning on doing the job yourself?"

"Well, I don't want her causing any more damage to others' lives than she already has. You know me, Kin. I'm always looking out for the other guy."

"You are truly knight-worthy, my shining-armored friend."

"Ya know, you are a good friend with the way you give me props so I don't accidentally pull any muscles patting my own self on the back."

"So you took her home. Then what?"

"I helped her stumble inside, helped her get undressed, and tucked her in. She asked me if I would mind staying and cuddling. She even came up with the brilliant idea that I could drive her to get her car in the morning and save her cab fare. An idea that I was more than willing to be party to, as it would make my job that much easier."

"I assume you had TINA with you, yes?"

"Never leave home without it."

The TINA that Kinley was referring to was the deadly poison that Harper used as his number-one means of assassination. A combination of thalamic acid and sodium, the mixture was both lethal and untraceable to even the keenest of medical examiners. When the formula was written out in chemical equation shorthand, it was written as $T1Na$, hence simply called TINA by the assassins.

"So, what happened?"

"I got in bed with her. I was, lit'rally, sleeping with the enemy."

"Two points for an extremely average movie reference."

"Thank ya, judge. Anyway, I was laying there for what may have been one of the most excruciating three minutes of my life while this chick is breathing her horribly horrendous halitosis all over my face—"

"Ew, the three 'H's. That's never good."

"Tell me something I don't know, chief."

"Elephants are the only mammals that cannot jump."

Harper looked across the table at his buddy quizzically. "Is that right?"

"Far as I know it is, yes."

"Hmm. Neat. Well, anyway, before too long this kooky woman finally passes out, which gives me plenty of time to move quietly around her place and find a suitable pair of footwear into which I can deposit TINA. However, it turns out that, apparently, this woman has been using most – if not all – of the money to buy shoes. I went into her closet and there must have been 70 pairs of shoes in there. Enough so that they had their own walk-in closet.

"Well, I couldn't just dump TINA into all of them. I didn't bring enough with me, for one thing. For two, even if I were to pour TINA into all 140-some odd shoes, she was only going to be wearing one pair. That would mean that after TINA had the desired effect on this woman I would still have to go back and clean it out of all the other shoes, and – no. Just no."

"So, what did you end up doing?"

"I was pacing around the room, back and forth, to and fro, and I started trying to narrow the field a little bit. This was the week before Halloween, and late October in Canada is pretty cold and rainy. So I ruled out any open-toed shoes, any extreme-heeled shoes, anything like that. Still it just left way too many from which to choose. And that's when I see them."

Harper paused for dramatic effect.

"Saw what?" Devereaux asked the obligatorily question.

"There under the bed. A pair of house shoes. It got me to thinking that with as drunk as this broad was, she probably wasn't going to be moving around too swiftly come morning time. I know that on the few occasions that I've been plastered like that, the only things I wanted the next morning were my fuzzy bunny slippers, my flannel robe, a strong cup of joe, some aspirins, and some toast and jam. I didn't want to get dressed, I didn't want to talk to anyone, and I sure as shootin' didn't want to be laying down. Lying horizontally the morning after I've tied one on always makes me feel nauseated."

"Yeah, I get that, too. Oh, and I get, like, these motion headaches. If I keep my head perfectly still then I have no pain at all, but if I even turn my head so much as to look at a clock on the wall it's like Paul Bunyan's axe is splitting my brain in two."

"Oh, those are the worst," Harper nodded empathetically. "Anyway, come morning time this woman wakes up hurting just like I figured she would, but I'm ready for it. Got the coffee brewin', got the toast ready, found a bottle of aspirin in her bathroom, found a robe on the back of her bathroom door, and, of course, I have her house shoes at the ready."

"And?"

"And she died. Face down in her jelly toast."

Devereaux shook his head. "You did all of that just for the promise of some favor in the future?"

"That's right."

"Sounds like a lot of work for no dough, bro."

"Man, I have enough money to last me three lifetimes. Like I said before, for me it's about helping the helpless; making a difference when other people can't. I loved working for my country when that was the path, but those days are gone, and they won't be coming back any time soon. Now God has set me on a new path where I can do the most good, and it's the one that I will stay on until it's time for the next path."

"I understand that. I most definitely do." Kinley checked his watch. "Got about twenty minutes until the witching hour of the new year. Hey, since we have a few more minutes let me ask you this: what did she look like? Your target in Canada?"

"She was a little woman – probably around five-two, five-three – blond hair, good build, very toned. Kinda reminded me of that Broadway actress, um, Kristine Jenowith? Something like that."

"Oh, yeah. I know who you're talking about. She's cute and all, but she has that voice that sounds like a strangled cat clawing at a blackboard. Your woman sound like that?"

"Geez, no. If she had I probably would've had to call an audible on the whole assassination method and switched to something that would be a little more succinct and direct. Maybe like dropping a piano on her head. Why do you want to know what she looked like anyway?"

"Oh, nothing more than to satiate my morbid sense of curiosity, I guess." Devereaux leaned back in his seat, stretched his arms straight up, and let out a big yawn. "Hey, weren't you going to contact your friend, Big James?"

"Well, if he is in the greater Rio area it's about 3 a.m. there right now. Being that it's New Year's Eve, I'm sure he's probably right in the middle of his celebrations. He's an equal opportunity partier. He'll ring in every time zone without any bias whatsoever. Besides, I don't actually contact him directly. He has an answering service that he uses. So I may as well go ahead and leave a message there now. He checks it frequently, so I would imagine that he will be back in touch with us before too long. Do you have a phone on this thing?"

"Yeah, there's a sat phone up in the cockpit. I'll go fetch it for ya." Kin stood up out of his seat and made his way toward the front of the plane where he disappeared into the cockpit. A few moments later he emerged with the sat phone. It was an older version of the device, big and bulky with a large retractable antenna on top of it.

"Holy Malone, dude," Harper commented upon seeing the device. "Where did you dig this relic up from? The Smithsonian?"

"Yeah, I suppose I am due for an upgrade," Kinley handed him the phone, then plopped back down in his seat. "Don't worry though. That thing works great, and it's like they say, 'It's not the size of the phone that matters. It's the size of the satellite network it's pinging off of'."

"Oh yeah? Is that what they say?"

Harper punched in the number and waited for some sort of answer on the other end. He was definitely in the minority when it came to automated messaging services; he actually preferred talking to the machines. "Machines are smart. Humans tend to be stupid," he had said on more than one occasion. Finally an automated voice came on the line saying, "Thank you for calling Dick's Automotive World. If you know the extension of the party you would like to reach, then please dial it now."

Harper dialed in the memorized extension: 120585. A few seconds later he heard Big James' voice on another recorded message. "Thanks for calling Dick's Automotive World. You've reached Otto Mobile in the classic cars parts department. Tell me what you need and when you need it, and know that I will do my best to get it to you in the time allocated."

"Otto, my man. It's Stewart Lytle. I've got some work I need to do on a 1967 Chrysler Newport Convertible. Gonna need some brake pads, a couple of new fuel lines, and a part for the carburetor. If you would be so kind as to give me a call back at–" Harper pulled the phone away from his face. "What's the number to this thing?" he asked his partner.

"He needs to dial his country code first. The country code for Brazil is 55."

Harper put the phone back up to his mouth, "–5-5–"

"Then the provider prefix. The one for that one is 8816."

"–8-8-1-6–"

"Then the eight-digit phone number. The number for that is 55550325."

"–5-5-5-5-0-3-2-5. I'll be patiently awaiting your call, Otto."

Harper disconnected the call, pushed the antennae back down into the phone, and handed it to Kinley. "If he's up and around – which I'm sure he is – he'll give a call back before too long."

"Then while we wait," Kinley said as he reached into the built-in refrigerator space under his seat, retrieved two small bottles of champagne and set them up on the table, "let's ring in the New Year together." He slid one of the bottles across to Harper.

"How much time do we have?"

Devereaux looked at his watch. "About 45 seconds."

"Any last minute New Year's resolutions?"

"The same resolution I make every year–" Devereaux popped the small cork on his bottle. "not to die."

"Hear, hear," and Harper mirrored his buddy's technique of removing the cork from his small bottle of champagne.

"Ten seconds – nine – eight – seven – six – five – four – three – two – one – Happy New Year!"

Kinley and Harper leaned toward each other and lightly clinked their bottle necks together.

"Here's to not dying."

CROOL ON THE HUNT

"Jeb, we just got the video in from Atlanta," David Baldwin said, sticking his head into Jeb's office. "I need to show you something."

"Well, get on in here and show it to me," came Jeb's invitation.

Baldwin double-timed it over to Jeb's desk and punched a few keys on his computer's keyboard. The screen changed a few times and in just a matter of seconds the video from the Atlanta police station was playing on Jeb's screen.

"How'd you do that so fast?" Jeb asked in amazed bewilderment.

"The keyboard is my home, boss. That's why you recruited me to be on this team." The two men watched as the video started playing. "Okay, this is the cops bringing Rowe into the station."

"That's definitely him, all right. I'm still trying to figure out just what he was doing there in the first place."

"At first I thought maybe he just got careless," Baldwin said.

"This is Harper Rowe. He's calculating even when he is being careless."

Baldwin hit a couple of keys on the keyboard again, and the image on the screen changed camera angles. "Okay, here's where Rowe goes into the bathroom. There are no cameras in there so we can't see for sure what he's doing, but since that's where the blast originated, I think it's safe to assume he wasn't just dropping a few kids off at the pool."

"Can you see anything that's different about him from when he enters the bathroom as opposed to when he comes out?"

"Took me a while but – yeah." Baldwin backed the footage up and paused it. "Right there." He pointed to Harper's left ear. "It looks like he is wearing some kind of hearing aid, but–", and Baldwin fast-forwarded the images to where Harper was coming back out of the bathroom, "it's gone," he said as he once again pointed to Harper's left ear.

"And they didn't notice that?"

"Like I said, Jeb, it took me a little while to pick up on it, too, and you know that I have a pretty keen eye for that sort of thing. Still, that isn't even what I wanted to show you." David leaned over and started tapping away at the keyboard once more. "Look at this. This is where his conspirator, AKA Jeff Samples from ATF, comes in."

"Wow, look at the hair on that dude."

"Yeah – whether it's real or fake – between that and the hat pulled down low, and this guy's complete awareness of where the video cameras were, I wasn't able to get one decent shot of his face.

"Nevertheless, you were asking before what Rowe was doing there in the first place? Watch this," and one more time Agent Baldwin's fingers did a little tap dance on Jeb's keyboard and pulled up yet a different camera angle. "This is the camera from the basement evidence room just after the explosion. See here? That's our Outback Jack fellow coming down the stairs to tell the evidence room custodian to get on up out of there. And here he is following the guy up the stairs to safety, but – wait for it – wait for it – there! Our furry little friend comes back down the stairs, blows right through the lock on that evidence cage, and a few seconds later emerges with what appears to be a sniper's rifle."

"Did you call down there to see what it was being held for?"

"Sure did. They said it was being held in the investigation of a possible assassination of a very bad man named–", David reached into his pants pocket and retrieved a folded piece of paper, opened it up and read, "Felix 'Nine Mil' Foster, a renowned drug kingpin in the area. Cop says it looks like the shooter just left the gun on the sidewalk. If the guy had come in to claim it, they're not sure if they would've arrested him or given him a medal."

"With a name like 'Nine Mil' I was kinda figuring him for an usher at the local dinner theatre. A drug kingpin, huh?"

"A renowned drug kingpin, at that."

"So, no good shots of Jeff Samples' face in any of this?"

"No. Whoever our mystery man is, he sure knows how to keep his face hidden."

"And he's pretty ballsy, too. I understand wanting his gun back, but setting off a bomb in a police precinct on New Year's Eve? I'm not sure just what it would take for me to pull a stunt like that."

"If whoever that guy is really is an assassin, then he probably knew that gun could be tied to more than a few hits."

Jeb ran his hand over his shaved scalp and leaned back in his chair. "Doubtful, Agent Baldwin. Most of the good ones use a different rifle for every job for that very reason – so if their weapon does end up in the wrong hands no other jobs can be linked to it."

"Really? I guess I just always thought assassins had their go-to weapon of choice that they used for all of their jobs."

"Well, that'll teach ya to think, Agent Baldwin." Crool looked at his computer monitor. "So you don't think that there's a decent enough shot on here of our bearded friend that we might be able to clean him up enough to see what he might look like clean shaven?"

"Sure isn't. Before I sent it to you, I went through all the footage looking for that very thing. Like I said before, this guy really knew how to avoid the cameras."

"In that case let's assemble a team and head to Atlanta. Maybe once we're onsite we can get a better clue as to who Rowe's bearded buddy is. Oh, and put in a call down to Atlanta to have their best forensics people gather any fingerprints or hair fibers that ATF Agent Jeff Samples may have left behind. Maybe we'll get lucky, and we can find some sort of DNA match on this guy."

WAKE UP CALLS

Kinley and Harper had dozed off to sleep after a little more conversation and finishing their respective bottles of champagne. The assassins were about two hours into their slumber when Kinley's cell phone went off. Harper woke up first, sleepily reached across the table and slapped Devereaux's shoulder.

"What?" was Kin's slow-witted response.

"Either your pants are ringing, or someone is trying to call you."

"What are you talking about?" Devereaux said, somewhat annoyed.

"Answer your stupid cell phone already, will ya? I'm trying to sleep over here," Harper said as he plopped back down into his seat.

"Oh. Sorry." Kinley pulled his phone out of his pants pocket and checked the number. "Hey, it's Chase," he said, and without waiting for a response from his partner he answered, "Is this DEA Agent Laurie Chase?"

"Is this Kinley Devereaux?"

"I can assure you that it's not Mother Theresa, Laurie."

"Dude, get a new line," Harper chirped from his seat.

Kinley shot him a look.

"Is that Harper I hear in the background?"

"That'd be him."

"Put me on speakerphone then. You're both going to need to hear what's going on. By the way, does he know why the two of you are coming this way?"

"I told him that you and I had been talking, and that you were in Rio doing a ton of recon on Tito del Fuento, and that he and I were heading there to see if we could help you out. Hang on a second," Devereaux said as he pulled the phone away from his ear and put it on speakerphone.

"Okay, Laurie, you're on speakerphone now."

"Hello, Harper," Chase said without any sentiment whatsoever in her tone.

"Laurie," Rowe returned in kind. "So start filling in the blanks a bit for us here. What is going to happen once Kin and I land there?"

"Kinley, your pilot has already sent me the coordinates to the airfield where you guys will be landing. Looks like I'll be seeing you in just under three hours."

"Well, I sure hope this time that your picking us up goes a little bit smoother than when you picked us up in Mexico City," Kinley chided.

"I don't anticipate any issues, dear. From there I will bring you back to my place," Chase paused for a moment and then began in on her plan. "Tomorrow evening on January 2nd, Tito del Fuento and about a hundred of his men will be leaving to go to Dresden, Germany, where he'll be meeting up with some major players in the European drug market. He'll be talking to them about becoming one of their larger suppliers of cocaine and hash."

"So is that where we'll be going? To Dresden? Take the guy out while he is on business?" Harper asked.

"No. We'll be staying here. With him and his men being gone that will leave somewhere between 150 to 200 soldiers behind to tend to the place."

"When you say the place, are you talking about his compound? His plantation? What exactly?"

"All of it. There's one humongo-sized mansion that he lives in. He keeps twelve servants inside at all times, and seventeen guards on the immediate premises. Then he's got two large industrial buildings – one for where they break down the crops into drug form, and the other is for packaging and storage. Add to that twelve good-sized houses where the field workers and their families stay. Then there's three barracks for his soldiers and guards. He's always got between twenty-five to thirty guards patrolling the fields, and he has another sixty or so manning the perimeter of the property. And then – there's the planes and helicopters."

"Oh, he's got planes and helicopters, too?" Harper asked in mock amazement.

"He has four Lockheed P-3 Orions. Two are in the air at all times doing low-level surveillance on the entire property. If they spot any irregularity at all, he dispatches one of his six S-70i Battlehawk helicopters to deal with it until a troop of his men can get there."

"What's an S-70i Battlehawk? I'm guessing that's not a good thing?" Harper asked.

"You remember that show 'Airwolf ' from when we were kids?"

"Oh, yeah. I used to love that show."

"A Battlehawk is like that helicopter on steroids," Devereaux said with a worried look on his face. "Definitely not a good thing."

"So," Chase continued, "he has a hangar for all of these right in the middle of his land. He has soldiers guarding that place like it was Fort Knox, and the pilots stay in bunks that are in the hangar. More than that, these chopper pilots sit in the choppers on 8-hour shifts, 24/7. If and when they get a call from the P-3, they fire those bad boys up and go."

"Well, how big of a plantation are we talking about here, Laurie?"

"It's a little over five square miles."

"Ho-ly crap!" Harper exclaimed. "That's, like, three times the size of Hollywood!"

"So, it's big," Devereaux stated.

"Big, yes, but not so big that one of those Battlehawks can't be anywhere on the property in under a minute."

"So, even with del Fuento being out of town, this still sounds like a pretty tall order to fill, Laurs."

"Wait," began Harper, "if we're doing this while he's out of town then what's the point? I thought the whole goal of this little shindig was to put that jackass six feet under?"

"And that will be the endgame, Harper, but timing is everything. My plan is to get this going just about the time he's headed back. When he leaves town he will be taking his best men with him. We'll start our initiative then. Hopefully, by the time he gets back, things will be in such disarray and chaos that he will be ripe for the pickin'."

"Even if we work the timing out right, Laurie, this sounds like a pretty big job for just the three of us," Kinley said.

"We're going to need a lot more than just the three of us. We'll need a plane, some explosives, probably some ground-to-air missiles, weapons, and if I had to ballpark it – somewhere between ten to twelve people to pull this off. Oh, and we'll need it fast. I've made some contacts since I've been here, and I've got a lot of guns and ammo, but the bigger stuff – I knew if I made a play for that too soon it would draw a lot of unwanted attention to me that I just don't need."

"We might be able to do something about that," Kinley said assuredly. "Harper knows a guy."

"What kind of guy?"

"He's a weapons guy," Harper answered. "Hey, Laurie, let me ask you a question. Have you taken any of del Fuento's guys out since you've been down there?"

"I have. Twenty-three of them, to be exact."

"Wait, if you're poppin' his guys isn't that going to make him a little bit on edge? Maybe want to heighten his security even more than it already is?"

"Not to fear, boys. I stopped dropping his crew about six months ago. There was this two-bit drug dealer named Javier Salvador. His M.O. was getting young girls – we're talking fourteen, fifteen, sixteen year olds – hooked on the smack. Then he would pimp them out in return for supporting their habits. I took the rifle that I used to take out del Fuento's twenty-three guys, and I planted it in Salvador's apartment. I made a well-placed call and the next thing ya know that son of a bitch Salvador is no more. I got rid of him and made Tito feel like everything was back to good all in one fell swoop."

"Well, it's good to know that you haven't just been soaking up the sun and drinking Mai Tais since you've been down there," Harper joked.

"Tell ya what, I'm gonna hop off here and do a little bit more tidying up around the place. I will see you two in a few hours."

"I'm excited. Till then, Laurie," Kinley signed off and disconnected the call. With raised eyebrows he looked at Harper and said, "We really got our work cut out for us, kid."

"Won't be the first time, Kin."

"So – if you don't mind, and even if ya do – let me ask you. After we parted ways you went around and did a great job of sealing up all the loose ends from Mexico City–"

"Yeah?"

"Why didn't you ever bother to go after Chase? And what about that fed? Crool?"

"Well, number one, I would never kill a federal agent. That's just a whole bag of albatrosses that I don't want hanging around my neck. Plus, I need that guy alive and coming after me. As far as he knows, you and Chase are dead. I don't want him getting bored with me and getting a wild hair up his can and go snooping around for something that just isn't there."

"Sure. I get that. Still, why not Chase? She could've buried us, dead or not."

"Kin, part of my tying up the loose ends was going back to Mexico City and making sure you and her were dead. I used every trick that I knew to get back up on that rooftop to make sure that two of those dead bodies were you and Laurie. So, why would I go through all that trouble if I was just going to finish her off myself? Besides, I knew you and her had a bit of a connection back in ol' Me-hee-ko. I couldn't come between my best friend and his next best shot at finding happiness with someone."

"Harp," Devereaux said somewhat frustrated, "I swear, sometimes you get under my skin like an army of burrowing red ants."

"Yeah, and believe me – you're not the first girl to tell me that," Harper chuckled.

Kinley dismissed the comment and said, "We've still got a few hours till we touch down in Rio. Better take advantage of them while we can. Who knows if or when we'll get a chance to sleep again once we meet up with Laurie."

"Not going to argue with ya on that one." Harper closed his eyes and began to think about the girl of his dreams, and within minutes he was asleep and on a Caribbean shoreline laying in the arms of Minnie Dri–

The sat phone rang. Harper's eyes shot open. Shaking out the mental cobwebs, he sleepily grabbed the phone off the table. "Yeah?"

"Harp?"

"Big James?"

"Yeah, brother. Sorry it took me a bit to get back to ya, but I was ringing in the New Year with some Filipino friends of mine. Just got back from a job in Manila a few days ago, and I brought some women back with me to keep me from getting too lonely on New Year's Eve. We rang in the Filipino New Year about fifteen hours ago, killed about nine hours – if ya know what I mean? – and then clanged in the Rio New Year about six hours ago. Where you at that you've got me calling you on a sat phone?"

Harper was still rubbing the sleep out of his eyes when he said, "My buddy and I are winging our way to you in Rio." Harper took off one of his shoes and threw it at the still-sleeping Devereaux. Barely opening his eyes, Devereaux reached up with his right hand and snagged the shoe before it hit him.

"Don't do that," Kin growled sleepily. "Just don't – don't do that."

"Wake up, champ," Harper said in a hushed tone. "I've got Big James on the phone."

"Then put him on speakerphone and leave me alone," Kinley advised.

"You still there, Harper?"

"Yeah, I'm still here, chief. Hey, I'm going to put you on speakerphone. You'll be talking to me and my partner, Mr. Player To Be Named Later. You cool with that?"

"Heck, yeah, the more the merrier."

Harper pressed the speaker button on the sat phone. "Say hello to my partner."

"Hello, partner. So, Harp, that message you left me makes it sound like you two are headed this way with a mission in mind. What's going on, boss?"

"You know a drug guy named Tito del Fuento?"

"Absolutely. Ha! That would be like me asking you if you'd ever heard of a crime boss named John Gotti. Why do you ask?"

"We're winging our way to you. Probably a suicide mission, but we have somebody that's been in play down there for a little over a year. Based on their intel, we are looking to take out Tito del Fuento. Do you think that's possible?"

Big James laughed and then he straightened up. "Yeah, you can definitely do that." And then he laughed again.

"Stop screwin' around. Is this doable or not?"

"It's definitely a suicide mission, my brother, but if someone was willing to do it – I would be all in. Del Fuento is a big time bad guy, and from what I'm hearing on the waiver wire he's making plans to get even bigger and badder. He's been trying to make some business acquisitions in the European drug trade that would pipeline a decent chunk of their business over here.

"Truth be told, the guy's already got everybody and his brother in his back pocket: the local federales, the railroad cops, judges – both federal and civil – international agents, the post office, the FAA. If this deal with the Europeans goes through, del Fuento is going to have more money to pay off even more people, and the guy already comes and goes when he pleases as it is."

"Well, I guess that answers the age-old question, 'What do you get the man who has everything for his birthday?' A judge."

"Big James, this is Harper's partner. You can call me Jeff Samples. Harper says that you're a weapons and arms dealer. Is that right?"

"Best in the business, Jeff."

"Like Harper said, we are going after del Fuento to take him and his entire operation down. I don't know the whole shopping list, but for starters we're going to need some man-portable Strela-3 surface-to-air missiles, about six or seven FIM-92 Stingers, and enough automatic weapons, grenades, and body armor to gear up ten to twelve people," Kin paused. "Oh, yeah, and we're going to need a plane big enough to carry enough explosives to take out, roughly, five square miles. Oh, and also – we'll need the explosives, too."

"And that's just for starters?" James asked.

"For now, that's what we know we'll need," answered Kin.

"One other thing, Big James," Harper cut in, "as far as that ten to twelve people thing, do you know about six to eight people that might be daring enough to go in on this suicide mission with us?

Because right now it's me, you, my partner, and our person on the ground there in Rio."

"You covering the tab on this?"

"I am. So, don't fret about the cash, James. You will be rewarded handsomely."

"How soon are we talking here? A week? Maybe two? For me to get all of this together?"

Silence reigned for a brief moment before Kinley said, "More like twenty-four to thirty-six hours."

More silence.

Suddenly, Big James burst into a hearty laugh. "Twenty-four to thirty-six hours – that's a riot. Harper, you didn't tell me that your partner was such a comedian."

"Believe me, he's not. He's about as funny as two dead elephants at a railroad crossing."

"So – you really do need this shopping list that fast?"

"It would certainly appear that way," Kinley answered. "We're meeting up with our contact in Rio in just a few hours. She's the one putting this whole plan together. Once we find out all the details we can give you a more detailed list with a better timeline, but with the little bit that we know right now, I'd say the twenty-four/thirty-six time frame is relatively accurate."

"You can do it, big guy," Harp said assuredly. "You're the best in the business, remember?"

"I can probably scrounge up most of the weapons we'll need, but finding some quality people that will be willing to drop everything that they're doing to go in on a high-risk mission such as the one you are proposing is going to be a challenge."

James paused for a moment. "However, I did do a job with these four Americans a few months back – three dudes and a chick – and they were some straight up, badass soldiers. Ex-Delta force types. Their last six months working for the U.S. military they were in and out of North Korea on a relatively regular basis, doing intel work, pulling out high-ranking officials that wanted to defect to the States, performing other classified assignments that they couldn't tell me about. Now they've taken their skills into the private sector doing all kinds of work. They're based out of a town called White Pines, but they do jobs all over the place."

"White Pines – now that's a pretty ritzy town, not to mention a suburb to one of the biggest cities in America. Seems they were smart enough to go where the money is," Harper said.

"So, what kind of jobs do they do now? What are they, like mercenaries or something?" Kin asked.

"No, more like good Samaritans. They work under the moniker of Dragon's Men Protection Agency. Kind of a silly name, I know, but it's not like they have a big banner over their office door or an ad in the Yellow Pages or anything like that. They work off the grid for the most part. I do know, though, that they pick up a lot of work from the police there in White Pines. You know, the kind of people that fall through the cracks. The kind of people that are in just enough of a pickle to be in legitimate danger, but not in enough of a pickle that the police can help them.

"For instance, say you saw a pro take somebody out, and the pro knows you've seen him, but because he is a pro he tidies up his mess. No body, no evidence, no nothing, so that when you go to the police to report this supposed crime that you saw, well, there's nothing there for the police to investigate. Now not only do they think you're full of horse squish, but they, for sure, are not going to give you any sort of police protection for when this pro comes looking to tie up the loose end that you've become."

"And that's where these Dragon's Men people come in?"

"Then and there, and like I said they do a bevy of other things, too. We crossed paths down in Sydney. I was tracking a shipment of weapons that was headed for a sleeper cell there. I was going to intercept the package and use it for myself, to be honest with ya. Ends up, these four are down there tracking the very same package, too, but they're not tracking the weapons so they can take them for themselves. No, they're tracking the package hoping it will lead them to the terrorists so they can take those daffy dicks out of commission. They told me that it might be in my best interest to give them a hand taking out the bad guys so that when I took possession of the weapons I wouldn't have to be looking over my shoulder the rest of my life should they ever find out that it was yours truly that pilfered the package."

"How many were in the terror cell?"

"Twenty-one."

"And of you guys?"

"Just the four of them and myself. Really, I thought the odds were stacked against us, but the way they took care of business, heck, there could've been forty members in that cell, and they still wouldn't've stood a chance. Talk about poetry in motion. The really great thing about them – they were cool. Not your typical military full-of-bravado pickle smacks."

"Yeah, but that name – Dragon's Men? Just sounds a little cornball-ish to me. I mean, where do you even get a name like that from?"

"Well, the guy that sort of runs the show – his name is John Watkins – he's about as levelheaded as they come, but when he does get angry he's got this thing that he does where he breathes through his nose real hard, kinda like a dragon breathes fire out of his or her nostrils. And, no – before you even ask me, Harper – I never actually saw fire come out of the man's snout.

"So, there's that, and probably because the guy, Watkins, has five or six degrees of varying black belts in differing styles of the martial arts. But, yeah, like I was saying, these cats are about as cool as they come. I might like our chances about fifty percent more if we could get them on board."

"Sounds promising," Kinley said with some hope in his voice.

"I know you'll do your best, Big James. Once we get on the ground and have a better handle on what's going on and when, we will be back in touch. Till then enjoy your lady friends."

"Oh, I've been enjoying them ever since I've been on the phone with you. I guess you could say that I've been doing a bit of multi-tasking. Nevertheless, I'll wrap this up soon, get about forty winks, and then get it in gear on that weapons list. I'll hear from you when I hear from you. *Tchau, meu amigo*," and Big James was gone.

"Well?" Kinley asked.

"Well what?"

"Do you think your boy is going to be able to come through for us on this or not?"

"He said he's going to do his best. I've got no reason to think otherwise."

"Cool. I'm back to sleep then." Devereaux looked at his watch. "Looks like we've still got a couple three hours till we touch down."

DRAGON'S MEN

Big James finished up his business with his two Asian friends, took a quick shower, then grabbed his cell phone. He ambled over to his desk and plopped down in the chair. Thumbing through his rolodex, he patiently looked for the phone number of the Dragon's Men Protection Agency.

Big James found the number, dialed it, and then waited – and waited – until it rang, several times. And then–

"Protection agency, John Watkins speaking."

"Johnny! It's Big James from Rio. You remember me? We did that–"

"What's going on, Big James?" Watkins said affably. "Yeah, I remember you. Ya got something for me?"

"Yeah, you got a few minutes? I think I might have a pretty big job for you and your crew. It'll be a pretty big payday, too."

"I have a few minutes. What's going on?"

"You and your gang looking for a quick score?"

"Sure. Tell me what is on our end. What do we need to bring to the table?"

"You and your team's expertise. I have a small crew that is looking to take out a major drug lord here in the outskirts of Rio. It's a trio. I know the one of them to be a top-notch former U.S. military assassin, and he's loaded. The other two, this guy vouches for. I know him well enough to know that if he is calling me in, and he is fronting the money, this will be a good job for you and your team."

"So, who is the bad guy?"

"Drug lord named del Fuento. From Rio. Ever heard of him?"

"Tito Javier del Fuento IV? Father's name is Tito Javier del Fuento III. Mother's name is Gloria Bradford del Fuento. His father met his mother when he attended the University of Tennessee here in the States for a semester back in 1964. Tito is the youngest of five siblings and, oddly enough, the only one still alive–"

"So, I'll take that as a yes, you've heard of him?" Big James interrupted.

"Yeah, my crew and I are very aware of who he is."

"And do you think you and your crew might be on board for taking this joker out? Out of commission, I mean, not out on a date."

"Well, they're out ringing in the New Year and I'm back here holding down the fort. I'm already looking at del Fuento's arsenal. It would appear to be rather spectacular, as well as somewhat daunting. So, it would be your three people, you, and us?"

"Far as I know. And it has to be quick. They are looking at a day, day and a half to get this thing rolling."

"Your guy pays well, you said?"

"Let's put it this way: I did a computer hack on a hotel key card one time for this dude. Yeah, it wasn't easy, but I would've been happy with 10 gs. And this guy walks up to me and hands me fifty large. Granted, he has told me it was the best investment he ever made, but, still – he paid me five times as much as it was worth."

"Still doing some digging on del Fuento. Certainly looks like the kind of guy I wouldn't mind taking out, and it sounds like your friend will ante up the cash we would need to come down there on short notice."

"So, you're in?" Big James asked.

"Yeah, we're in."

"Don't you want to talk it over with the rest of the squad there?"

"Squad? We're not a group of cheerleaders, James."

"Well, I just meant once your people got back home from – ah, never mind."

"We should be wheels up and winging our way to you in less than an hour. I'll page them to get back here asap. Probably looking at a ten-hour flight – that should give them plenty of time to sober up. You're one time zone ahead of us. Look to hear from us around 3 p.m. your local time. You'll have a place for us to land, yes?"

"Roger that, Johnny."

"Any requests?"

"Yeah – bring everything ya got."

Back with Chase Again

A voice came over the intercom system back inside the plane's cabin where Kinley and Harper had been fast asleep for the last two hours.

"Guys, you still with me back there?" the pilot asked. "Gonna need you to buckle up if you're not already there. We're looking to be touching down in just about fifteen minutes. We'll be beginning our descent here real soon."

Harper awakened first because his head was resting right next to the intercom speaker. He lazily moved his hand to the intercom button, pressed it, and said, "Ten-four, captain. We're buckled in."

He propped himself up and hollered at his partner, "Kin! The pilot wants us to buckle up. We're getting ready to touch down."

"I'm already buckled in," came the tired and irritated reply.

Harper stood up and looked over the table that separated him from his partner to see if Devereaux actually was buckled in. "Doesn't look like you're buckled in. Looks like you're just lying there sleeping."

Kinley raised his right hand with little to no effort and extended his middle finger toward his friend. "How's 'bout now? Does it look like I'm buckled in now?"

"Eh, what does it matter if you're buckled in or not. If the plane crashes upon landing, I'm pretty sure being fastened to your seat by a three-inch-wide piece of fabric isn't going to do much for ya anyway." Harper sat back down in his seat and buckled up. "Nevertheless," he sighed.

Twenty minutes later, the plane came to a halt and the side door of the aircraft slowly opened. Devereaux moved upright in his seat, rubbed his eyes, and said, "Looks like this is our stop, Harp."

"Yeah, you won't mind waiting up for me while I unbuckle my safety belt, will ya?"

Devereaux made his way over to the open hatch of the plane and cautiously looked out. "Take your time, dude, just looking over the lay of the land to make sure Chase didn't bring any more hellbent terrorists with her like last time."

"Pretty sure they were drug dealers last time," Harper replied as he stood to his feet and made his way toward the door.

"Drug dealers, sex traders, Jehovah's witnesses – whatever they were, I felt pretty frickin' terrorized."

"I get that, I do. Especially having to have our butts saved by the flight crew. That was just downright embarrassing. How's it looking this time?" Harper asked as he crowded behind his partner.

"Good. I see Chase. She's outside of her vehicle. I'm checking the peripherals, and I'm not seeing any traffic going in or out of where we have landed."

"So, in your opinion, it's okay to deplane?"

"I have to go up and talk to the pilot for a few. Pay the money that was needed to make this voyage. You go ahead on, I'll be along rightly."

"Pretty sure she would like to see you first. As a matter of fact," Harper noted, "I'm watching her right now. Hmm, looks like she lost a little weight."

Harper waited patiently for Kinley to come back out of the pilot's cabin. About five minutes later, Kin emerged and joined his friend.

"You still have eyes on her?"

"Sure do," Harper replied. "She's right down there. There's no way that I was headed down this particular set of stairs without you leading the way."

"Dude, lighten up. She'll be just as happy to see you as she is to see me," and Kinley started to make his way down the stairs toward Laurie Chase.

From behind, Harper watched as Kinley walked right up to DEA Agent Laurie Chase without falter and wrapped his arms around her.

"It's good to see you again, Laurie," Kinley smiled during his embrace. "Happy New Year, kid."

"Happy New Year to you, too," she said, smiling excitedly. Laurie pulled back from him, looking at his long, shabby hair and beard. "Wow, you really let yourself go, didn't you?"

"Just trying to stay off the radar is all. Besides, if need be, I can trim this, dye it, shave the head and keep the beard, shave the beard and keep the hair – the options are a-plenty."

Harper was off the deplaning steps and on the ground just seconds later. "Hey, Laurie," he said and opened his arms for a hug. Laurie, without ending her hug with Devereaux said, "Good to see you again, too, Harper."

Devereaux released Laurie and said to his partner, "Dang, dude, you haven't even been off the plane thirty seconds, and you've already been shot down."

"Good to know that some things never change," Harper smarted off as he headed toward Chase's van. "Good Lord, it's hot down here for January first. I'll be in here when you guys deem that it's time to go."

Laurie looked at Kinley. "It's probably time to go. We'll have time for catching up on the ride back to my place. Let's get your bags, and we'll head out."

"Things got a little hectic before we caught our flight here so we didn't really have time to pack, but, hey, we're in Rio de Janeiro. I've seen those really cool open markets that they have down here. We were just going to go check out a place like that to see if we couldn't find a few things to tide us over. Maybe some tee shirts, a tooth brush, maybe a black market DVD version of *Cool Runnings*."

"We don't really have time for that right now, and where I'm staying is a little bit outside of the city."

"How far outside?"

"About forty-five minutes outside."

"Ah, for crying out loud," Harper moaned, "you mean to tell me we're gonna have to wear what we have on for the next two days? Why does this sound tragically familiar to me, Kin?"

"Don't worry, boys, since I know your penchant for not packing for the occasion I took the liberty of picking up a few things for you in advance. It'll be more than enough to get you through the next few days. I was just hoping that neither one of you had let yourself go over the last year and a half."

"The only thing that got fat is the hair on Kinley's dome."

The Fourth Ace

It was a different country.

It was a different set of circumstances.

It was a different van.

Still, the players were the same, and the stakes were just as high.

Laurie Chase drove the van, Kinley Devereaux rode shotgun, and Harper Rowe made himself comfortable in the bench seat directly behind them. The usual quips and pleasantries were exchanged as they rode toward Chase's place.

"Got any AC in this jalopy, or do we need to roll down the windows? It's a little humid in here."

Laurie reached up to the climate controls, pushed a button, slid a lever, and turned a knob. In a few seconds cold air was blowing out of the van's vents. "Better?"

"Like winter in the Adirondacks."

"So, how long after we parted ways did it take you to get down here, Laurie?"

"About two days – oh, and by the way, not a day too soon – since I found out shortly thereafter that I was dead."

"You're welcome," Harper smiled from his horizontal position in the middle seat.

"I'm welcome? How am I welcome? If I hadn't gotten everything together and left the States when I did, I could've been stuck inside the country. Who knows where I'd be right now? I could be stuck in Cowhole, Massachusetts or even worse – a Kesha concert."

Kinley turned around in his seat and said to Harper, "Told you that you were alone on that Kesha thing, chief."

The van hit a series of potholes and practically jostled Harper off the middle bench seat and onto the floor. "Whoa! Laurs, are you driving this thing, or is it driving you?" he asked as he clambered back into a sitting position.

"Sorry. Once you leave the main roads around here, pavement is more of a wish-list item than an everyday amenity."

"He's fine," Kinley said. "What I'm more concerned about is what is going down in the next day, day and a half. I know you've been down here for a while getting everything set up for this, but still, it seems like a pretty big undertaking for just a handful of people."

"You're right, I've been down here for a while. I know Tito del Fuento inside and out. I know where he's going, when he's going there, and why he's going there. I've got this, boys," she said reassuringly. "Also, I've got the fourth Ace."

"The fourth Ace?"

"Yes, the fourth Ace. Ever play cards, Kinley?"

"A few times, yes."

"The fourth Ace comes into play when you have three Aces, and you're just so sure that you have the hand won – but I have the fourth Ace – which happens to be the same suit as my 10, my Jack, my Queen, and my King," Chase smiled.

"Completing your Royal flush – the unbeatable hand," Harper commented.

"So, you have the card that makes your play unbeatable?" Kin asked. "Care to explain?"

"My fourth Ace is named Diego del Fuento."

At that remark, Harper resumed his reclining position on the van's middle seat and said, "Oh good. He's kin. What could possibly go wrong here?"

"Harper, every third person's last name down here is del Fuento. I'm sure they're not related at all. Right, Laurs?"

"First cousins, actually, but more like brothers. Tito and Diego grew up together, went to school together, had a double wedding even. When Tito started his next-to-nothing empire, Diego was right there with him through it all, thick and thin.

"He was Tito's right-hand man for years, but then one day Diego got a look at Tito's books and realized that Tito was treating the hired help just a little bit better than he was treating his own blood. Diego brought to Tito's attention all of the things he had done for him through the years, and Tito let it wash over him like water off a duck's back."

"And Diego was relatively pissed, I guess?" Harper smiled. "Pun intended, of course."

"It went like this," Chase continued, dismissing Harper's remark, "Diego went to Tito, told him he felt like it was time for them to go their separate ways, they hugged, wished each other well, and said good-bye. Twenty minutes later when Diego got home, his wife and four children were dead. Then, to top it all off, Tito put a bounty out on Diego's head."

"How did you find out about that?"

"Oh, believe me, when Tito del Fuento puts a contract out on your life, he makes sure that everybody knows. And make no mistake about it, everybody tries to collect, too. You've got mothers of small children out there trying to whack someone because they know that when it comes to Tito del Fuento, crime definitely pays."

"Plus, del Fuento gets his man – or woman – dead, and he never has to worry about sullying his guilt-free hands," Kinley added.

"Okay," Harp spoke up, "so where do you come into all this, and what does this have to do with your plan to get del Fuento?"

"I'm getting to that just now. I knew if I could get to Diego before anyone else I might be able to use his help. Now depending on your philosophical beliefs, it was either dumb luck or divine intervention, but I took a stab at staking out the local florist shop near his house. His wife and children had a traditional Christian burial in a nearby cemetery, and I figured at some point he would be sending someone to put flowers on their graves.

"Obviously, Tito would have eyes on the cemetery so there was no way that Diego could put the flowers there himself, and since that was the case he would, at the very least, want to pick the flowers out himself, especially since he knew that the only way he was going to survive was to go on the run. He'd have to leave their graves behind. This opportunity might be the only one he would have to somewhat pay his respects.

"So, I sat on the florist shop for a couple of days. I was starting to get worried because I knew he would be in disguise, and I was afraid that he had slipped past me. Then about 9:30 in the morning on day three – just after the place had opened – I see this guy who's got on this weird-looking hat and some sunglasses and hair that, to the trained eye, just doesn't look natural. So, I get out of the van, and I go into the florist's shop to get a closer look to see if what I see is what I'm really seeing."

"I see," remarked Devereaux.

"It was definitely a disguise – and a good one, too, because even knowing it was a disguise I still couldn't tell if it was Diego or not. But I just figured who else was going to be wearing a disguise into a flower shop at 9:30 in the stupid morning."

"Dang, baby, you are good."

"So, did you approach him in the flower shop or did you wait until he was outside?"

"When everyone in town is looking for this guy I'm not going to stop him in the middle of the street and ask him if he would trust a perfect stranger to keep him safe and help him get his revenge on his cousin. For one thing, he'd probably run, and it's too hot down here for that kind of nonsense. Plus, if he ran, there was an outside chance that he might have people of his own keeping an eye on him. So now not only am I running and sweating, but I also have people of the 'shoot first and ask questions later' variety with weapons trained on me. I didn't come down here to go out like that.

"I absolutely approached him inside. I came up to him on his side that was closest to the door so that if he was going to make a break for the door he was going to have to do it through me. I told him in Portuguese to not be afraid, that if I wanted to kill him I would've done it already, and then I asked him if he spoke English at all because at that time my Portuguese was sketchy at best."

"What's the Portuguese word for sketchy?" Harper asked.

"I didn't say that part to him, you moron. I was just saying it to you guys so you would know why I had asked him if he spoke English."

"Oh, *mea culpa*. As you were then."

"And FYI, the Portuguese word for sketchy is *impreciso*. Anyway, he does the first thing that I figured he would do, which is tell me that I have him confused for someone else, and that if I don't leave him alone he will call the police. To which I reply that maybe I do have him mistaken for someone else, but I can't tell because he is wearing a disguise."

"Are we still talking in Portuguese?"

"Up until that point, yes," replied Chase, who then proceeded to tell them just how the conversation went between her and Diego del Fuento.

"Yes, I speak Engleesh," Diego said in a hushed voice, with a thick Portuguese accent. "Who are you? Who do you work for? What do you want with me eef you are not here to keell me?"

"As you well know your cousin has plenty of enemies. I'm one of them. I want to offer you protection and a chance to avenge your wife and children. In return, you will help me put together a plan of attack to destroy him and everything he has."

"You are American. I do not trust Americans."

"Well, I'm pretty sure that you can't trust anyone right now, but I'm the only one that's offering to keep you alive and offering you a shot at redemption. C'mon, I know you have to want that."

"What I want, mees, ees to put flowers on the graves of my dead wife and cheeldren, but Tito weell be watching for me to show up there. But he ees not looking for you. You weell do thees for me, okay? You help me to do thees, and I weell help you to get Tito. When eet ees over you weell help me move to America, yes?"

"I would love to help you move to America, but the truth is, Diego, I'm not really allowed back there myself. It's a long story, but let's get some flowers and get them to where they need to be. Did you walk here?"

"No, I take cab. Was hoping the driver would not recognize me. When I get eento cab I see the cabbie has picture of me on hees dash and a *pistola* on his seat. I ask heem who the man ees een the picture, and he say, '*homem morto*' – Portuguese for a dead man."

"Let's find some flowers, and we'll get out of here. I have a van right outside."

So that, my good men," Laurie said with a smile, "that is how I got Tito del Fuento's right-hand man to work for me. Sometimes I'm not sure who is more excited about Tito's demise, me or Diego, but I do know this much: I couldn't've gotten this far without him."

"Well, hurray for the fourth Ace. Where is he now?"

"Back where I'm staying."

Kinley and Harper thought the drive out of Rio had been a very bumpy one, so they were somewhat surprised when they heard

Laurie say, "Better hang on tight for the next few minutes. It gets kinda bumpy on this stretch. We're gonna be leaving the pavement for a couple of miles."

"Oh, man, I thought we had already left the pavement about five miles back."

And before another word was said on the topic the van started jostling the three around like ping pong balls in a lottery machine.

"I can't imagine this is too good for the suspension."

"Oh, don't I know it. I've had to change out the suspension twice on this thing. You should've been with me the first time I came out here. It was nothing but weeds and vines and small trees. I had to get a big truck, tie a cement pad onto the back of it, and run up and down this stretch for an entire day just to get it this good."

"Geez, Laurie, maybe you should've gotten a jeep instead of a cargo van."

"How fast are you going?" Harper asked over the noise of the jarring ride.

"Oh, about seven." Chase replied loudly.

The trio rode over the rough stretch of terrain without saying much else in the in the noisy van. Harper was making guttural noises behind Laurie and Kinley to emphasize how much his body was being rattled around. Then, just as fast as the noise and shaking had begun, it ended and they were back on a paved road.

"So what's the deal? They never finished paving this road or something?"

"There's hundreds of roads like this. Roads that were meant to connect at some point or another, and they just never did. This road had a road block up back there the first time I came out this way. I had to move it so I could get through."

"Why would you ever want to do that?"

"Because I stole some images from a DEA satellite, and I saw something, and it looked peculiar, and I wanted to get a closer look," she said matter-of-factly.

"So? What was it? Some kind of nuclear facility or something?"

"It looked like buildings, and it had a road coming out of it, and the road just stopped. I made a map, drove to the dead-end road, and then I drove in the general direction of where I thought this road was. It took me a while, but I found it."

"And where does it go?" Harper inquired.

"There," she pointed. Devereaux rolled down his passenger window and Harper moved up between the driver's seat and the passenger's seat. They both gawked at the structure as the van approached it.

"Dude, where are we?"

Chase pulled off the overgrown broken-pavement road and into an equally-overgrown paved parking lot. Kinley could see a well-beaten path through the tall weeds from where Laurie had been driving repeatedly during her stay there.

"We're about forty-five miles outside of Rio, and about eight miles from del Fuento's compound."

"So, this is your *house*?"

"These warehouses have been abandoned for almost three years. I tracked down the owner of them and worked out a lease agreement. I bought in for a year and then month-to-month after that," Laurie stated as she pulled to a stop.

"You're renting all of these?" Harper was amazed.

"No, just part of one. She was getting nothing for any of it, and until they come and tear it down she said I could stay here as long as I liked. I told her I was writing a book, and that I needed someplace out of the way where I could think. She was a sweet old lady. Funny name though: Alicia Greenmint."

"Wait, you mean to tell me your landlady's name is Alicia Greenmint? That's hysterical."

"I know, right? And you would think that a name coincidence

like that would only happen once in a lifetime, but – no lie – I know a guy named Skip Church, and he's an atheist."

Chase pulled the van up to the front of a warehouse that was located to the far right of the six warehouses and office buildings that were lined up adjacent to one another.

"I'm going to let you two out here. See that door right there?" she asked, pointing to a battered door that was to the right of where they were stopped. Before either of them could answer, Chase pointed to a parking garage that was attached to the right of the warehouse. "I'm going to park in there real quick – keeps the van out of sight from any onlookers – and I'll come around and let you guys in. Cool?"

"Cool," Harp replied as he scooched himself toward the van's side door. As he opened it, he asked Kin, "Cool with you, boss?"

Devereaux opened his door and hopped out. He turned back toward Chase and said, "How long are you going to be?"

"About five minutes, tops. Why?"

"Because if you fall and break your neck on your way back to us, I don't want to be standing out here with Harper for an hour going, 'She'll be here any minute now. I just know it.' If we don't see you in ten minutes then we're going to start making plans for an immediate evacuation out of here."

"Shut the door already, will ya? I'll see you in a few."

Devereaux slammed the door and watched the van pull off. He turned to his partner to make a comment only to see Harper staring off into the distance. "Whatcha looking at, buddy?"

"Holy Malone, we are seriously in the middle of nowhere," Rowe replied as he raised his left arm and pointed at nothing in particular. "I can see why these warehouses went belly-up. There is, lit'rally, nothing around here."

Between regaining their bearings from jet lag and their conversation with Laurie Chase, neither Kinley nor Harper had realized how far the trek from the airstrip just outside of Rio to the warehouses had taken them up and away from the city.

"I mean I was kinda into this whole thing when you said Rio de Janeiro, but, like Chase just said, we're a little bit outside of the Rio de Janeiro jurisdiction at this point," Harper said solemnly.

"Well, technically, we did land in Rio, and hey, look at the bright side. This place does look bigger than her shanty in Mexico City."

"Oh, that has me doing backflips over here, I'm so excited," Harper said flatly. "Had I known we were going to be so far outside of the city I might've packed a little more."

"Yeah, I was just thinking that, too. Eh, it'll be okay. She said she got us some stuff."

"That would make me feel better if she didn't have the fashion sense of a blind wookie."

Just then a service door on the front of the warehouse opened. Laurie Chase stuck her head out and yelled, "Door's open, fellas. C'mon in."

When they walked into her place, Kin and Harper looked around in disbelief. It was enormous and spacious and set up like a war room in the Pentagon.

"Wow. Who's your interior decorator? Sergeant Slaughter?"

"Like what I've done with the place?"

"Yeah," they both answered simultaneously.

The room where they now stood was the main warehouse floor. It ran some seventy yards deep by forty feet wide. Along the right side wall, three individual sets of stairs led up to a bevy of overhead offices.

On the main floor were several different types of dioramas, except this time they were not the electronic types like Chase had in Mexico City. This time they were actual models – and a lot of them.

"Is that the compound?" Kin asked.

"It is," she said.

"Are those trees?"

"And fields, too, on some of them."

"It looks like you've got a lot of them. These little model thingies."

"They're called dioramas, Harper. Geez, I would have thought you would have learned what they were called by now," Laurie said in exasperation.

"He knows, Laurie," Devereaux said covering for his friend. "He's just messing with you. He's missed you."

"And I suppose that I've missed him, too – like I've missed an unscheduled enema."

"*Olá*, Laurie," a voice seemingly came out of nowhere. Then from the back of the warehouse appeared a short, thin Portuguese man.

"Hey, Diego," Chase turned to greet him. "These are the two men that I was telling you about. The two men that will help us with getting Tito. Kinley Devereaux," she pointed to Kin, "and Harper Rowe," she said, pointing to Harp.

"Eet is wonderful to meet you," Diego said in his thick accent as he approached both men with his right hand extended. Kinley met Diego's handshake with a firm grip and said, "Good to know ya, brother."

Diego turned to Harper, right hand extended. Harper grabbed Diego's hand with both of his and shook it vigorously. "We're going to get your cousin, and if I have any say in the circumstance, I hope you get to pull the trigger on the shot that sends him straight to his grave."

"To me, eet does not matter who sends heem to his grave just as long as he gets there. I weell hope that my wife and children weell be waiting for heem when he crosses over. I hope they are there, and I hope they are the ones who get to toss him eento the fiery peet."

"Well, we're all here now. Let's get things rolling."

"Before we delve too deep into this plan," began Chase, "let's get situated first. Diego has a cot in the back – in what was supposed to be a break room, I guess – and I sleep up there." Chase pointed up toward the offices that overlooked the entire warehouse. "I set up a room up there for the two of you, as well. That's where you'll find the clothes that I got for you."

"How do you have electricity in here? There aren't even electric poles outside."

"Well, they put in all underground wiring – don't ask me how with the craggy mess this place is built on – they just never hooked it up. I hooked it up. Only took about two days – and about seven different electrocutions of one form or another, but hey, I'm still here and I have electricity in this mess."

"Good golly, is there anything you can't do?"

Laurie smiled. "Get washed up, get settled in. Diego and I are going to get things set up down here."

"Cool. We'll be back down in a jif."

CROOL AND BALDWIN TO ATLANTA

By the time Jeb Crool and his right-hand man, Agent David Baldwin, had made their way downtown to the APD 5, most of the mess from the calamity of the night before had been cleared. But the chaos from members of several different law enforcement agencies milling in and around the crime scene still remained. It was a chilly January morning and both of the agents were wearing their heavy NSA jackets.

"Well now, doesn't this just look like a whole new kind of stupid," Crool said under his breath to Baldwin.

"Who are we supposed to be looking for again?"

Crool scanned his memory the best he could. "Uh, Daltry, Dauber, Daugherty. That's it. Jerry Daugherty."

"You sure?"

"Yeah, flash your tin and ask for a Jerry Daugherty."

Crool and Baldwin meandered around the parking lot full of agents, officers, and emergency crew workers until they saw someone that looked like they might be the highest ranking official on the scene. She was a tall, lean blond-haired woman that a lot of people seemed to be walking up to, bantering with, then walking away.

"She looks like the big badge here, Dave. See if she can get us to Daugherty."

Baldwin stepped up to her and said, "Agent David Baldwin,

NSA. Are you in charge here, ma'am?"

"Agent Phelps, Georgia Bureau of Investigation," she said in a voice dripping with Southern accent, as she eyed Baldwin up and down and shook his hand. "I'm guessing since you're from the NSA that my being in charge here is going to be rather short-lived, huh?"

"Oh, no, ma'am. That isn't the case at all. My boss," Baldwin turned and gestured to Jeb, "and I are just down here to find an officer Jerry Daugherty."

"He was here earlier. I took his statement, and he showed me the video footage of what the security cameras in the precinct had picked up of the incident. He did tell me that he had talked with someone from the NSA, and that they would be coming here to look over said video footage."

"Yeah, that's us, and that really is pretty much all we wanted. Maybe see what the forensics guys came up with, too. Can we do that? Soon?"

Phelps looked around at the disorder and disarray surrounding her. She turned back to Baldwin and said, "I don't seem to have a needy agent trying to garner milk from my proverbial teet at this particular moment. Perhaps now would be as good a time as any to go check out that beautiful bomb footage." Without waiting for an answer from either Baldwin or Crool, Phelps started walking toward the precinct.

"Hey, is it safe to go in there?" Crool spoke up.

Phelps laughed out loud.

"Agent Crool, is it?" she stopped short in front of the two men.

"Last I checked."

"Your guy – the one that you're trying to track down – Harper Rowe? Yes?"

"He'd be that. That'd be him."

"Not that I would have ever thought anything less, but oh my, he is quite good, isn't he? He had Jerry in quite the foul mood when

I got here this morning. Oh, and his partner is also quite good."

"What are you getting at, crazy lady?" Crool said, growing short of patience. "Of course I know Harper Rowe is good. It's why I'm here, and he's still on the run. As far as his partner? I have no idea who this man is. I know Harper's former partner was killed up on a rooftop in Mexico City about a year and a half ago. Who he's working with now? Like I said, that's what I'm here to find out."

"Gosh," Phelps chuckled. "Lay off the caffeine, will ya? All I was getting at was that the little scene they caused last night was seemingly well played out. Big boom, big ruckus, big disturbance, very little damage. It looks like Harper got himself arrested, came in here with the explosives on him–"

"Right," said Baldwin, "with the detonator that was posed as a hearing aid."

"Oh good. You caught that, too. Yes, their actions last night were meant to cause enough of a distraction for them to specifically get a rifle out of the evidence cage. This wasn't an act of terrorism, and as long as you boys are okay with that then that's just what I'm going to tell the press." Phelps began walking toward the precinct building once again. "Rowe brought the explosives in, detonator and all, got himself just enough time alone in one of the bathroom stalls and planted them. The second man came in. He had the switch. Looks like he made sure everyone was free and clear of the blast before he hit the button. Very humane for domestic terrorists, wouldn't you say, Agent Baldwin? Agent Crool? I mean, that is why you're looking for Harper Rowe, isn't it? Because he's the one behind the assassination of former Secretary of Defense Paul Michaels, isn't it?"

"He's definitely a person of interest, and the fact that he hasn't turned himself in or even bothered to contact me about it at all makes me very suspicious of why he was seen talking to Michaels just before Michaels got gunned down. He knows something, and I want to know what it is."

"With all of the things that have come out about Secretary Michaels since his assassination, I can't help but wonder if your Harper Rowe didn't do us all a big favor."

The trio arrived at the open entrance of the precinct building. "Watch your step," Phelps said as she began to tiptoe around the rubble in her brown pumps that coordinated perfectly with her tan skirt and white blouse.

"You sure it's safe to be in here?" Baldwin asked.

"Stay on my skirt, Dave. You'll be fine. Like I said before, your boy did a nice job of creating havoc without really destroying anything."

Agent Phelps walked down a hallway that originated to the right of the precinct's lobby and ended up in what looked like a cul de sac of offices. "The video footage that you will want to review is in here," she said as she walked into an office and flipped on a light switch. She turned to the two agents, smiled and said, "Oh, by the way, Agent Baldwin and Agent Crool, Happy New Year."

"Yeah," Jeb said in his usual droll tone, "welcome to the year two thousand and sunshine."

The room they entered was big enough to hold eight or ten people. There were chairs arranged sporadically about and a big-screen TV was attached to the far wall. Video viewing equipment of all sorts was scattered on a table that was close to the wall immediately to their right.

"Have a seat anywhere," Phelps instructed, "and I'll pull up the video from last night – slash – early this morning."

"Any popcorn with this matinee?" Crool asked as he and Baldwin discarded their coats onto nearby chairs.

"Oh my gosh," Phelps said as she smacked herself lightly in the forehead. "It totally escaped my mind that you guys have been up all night making your way down here. Do you need some coffee or anything?" Her Southern accent made the gesture sound genuine.

"I could probably use a bathroom," Crool said. "I have to pee so bad that I may actually have to sit down to do it."

"Any chance you have a cappuccino machine?" Baldwin asked.

"Why? Is that where your boss is gonna take a leak?" Phelps laughed at her own humor. "Sorry. I'm a little slap-happy myself. Seriously though, they're both down that hall on the left. One a little further than the other. I'm sure the two of you can figure out which is which."

Without further fanfare the two agents turned on their heels and headed out of the office and down the hall. Once they were out of sight and earshot of Agent Phelps, Crool said in a hushed tone to Baldwin, "Well, ain't she just like a Dyson vacuum–"

"What?" Baldwin asked in bewilderment.

"She sucks, agent. She's about half daffy and just a few flavors short of being a complete box of Fruit Loops."

"What do you want to do?"

"Not much we can do, I guess. I mean, it's not like she's giving us any resistance about what we came down here for. I just wish she was – I don't know – a little more professional."

"It's New Year's Day, boss. Ain't nobody wants to be here today."

Just before he walked into the men's room, Crool looked at Agent Baldwin and said in all seriousness, "I do. I want to be here, because here is a little closer to getting Harper Rowe, and getting Harper Rowe may finally clear up a whole bunch of questions that this country has needed answered for a while now. We finally nail some of this down, then maybe by Valentine's Day – maybe we both can have the night off."

With that Crool entered the bathroom.

Baldwin laughed. "My wife would love that."

Through the closed bathroom door, Dave heard Jeb's muffled voice, "I didn't know you were married."

BACK IN RIO

Up in the room that Laurie had prepared for them, Harper and Kinley were finally alone and able to talk to each other.

"Wonder if she rat-proofed this room?" Harper started.

"I'm sure it's fine. I hear most rodents are afraid of heights anyway."

"Really?"

Dev looked at Harper incredulously. "No. Not really. I swear, Harp, sometimes I wonder if you've got a brain in that head of yours or just an overused urinal cake."

"Mock me all ya want, boss, but I'm anything but happy with this trip so far. I had a perfectly beautiful girl back in Johannesburg that I was more than willing to spend the next two weeks with until you called me in the middle of the night about all this bull crap."

"Yeah, I know, buddy. This is definitely not what I thought it was going to be either. I just figured we owed her, ya know?"

"Yeah, I know," Harper admitted.

"Just gonna take a little getting' used to, is all. We'll wash up and head back down and see how her presentation goes. Hopefully, it will win us over. I know that you're itching to get back up with Big James to let him know just what we'll need and when."

"Not to mention finding out when his friends will be able to make it into town."

Harper and Kinley went through the things that Laurie had bought for them. Most of them were black tees, lightweight cargo pants, and some underwear and socks.

"What do you think of that guy, Diego?"

"I met the guy for, like, ten seconds, dude. What do you think I think of him?"

"He seems like he's on the up and up, but gosh, how reliable is this guy gonna be when we get into the heat of things?"

"Not sure what ya mean, bud?"

"I'm just sayin'," Harper began to explain, "what if the fit hits the shan and it comes down to us or him, and he has his shot to kill his cousin? He leaves us hanging to get what he wants, our well-being be damned. That's what I mean."

"I highly doubt that's going to happen. Pretty sure."

"Next question. She's been down here for a decent amount of time. What if she shows us her plan, and we see an obvious hole or a flaw in it? Is she going to listen to what we have to say?"

"Of course she will. That's why she wanted us to come down here in the first place. She trusts us, and she needs us."

"Is that what she told you, or is that what you think? I mean, how much did you talk to her about this whole ordeal? Please, please, please don't tell me that we're down here on a blind whim that you're having because, once again, you think we owe her because of Mexico City."

"We do owe her."

"Kin? Please tell me that this isn't some kind of moral obligation that you think you owe this girl, and that is why we're here."

Devereaux sat down on one of the beds in the makeshift bedroom. He was quiet for a while until Harper sat down on the other bed and broke the silence. "Is that why we're here?"

"Yeah," Kinley finally came clean.

Harper took off one of his shoes and fired it across the room, nailing Kinley right in his ribcage.

"Ow! Ya little dope."

"You deserved that. You probably deserve a lot more than that."

Devereaux sighed, picked up Harper's shoe, and tossed it back to him. "I'm sure I do."

The duo was silent again for a while as they stared at each other.

"Eh, we've been in worse situations, right?" Kinley proffered.

"By a long shot," Harper laughed. "I'm sure in forty-eight hours we're going to be laughing our heads off about this."

"She's been down here for over a year doing her homework. She's got del Fuento's right-hand man on our side. We got Big James, and Big James has his guys. We got this."

Harper stood up from his bed, crossed the room, and patted Kinley on the shoulder. "We got each other. That's all that we'll need."

"While I'm getting cleaned up, give your guy a call and let him know we've landed and are getting settled in. See what the ETA is on his guys getting here, too."

"Roger that, Rabbit. I'm guessing we're going to have to meet them at some point. It's not like he's going to be able to find this place with a GPS."

"Not unless he's got a GPS that uses the same DEA satellite system that Laurie used to find it." Devereaux picked up one of the changes of clothes that Chase had gotten for the duo and said uneasily, "I sure hope that she's de-ratted this place."

PART OF SOMETHING BIG

Samuel Hawkins was at the controls of the airplane that was flying the quartet known as Dragon's Men toward Rio de Janeiro. Daniel Sloane was in the co-pilot's seat watching Hawkins' every move.

"Ya know, Daniel, just because I'm teaching you the art of flying a plane, it doesn't mean that you have to sit there and stare at me with the piercing stare of a psychopath."

"I'm not staring. I'm studying. I just don't want to miss anything."

"You're not gonna miss anything, boss. What? Do you think that I'm just going to land the plane when you're not looking or something?"

"I still have no idea how you do this stuff," Sloane said. "Not just the flying stuff, but – like – how do you get a flight plan OK'd from the FAA on such short flippin' notice?"

Samuel Hawkins was a tall, lean black man with the distinction of having a very bass, very Barry White voice.

"I still use my military clearance. It works, even today."

"What?" Sloane asked, confused. "Military clearance?"

"Yeah, you had it, and I still have it – and I use it. Especially when it comes to getting things accomplished as far as getting a flight plan OK'd in a jif."

The door to the cockpit opened and John Watkins appeared. "You guys okay up here?"

"We're landing where we always land when we visit Rio, right?" asked Hawkins.

"Yeah, that's exactly what we're doing."

"Where's Merc?" Sloane asked, referring to the fourth member of the team, Dr. Mercedes Lara.

"She's sacked out in the back," Watkins confirmed.

"So it's just us boys up here talking?" Hawkins asked blankly as he studied the ILS readouts of the plane's gauges.

"Yeah, it's just us."

The three men were silent for a few moments before Sloane picked the conversation back up again. "And remind us again why we are winging our way to Rio on the first day of this fine new year?"

"For real," chimed in Hawkins. "I mean, I know we've had a few days off, but it's the end of the year holidays, John Boy. I didn't feel my skills getting any rustier just because I was enjoying a few cups of eggnog."

"This is a shot at getting a big-time bad guy. We have all heard of Tito del Fuento, the Brazilian drug lord that's only getting stronger."

"I've heard of that guy, yeah. He's a real turd stain on the tighty whities of life."

"So, what's the plan then?"

Watkins took a breath before saying, "I'm not sure."

"We are callin' the shots on this, right?" asked Sloane, becoming a bit uneasy.

"Not this time," answered John.

"Whoa, whoa, whoa," Hawkins turned around in his pilot's seat. "I thought we were doing what we're doing so that we would always be the ones calling the shots. No more of this getting out-ranked bull crap."

"We are," John reassured him, "but you remember the last time we were in Rio? We worked with that guy Big James?"

"The Brazilian black ops guy," Mercedes recalled as she sneaked past John in the cockpit doorway and took a seat in the navigator's chair. She looked around at the other members of the team. "What? You didn't think I was going to just let you three leave me alone back there with my dreams, did you?"

Without batting an eye over Merc's sudden presence, Hawkins asked, "So? What? Big James is the one calling the shots on this particular endeavor?"

John shrugged his shoulders and shook his head in uncertainty. "No, I don't think he's calling the shots either."

"Then who's runnin' this show?"

"Guess we'll find out when we get there."

"Oh, that's just great," Mercedes said in her usual cynical tone. "We get yanked out of what was looking to be a pretty kick-ass New Year's Eve party to head to South America for a job that we not only know nothing about, but we're also taking orders from some unknown person that may or may not have our best interests in mind. Yeah, that's just great."

"Good to see that the New Year hasn't brought any unwanted changes in your sunny disposition, Merc," Sloane smirked.

Besides being the team's resident physician, Dr. Mercedes Lara was also the unit's munitions expert and overall pessimist. While her attitude was usually a pain in the neck, it kept the group grounded and free of delusions of grandeur. Plus, she had patched up John, Danny, and Samuel so many times over the years that she had more than earned her spot in the troop, regardless of her attitude and outlook.

"I'm just saying that I thought we had given up being someone else's rag doll when we left the military."

"Thank you," agreed Hawkins, "that's exactly what I said."

"Couldn't we have taken a vote or somethin', at least?"

"What's there to vote about?" John asked rhetorically. "We said when we started our venture together that we wanted to do it so that we could make a difference – really do something that would help make a change for good in people's lives. Tito del Fuento is a peddler of goods and wares who ruins lives and gets people killed every day. He's the rotten egg at the bottom of the wastebasket that's stinking up the whole house, and now it's time to take out the trash. We won't get an opportunity like this again, and I am for sure not going to let it pass us by."

"Hey, Johnny, we hear ya. But it's just that when taking a big risk like this it's usually in our best interest to sit down and map it out first."

"We will. We'll get down here, hook up with Big James and whoever else is in on this operation, and we'll put together a plan of attack. If for some reason the plan seems outlandish and undoable, then we'll bail. But I highly doubt that is going to be the case. Yeah, Merc, they may not have our best interest in mind, but I always do. So, if this is an effort that's going to bring this guy down, I want to be a part of it."

27

DEVEREAUX CLEANS UP HIS ACT

James Gray was out like a light when his phone rang. He didn't even bother to open his eyes while he reached over to his bedside table and fumbled around for the cellular device. Once his fingertips felt the familiar apparatus, he propped himself up on one elbow and, with eyes still closed, answered groggily, "Yeah?"

"Big Time, it's Harper. Just callin' to let ya know that we've landed."

"Good. That's good," the big man said as he flopped back down onto his pillow.

"This a good time? Are your friends from Manila still there?"

Big James lifted his head off the pillow and took a quick scan of the room. "Nah, looks like they left," and back to the pillow his head went. "Where are you and your crew?"

"Somewhere left of Albuh-koykee," Harper said in his Bugs Bunny voice.

"Well, my guys are enroute here via plane. What time is it anyway?"

"A little after 1 p.m. local time."

"Okay, so if their ETA is accurate, then they will be here in less than two hours. Where do you want to meet us?"

"Man, I have no idea. Where are you meeting your guys?"

"A small airfield about 60 kilometers outside of Rio called the *Bartolomeu de Gusmão* Airport. It was being used for the Santa Cruz military. They stopped using it about ten or twelve years ago, give or take, but it's still usable. It's where I have people fly in with shipments I don't want to have picked up by the authorities."

"60 kilometers. That's what, about 35 miles or so?"

"Yeah, to the west and a bit north. You say your person's been down here for over a year?"

"Right."

"They'll know where to find it then."

"And you said you're meeting them there at three-ish this afternoon?"

"Roger that, corpsman."

Harper took a quick glance at his watch. "We'll be there, too, then."

"I'll see ya then, chief."

Harper hung up the phone and made a beeline to the bathroom where Kinley was showering. He knocked on the door and said, "Wrap it up, Kin. We've officially got someplace to be."

"Hang on," Harper heard his friend's voice through the door. He heard the shower cut off, the shower curtain open, a few ambiguous noises, then the door opened to reveal Devereaux wearing nothing but a towel around his waist. That was not what grabbed Harper's immediate attention, however. "Holy cow! Ya shaved!"

"It's just too humid down here to keep that look goin'. Besides, I was getting tired of looking in the mirror every day and not seeing myself looking back. And we're meeting new people today. I wouldn't want to give them the wrong impression."

"What impression is that? That you might whittle them some kind of duck decoy?"

"I hate that feeling your skin gets after you shave a beard off, too. You know what I'm talking about? That weird, numb, tingling feeling?"

"That is irritating, true, but it's not as bad as when you shave your back and shoulders, and that same effect is made infinitely worse by having a shirt rubbing against it all day."

"Agreed," Devereaux said. "So why was it that you were banging on the bathroom door in the first place?"

"I talked to Big James. He's meeting his guys over at the old Santa Cruz military airport. If I'm remembering correctly that's not too far away from here."

Kin took the second towel that he was using to dry his hair and upper torso and draped it across his right shoulder. "If you don't wanna see anything that's a bit too unsightly, you might want to look the other way."

Harper turned 180 degrees on his heels. "Anyway, Kin, I was going to go down and tell Laurie to hold off on the presentation of her awesome plan, and we could all head to that airport together. That way everyone could be present and accounted for once we get back here and Laurie and Diego go over the details and fine minutiae of the operation. I mean, that seems like the best usage of time, don't you think?"

"In the grand scheme of things, I think that definitely sounds like the best usage of time. So, what time are they due to show up over there?"

"Three o'clock local time. That's about an hour and a half from now."

"In that case, I'm going to do you a favor. I'll get dressed and go down and inform them of what has happened and what is going to happen. This way you can do all of us a favor and take a shower. You still smell like someone dumped alcohol all over you about eighteen hours ago. It was tolerable on the flight down here because we were in an air-conditioned cabin, and it was bearable on the ride here because Laurie had the AC on, but now that the air is thick with heat and humidity, your stench has become quite unmanageable."

"After that little fiasco in Atlanta I don't care if I inhale the aroma of tequila ever again."

"I'm kinda right there with ya," Devereaux said as he exited the bathroom and began making his way back to the makeshift bedroom that Chase had set up for him and Harper. Harper fell right in behind him.

"Fine by me you telling her to hold off on her plan. I somehow get the feeling that if that request came outta my mouth it would be met with all the grace of an angry hippo. But coming from you? Oh no. Coming from you – I'm sure she'll be doing backflips and cartwheels from one side of the building to the other."

"Hey, maybe if I ask real nice she might put on a two piece and lather herself up in baby oil when she is doing those cartwheels and backflips. Yeah, I think I'll do that."

"Don't placate me, Kin. You know if there's one thing in this world that burns my butt like a three-and-a-half foot flame, it's when you try that crap."

"Fine. Then let me ask you this: do you think I look like Tom Cruise?"

"That's not th–"

"Eh, eh, eh – answer the question. Do you think I look like Tom Cruise? Or maybe one of those up-and-comers in those dreadfully boring vampire and werewolf movies? Is that what you think I look like?"

"No."

"Exactly. I do not look like them. Yet for some unimaginable reason you seem to think that every woman that I meet just fawns all over me like I'm some pin-up model on every teenage girl's bedroom wall. You used to do the same thing with me and Kelly Campbell. Now you're doing it all over again with Chase. And let me tell ya, bud, that stuff gets old."

"Ah, I guess you're right. This time, at least, you like the woman back."

Kinley shook his head incredulously. "Are you going to go get a shower anytime soon, Brewmaster Bill?"

Rowe grabbed his clothes off the bed. "Hey, did you leave all the shower amenities in there?"

"Yeah, there's some soap, shampoo and conditioner, some shaving cream, razors, balm. Everything you'll need."

"Excellent. I will see you downstairs in just a bit."

When Kinley finished his trek down the stairs he saw Laurie and Diego standing by the dioramas, talking quietly to each other.

"Hey, what's going on?" he asked as he moved across the warehouse floor toward them.

Laurie turned to look at him and smiled. "Wow, that really was you underneath all that hair. I was worried for a minute that we may have been infiltrated." She walked up to Devereaux. To his surprise, she raised her hand to his face and slowly ran her fingertips across his left cheek, down to his chin, up around his right cheek, and then took one fingertip slowly down across his lips. "Mmm, smooth."

Kinley found his eyes locked on hers, entranced, even hypnotized. Then she quickly pulled her hand away from his mouth. "So," she smiled, "where's Harper?"

"He'll be down in a bit," Kin said, quickly composing himself. "He's getting a much-needed shower."

"Good. I'm excited to show you what Diego and I have come up with."

"Well–" Kinley started slowly, "we're excited to see what ya've got going on, but there's been a change in the plan for the time being. Harper's got a guy, and he's bringing in four guys from the States. They're landing over at the old military air base."

"Okay. How soon?"

"Three."

"Three? Three what? Three o'clock or three hours?"

"O'clock. Three o'clock. The guys that Harper's guy is bringing in. They're going to be–"

Kinley seemed unable to speak coherently because he was thinking about how Laurie had touched his face, and how he felt about her, and what Harper had said about how Devereaux loved Chase, and how at least this time the woman loved him back.

Laurie snapped her fingers in front of Kin's face. "Hello. Earth to Kinley Devereaux. They're going to be – where?"

"The old Santa Cruz Air Force Base. You know where that is, yeah?"

"Oh, very good. Yes, indeed, that is a great place to bring in outside planes. So many different companies that need to do quick drops or planes that have to do emergency landings use that all the time. I mean, the thing's been shut down for a while, but it's a big airstrip, and around here these days it gets patrolled less than a church parking lot on a Tuesday afternoon."

Laurie turned and in a hushed voice said something in Portuguese to Diego. He replied in kind. She nodded. He smiled and gave a thumbs up.

"Diego's going to stay here to keep the home fires burning while we run down and get your friends." Chase said to Kin. "I'll go get the van ready for another road trip," she walked past Kin and ran her fingers across his ribcage.

"Need any help?"

"Just go make sure your boy doesn't use up all the hot water. Wouldn't be proper to have guests over and have to give them the no-frills package here at Casa de Chase."

Two Friends at a Café

She returned to the café table with orange mint tea for her dear friend, Eliska Lukasik. For herself she had ordered a triple espresso. She set the two drinks down on the corner table before taking a seat herself.

"So, we're here. We're safe. Let's enjoy the day."

"I do not understand," Ellie smiled nervously. "I already do enjoy day."

"Relax," she said and smiled. "We are safe. We can talk. You can talk to me about why you called me – why I'm here. What has you so spooked, baby girl?"

"I am very afraid for friend. She has seen things she is not to see, and now she is in much danger. She tell me what she see, and now I am very afraid for own life, too."

"Oh my, Ellie, what is it that she saw? Can't she just go to the police and ask for help?"

"No, no," Lukasik said adamantly as panic covered her face. "No police."

"Then tell me what's going on, Eliska. What in the world did your friend see that she wasn't supposed to?"

"My friend – her name is Anezka – she has little daughter who make friend with another little girl that live in children's home. She is orphan. One day Anezka's little daughter – her name is Jana – see that orphan girl very bruised and beaten. She ask orphan girl how come she to be like this, and the orphan girl cry and run away. When Jana tell Anezka, she go to children's home to see if little girl is okay. People at the children's home tell her please leave. They argue with Anezka and call police. Police make my friend leave or arrest her. She leaves, but come back later that night to see in windows maybe find out why little girl is beaten and if more children beaten, too."

"Did she see anything?"

"Yes, she see many things. Many bad things."

She could hear the fear and trepidation rising in Eliska's voice. "What did she see, Ellie? Did she see them beating the children?"

"She see – she see older men with little girls, and older women with little boys, and they are smoking illegal and drinking alcohol. The men and women are naked and the children are make to touch them in bad ways."

"What? Oh my Lord God. What did she do?"

"Is bad. Someone see her and chase her. She drove back to home, but when she get there, the police, they are already there talking to her sister. They tell her sister that they have warrant for Anezka for trespassing."

"What did she do?"

"She wait for them to leave then go inside. She packed bag for her and Jana, and she left."

"Oh, dear God. How did you find out about all this? About what happened and what your friend saw? Have you talked to her? Do you know where she is?"

"Yes, I talk to her and know where she is."

"Well, where is she?"

Eliska hesitated for a moment. "She and Jana are at my home. They stay with me two nights. I tell her that she need to leave country, but she has no one. No family besides sister. This is why I call you. I am scared for them and do not know what to do."

She reached across the café table and squeezed Ellie's trembling hands. She looked thoughtfully into her friend's eyes before calmly saying, "It's going to be okay. I know someone that can help."

"Not police."

"Oh no, sweetie. This guy is definitely not the police," she smiled. "Hey, let's finish up here, and we can go back to your home, okay? I am going to have to make a phone call to find this man that can help. It might take a day or two, but he will know what to do when I tell him about this."

Eliska reciprocated the squeezing of her friend's hands. "Thank you. I feel better to know that you are helping."

"You're my best friend, Ell. Heck, you're pretty much my only friend. I feel like crap that I haven't seen you in so long, and that it takes something like this to get us together again."

"Is okay, *přítel*. We always find way back to each other. Is what friends do."

A Nice Place to Hangar Round

Big James Gray drove his faded gray clunker of a minivan through one of the many unmarked entrances to the former Santa Cruz Air Force base. Just as he was pulling onto the property, he looked up to see the plane that was carrying the Dragon's Men come in for a picture-perfect landing.

Big James knew where they were going and so did they. As the plane touched down and headed for the end of the runway, it made a right turn toward the airport's hangars. James gunned the engine of the Dodge Caravan and made a beeline toward the same destination.

"Coming to meet ya, crew," he yelled inside of his vehicle as it bounced over the grassy field, arriving at the hangar just about the same time as the plane. He pulled up outside the building, exited the van, and watched as the big plane maneuvered itself into the hangar and out of sight.

As excited as Big James was to see his friends again, he knew it was best to approach with caution. He ambled his way up to the building and waited as he watched the bay door on the back of the plane open slowly and descend to the hangar's cement floor. He smiled as he saw John, Daniel, Mercedes, and Sam come walking down in a standard two-by-two formation.

"Don't shoot," he said just loud enough to be heard from the hangar entrance.

"Is that you, big fella?" asked Sloane, donning a pair of aviator sunglasses.

"It is, it is. Anything I can help you with? D'you guys have a safe flight?"

"We're here, ain't we?"

Big James trekked across the 400-foot construction toward them. Suddenly, the four all went for their weapons at the same time.

"James, get down!" Lara yelled.

The fat man hit the deck with astounding agility, covered his head, and yelled, "What? What the crap?"

"Spread!" Watkins ordered. He hustled up to James, extended his hand, and said, "Take cover with me, boss. Looks like you were followed."

"What? No," Gray said as he took John's hand and stood to his feet. "No one even knew that I was going to be–", James stopped short. Without turning around he said to John, "Crap, tell your gang to stand down."

"What? You sure?"

"Yeah." The gentle giant turned around to spot a white van that was parked just outside the hangar.

"Stand down," Watkins said quietly. "Stay tight."

"Roger that," John heard from a trio of voices through his com as he watched James Gray start making his way toward the front of the hangar.

"Hey!" James hollered as he began a husky jog, "holster your weapons!"

Laurie sat behind the steering wheel in the driver's side of the van. She smirked, "Is that your guy? The chubby one headed this way?"

"That'd be him," acknowledged Harper. "I'm going to go give the guy a hug before he collapses," Harper said as he opened the sliding door of the van. He hopped to his feet and double-timed it up to Big James. "Big Time!" Harper prepared for impact.

Gray wrapped his meaty arms around his friend and lifted him off of the ground with a fervent embrace. "Good to see you, bud! Good to see you," James patted him on the back.

"I'm equally as excited," Harper gasped. "Now, put me down, Nanook."

From inside the van, Laurie said, "He's going to let him breathe, right?"

"He's Harper's friend. I'm sure it will be fine."

"Oh, crap," Laurie replied. "He's not gonna hug *us* like that, is he?"

"Well, just on the outside chance that he's an equal opportunity hugger, I'll let you go first."

"You're such a pussy."

Kinley looked at Chase and said, "That seems a bit harsh. I was just joking around."

"Oh, you so were not, and just to make you look like the smaller man–" Chase opened the driver's side door and hopped out of the van.

"Oh, no, you don't," and Kinley opened the passenger's side door and made an equally quick exit out of the van. He met Chase stride for stride just up until she leapt into the big man's arms.

James Gray was taken a bit off guard by Chase's enthusiasm. He caught her out of midair and squeezed her tight. "I'm guessing you're Laurie?" he said as he patted her on the back with his big meaty paws. "It's nice to meet you."

Chase gasped for air as she said, "Good – to meet you – too."

As Big James set Laurie back down on her own two feet, Kinley stepped up, extended his hand, and said, "Nice to meet you, Mr. Gray. I'm Harper's partner, Kinley Devereaux, a.k.a. Jeff Samples. How's it goin'?"

James met Harper's hand with a firm handshake. "Good to meet you, Mr. Devereaux. I've heard a lot of good things about you."

Kin looked at Laurie and gave an imperceptive wink. "I'd give you a hug, too," Devereaux continued, "but I've got a bit of a rib condition–"

"Think nothing of it, sir," James butted in, "I've been told that I'm a bit too much of a hugger as it is. I've been trying to quit, but heck, I just love people."

"Well, shucks, James, I don't want to keep you from fulfilling your prophecy," Dev smiled.

"Don't you do it," Chase said curtly under her breath.

"You can give my hug to her."

Laurie shot Kinley a look that could kill, but before the proceedings could go any further, Harper stepped up and said, "So, where are your guys, Big Time?"

"They're right here," he answered. "Johnny, it's okay," he yelled, and from seemingly out of nowhere the quartet that made up Dragon's Men appeared.

"What in the world?" Kinley said out loud as he looked around the hangar, expecting more people to come walking out of the woodwork.

"I'm John Watkins," John said as he approached Devereaux.

"Nice to meet you, John. I'm Kinley Devereaux, and my secondhand smoke friend here is Harper Rowe."

The introductions amongst the cast of characters that filled out the group that would be embarking on the mission to annihilate Tito del Fuento and his drug empire from the face of the earth took about five minutes, with handshakes aplenty, and yes, more hugs from Big James Gray. He hugged John, Hawk, Danny, and Merc because he knew them from prior dealings. He restrained from hugging Kinley, being unfamiliar with him and not wanting to create an awkward situation right out of the gate.

"So, does everybody call you Big James, Big James?"

"Pretty much."

"Well, why wouldn't they?" Harper asked rhetorically. "His name is James, and he's big. Although, I guess some sort of variation of big could be substituted. Like – huge, gargantuan, enormous, gigantic, etc."

"And James is actually my middle name."

"Really?" Harper asked, somewhat surprised. "James is my middle name, too."

"You're not going to tell us that your first name really is Big, are ya?" Hawk asked.

"No," the big man laughed.

"Then what is your first name?"

Big James gave kind of an uneasy look to everyone before he finally said, "My first name is Leslie."

An awkward silence filled the hangar until Harper asked, "Is that a family name?"

"Yes, it is. I'm actually Leslie James Gray IV. I went by Les for a while, but then everybody started calling me Lester. I didn't want to correct them because that would've defeated the whole purpose of going by Les in the first place. So, when my parents died when I was twelve years old, and I went to go live with my grandma, I just started going by James."

And with that bummer of a story, any thoughts of smart aleck comments in regards to Big James' first name quickly evaporated from everyone's mind.

"So," Daniel Sloane spoke up to break the silence, "is this everybody that's in on our bad guy venture?"

"All but one," Laurie said. "We have Tito del Fuento's, former right-hand man – his cousin Diego del Fuento – back at the place we're heading to now. We'll be there in a few minutes."

"Are we sure he's on our side, and not just blowing smoke?"

"I'm sure," Laurie confirmed. "He's given me way more intel than any double agent would have ever dreamed of. He's Tito's cousin. They grew up together, worked together, and then at the first sign of Diego's objecting to anything, Tito had the guy's family wiped out, and even now has a national hit out on Diego's life. Yeah, he's 100% on our side."

"Tell ya what," Harper said as he walked slowly towards the aircraft, "this plane is huge. How did you ever come upon a craft like this?"

"We bought the plane, and then Danny here," Watkins said as he pointed to Sloane, "stripped it down and modified it into what it is now. The body type is a Douglas DC-3."

"What kind of modifications did you do to it, Danny?" Harper asked.

"First thing I did was pull the engine and the exhaust system, then pulled any of the unnecessary components to try to make it as light as could be. After that I installed a jet propulsion engine and exhaust so that it could still carry some payload while making good time. I then modified the wings so that we could attach some Bulava missiles, the lightest missile of its kind."

"Wait, what?" Devereaux asked in disbelief. "The Bulava missile isn't even in use yet. The U.S. shut down the manufacturing of those missiles months ago. Plus, they're nuclear missiles launched from nuclear subs anyway. How the heck are you making them compatible to be fired from an airplane?"

"Because when they are fired from a sub they are nuclear, but when you change out the payload ratio from nuclear to auxiliary, it makes the missile itself light enough to be fired from a plane. Not to mention a heckuva lot more of a controllable strike. I also re-wired them to be heat-seeking missiles, as well."

"Where do you even find Bulava missiles these days anyway?"

Hawkins started laughing and said, "You might wanna make sure who these cats are, John, before you go spillin' them beans."

John turned to Big James for a look of approval.

The big man nodded and followed up by saying, "I vouch for their trustworthiness a hundred percent without hesitation."

"Okay," John exhaled. "See there are these highly-classified military government junkyards. Ya won't find them on a map or a GPS or get directions to them from anyone that happens to work at a nearby BP station because, frankly, they just don't exist. The only way that you'll ever hear about them is from someone that is looking to cut a deal in a late-night back alley non-sanctioned torturous interrogation that, by the grace of God, you happen to be privy to."

"And where, pray tell, does this secret hidden government junkyard exist?"

"Oh, no, no, no, my friend. You know how you might hear of a sunken treasure ship off the coast of Aruba, and you want to get a party of people together that can help you find such a treasure, but you keep it to the bare minimum so you don't have to share it with any more people than you have to?"

"So you want us to believe that it exists, but you're just not going to tell us where, huh?"

"Let's just put it this way. If you were to ever try to break into a place like this and get caught, they might do you the favor of questioning you about how you found out about the place before they kill you, but you're going to wish that they had just killed you. Being under such duress during such an interrogation, you would probably give up the info that they are seeking, and that info would be us," John said in reference to himself and the other three members of his team. "So just consider me not divulging the whereabouts of such a place a favor to you and us both."

"And in this so-called government junkyard is where you found these Bulava missiles?" Laurie asked.

"Yes, these 'so-called' government junkyards are where the U.S. Government scraps all of its state-of-the-art technology that it can't quite figure out how to make work. They're actually more of a storage area for them to put their crap until someone else figures out a way to make it work. Just so happens that as far as the Bulava missiles go, we were the 'somebody' that figured out how to make them work," Dr. Lara put in her two cents.

"As much as I love my country," spoke up Sloane, "I just can't be the one to bring this particular project to light to them."

John Watkins wrapped it up. "The security on this place is as tight as a drum, but we found an ant hole of vulnerability to get in. We find something that looks fixable and move it out without being caught. Tell ya right now, those Bulava missiles aren't the first nor the last things that we have confiscated from there."

"Yeah, we keep this sucker fully stocked so that when we need to get somewhere in a hurry, we know that we have all of the same weapons available to us wherever we are going that we would have available right in our own office."

"Whatcha got in there?"

"Oh you name it," started Hawkins. "Munitions, computers, a couple vehicles, weapons, a fully stocked fridge with everything we like. I mean, the list goes on, man. We could spend a fortnight here going down everything we have on that bad boy."

"And we could stand around here bantering all afternoon, as well," Chase pointed out, "but we have things that we need to be doing. You said you have a couple vehicles on that thing. What kind?"

"We have a soft-top jeep that's great for off-roading, and we have a Humvee that is fully bullet-resistant, heat-resistant, and gets about three miles to the gallon. So we only like to use that if we know we will be facing imminent peril."

"The path up to where I have our headquarters set up is definitely the road less traveled, but I'm pretty sure you can make it up there in a jeep." Then Laurie looked at Big James. "As far as your soccer mom minivan goes, big guy, you may want to catch a ride with us or them."

"Actually, I'm gonna let all of you take the trip back to your fortress of good, Ms. Laurie, and I'm gonna go run some errands – which is to say, I'm going to go pick up the items on the grocery list that you guys," and he nodded to Harper and Kinley, "gave me on your way down here. You get to where you're going, start making plans, and figure out we're gonna need something that's not on this list, then be sure to raise me on the horn. Other than that, I will let you know when I've got what I've got."

"The party just won't be the same without ya, big guy," Harper slapped him on his billboard of a back. "Try to get us some stuff that isn't going to blow up on us as soon as we light it like that junk you procured back in Tangiers in 2000 and whatever."

"It was just three years ago, and the reason all the stuff blew up as soon as we lit it is because you cut all the daggone fuses too short, ya jackass," the big man laughed as he started off toward his minivan, and waved a pleasant goodbye to everyone.

Once Big James was gone, Kinley turned back to the group. "Hey, why don't we let Harper ride with you guys, and one of you guys can ride with Laurie and me. Give us an opportunity to get to know each other in what little time we have. Sound good?"

"I'm down," Hawkins stepped up. "I'll ride with you and her. Shi', boy, give me some time away from these fools."

Sloane turned to Watkins, "Finally some peace and quiet, boss."

They exchanged a brief smile before Daniel Sloane started back up the plane's rear bay door. "I'll bring out the jeep," he hollered back.

The Drive Back to Chase's Place

A few minutes later, Daniel Sloane pulled the jeep out of the hangar and positioned it to the rear of the van that held Laurie Chase, Kinley Devereaux, and Samuel Hawkins. As they drove off, he did not follow too closely because of the amount of dust the front vehicle kicked up. Next to Sloane sat Dr. Mercedes Lara. John Watkins sat in the back behind Merc, and Harper was behind Sloane.

Mercedes turned around in her seat and gave Harper a long, hard look.

"Like what ya see, girlie?" Harper asked in his usual slack-jawed way.

"You're him, aren't you?" she asked loudly over the noisy jeep.

"I'm sorry, what?" Harper yelled as the vehicle began to gain speed.

"You're Harper Rowe. The guy that they're looking for in regards to the death of Secretary of Defense Paul Michaels."

"Oh, that," Harper said dismissively. "Believe me, it's not as glamorous as it sounds. Besides, even though this trip to where we're going is going to seem like an incredibly long time, I assure you – it won't be long enough for me to tell you just exactly what went on in with the Secretary of Defense. It's been so long ago, I don't even know if I remember what happened on that kooky elephant of a day myself."

"Your partner shot him, didn't he?" Watkins asked.

"Not sure what you're asking," Harper deflected.

"Kinley Devereaux and Laurie Chase – the NSA agent and the DEA agent that were killed in Mexico City just about a year and a half ago. That's who we were just talking to in the hangar back there. And who are in that van right up in front of us. So, if they're still alive, how come you're the only one that the U.S. Government is coming after?"

"Well, like ya said, the U.S. Government thinks they are dead so why would they be coming after them? Besides, it's just the way my life goes, I guess."

"What does that mean?" Sloane asked.

"This is how my life goes. When I was in high school we had this guy named Jeff Skills. Jeff was a pro baseball prospect from the time he was in sixth grade. Every year, Jeff was knocking the ball out of the park and the best fielding shortstop in the state. Right after our junior year, over the summer, Jeff is in a terrible car accident. His knees are mush. He has about seven surgeries to try to get him back to working order. He works as hard as anyone, and about halfway through our senior season, Skills makes it back to good.

"He gets back out there on the field – and he's just as great as ever. We make it to the state finals, two down, winning run on third, ninth inning. Skills is up. The pitch comes in and Skills takes a mighty swing. Fouls the ball off his kneecap and crumples to the ground. They carry the dude off the field. I'm at the other end of the dugout making paper airplanes out of the scorecards, and the coach tells me to go in and finish the at-bat.

"I'm blank as a fart. So I get a bat, stumble out to the batter's box, and the pitch comes in. I'm so scared – I swing. The ball lands in center field, the winning run scores, and I'm carried off the field the conquering hero. My picture is in all the local papers, I'm as popular as ever. Skills – he never walks again. And this is how my life goes. I don't want the attention or the action, but, as you can tell from that story, it's just sorta been that way since I was a kid."

"I understand. Well, ya needn't worry about any flack or loose lips from us," Sloane assured the assassin.

"So, what are the numbers looking like in this particular go-round with fate? Do we have a puncher's chance against del Fuento and his men?"

"Chase says that we're going up against roughly two hundred bad guys. And they're heavily armed, have airplanes and helicopters, and home field advantage as they certainly know the grounds better than we do."

"We've been up against worse. How long have you guys been planning this out?"

"Well," Harper began, "Laurie's been here for about a year and a half doing her homework. Kin and I just got here less than twelve hours ago. As we were flying in, we contacted Big James – gave him a list of weapons that we're going to need – so it's been pretty quick with all of what we're trying to get together here."

"What do you think?" John asked Harper straight out.

"We're going to where she's been staying – Laurie Chase – and she has things kind of set up in a diagrammer that's scaled down, and she's going to–"

"Wait, what?" Mercedes asked confused. "What's a diagrammer?"

"You know. Like a model."

"Are you trying to say diorama?"

"Yes, right, a diorama."

"You're the low rung on the mental ladder, aren't you?" Lara asked, somewhat concerned.

Harper laughed out loud. "Oh, you better hope I am."

Meanwhile, in the van that Laurie Chase was driving, she, Kinley, and Samuel Hawkins were having a similar conversation.

"So, that dude ya'll hang out with, Harper Rowe, isn't he the one they think killed the Secretary of Defense a while back?" Hawkins asked.

"They just want him for questioning. He's what you would call 'a person of interest', but they know he didn't actually do the shooting."

"So, why's he been so elusive? I mean, what's up with all the cloak and dagger stuff if he didn't kill the guy?"

"Well–" Chase began cautiously.

"Yeah. 'Well' is kinda the right answer there," Kinley affirmed. "Let's just say that he really can't answer the questions that they want to ask him."

"Because?"

"Well, now you're asking me questions that I can't answer," Devereaux answered mysteriously.

"So, how's 'bout you, Ms. Chase? Can you answer any of my questions?"

"Harper has a pretty tough time just talking amongst friends without pissing them off. I'm pretty sure that if he tried to talk to an interrogator, he would really get them into an uproar."

Hawk knew that he was being shut down so he opened a new line of dialogue.

"I get it. You two don't want to talk about that. I'm cool. I'm certainly not one of those people that pokes and says 'Come on' and pokes again and says 'Come on' and just gets on your nerves over and over again. So, let me ask this question: How many baddies are we up against when we go to take down this guy del Fuento?"

"About two hundred," Kinley said uncertainly as he looked at Chase. "Right?"

"Once Tito leaves with his traveling entourage, yes, about two hundred guys."

Hawkins began to move uneasily.

"I'm sorry. What?"

"What?"

Hawkins looked at Laurie and asked, "Did you just say that–" and he looked at Kinley, "Did she just say–"

"That Tito isn't going to be around once we strike? Yes, that is exactly what she said."

"I thought that's who we were down here to get." Hawkins' voice hit a high note. "That Tito guy."

"It is. We will."

"Call me old-fashioned, but I kinda remember back in my grampy's days–" and Hawkins took on a stereotypical-sounding voice of an old negro slave and said, "when people would attack a drug dealer's compound in hopes to level a feller and the feller's doin's – it was kinda mandatory that the feller would doggoned-well be there." He went back to his normal voice to say, "When did I miss the handbook change?"

"No, you didn't miss anything," Chase answered.

Silence filled the air before Kinley said uneasily, "I was kinda on the same line as Hawkins. Why are we doing all of this if del Fuento isn't going to be there?"

It was just about that time that the van hit the "off road" portion of the way back to Chase's headquarters. She held tightly to the steering wheel while she tried to explain to Hawkins and Kinley what was going on. "Did you ever – wonder," she stopped talking while the van bounced wildly along the path that she had driven so many times before.

From the back Hawkins held on tight and said, "Holy Jew, are we gonna die? Is this even normal?"

"Hang tight, Hawk," Kinley said reassuringly. "It'll be over soon."

"I shoulda ridden this ride with my boys," Hawkins said as he held on tight to his seat. "Ya'll are gonna get me killed."

"You'll be fine," Chase said as she finally pulled the van back onto the paved part of the road. "See?"

Kinley sat back up straight and gave Laurie a hard look. "I think you probably could've taken that patch of off-road a little bit slower than ya did. Pretty sure my C-7 just fused with my C-8, 9, and 10."

"Oh, that's not good," Hawk spoke up. "I know a guy that had to have several of his C-spines fused together. Now the joker can't even bend over to pet his dog. You better have that looked at Kinley. Ain't nothin' to play around with."

Kin looked over his shoulder at Hawkins in the back seat, and then over to Laurie and said, "Honest to God, I never thought I would say these words: I kinda wish Harper were here."

To which Samuel replied, "Oh, your partner. Yeah, he all right back there," Hawk said as he pointed over his shoulder with his right thumb. "I mean, John and Daniel and Dr. Lara don't necessarily have the people skills that I do, but they some good people. Your partner's in good hands. Tell ya that right now. Tell ya 'nother thing, too, and that's what we were talkin' 'bout before we hit that stretch of outer Mongolia back there. Whassup with Tito del Fuento bein' absent from his own retirement party?"

Chase gave a frustrated sigh. "I understand your concern, Mr. Hawkins, but I assure you that Tito's being gone is of the utmost importance. Once we get to where we're going, everything will be explained."

"Did you know about this, Devereaux?"

"I, too – much like yourself – am still waiting to be enlightened."

"And where in the Hades High School are we going? I keep waiting for those dinosaurs from that movie to come barreling out of the woods at us."

"We're almost there," Chase said. Right on cue, Hawkins' cell phone rang.

"It's Johnny," he said as he put the phone to his ear, and said, "How are you guys doin' back there?"

"Are we almost there?"

Hawk pulled the phone away from his mouth. "How much longer till we get there, Ms. Laurie?"

"Less than five minutes."

Hawk put the phone back to his ear. "Less than five, boss."

"Good. Even though it's about five minutes too long."

"Hey, Johnny, this woman just filled me in that del Fuento isn't even going to be at his compound when we raid it."

Laurie shot Hawkins a dirty look in the rearview mirror and snapped, "Dude. Did you just freaking tell on me?"

"What do you mean he's not going to be there?" asked a confused Watkins.

"No, it's okay," Hawk went on ignoring Chase and answering John. "I've been informed that once we get where we're going, all will be explained."

"Oh, and there better be a real good explanation for it, too."

Crool and Baldwin Check the Video Footage

Agents Jeb Crool and David Baldwin had returned to the video viewing room, Crool with a hot cup of black coffee and Baldwin with an almond mocha cappuccino. The two agents found comfortable chairs in which to sit and had their notebooks and pens out and ready. Agent Virginia Phelps sat on a stool next to the video equipment just to their right. "Are we ready to begin?"

"Let 'er rip, Agent Phelps," Crool replied.

As the video began to play on the screen in front of them, Phelps explained what they were viewing. "This is when Harper Rowe is first being brought into the precinct for suspicion of DUI. He seems to like the cameras."

The trio watched as the handcuffed fugitive was walked into the precinct. Harper did not miss an opportunity to flash a smile at every video camera that he walked past. Somewhere around the fourth or fifth camera he actually lipped something through a big grin.

"Whoa, whoa, whoa," Crool perked up. "Did you get what he said there, Agent Phelps?"

"Yes. Yes, we did."

"What's he saying?"

"It would appear that he is saying, 'See you soon, Agent Crool.' Would you like me to rewind it so you can see for yourself?"

"No, that won't be necessary. It's kinda what I thought he had said, too," Crool leaned back in his chair. "We can keep going."

"As you can see here, this is where he was seated during the time leading up to his request to use the restroom. His communication between the officers is rather relaxed and casual."

"Geez, just look at that little turd, will ya, Dave. Sitting there smiling like a Cheshire cat, not a care in the world. He's just the biggest piece of shi–"

"Hey, can you rewind that for a second, Agent Phelps?" Baldwin requested.

"Sure. How far back?"

"Take it back about ten seconds. Notice when he puts his head down and appears to be looking at the floor he says something, but there doesn't appear to be anyone in the room with him at the time."

Phelps took the video back to the appropriate playback spot and the trio watched intently to see what David was referencing.

"Right there," Baldwin pointed to the screen.

"Yeah, I see it," Crool acknowledged. "Actually – it looks like he said two different things. Play that back again."

Again the three agents watched the piece of footage closely to see if they could figure out what Harper Rowe was saying.

"Any way to zoom in on that, Agent Phelps?"

Within a few seconds Harper's image was tripled in size. They watched again to see if they could decipher his words and to whom he was saying them.

"It looks like he might be saying, 'Not yet', pauses, and then maybe says–" Phelps strained her eyes, "'Probably. I'll let you know' – something after that, too, but I'm not sure."

Rewind. Play.

"Yeah, it's something close to that. Just too hard to say, at this juncture, but he's definitely talking to someone that's not in the room there."

"He must've been wearing a com in his ear."

"Sorry, agents," Phelps apologized, "I'm guessing the Atlanta PD doesn't bring in a lot of suspects from sobriety checkpoints that are already pre-wired with communication devices."

Rewind. Play.

"I'm just trying to see if we can catch him saying a name or something," Baldwin said. "Get some idea who he's talking to."

"Probably whoever Jeff Samples from the ATF is."

"Just let it play on through, Agent Phelps. Maybe we can catch him saying something else here in a few seconds."

Crool, Baldwin, and Phelps watched as the scene played out. They watched as different officers talked to Rowe, questioned him, had him sign some papers, and then when he was finally allowed to use the bathroom, an officer escorted him there. Nothing else of any real substance appeared on the video.

"I'm guessing it's too much to hope that there are any cameras in the bathroom he used, eh?"

"There are cameras in the bathroom, but nothing in the stall where it would seem he set the explosives. So, no, there's nothing video-wise to show him doing anything pertinent in there. The next thing we'll see is when he comes back out of the bathroom – like you noticed earlier – he no longer has the hearing aid that he was wearing before he went into the bathroom."

"You or anyone else see anything more on the Harper Rowe footage that might be of importance, Agent Phelps?" Jeb asked.

"Not really, but then again, we didn't catch him talking to his partner either, and you guys did. So there might be something we missed."

"Fair enough. We can come back to this in a bit. I'm actually more interested in seeing the footage of the other guy at this point.

The man claiming to be Jeff Samples from the ATF."

"No problem, agents. Just a moment–" Phelps punched a few buttons on the equipment and, "there you go, gentlemen."

As they watched the video of the unkempt, heavily-bearded man enter the police precinct, Crool commented, "Wow. I did not realize the ATF was hiring homeless people these days. That's a shame."

"My people did confirm that there is no Jeff Samples that works with or in conjunction with the ATF."

"That's great work, Agent Phelps. Just spot on terrific," Crool said with sarcasm dripping from his statement, "but he had the credentials, and he knew procedure which tells me that whoever this guy is he isn't just some slob pulling a New Year's Eve prank."

"Which leads to what I'm going to tell you now," the GBI agent went on. "There was a Jeff Samples that worked with the ATF from 2007 up to March 12, 2014, which was when he went missing during an assignment and has not been seen nor heard from since."

Jeb turned in his seat to face Virginia. "Really?"

"Really," she responded flatly.

Crool gave Baldwin a look of disappointment.

"Seems that ATF Agent Jeff Samples' car was found in a surveillance area near a known militia member's house. There was a bullet hole through the front windshield, blood – his blood – found on the interior of his car, but the agent, his ID, his gun, and his keys were all missing from the vehicle and have never been recovered. Also, according to the report we uncovered, the bullet that went through his windshield was fired from a great distance away. It was believed to have been a sniper's bullet."

"A sniper's bullet." Crool repeated softly as he squinted his eyes ever so slightly in thought. "Agent Phelps, can you get a clean shot of that guy's face and zoom in on it, please."

Phelps did as directed.

"What is it, Jeb?" a perplexed Baldwin asked.

Crool did not answer immediately as his eyes were keenly fixed on the image that appeared on the 60" video screen in front of him. Baldwin and Phelps were moving their own eyes back and forth between looking at the man on the screen and looking at Jeb Crool looking at the man on the screen. Finally, after close to five minutes of silence, Jeb simply said, "Unbelievable."

"What?" Phelps and Baldwin asked in unison.

"Kinley Devereaux didn't die up on top of that building in Mexico City two summers ago."

"What makes you say that, boss?"

"Because that–" Crool said loudly as he pointed to the enlarged still image on the video screen, "is Kinley Devereaux."

The Call

He always kept the phone with him, and even though it had never been used, he held out hope that one day it would ring, and she would be on the other end – the woman who he had, surprisingly, become a good friend to. True, it had been some time since they had seen each other, but he never for a minute doubted that she would use the phone that he had given her all those months ago if she were ever in trouble.

However, today of all days, he had not expected the phone to go off. But careful as he always was, he had the ringer set to vibrate, and when it vibrated in his left front pants pocket, he was the only one to know it.

He did not need to look at the caller ID. He knew exactly who it was.

Still, right here, right now, there was just no way that he could answer it without making a scene and getting a lot of unwanted questions. So against every fiber of his being, he had to let the call go to voicemail.

It was, of course, no ordinary voicemail.

Knowing that one day she would call, and there always being a good chance that he would be in a situation like he was in now and would not be able to answer the call, he had set up a voicemail greeting specifically for her.

After all, she was the only one that had this number.

The greeting went thusly:

"I know what you're thinking at this very second. You're thinking, 'How in the world could this idiot let my call go to voicemail when he assured me when he gave me this stupid phone that I could reach out to him in my time of need?' I assure you that nothing would please me more than to have picked up your call on the very first ring. Apparently, though, I am in a situation at the present moment that prevents me from answering right now. But I promise you this: I will call you back within fifteen minutes. Somehow, someway. However, if you don't hear from me within the next fifteen minutes, then sadly, it means that I am dead or am getting ready to die. Because, frankly, Scarlett, that's the only thing that would keep me from getting back to you in the timeliest of manners. Yes, I'd rather be dead than to let you down. So, be patient and hang tight. I will talk to you in just a few minutes."

And when the phone stopped vibrating in his pocket he smiled, knowing what she was about to hear.

He hoped that she would be smiling, too.

When the two vehicles pulled to a stop in front of the vacant warehouse, Chase turned to Hawkins and said, "Tell your guy to follow me, and I will get us parked inside." She looked at Kinley. "You wanna hang here with me or get out with the rest of the Little Rascals?"

"While it's tempting to stay in, I think I'll get out this time around, but thanks for the invite, Darla." He opened his door and looked back at Hawkins, but Samuel was already out of the vehicle and heading over to tell Sloane to follow Laurie into the vacant complex.

Kin looked back in at Laurie. "Tell Diego to unlock the door, and I'll get everyone inside."

John Watkins, Dr. Mercedes Lara, Samuel Hawkins, and Harper were all making their way towards him as Chase and Sloane pulled away from the scene and out of sight behind the side of the warehouse. About half a minute later Diego opened the front door to the building and Kinley led everyone inside.

He waited until Chase and Sloane were back inside and Laurie was introducing everyone to Diego and giving them a tour of the premises before he slipped away. The warehouse was huge, so finding a secluded spot was not that difficult. He pulled the cell phone from his pocket, checked the time, checked the time of the call, did the quick math and figured he had about a minute and a half before the fifteen-minute time frame he had set for himself expired.

He dialed her number and smiled when she answered, "Good to hear from ya. In just about another thirty seconds I was actually going to get concerned for your well-being."

"Well, for now, I'm still in the upright position. Hey, I'd love to chat it up with you to see how you've been since the last time we talked, but my present situation is rather time sensitive. Still, knowing that you probably didn't reach out to me just to shoot the breeze, I'm sympathetic to the fact that you must be in some sort of serious plight yourself."

"Well, truth be told, it's not really me. It's a friend of a friend."

"Must be some friend for you to reach out to me like this."

"You gave me this stupid phone for a reason, didn't you?"

"And now you're using that stupid phone, aren't you? What's going on?"

"I'm going to need help with an extraction, and–" she hesitated for just a moment before finishing, "I'm probably going to need your partner in on this, too."

"Seriously?"

"Are you two still an item?"

"Yeah, we're doing a job right now, as a matter of fact."

"Good to know that some things never change," she laughed.

"So, this extraction – where is it that we'll be extracting this friend of a friend *from*, and where will we be inserting her *into*?"

"My friend, her friends, and I are in Prague. As far as where they need to get? I was thinking the States or Canada. They're going to need someplace where they can disappear. A whole new identity. A whole new look. The works."

"How soon?"

"Once you and your boy are wrapped up with whatever it is you have going on, take the next flight here. Where are you, by the way?"

"Rio."

"Oh, nice. Wish I was there instead of here."

"Yeah, well, you may actually need to come here."

"Why?" she asked.

"Eh, just the situation we're in – it's kind of intense. Seriously, our survival chances are probably somewhere in the thirty-five to forty percent range, and if we do survive, I'm not sure I can just get my partner to hop on a plane to Prague and be all happy, happy, joy, joy about it on such short notice. It would be like, 'Hey, I know we just jumped out of the fire and into the frying pan, and then we jumped out of the frying pan just before we were served up for supper, but how 'bout we hurtle headlong into another life and death situation before we've had time for a good nap?' I mean, sure, we all know my partner is always up for the next great adventure – crazy loon that he is – but I think you see my point. You probably should come here for a face-to-face and argue your problem to him in person."

"Okay," she said disappointedly. "Let me get things squared away here as much as I can. Once I do, I'll wing it to Rio. Call you on this line when I land."

QUESTIONS

By the time he got back to the group, they were just beginning to huddle around Chase's diorama of del Fuento's compound. Once everyone was positioned to have a good look at the setup, John Watkins asked, "Okay, before we get started with all of this, I have a couple of questions I'd like to ask just to kinda clear up some things."

Chase answered, "Absolutely. Ask away."

"Why us? Why now? I mean, we're eight people going up against, what, about two hundred, right? If you think that we can do it now, then how come no one else has done it before us? And I'm not talking about the United States DEA or the CIA or Interpol. I mean, anybody that has just the least bit of technology and a decent army? Why?"

Chase did not back down from the question. She immediately responded with, "Larger criminal organizations have tried and failed. Mainly because they were larger. That's one of the many advantages that we have here among the eight of us. It's just us. Anyone that knows about this operation is standing right here. Del Fuento has so many people of authority in his pocket that it's impossible to know who is going to sell out the operation next. So, that kills off any country with a decent-sized army or the kind of manpower needed for something like this. As far as a well-armed troupe of a few like ourselves? It's because it's a numbers game. He has about three hundred highly-trained, combat-proven soldiers on the premises at all times. Usually."

"Usually?" questioned Sloane.

"You want to know why del Fuento isn't going to be there when we attack? It's because he's taking a business trip to Germany, and when he goes on business, he takes about a third of his little brigade there with him. If he's here when we go in – him and his mighty three hundred – we don't stand a chance."

"And because you've been here doing your homework for the last eighteen months you know that he's going to be gone soon?" asked Watkins.

"Yes, he'll be flying out–"

"Him and his mighty hundred," Harp interrupted.

"Tomorrow morning at 8:15 sharp," she finished.

"And how did you come across this information? How did you verify it, I mean?"

"Diego knows Tito's FAA flight plan identification number. When Tito gets ready to make a trip he files his flight plan three days prior. Once we had finalized our plan of attack it was just a matter of waiting for that ID number to show up on the FAA's flight plan site. We've been checking it every day – just about every two to three hours – and it finally showed up two days ago, complete with times, dates, and destinations. He filed for two planes, as well, so we know that this isn't just some quick getaway for him and the Mrs."

"And that's when you called me," Devereaux stated.

"Yes," Chase confirmed, "and Diego has been monitoring the situation to be sure that nothing has changed."

"So, where's he jetting out from?"

She pointed to the diorama – the airstrip, specifically – and said, "From right here. He has three jets. Two of the jets are jumbo, and then he has one for himself and his family, close friends, etc."

"I'm guessing this is the hangar for those," Watkins pointed to a building adjacent to the airstrip. "What else does he have in there?"

"Two patrol planes sometimes, but they are usually outside. He has four of those total. He keeps two in the air at all times to patrol the skies and the traffic on the ground. The two on the ground always take off before the two in the sky land so that there are no holes in the coverage."

"What kind of birds are we talking about here?" Hawkins asked.

"Lockheed P-3 Orions."

"How high up do they fly?"

"Not very. Usually less than a mile to avoid any commercial traffic. Plus, they stay close just in case there should be an issue on the ground. He also has six S-70i Black Hawk attack helicopters, and, believe me, they strike fast and hard."

"With that much firepower on the ground it seems like there would never be cause for the Orions to do any ground work, and sweet mother of Mary, that is a lot of firepower." Harper said as he rubbed the back of his neck.

"And you're trying to tell us that you have some sort of plan of attack that the eight of us can somehow win the day on this one against – two-hundred some soldiers, P-3 Orions, and six Black Hawks?" Mercedes asked with her usual skepticism. "Because this I have to see."

"Yes, I do," Chase said forthrightly. "I absolutely do."

"Plus, it's nine of us," Sloane pointed out. "Don't forget Big James."

"Well, I think we've danced around this diuretic thing long enough," Harper said. "It's about time to get down to the whens and the hows of this attack."

"Diorama," several of them said under their breaths.

Laurie, who had been standing at the back left of the diorama, made her way front and center and began to explain the details of the attack. "Tito and company will leave tomorrow morning at or about 8:15 a.m. But we will not begin our attack until nightfall. Diego, tell them why."

Diego mustered a meek smile and said, "Cuss while da boss ees away, dee cats dey weell play."

"Meaning that his men like to party it up a little when left on their own. It's not their fault, really. It's just that if Tito catches even a hint of a whisper of some sort of trouble coming his way, he's as cautious as a porcupine in a balloon store. He wouldn't even consider leaving his place if he thought there might be an impending situation. Hence, if he feels safe enough to go away, his men feel safe enough to tie one on every night. Also, it's January so there's neither sowing nor reaping going on right now in the plantation fields. So the migrant workers' quarters are empty. Since these buildings are on the east perimeter of the property, this will be a good place to retreat to, if need be." Chase pointed to the right side of the diorama. "It's those twelve buildings right there."

She looked around the table and received nods of acknowledgement and understanding from the others.

"You tell her this, Diego?" John asked.

"*Sim*, I deed," Diego smiled.

"Nice."

"Since we know Tito leaves tomorrow morning, then it only seems the natural course of events that we attack tomorrow night when the majority of the men left behind will be inebriated and unsuspecting."

"The planes will still be in the air though, right?"

"Yes."

"And the helicopter pilots? Do they get in on the drinking and partying? Or do they stick to their posts?"

"Diego says that the pilots alternate nights so, yeah, there will be pilots to fly the Black Hawks."

"Well, where do we start then? What's the initiation point of the attack? And how do we avoid being detected by the planes?" Watkins fired away, but then realized he was taking things a little too fast. "Sorry. I should give you time to explain what you have in mind."

"We're good," and Laurie took a breath as she scanned the seven faces that surrounded her and her diorama. She purposely waited to look at Kinley last, and when she did, he gave her a nod of confidence. "It will go like this," and she was off and running with her plan.

It would start with a truck.

SHE MEETS ANEZKA AND JANA

She walked into Ellie's living room. "I have news," she said.

"I have Anezka and Jana," Eliska replied. "To-Day!" Ellie said, in her best attempt to say "Ta-da!"

"I get that," she smiled.

"So what is news?" Ellie asked. "You talk to friend, yes?"

"Yes, I talked to my friend."

"He will come here? Help Anezka and Jana?"

"He will – sort of."

"Sort of? What sort of mean?"

"I'm going to have to go to him. But I'll come back with two experts that will help out." She suddenly realized that Anezka and Jana were right there next to her. "Do they speak English?" she asked Ellie.

"They understand."

She looked at the two of them, a mother-daughter combo with their red hair and their ginger looks.

"I'm going to go get some help for the two of you," she paused. "I'm going to make sure you're safe." She hesitated again, looked at Anezka and Jana, and then said, "Before I do, however – I think I can do a few things myself."

The Plan

"Okay, so while the workers' quarters are empty, and there just isn't a whole lot going on, Tito has delivery trucks come around to re-stock everything," Laurie Chase continued with her explanation. "They carry everything from household supplies to ammunition to fertilizer. There is a truck scheduled for tomorrow evening at 8 p.m."

"How big of a truck?"

"Eighteen wheels' worth. Big truck. There's about a two-mile blind spot between where the truck will leave the main highway and where it gets into the sight line of del Fuento's security cameras at the front gate. This blind spot is where we'll take the truck."

"You say we'll take it – who's the *we'll* part of that?" asked John.

"What do you mean?"

"He means that we can't all take the truck," Merc explained. "Who's going to take the truck?"

"We're going to split up into teams, right?" Harper asked.

"Judas Priest, people!" Dev shouted, "Can we just let her explain what she has planned here?"

Everybody quieted down and Laurie began again. "Okay, so like I said, there's a truck that's coming in with supplies around six o'clock tomorrow evening. With the exception of your weapons guy and Diego, we'll all take the truck. Harper and Kinley will ride up front, and the rest of us in the back. Harper, you're the linguist. How's your Portuguese?"

"*Excelente, meu querido.*"

"Good, because we're going to need you to talk to the guards at the gate. Diego says that they will be expecting a regular guy, a local who speaks the language, so that is where you will be most useful."

"So, you admit you finally need me. It's going to be a good day, kids," Harper looked around at the rest of the group. "I don't even care if it is just to talk to the Mannys."

"The Mannys?" a few of them asked in bewildered unison.

"Yeah, the Mannys. What? You've never heard that term before? It's a slang term for Portuguese dudes–"

Blank stares.

"Because they're all named Manny. Hey, Diego, back me up here. How many guys Tito got working for him named Manny? A bunch, right?"

"*Sim.* He has a lot of guys named Manny."

"I know my Portuguese people, people."

"Can we get back to the plan sometime before Christmas?" Merc asked.

"Okay, so the truck will be coming down this road here," Chase pointed to the very front of the setup. "And right here is where we will have an opportunity to take it because it will be off the main road, but still out of range of the Orions."

"How many guys will be on that truck?"

"Somewhere between seex an' eight guys – one een the cab and the rest een the back," Diego answered. "They weell be armed. Steell, I no think that they weell be any pro'lem. I remember them being mos'ly young. Plus, they weell know that Tito weell be gone so they weell be thinking about the party they weell be going to. The seven of you weell be able to take them. I know eet."

"Once we have the truck and Harper gets us past the security at the gate, we will drive to here. This is the munitions building." She pointed to the corresponding building. "We will put a rocket into that thing and cause a pretty immense disturbance. Hopefully, by this time most of the soldiers, lookouts, guards, and military personnel will be decently inebriated. Diego says that they will be by then."

"You've drank with these ass clowns when Tito has gone away before, boss?" Sloane asked Diego. "How much can they put away?"

"*Sim*, I drink weeth them before. By thee time we make entrance weeth thee truck, they weell be very *bêbado*."

"That will be enough to get the attention of the Orions overhead. At this point, Diego and Big James – is that his name?"

"Yeah, Big James."

"Diego and Big James will cut through the west perimeter – Diego knows a place to do this – and they will use ground-to-air missiles to take out the Orions." Chase turned to Harper and asked, "Your boy will be able to get us some ground-to-air missiles, right?"

"I have no doubt in my mind. Not only will he get us the ground-to-airs, but he will get us the top of the line ground-to-airs."

"Wait, how far are they going to have to drive to get within range of the overheads?" Kinley asked.

"Probably about two miles."

"Geez, I hope James doesn't plan on using his soccer-mom mobile for this."

"That's going to have to be a heckuva shot to knock an Orion out of the sky with just some GTAMs," Hawkins spoke up. "I've flown a Lockheed P-3 before, and I've got three words for ya: Hard to Kill. Plus, if you shoot one and miss, it's gonna be lights out for you. They have air-to-surface missiles – AGM-65 Mavericks, AGM-84 Harpoons – they will take you out."

"Well, I guess they better not miss then," Laurie answered matter-of-factly. "While they're bringing down the Orions, we'll need to move as fast as we can to the airstrip to take out the Black Hawks before they can get into the air. If they get up on us then it will be lights out – for all of us. Needless to say, taking out the Black Hawks is the most important part of getting this thing done."

"You mean besides shooting down the overhead planes, and Harper getting us inside?" Hawkins asked.

She looked at John and his crew. "This will be your job, as Kinley, Harper, and I will lay down ground fire to cover you as best we can. If things go right, I hope we will have commandeered one of their vehicles to transport back to the hangar. By this time they will know we are there, so you're going to need something. It's too far to make it on foot."

"I'll get us something," Sloane said, "but what are we supposed to use to take out those helicopters? Those things are pretty big. I don't think hand grenades and handguns are going to keep them grounded for very long."

"How many rockets do you think we'll have? Because that's the only thing that's going to keep them down," John said.

"I'll give James a call. Make sure he gets us plenty," and Harper was immediately on the phone.

"How far back to the hangars from the munitions building?"

"About 500 yards. You'll get some resistance from the pilots, too."

"How many of them?"

"Twenty. Twenty-five."

"Wouldn't it be easier to just take out all the pilots instead of the Black Hawks?" asked Sam. "I mean, what do you call a fully-armed, indestructible attack helicopter that doesn't have a pilot?" Hawkins tarried a second before he answered his own question. "Useless."

"Hmm, ya gotta point, but let's get as many RPGs and Stinger missiles as we can. If we can avoid taking out those Black Hawks, we may be able to use them later to rip up Tito's fields and land."

Harper repeated into the phone what Laurie had said, "RPGs and Stingers, babe. As many as you can get."

"All right. So quick recap on what we've covered so far, James," Harper began. "We're going to go hijack a rig – the seven of us – take it up to the front gate, weasel our way in, and go blow up a munitions building, thus causing a huge upheaval in the tranquility of the night at *la plantation del Fuego*. At this point, you and Diego will be moving in from the west to take out the overhead flying planes. From there, the Dragon's Men and Woman are going to hightail it on over to the hangar to take out the pilots and/or the Black Hawks while we commence mowing down the soldiers that will more than likely be on us like stink on a pig by then. Does that sound about right?" he double-checked with Laurie.

"That sounds like it," Chase agreed. "So far."

"Did you catch all that, big guy?" Harper asked into the phone.

"May as well keep him on the line while we go over the rest of the plan," Watkins suggested.

"Do you have a few minutes to hang on the line? Get filled in with the rest of us as to what's going on?"

Harper nodded and then said, "Okay, sounds good. Go do your thing, and we'll hear from you in a few." He tapped his phone and said, "Man was in a time crunch. He had to go. Said he'll call us back when he's got everything we need. Be about a few hours."

"In that case, let's get to the rest of this plan then."

Laurie moved back to her diorama and started explaining the remainder of the attack plan. "Once Big James and Diego have successfully taken out the overhead planes, they will move down to here," she pointed, "to the extent that they will be flanking the soldiers that Harper, Kinley, and I will be engaged with. This should be what we need to swing things in our favor if they aren't already in our favor at that point anyway. Of course, also at this point is when we're going to start seeing engagement from whatever soldiers have been standing guard at the various posts around the compound. As best as Diego and I have figured, that's going to be around forty to fifty more guys. Some will be closer than others so, obviously, others will show up sooner rather than later. We'll need to be prepared for this."

"Let me ask you this, Miss Chase," Watkins interrupted, "is there a centralized location to where all of this will be going on? Someplace that might have a spot high up where we can put a sniper that can act as a lookout and take out any potential threats that might be trickling in from outside the main fray? Because it looks like this building here might be good for that." John pointed to a specific building on the diorama.

Laurie hesitated uneasily for a moment before answering, "Uh, yeah, that would definitely be the building to do that from, for sure, but–"

"But what? We've got three professional shooters right here. I say we put one of them up there as soon as we can so as to have our proverbial backs covered. What's the issue?"

"I would really like to keep as much action away from this building as possible if we can. That building you're referring to there is where Tito keeps his money. Ergo, that's our payday. The thing is he has it all stacked on wooden pallets wrapped in cellophane so if even the slightest spark gets in there, it would mean that we'd be witnesses to the world's most expensive bonfire."

"How expensive are we talking about?"

"Around five hundred million, give or take."

Harper's hands shot up into the air as he exclaimed loudly, "Thank you, Good Lord in Heaven!"

Then he looked around at everyone in the room and said, "Okay, Rule Number One for tomorrow evening's skirmish: no one goes anywhere near that building, and if for some reason we've got combatants that are firing at us from that building, then – you let them shoot you."

"Wait. So this guy's sitting on half a billion in cash, and his storage method is some wood pallets and Saran Wrap?"

"Well, it's probably hard to find a safe big enough to hold that amount of green, kid," Sloane smirked. "Still, you'd think the guy would make some sort of an underground bunker to store it in, you know, just in case some crazy-assed Americans get a wild hair up their butt and want to come storming the place."

"Or a bunch uff drunk *mijos*," Diego chimed in and laughed.

"The man makes a valid point," agreed Kinley. "So, there's really that much money in there? I mean, have you seen it? Or are you just kind of going on a hunch here?"

"Oh," Diego said nodding his head fervently, "ees there all right. I know. I put mos' of eet there myself."

"And we've kept a good eye on it, too. I, personally, have seen a ton of money go in there, but very little make its way back out. He hoards it because, well, the banks here are just as crooked as he is. The only difference is that Tito doesn't try to hide the fact that he's a scumbag while the bankers and bank managers around here will gladly lie right to your face and flash a toothy white smile the whole time they're doing it."

"I don't like banks. You give them your money, and then when you want it back you have to spend two hours filling out paperwork and proving that you are, in fact, you," Merc complained.

"Maybe we should get back to the rest of our plan, and then we can have question and answer time afterwards. Cool?"

"Yeppers."

"Coo–"

"The floor is yours, m'lady."

"As you were, Ms. Chase."

"So, as I was saying, Big James and Diego will be flanking down from over here. I'm going to want them to have plenty of firepower – number one to make sure that they can back us up properly, and number two I am going to want them to start blasting these buildings along in here," and Chase once again pointed to specific buildings on the layout of del Fuento's compound. "We take those buildings out, then those jerks won't have anyplace to retreat to."

"Good. Nice. I like that," Hawk said rubbing his hands together.

"John Watkins, when you and your team successfully take the hangars, I think that getting one of those Black Hawks up in the air as quickly as possible will definitely be the defining moment in all of this. That's a really good idea."

"So, is that it? Is that the whole plan?"

"It is – and I'll tell you why. I've been down here for a year and a half coming up with a different plan every third day. Each one better than the last, but each one having so many steps to it that the certainty of failure was almost guaranteed. Then one day I just figured out the plan with the least amount of steps – modified it a little more – and this is what I came up with." She looked at Diego. "*We* came up with."

"I like it," Harper said agreeably. "You like it, Kin?"

"I like it, sure, but let's not deceive ourselves here. It's going to have to go right as rain all the way from the moment we take that truck to finally getting those Black Hawks up in the air. One false move, and we're all dead. Not to mention, we die doing this tomorrow night you can bet your bottom dollar that no one will ever know about it. We'll just be gone. Gone and forgotten."

The room fell quiet and solemn while they let Kinley's words settle in. And then because Harper is Harper, he started clapping loudly and said, "Kinley Devereaux, ladies and gentlemen. He'll be here all week. Hey, Kin, maybe tomorrow night you can break out the ukulele and we can sit around a campfire and sing songs about the Holocaust."

"Come on, man. Take it easy. Dude's just saying what we're all already thinking."

"Don't sweat it, Hawk," Kinley smiled. "I'm used to this monk-tard's antics by now," Kin turned to Harp, "but that Holocaust camp fire song line – don't think I've heard that one before. You been working on that for a while?"

"Yeah, it's kinda edgy. Really wanted to wait for the right time to debut it. I figured with the distinct possibility that this could be my last night on earth, that I'd run it up the ol' flagpole and see who saluted. I mean, what's the worst that could happen? You all get mad at me and make me stay home tomorrow night and not let me play in this most epic of reindeer games?"

Hawkins laughed a ridiculous laugh before saying, "Man, don't you know the four of us were in the military for years and years? Trust me, we've heard a lot worse than that."

"And a lot better," Mercedes followed up as she cracked a rare smile.

"Okay, so that's the plan. I guess now we can go around the room and see who might have any questions or ideas that could shore this thing up even more."

"Well, Miss Chase, Kinley's right. The steps to this plan are few, but they do seem like they will be effective. Still, everything has got to go just next to perfect for us to come out on top. I think that we might have something on our plane that could really give us a leg up on this attack."

"Is it a nuclear bomb? Because you could tell me that you have a nuclear bomb on that plane of yours, and I would absolutely believe you because you guys sure seem to have every other thing on there."

"No, Harper, it's not a nuke. In point of fact, I would say that it's even better than a nuke. Safer, at least. Let me ask you this: have you ever heard of an EMP device?"

"Heard of them – in the movies. They were once thought to be the up and comer in the next wave of terrorism, but the only problem is that they only seem to work in theory. I haven't ever heard of one actually working the way it was supposed to."

John smiled a wry smile. "Well, that might be getting ready to change."

"Are you serious?" Kinley asked in disbelief.

"Oh, he's serious, alright," Daniel Sloane said, backing up his boss.

"Escoos me," Diego spoke up with a look of uncertainty, "but wha's an EMP device?"

"EMP stands for electromagnetic pulse. It's a device that can send out a wave of electromagnetic energy to a surrounding area, and this wave of energy will disrupt or damage most – if not all – of the electronics in the area. The bigger the device, the bigger the affected area is. The one we have is about the size of a cast iron bathtub, and when we used the first one, it knocked out an area about the size of a city block."

"Does eet uh-splode? The EMP?"

"No, it doesn't explode," smiled Daniel Sloane. "It's pretty much invisible. We have a remote switch that we use. When we're ready, we hit the switch, the device activates, and out go all the lights, computers, and electronics in the affected range. So, basically, that's an EMP device."

"And don't even ask them how they got it to work," spoke up Dr. Lara. "I've heard them tell the story about ten times now, and I still think they're full of crap."

"How can you say that, Merc? We've already showed you the proof in hard, fast, documented form. You saw the thing work. How can you say that we're full of crap?" Sloane asked in protest.

"I'm not saying it didn't work. I'm just saying that the story you told me about how you got it to work is just pure malarkey. With technology the way it is these days you can falsify any documentation or article or piece of literature that you want, and I know that's what you did."

"Whoa, whoa, whoa," Laurie Chase interrupted, "so you're saying you've made a functional EMP device?"

"Three of them, actually," John answered, "but if you're at all versed in EMP devices then you would know that it's a one shot deal. Kinda like a hand grenade. So, yeah, we made three, used one, and have two left, and one of them is on our plane in that hangar that is seemingly 800 miles of bad road from here."

"And it works?"

"Well, ma'am, we made all three of them the exact same way using the very same techniques on all of them, so, it would just go to reason that if one worked then the other two would work, as well."

"But like ya said it's a one shot deal."

"My apologies to you, Mercedes," Harper winced, "but I gotta know – how did you guys figure out how to make a working EMP device?"

"And here we go," Merc gestured with her hands as if she were bringing to stage the main act of the evening.

"We followed a design that was published in the September 2001 issue of Popular Mechanics. Using some inexpensive supplies and rudimentary engineering knowledge, we tweaked the original plan until we knew it would work."

"Tweaked?"

"Come on, man, do you really think they're going to actually publish a design of a working EMP device in Popular Mechanics?" Hawkins asked Harper incredulously. "What they did was put something in there that would work in theory but not in reality – unless – you knew what they had left out of the design."

"And you three figured it out? How long did that take?"

"The two of us," Watkins said gesturing to himself and Hawkins, "were pretty much there to fetch parts and go for take-out. Danny's the one that actually figured everything out. Took about two weeks of conjecture and speculation and tweaking before we felt good about trying it out."

"Where did you try it out?"

"A Biebs concert." Watkins smiled.

"What?"

"Oh, no, way," Laurie looked to Mercedes for some confirmation. "Did they?"

"Not they. We."

"Absolutely. When we do something that galactically stupid, it's all of us or none of us."

"Ya know," Kinley said, "I remember hearing about that now. That was in San Jose, right? End of last summer?"

"That's the one."

"At 5:34 p.m. Pacific Daylight Time."

"Wait? You pulled something like that off in the late afternoon?" asked Chase.

"Well, yeah," answered Hawk, "I mean, we might be a bit ludicrous in our actions, but we're not going to be putting people at risk with them. If we had pulled that stunt off at ten o'clock at night, I mean, that would have been tragic in its aftereffect."

"No, I was just thinking that you pulled something like that off in the middle of the day under everybody's noses and got away with it, is all."

"It was one of our finer moments, to be sure. Nevertheless, it worked, and it leads me to believe that the other two we have should work, as well." Watkins said.

"So, having something like this at our disposal, let's figure out the best way utilize it to our advantage tomorrow night. What were you guys thinking?" Kinley asked the Dragon's Men quartet.

"First of all, we need to figure out how to get it there. I am pretty sure that if we pull all the seats out of the back of your cargo van, Laurie, we shouldn't have any trouble getting it in there. Granted, it's probably going to kill your gas mileage because the thing weighs in at around 800 pounds or so." Watkins paused to think for a second before beginning again.

"When we take that truck, one of us will need to stay back with the van – follow at a distance heading up to the front gate of del Fuento's compound. Once the truck is through and the fighting begins, that's going to be the best time to set the EMP device off. It will kill their lights, their communications will be out, and it will take out the tracking and instrument landing systems on the planes overhead."

"How long will it take them down for?"

"In San Jose it took about thirty minutes before things started powering back up again."

"What about us, though?" Harper asked. "If it's going to knock out all of their electronics, isn't it going to zap ours, as well?"

"In theory, yes, but there are ways for us to protect our own stuff from the effects of the blast. We have some small boxes that attach right to your hip. Put your coms, batteries, and whatever else in them. They're insulated against the pulse so once it goes off all you have to do is pull them out of the box, put 'em in, turn them on, and you're good to go. We have a com system that we can use tomorrow. The main com switchboard has already been built to withstand an EMP blast."

"Judas Priest," Harper exclaimed, "you guys are like James Bond and the A-Team all wrapped into one elite killing squad."

"The A-Team's got nothing on us," the doctor said dismissively.

"Although, we do have our token black guy," Sloane laughed at Hawk.

Laurie was looking something up on her phone. "Hey, sunset tomorrow night is 7:42 p.m. So if we hit around eight, that should be plenty dark enough so that it makes a pretty good difference."

"Will this EMP device take out night vision goggles, too?"

"It will take out their batteries, yes. Anything electronic or battery powered."

"So, hold up," Hawk said with a pensive look, "that EMP blast is going to render those Black Hawks just about worthless, isn't it?"

"If the timeline from San Jose holds, then I'm thinking that by the time we get back to them, it's going to be close. It may take a few minutes, but the electronics of those birds will definitely be back up and running soon after we get to them."

"So, this EMP blast, it doesn't destroy electronics?"

"I can't talk for every EMP device that has ever been or ever will be made, but ours just knocks out batteries and electricity for a short period of time. Basically, renders all the systems helpless. After the effect of the blast has worn off, things will begin to regenerate and come back into use."

"Laurs, how long do you estimate it will take us to pull this whole shabang off if everything goes halfway decent?"

"From first shot to final exodus," she said firmly, "we need to be in and out in less than an hour."

"I'm not sure about your math, Ms. Chase," John countered. "An hour? I'll figure out the attack ratios and the time schematics in a bit, but I can tell you right now that if we are still fighting them after an hour, we won't win."

"The police won't be there immediately, but eventually, they will send somebody out there to see what's going on," Kinley added.

"Seence Tito ees going to be out of town, thee *policía* weel be slow to respond. They know hees men like to party while hees gone," Diego explained.

"Yet another thing that will play into our favor."

"What's the escape strategy? Like you said, eventually the authorities are gonna show up. Do we have a specific plan of escape?"

"Once we have control of the compound, there will be a myriad of escape routes. We certainly won't have to leave the way we came in. When the authorities eventually show up, it will be well after dark. And then the last thing I want to do before we get out of there is set fire to all his frikkin' cocaine fields. Destroy all of his crops. Destroy everything."

"If I'm up in the air in a Black Hawk," Hawkins said, "I'll light up his fields like it's Independence Day. Bing, bang, boom!"

"Hey, I just thought of something," Sloane smirked. "Black Hawk will be flying a Black Hawk! That's like poetry or something."

Devereaux leaned over and whispered to Harper, "I think you may have just met your intellectual equal, and I don't know about you, but I was kinda hoping that day would never come."

"You want to tell him he's a big dope then you go right ahead," Harp whispered back, "but I'm not sure if you've noticed the gun show that guy's walking around with. His muscles have more ripples than a topographic map."

"With all of the perimeter guards taken out," Laurie continued, "we will have our choice of escape routes. Still, for the sake of continuity, we really should pick one. Maybe an alternate, just in case."

"At this point, we should have Big James' vehicle and your van, right?"

"Should. Hopefully they won't take any major damage during the attack."

"Even if they do, it's not like there's going to be a shortage of vehicles around the compound. We can take any one of those. Things go according to plan, I'm pretty sure del Fuento's guys won't have any use for a set of wheels."

"We can just go right back out the same way Big James and Diego will have come in," Laurie said. "It's a direct shot right back to the main road, and we'll be going in the exact opposite direction that the police will be coming in from. We'll be clean away with little to no resistance."

"All right, it sounds like we've got a pretty good jump on this thing," Samuel Hawkins was excited. "For now, however, I would just like to proffer that maybe we run back over this plan one more time, and then how's 'bout we get on up outta here and go enjoy the nightlife of beautiful Rio de Janeiro for a while. Ain't nobody got to be anywhere early in the mornin', do they?"

"I'm down with that," Harper agreed. "Let's give this whole thing a quick run through one more time and then go have some fun. Besides, we've still got all day tomorrow to fine tune the plan. I came here to help Laurie out, but I was kinda hoping to take in the sights for a bit, too. I'll send a message to Big James to let him know that we'll be making our way back into town, and we'll meet up with him there."

"You have any recommendations for a good place to hang out for a few hours, Miss Chase?" John asked.

"Recommendations? Yeah, it's Rio. I recommend the whole place," she laughed.

Group Chatter

The group went through the plan of attack one more time. They were thorough, asking a few more questions and tweaking it until they were content that the model would work.

"Got someplace my crew and I can get cleaned up before we hit the town?" John asked Laurie.

Unlike Kinley and Harper, Dragon's Men had come prepared with just about everything they needed, including a pack in their jeep containing spare clothes and shower and bathroom supplies. So when Laurie showed them where they could clean up, John Watkins and crew were about their business with no further facilitation needed.

Finally alone amongst themselves, Laurie, Kinley, Harper, and Diego began to speak about their newfound cohorts.

"Wow!" Laurie was the first to speak.

"Yeah, wow," Kinley seconded. "Those guys are something else."

Laurie looked at Harper and asked, "Where did your friend Big James find these people?"

"I'm pretty sure it wasn't in the Yellow Pages," Harper replied.

"Being around them, I feel like the school nerdette going out with the starting quarterback of the football team," Chase smiled.

"Nerdette? What exactly is a nerdette?"

"A female nerd," Chase stated. "What else would it be?"

"Man," Kinley laughed, "the nerd culture must've run pretty deep in whatever institution of learning you attended in your formative years."

"Oh, and why do you say that? Because you've never heard the term nerdette before, so it must not be a real thing. Is that it?"

"It's not a real thing, Laurs," Harper uttered. "The word nerd is all-gender encompassing. Kinda like the word chef or the word pilot. There's no such thing as a pilotess or a chefette."

"Whatever," Chase said dismissively.

Kinley looked at Diego. "Diego, when you were learning English, did you ever hear of the word nerdette?"

Diego furrowed his brow. "No, Meester Keenley, I do not know of thees word."

"There ya go," Kin said to Chase.

"What? No. You can't ask him. He barely knows English at all," she protested.

"He knows it well enough to know that nerdette isn't a word," Devereaux said, reaching over and playfully poking Laurie's rib-cage. "Nerd."

"Hey," she feigned objection and tickled Devereaux's stomach. "Jerk."

"Oh, I'm a jerk, huh?" Kinley laughed as he gently grabbed her wrist and moved closer to her.

"Aww, good gosh," Harper sighed, "I don't need an R.S.V.P. to know that I'm being cordially invited to make myself scarce." Rowe looked at Diego. "Wanna go see what we can scrounge up to eat around here, *mi amigo*?"

"*Sim*, Meester Harper, I have some leftover Portuguese *chouriço* and peppers. Ees *muy bueno*," the diminutive man said as he walked over to Harper, patted him on the back, and led the way toward the kitchen area of the huge building.

John, Daniel, Samuel, and Mercedes all crowded into the upstairs bathroom and began their own conversation.

"They seem confident that the nine of us are going to be able to mow down two hundred trained soldiers tomorrow night," Dr. Lara said with a slightly doubtful tone. "I don't care how much the soldiers have been drinking, or that we've got the advantage of surprise on our side, the numbers don't lie. Everything's going to have to go off without a hitch in order for us to all make it out in one piece."

"Eh, we've fought more with less, Merc," John answered. "I know a little bit about what went on in Mexico City a couple of years ago, and the three of them were up against some pretty heavy odds then, too, and they managed to pull it off. If that EMP device works the way it should, this might even turn out to be somewhat of a stroll in the park. No, what I'm more concerned about is that we came down here to take out Tito del Fuento. Not his men. Not his property. Not take his money. Big James said we were going to be taking out the boss himself, but there's been no mention of when or how we plan to do that as of yet."

"Maybe James is being kept in the dark just like we are," Sloane suggested.

"Yeah, or maybe she just wants to wipe out everything the guy has, but leave him alive to live through the aftermath. Kinda like he did to her when he slaughtered her DEA team," Hawkins offered. "Besides, as long as we don't blow up the building with the money in it, we're gonna walk away from this with a pretty big payday in tax-free, cold, hard, dollah-dollah bills, ya'll."

"Amen to that."

"That's all fine and well, but leaving del Fuento and a hundred of his best men alive isn't exactly my idea of ending this guy and his drug empire, ya know?" John stroked his clean-shaven chin in thought. "Sammy, tell ya what, why don't you buy the first couple rounds of drinks for everybody and let's see if some liquor doesn't get Ms. Chase's lips a little looser. Find out what her endgame is in all this."

"I'm all in for that," Hawkins smiled a pearly white grin.

"Merc, see what you might be able to find out from Harper Rowe. I'm sure you probably noticed that the guy seemed to take a bit of a liking to you."

"Noticed? Of course I noticed. Just because I hang out with you guys doesn't mean I lost my female Spidey-sense," the golden-haired beauty acknowledged.

"And about the money. Chase seems to think that we're all going to need to make a quick exit out of there once the fighting is done. I'm thinking that once the four of us take that hangar and get Sammy up in the air, Merc, you and I will head back to the main fray. Daniel, I want you to head to the building with the money and get that stuff packed and ready to load."

"You know, she said she thought it would take about an hour for all of this to play out. I just ain't seein' it that way, boss. If it goes the way that woman says it is, I gotta figure twenty, twenty-five minutes tops."

"Yeah, and there's more than just a little bit of sexual tension between her and Devereaux."

"Yeah, I guess they got their own thing goin' on," Sloane noted. "I don't really care as long as it doesn't get them distracted tomorrow night. Let's get this outta the way, and they can get back to their regular thing after that."

Mercedes laughed softly. "Those two don't have a regular thing. My money's on that they've never been intimate with each other even once."

"What makes you say that, Doc?" Hawk ask a bit bewildered. "They seemed pretty friendly with each other to me."

"I wouldn't be much of a doctor if I didn't know how to read people, and I'm telling you right now that with the level of flirtation they've got going on with each other, as far as any intimacy is concerned – that's undiscovered country, boys."

"Now, Doc, c'mon. You may be able to tell the difference between a lacerated spleen and a ruptured appendix, but I know the difference between beginner's flirtation and people that been at it for a while, and I'm tellin' ya those two ain't just startin' out."

"Oh you're so sure, huh? Well, in that case, do you care to make it interesting?"

"Sure," Hawkins smiled. "Whatcha got in mind?"

"Winner gets ten grand of the other person's split of the money we take tomorrow night. Sound fair?"

"Oh yeah," he rubbed his hands together, "this is going to be easy money, baby."

"Oh no it won't," John said sternly. "I'm not letting you two bet any amount of money on something. Especially something as arbitrary as this. You guys make a bet like that, and I don't care who wins or who loses, it's going to cause some friction, and I'm not just going to stand idly by and allow that to happen."

Sam and Mercedes sighed, knowing Watkins was right.

"You wanna wager something, then make it dinner. Make it foot rubs for a week. Make it that one–"

"Foot rubs!" Hawkins and Lara said at the exact same time.

"I'm down with that, Doc."

"Me, too. I'll even make sure I wash them real good before you have to work on them."

"Twenty minutes a pop sound proper?"

"Indeed."

The two shook on it and Mercedes said, "Now if you boys don't mind, I'm going to play the 'ladies before gentleman' card and grab my shower first."

"You coulda played the 'age before beauty' card and also gotten away with it," Sloane said on his way out.

"Easy, Danny, it's not her fault she was born in the 1940s. It's just the way it worked out," Hawkins chided.

"I'm barely old enough to run for President!" she exclaimed as she kicked Sam in his butt. "Get outta here already, will ya?"

BRAND NEW LOOK

"Oh, my goodness!" Ellie gasped as she looked at her friend and her daughter. "They do not look like same people."

"Yeah, it's called a cut-and-dye job," she smiled. "Nice, huh?"

Anezka and Jana, the mother-daughter duo that had previously both had long red hair, were now polar opposites. Anezka now had butch, black hair and a pale complexion. Her daughter was now sporting mid-length blond hair, an olive complexion, and a pair of librarian glasses.

"Look like different people from different country," Ellie confirmed.

"That's what I was going for."

"Did good job."

"Good. In that case get off your ass and help me move them. You take one and go somewhere – don't tell me where – and stay as far off the radar as you possibly can."

"Then what?"

"If it's safe, you will hear from me."

"If I do not hear from you?"

She furrowed her brow, picked up the nearest loose object that she could find and hurled it in Eliska's direction. "Then it's not safe, ya goof!"

Ellie ducked as whatever it was that was hurled at her hit the wall behind her. She stood back up, looked at her friend, and with a fantastic amount of enthusiasm said, "This will go well. Am sure of it."

A Passionate Moment

"You know we can't tell any of them about us, right?" Chase was trying to be cautious. "If any of them ever knew–"

"Harper already knows," Kinley said as he shook his head.

"How could he know? I didn't even know. Who is he? God?"

"He ain't God. He ain't Elvis. He's Harper Rowe, and he knows everything. I don't know how he knows. I guess he's just intuitive – but he knows."

"Do you think he'll blab?" Chase asked.

"I've known the kid for a few years and I've never known him to blab about anything. Our secret is safe. I think he likes it that we love each other."

"Whoa," Chase said in surprise. "Love?"

"Well, highly in like with each other," Kin corrected. "Really, we needn't assign any sort of label to any of this. Let's just be cool, enjoy each other, and hope we get through the certain–"

"Love's good," Chase said, jumping into his arms and wrapping her legs around his waist. She began kissing Dev passionately, and he did not resist. He squeezed her so tight that he actually felt a tendon in his elbow pop ever so slightly.

It was one long kiss, replete with lip-biting and a few indistinguishable barnyard noises.

Chase finally pulled her head back, loosened her grasp from around Kinley's torso, and lowered her legs back to the floor. She was out of breath.

"Wow," she breathed out.

"Yeah, wow," he concurred. "That was nothing short of extraordinary."

They leaned against each other, still wrapped in sweet embrace.

"Quick question," Laurie seemed a bit confused.

"Yeah?"

"About twelve seconds into that – did you moo, by any chance?"

Devereaux tried to repress a smile as he replied, "I would answer that, but I'm pretty sure that falls under 'kisser-kissee privilege', and therefore, I am not at liberty to divulge that information at this juncture."

Chase smiled. She kissed him again before reluctantly saying, "We should probably chill with this for now. No telling when anyone of the others will be making their presence known, and I don't need them to think that this," and she pointed back and forth between herself and Devereaux, "is going to make tomorrow night's events anymore complicated than they already will be."

"Absolutely," he agreed.

"We should–" she started to say.

He kissed her again playfully.

"–probably get ready to–"

Unable to resist, she kissed him back.

"–get going."

"I agree," he smiled. "Besides, I'm sure Harper will be back here soon enough, and that dude never listened to Billy Joel's advice of leaving a tender moment alone, ya know?"

"More than likely it's because Harper wouldn't know a tender moment if it kicked him in the shins."

The Playful Doctor Lara

The whole group was headed back to Rio. They had spent several productive hours at Chase's home base up in the hills – way up in the hills, for that matter – and the plan had been rehearsed, refined, and agreed upon.

New alliances had been made. Friends even, maybe. A new romance had finally come to fruition. Everyone had had a chance to clean up, refresh, and reset. Now the lot of them were carefully making their way back down the mountain and into the heart of the city.

Once again they were in two vehicles – Laurie driving the white cargo van with Kin riding shotgun and Samuel Hawkins in the seat behind them – and the black jeep riding in tow with Daniel Sloane behind the wheel, John Watkins riding in the front passenger's seat, and Merc and Harper cozied up in the back seat.

Harper did not mind the arrangements, as he found Mercedes Lara and her golden-haired, bronze-skinned features to be some of the best he had ever laid eyes on. Mercedes welcomed the closeness because she was getting ready to try to pump Harper for some information, and she knew her sex appeal was among the best in all the land.

"Nice night before a slaughter," she said to him with a smile.

"Yeah," Harper agreed, "even if it is us that gets slaughtered tomorrow, it's definitely a nice night tonight. The stars look as if someone just gave the earth a big roundhouse punch right in its kisser."

Somehow that made her smile. She had never heard that line before, and she had to think that this idiot could not have been the first one to have come up with it, yet something in his delivery made it sound fresh and unrehearsed.

"As much as I'd like to just slouch down in this seat and cuddle you like crazy, I'm probably not going to do that because it would be rude to your fellow Dragon's Men guys. Nothing burns my butt like a three and a half foot flame more than a couple of yutzes that don't know how to place manners over magnetism."

Without hesitation, Mercedes asked John and Daniel, "You two have any issue if I playfully coquet with our friend back here until we get into town? I promise not to use any tongue." Truth be told, she was not finding Harper Rowe too hard on the eyes, either.

"Knock yourselves out, kids," Danny replied. "Let me know if you get naked so I can make sure to adjust the rearview mirror just so."

Watkins looked quizzically at his sinewy friend, "Just so how?" he asked.

"Just so I don't accidentally see it and end up puking on my shirt." Sloane imperceptibly nodded down toward the tight black tee shirt that was glued to his upper torso.

"Good enough," Watkins said as he laid his head back against the headrest and closed his eyes. "Gonna catch a few winks on the way. I'm tired as crap."

Mercedes moved in closer to Harper. "See? They're cool with us getting to know each other a little better." She took Harp's arm and put it around her neck. "And so am I."

"Mmm," Harper sighed as he settled in next to her, "you're like a bearskin rug, a bottle of wine, and a crackling fire all at once. You feel like home."

"Nice. You use that one a lot, do ya?"

"Only when inspired to do so," Harper acquiesced, "but I change it up depending on the situation. Sometimes it's a grassy field, a warm summer breeze, and a blanket. Sometimes it's the middle of nowhere, a secluded waterfall, and a bar of soap. Sometimes – it's other stuff." Harper looked into Merc's eyes and smiled warmly. "I haven't been home in so long, I almost forgot what it felt like till now."

"Daggone," Sloane said to himself, "this guy is layin' it on thick."

Mercedes thought so, too, but in the spirit of keeping up the charade so that she might be able to pick the assassin's brain later on, she played along.

"Glad I can do that for ya."

"So how long are we going to keep this up until you start trying to verbally frisk me for information?"

"Ooh, she was doing good up to there," John said from his position of slumber.

"Is that what you think I want?" she asked Harper as she moved her mouth closer to his lips.

"It's not like I'm objecting or anything."

Just then the phone in John Watkins' shirt pocket rang. He sleepily pulled it out. "Yeah, Hawk, what's up?"

"What's goin' on back there? Whatcha'll into?"

"Apparently, we are on a really great episode of 'Taxicab Confessions,' as far as I can tell," Watkins answered quietly.

"What? Shi', boy, I wanna be back there witchoo. We ain't doin' nothin' up here but talkin' shop. Kinda bor'n', really."

"Well, hang tight, Sam. We'll all be together soon."

Hawkins hung up the phone and said to Laurie and Kin, "Yeah, it sounds like you two are right. Definitely some noise going on back there. John boy called it taxicab confessions, so, yeah, it sounds like you two nailed it with Merc and Harper hooking up." Hawk kept it to himself that that was the plan all along, a little touchy-touchy, kissy-kissy to get just a little more information, a little more insight into tomorrow night.

"Mind if I ask you a question, Mr. Hawkins?" Dev inquired.

"By all means, please do."

"What is it that your doctor is trying to get out of Harper that you couldn't just ask us right up front?"

Hawk squirmed in his seat for a second or two before asking, "So, we getting close to our destination? Cos I know I am parched as the Sahara. Could definitely use a drink right about now."

"I mean, she just doesn't seem the type to be throwing herself at someone like my friend, ya know?"

"Oh, you'd be surprised what she throws herself at sometimes. Woman's got a mind of her own. Besides, your boy back there ain't half bad lookin' either. I know I wouldn't want to leave my girl alone with him for more than half an hour, tell ya that much." Hawkins laughed nervously and tried to move on to a new subject. "Hey, where we goin' anyways?"

"It's a nice little beach club called Espetto Carioca. It's open-air right on the beach," Laurie answered.

"Carioca? You mean it's a karaoke bar?" Devereaux asked.

"They have that there, yes, but I just like going to this place because of its exposure to the beach. I mean, it opens right up to the white sand of Copacabana Beach. It's relaxing, laid back, not too loud. We'll be able to talk some more about tomorrow."

"So, you've frequented this spot before?"

"Of course I have. Since it's January first most places will be kind of low key after all the partying from last night. But this place should still be pretty busy, so we'll be able to blend in okay."

"But there will be some beautiful Brazilian babies there tonight, right?" Hawkins asked from the backseat.

"Really?" Laurie asked incredulously. "Please tell me that you aren't actually thinking about getting laid at a time like this."

"Hey, now, I ain't gonna sit around and let you two be the only ones gettin' happy later on tonight."

Chase and Devereaux exchanged looks.

"I'm sorry – what?" Laurie asked, somewhat bewildered.

"I said that I'm not gonna be the only–"

"Yeah, we heard what you said," Kin interrupted. "We're just not real sure where you got your information."

Hawkins laughed slyly. "Aw, c'mon, you two. Y'ain't gotta play with me like that. I get that ya'all might be tryin' to hide it from the others for whatchever reasons ya may have, but I'm cool. You can let your guard down around ol' Hawk. I won't say a word nor a syllable."

Kin furrowed his brow. "Did Harper say something to you about Laurie and me being an item?"

"Harper? No. Shi', boy – and girl – ain't nobody had to say anything to anybody. Plain to see that you two's got your own thing goin' on."

Dev looked at Laurie. "D'ya hear that? We apparently got our own thing goin' on."

"Oh, but it's okay because we can let our guard down around ol' Hawk. He's cool."

"Well, thank God and Trailways for that," Devereaux laughed.

Hawkins moved uneasily in his seat as he thought about his bet with Mercedes. "I get it. You all wanna be private about your relationship. I respect that. I do. I feel bad now that I even brought it up – the two of you being together."

"If you mean the two of us being together as in doing the dirty then, no, Mr. Hawkins, I can honestly say that we have not ever been together," Laurie confessed.

"Okay. Okay. Well, I get that. Savin' it up for marriage. That's the honorable and right thing to do. Kudos to y'all for that. Still, doin' the dirty aside – how long you two been together as a couple?"

Chase laughed. "This guy's just not getting it."

"It's almost like *he* wants us to be together more than you and I want us to be together."

Laurie was quiet in thought for a moment as she took in what Kinley had just said.

And then she suddenly burst out loud, "Oh my gosh, no way!"

"What?" asked a confused Kinley Devereaux.

"What?" asked an even more confused Samuel Hawkins.

"Mr. Hawkins, do you and your little teammates have some sort of bet going on about Kinley and I being together?"

"What? No," Hawkins shook his head adamantly. "That's just crazy talk."

Kinley looked at Laurie and said, "Methinks he doth protest too much."

"Okay, hold up," Hawkins said loudly as he slid forward in his seat. "Number one, 'at ain't even what that sayin' means. Number two, I totally resent ya'll referrin' ta John, Danny, and Merc as my li'l teammates. Not sure if ya'll noticed this or not, but we ain't the girls JV basketball squad. Seems to me the three o' yas might be straight at what ya'll do, but lemme assure yer white hides that we are also quite good at what *we* do."

"So what's the bet?"

Hawk flopped back in his seat and sighed, "Foot rubs."

"Really?"

Laurie looked at Hawkins in the rearview mirror. "I'm going to take it that Mr. Watkins and Mr. Sloane are not a part of this particular wager."

"No, it's just me and Merc, and I do not want her to win. I know her, and she will not cut her toenails or wash her feet for about two weeks leading up to me touching those things!" He cringed at the mere thought of it.

"So, that's what she's doing back there with Harper? She's

trying to pump him for information about us?"

And even though Samuel knew full well that this was not the reason that Dr. Mercedes Lara was pumping Harper Rowe for information, he unapologetically and emphatically answered, "Absolutely."

"Oh, man, that's rich. Harper's going to know what's going on and he's going to lead that poor woman right through the wide gate and down that broad road that is the path to destruction – and many are the women that have entered through it."

"Well, that's what she gets," said Chase matter-of-factly. "Can't just be going around making wagers on other people's love lives."

Hawkins was quiet for a minute before asking once again, "But there will be some beautiful Brazilian babies there tonight, right?"

A Night at the Espetto Carioca

The group parked their vehicles about four blocks away from the Espetto Carioca beach club and took their time walking through the warm night air. Chase was right about the town being quiet since it was the evening of January first. Still, the small crowd on the street buzzed with mirth and merriment for the New Year.

Harper and Mercedes walked close to one another, arm in arm. Laurie and Kin were not nearly as proximate as they followed side by side. John, Daniel, and Sam brought up the rear with Sloane stopping a time or two to light his cigarette. The septenary was dressed in casual attire; Harper and Kinley had donned matching black tee shirts which they wore untucked over their khaki pants. Laurie and Mercedes both wore dark short-sleeved sweaters with short skirts over black leggings.

John, who always said that he represented the agency with his actions, appearance, and demeanor, and that one should never question the importance of those three things to him, wore a button-down blue Oxford shirt tucked into his gray Traveler wool pants, covered by a loose-fitting sport coat. This may have been a bit much for such a warm night, but when Johnny went out he always made it a point to look good.

As for the other members of the Dragon's Men Protection

Agency, John did not really care how they looked unless they were going out on their own to meet a new client. Hence, Samuel was attired in dress shorts, a three-button, three-quarters-sleeve gray Henley shirt, and a pair of Ecco Biom golf shoes. Daniel, who was not much for dressing up unless it was to meet a new business prospect for the agency, wore a black tee shirt with blue jeans and a pair of concrete white Jordan 3 high tops. Nevertheless, with his Atlas-like physique, he made slummin' it look good.

As the group made their way up the street to the Espetto Carioca, they passed several tinted storefront windows. It made Mercedes smile, the way Harper would check his reflection in almost every window they passed. She was discovering that getting close to him was not as bad as she had anticipated. His colorful personality intrigued her, along with the fact that this was, indeed, the man that had first-hand knowledge of the assassination of former Secretary of Defense Paul Michaels. She did not usually go for the dangerous type, since she had plenty of danger in her everyday life. But for some reason she was feeling a strong attraction to Harper.

"Well, here we are," Laurie announced as she walked past Harper and Mercedes and opened the door to the club. She led the group inside the well-lit restaurant that had tables and booths to the left and a large horseshoe-shaped bar to the right. Straight ahead of them was a large dance floor, and on the far side of that was a huge stage that currently featured a young man and woman singing Jimmy Buffet on the karaoke machine.

Just past the tables to the left was a large set of French doors that led to the alfresco seating area. Here, twenty-some umbrella-covered tables were randomly spread out over rubber outdoor flooring that ran about thirty yards wide and fifty yards down toward an outdoor dance floor. The dance floor extended another ten to fifteen yards toward the ocean before it disappeared into the white sandy beach. On each side of the table area were eight-foot-high red-slatted fences dotted by silver light posts that lit up the entire area. The huge speakers in front of every light post pumped out vocal trance music that drew people out of their seats and onto the outdoor dance floor.

"Everybody cool with sitting outside?" Laurie asked. "It would make for better conversation."

"Sure."

"I'm down."

"Sounds good."

With everyone in agreement, the gang went outside and found a table that would fit all of them comfortably.

The night air was warm, and the breeze coming off the beach was perfect. A waitress came by, handed out some menus, and took everyone's drink orders. It was not long before conversation began flowing again.

"So, what is it that you all do?" asked Kinley. "I mean, I understand that you all were in the military together, but now that you are back in the States and civilians, what does your protection agency actually do?"

John was quick to answer. "We do what needs to be done to ensure the safety of our clients, who are mostly people that fall between the cracks of the law. These are people who are in danger, but it's just not dangerous enough for the law to help them. And that's where we come in."

"I guess a job like that can get pretty intense sometimes, huh?" Laurie asked.

"Sometimes, but if we're on top of things we can usually prevent things from escalating to that point."

"Which is most of the time," Sloane was quick to point out.

"Ever get a case that was a lot more than you thought it was going to be?" Kin asked. "One where you had to chew a lot more than you thought you had bitten off?"

"Few times."

"Like what?"

"Had a run-in with the Russian mafia one time," Merc said.

"Really?"

"Had a run-in with the Chicago mafia one time, too." Hawk put in.

Kinley looked at Sam and asked, "So, if I may ask, what was the biggest difference between the two?"

"Oh, yeah," piped up Harper. "Now there's a question you don't get to ask every day. Ever."

"Easy," Hawkins replied without hesitation, "the Russian mobsters had a much better grasp of the English language. Those jabronis from Chi-town may as well've been talkin' Pig Latin for as much as I understood what they were sayin'."

"Hey," Sloane said as he feigned looking around in a panic, and then in his best Chicago accent said, "Be careful what you're goin' on about. They very well may still be watchin' us."

Harper gave an obligatory laugh to which Mercedes responded, "He's not kidding. That was about five months ago, and I'm still looking over my shoulder on a regular basis expecting to see someone that I don't want lurking around in the shadows."

"Really?"

"Really. Those Russians show up, handle their business, and then they're gone like smoke in the wind. The Chicago mobsters? They do whatever it is they need to do, but then they leave a presence behind that lingers like a fart in a phone booth. I have not slept well since that particular job."

"I definitely get that," said Chase. "Lord knows I haven't slept well since my team was taken out by Tito and his crew back in Mexico City, and that was over a year and a half ago. Which is why I just—"

The waitress returned with a busboy in tow. Both of them were balancing trays of drinks for the seven of them. "Here we go, gang," the waitress said. Her Brazilian accent was slight but noticeable enough. She was good though. She did not even have to ask for a reminder as to who ordered what. She distributed the drinks to whom they belonged, no questions asked.

Once the drinks were handed out, the busboy exited the scene and the waitress pulled out a small notebook. "And will we be ordering any food tonight?"

She was amazingly attractive, and Devereaux noticed how she was eyeing up Harper. Dev was also noticing how Mercedes was noticing how the waitress was eyeing up Harper. Knowing Harper's penchant for flirtation, Kinley wondered how this particular scene was going to play out, with Dr. Mercedes Lara hanging on Harp's arm like she was.

No one had actually looked at their menus yet, so when the question of food being ordered was brought up, they took quick sips of their drinks and picked up their menus.

Everyone except for Harper. He picked up on the eye contact that he was getting from the waitress, and returned it in kind.

"What would you recommend?" he asked. "I'm guessing you've eaten here a time or two, yes?"

"Here we go," Kinley muttered to himself. Fighting the urge to see if the rest of the group was picking up on it, too, he eyed up his buddy and continued the narrative in his head. "Don't let me down, don't let me down, don't let me down. Make this as uncomfortable as possible, buddy."

"Well, of course, I like just about everything we have. I do work here after all," she laughed playfully. "I think the real question is: What do you like?" she said, never breaking eye contact.

Kinley kept staring at the train wreck.

"I like something that's sweet and tasty yet not too heavy. Something a guy could really wrap his tongue around. Do you have anything like that?"

"So you're hoping to find something that will satisfy you now, but not stick around and make things uncomfortable for you later on in the night?"

"That is exactly what I'm hoping for," Rowe smiled.

Kin was loving this. In his head he was thinking, "Yes, yes, yes, buddy. Oh my goodness, you can't find theater this good on Broadway, kids."

"Then I would definitely recommend the lemon-butter tilapia. It's satisfying from the very first bite, fulfills the pallet, but won't haunt you later on. Does that sound like what you're wanting?"

"Perfect. Put me in for that, and if it's as good as you say it is, I'll be sure to thank you later with a very nice tip." And as everyone was waiting for Dr. Mercedes Lara to throw her drink in his face, Harper turned to Merc and asked, "Does that sound about right? A very nice tip? Later?"

"I think the rest of us might need a few minutes," Hawkins said, trying not to lend any sort of credibility to what had just happened. In his own head he was laughing, but he was unsure how everyone else taking the – what Hawk presumed was innocent enough – playful banter between Harper and the waitress.

The waitress, in turn, played it the same way. "I will come back in just a few minutes to see what you have selected." Before walking away, she said to Harper, "I'll go get to work on what you are wanting, sir," she paused for effect and then continued, "so that I can get that big tip later."

As she walked away, the tension and silence that she left behind could have only been cut with a freshly-sharpened machete.

Watkins was the first to speak. "Was that really necessary, Mr. Rowe? That whole back and forth between you and the waitress?"

"What? The back and forth between me and the waitress?"

"Sweet and tasty? Something to wrap your tongue around? A big tip later? That seemed just a bit rude to me when you've got a lady sitting right next to you."

"It's good. We're good," said Devereaux, covering for his friend. "We're good."

"Seriously, John," Merc spoke up. "The guy's just getting into the spirit of the night. Who knows what tomorrow holds. I'm all in – let's have some fun."

"John," Harper put his hands up. "Come on, man. She's just a nice girl trying to make a little coin waiting tables. All she wants are friendly customers, a nice atmosphere, and to not screw up our orders. On a normal day, that girl probably has to deal with butt monkeys about seventy-five percent of the time. I'm just letting her know that the lot of us – we're not with the butt monkey clan."

Watkins pursed his lips and gave a slight smile. He looked at Harper, then on to Daniel, and lastly, he looked at Merc, who smiled reassuringly back at him. "You're right," he said as his mood lightened. "That's me being in the wrong there. Sorry."

And just like that the tension broke and the good mood returned.

To get everyone in the spirit of the evening, Laurie Chase stood up, waited for a bit of silence, and said, "There is no way that I could ever thank all of you for being here and doing – well – doing what we will be doing tomorrow. So, tonight's on me. Let's enjoy Rio!"

Kinley looked at Harper and flatly said, "Harp, let's enjoy Rio."

Harper turned from Kin and to Mercedes and said with feigned sadness, "It is with deep remorse and a heavy heart that I regretfully inform you of the following: Dr. Mercedes Lara, let's enjoy Rio."

Merc turned to Daniel and in her best Terminator voice said, "Daniel. Let's enjoy Rio."

The group lightened up, and though they wanted to look at Watkins to see if he had chilled, no one did.

Watkins sensed the uneasiness. To break the tension, he quietly started singing in his off-key voice, "*Her name is Rio and she dances 'cross the sand...just like a river goin' through that dusty land.*"

His gesture worked perfectly as the rest of the gang began to sing along with him.

"*And yeah she shines and really shows you all she can...Yeah, Rio, Rio, dance across this Rio Grande!*"

Then, suddenly, from out of nowhere the group heard a booming voice from behind them. "Now there's a man who knows how to do some crowd control!"

It was Big James Gray. Everyone turned in unison to look.

"Hey now, " he laughed at the attention, "don't stop singing just because I'm here. I was just getting ready to join right in."

And for a moment it seemed like everyone was getting ready to resume singing again until Harper stood up and said, "Pretty sure they've already called Noise Control without you chiming in, ya big lug."

The two men embraced briefly. Laurie, who was already standing up, came over and got herself a Big James hug, too.

"Hey, now, we gonna hug it out all night or we gonna hit that dance floor and live for the night like they ain't gonna be no tomorrow?" Hawk asked as he stood up from his seat. "Cos, goodness knows, I'm ready to cut a little rug."

Mercedes grabbed Harper and said, "Dance with me, gorgeous."

Laurie took Kinley's hand and politely asked, "May I have this dance, sir?"

And as the music blared away through the loudspeakers, the gang made their way toward the dance area.

Even Sloane, who was the worst dancer ever, seized the moment. "I'm down." He looked at his boss, "Ya comin', John?"

"Think I'm gonna sit this one out. You go on and have some fun. I'll be along in a few."

Sloane knew John well enough to know when something was not sitting right with him. This seemed like one of those times, but for the life of him, Daniel could not figure out what could possibly be bothering John. Not here. Not now.

He knew that John was not still irritated with Harper about his little flirtation with the waitress in front of Mercedes. When John got upset about something, he would not make any bones about it, but when he was once again right with whatever or whomever had run afoul of him, he moved on from it. He did not hold a grudge or let things stick in his craw. Ergo, Sloane knew it was not Harper that had John in a somewhat-suddenly sullen mood.

Maybe it was still getting under John's skin that Laurie Chase did not have a definite plan about getting rid of Tito del Fuento. Yet somehow, Daniel sensed it was something else. He was just not sure what. Still – there was definitely something else.

"Ya sure?" he asked one last time, hoping Watkins might come clean. And he did.

"I think – we might be in danger."

"What? You mean tomorrow? When we go to take out del Fuento's guys?" Sloane asked, surprised by John's answer. "I mean, yeah, the plan is going to need some fine–"

"No, I'm fine with tomorrow, Daniel," Watkins answered, seeming a bit distracted as he looked intently past Sloane and toward the beach. "I think we might be in danger now."

"You think? Or you know?" Sloane asked as he slowly started to look around.

"Not to sound rude, bud, but I could explain myself to you now, and then you could go get everybody from the dance floor, and you could proceed to explain it to them. Or, you could just go get everyone, and I can explain it to all of you at the same time."

"In the interest of saving time – I'm just gonna go get everybody."

"Might wanna hurry," Watkins urged.

Here Comes Trouble

It did not take Sloane long to gather the gang from the dance floor. Once he told Hawk and Mercedes what John had said, it was just a matter of seconds before they all returned to the table.

"What is going on, John?" Merc was the first to ask.

"Sit," Watkins said without emotion.

Everyone sat.

"I think we might be getting ready to be in the middle of something here, people. Without making it extremely obvious, look down towards the beach – the shoreline – slowly. I know it's dark, but if you look hard enough you will see two men dressed in black. Do they look even remotely familiar to you?"

They turned their eyes toward the beach to see what Watkins was describing. By the light of the club's outdoor lamps, two darkly-dressed men standing down by the shoreline could be seen with relative ease.

Kin answered first. "Yes, when we were walking up the street to this place, I think I saw them. I mean, they are kinda far away so I can't say for sure – but I think I saw them standing outside a black van as we were walking up. They were smoking."

"Yeah," said Chase, "I saw them, too, and there were seven of them. Four of them were outside the van; three of them were sitting inside."

"Right," said John, "there were seven of them. So if two of them are down there by the shoreline, where are the other five?"

Harper looked at Kinley. "Maybe they're here for me."

"You think? How would they even know you're here?"

"I don't know, but this is what it looks like when the feds are getting ready to make a move on someone. They surround the place with guys, wait for the go-ahead from the AIC, and then they move in."

"No, Mr. Rowe," John said straight out. "They are most definitely not here for you. The guys in that van were casing this place long before we showed up. I could tell that they had been there a while by the large amount of cigarette butts that were littered around the outside of the van."

"So, you think we're looking at a robbery waiting to go down here?"

"I'm afraid so, and with those two guys being down there by the water right now, I have to think that their actions are imminent. I suppose that it's possible that the two of them are just down there scouting out the back side of this place, but their body language is telling me otherwise. They seem extremely skittish for two guys just out on a homework assignment."

"Oh, no, no, no, no, no," Big James said. "No."

"Yes," answered John. "Who's packing heat here besides me and my team?"

"Harp and I are."

"I've got a Glock 19 tucked in my waistband," Big James acknowledged.

"Wait," Laurie protested, "what is going on here?"

John looked at Mercedes and asked, "You good working with this guy?" And by "this guy", he meant Harper.

"With my life."

"Then you two get inside. I don't think it will be long now. First sign of strife or struggle, put 'em down, Merc. Shoot first – we'll figure out the questions later."

Harper was about seven steps ahead of John. He knew that whatever was going to happen, he and Kinley and Laurie could not be caught on video footage. It would not be the end of them, but it could certainly make things very uncomfortable if video footage of any sort was to find its way to Jeb Crool sooner rather than later. The extra twenty-four to thirty-six hours the trio planned to be in Rio after tonight would give Crool more than enough time to get down there and be hot on their trail once again.

So Harper began to direct his own situation.

"Kin – kill the guys on the beach and the security cameras. There are two covering that area. One on each of the light poles on both sides at the end of the fencing."

"Already planning on doing just that."

"Oh crap," John said as he realized the dilemma that Kin, Harp, and Laurie were facing. "You guys really can't be here, can you?"

"It's not that we can't," said Harper," it's just that we shouldn't. We could definitely use some ski masks for this impending little chore, if you know what I mean."

"If this goes down the way it appears it will, then everyone from the local cops to the feds to the national media is going to be swarming this place, wanting whatever video footage the security cameras pick up, and they will be going through it with a fine tooth comb, and it will be splashed all over media outlets across the world," explained Kinley. "However, to run away from a situation like this just to save our own hides – well – it's just not in our DNA."

"If this really is what it looks like it is, let's do what must be done, and then the three of us will have to hightail it on out of here. I mean, maybe we all should. We're planning a major move on the biggest drug dealer in Brazil tomorrow night," Chase said quietly. "I don't think it would be such a hot idea for any of us to be showing up on the 11:00 news tonight, ya know?"

"I think I can quash all your worries, gang," Big James said assuredly.

"And how's that?"

"I know the proprietors of this establishment. I was just yuckin' it up with one of them a few minutes ago when I was inside the restaurant on my way out here to meet up with all of you. Pretty sure if we keep his patrons from getting robbed or, heaven forbid, shot to death by these lowlifes, he'll be more than willing to help out in any way humanly possible. Plus, he can be bought easier than a crooked politician. Once I tell them that anyone else that's going to come through those doors isn't going to offer them a red cent for the video footage, I'm sure they'll find my offer for it more than fair." James looked at Harper. "I'll add it to my bill."

"Are you absolutely positive you can do that, Mr. Gray?" John asked.

"If I couldn't do this then I wouldn't've ever brought it up. I know what this means to all of you. Give me some credit, for crying out loud. Tell 'em, Harp."

"Yeah, we're solid here. If Big Time says he can eradicate the security footage then we're golden."

"Like a state warrior," Kin agreed.

"Then what are we standing around here for?" asked Big James. "If something wicked this way is coming then let's stop it, and you guys can all get on up outta here while I stick around and do damage control."

"I think it will be best if we advance in this manner," began John, "Kinley, you and Sam and Daniel take the two suspects down by the water. Move in a two-by-one formation. Danny, you and Sam take the lead and put those two down. Kinley, try to stay back and be sure that there aren't any more baddies lingering back somewhere that might come up on your flank and get the drop on the three of you. It's dark down there by the shore, so I think it goes without saying – keep your eyes open. I know you know what you're doing though, Mr. Devereaux."

Hawkins, Sloane, and Lara were all too familiar with John's way of telling someone what to do, admonishing them to do it right, but then letting them know that he had complete faith that they would get the job done correctly and effectively. Almost like a stern talking to and a pep talk combined, it was his way of giving out orders without sounding domineering.

Watch out for guys trying to sneak up on ya, Kinley. Don't let 'em kill any of my guys with a cheap shot from the bleachers, Kinley. I know it'll all be fine because you're the perfect man for the job, Kinley.

Mercedes took a quick peek at Danny and Sam just as they were taking a quick peek back at her. She knew that they, too, wanted to smile. It was funny to hear John doing it to someone else. Still, there was no arguing with Watkins' methods for handing out orders. It had gotten the three of them through a tour in Afghanistan, a stint in Libya, countless off-the-book military assignments that they knew all too well nobody else wanted – or probably would have even survived. Then there were all the incredibly dangerous situations through which they had to navigate in their current, post-military business. So, while John would never take credit for it, the fact that his leadership, mental acuity, and all around know-how is what kept everything and everyone in good working order was certainly not lost on them.

Still, it was refreshing to see that he was this way with everyone, and that this time the everyone was someone other than them.

"Merc, you and Harper go back inside through there," John continued as he nodded toward the French doors that led back inside of Espetto Carioca. "Scan the crowd. If I'm right about this then the other five members of this crew will be in there eventually. Some of them may be in there already. If they are, then you and Harper need to find them, mark them, and stay close to them until they make their move."

"What about me?" Laurie asked.

"You will be with me," Watkins answered. "We'll circle back around front to see what we can see. First thing is to locate the van they were in and around. If it's still parked in the street, and no one is inside of it, we might have time to toss it. Try to find out who these guys are. Hopefully, get an inkling as to what kind of firepower they're toting and see what we're up against."

John looked at Big James. "I need you to go inside and talk to the owner. Let him know what's going on, get him to someplace safe, and convince him to hold off on calling the authorities until–"

"Sure," James Gray interrupted, "until we know whether or not this is an actual robbery or what. I understand."

"Well," John said hesitantly, "I was actually going to say until we have these guys and this situation under control, I'd just as well leave the cops out of this. The last thing we'll need is more guys with more guns shooting up the place."

"I'll go have a talk with him now."

"When should we move down toward the beach, boss?"

"Give Laurie and me a chance to maneuver around front to their van. Not sure how much time we have here so we'll try to make it fast. Does everyone have Bluetooth?"

Everyone answered in the affirmative with the exception of Harper. "In the last several months, I haven't had a cell phone long enough to even bother activating it."

"It's all right. You're teamed with Merc. She can just relay everything to you. As for the rest of us, my number is 555-372-4667. Call it so I can conference everyone in."

Once that was taken care of, John looked around at the group – sans Big James – and asked, "Are we all good here then?"

The group nodded in agreement.

"One last thing, Harper," John spoke up. "You might want to find our waitress and tell her not to bother coming back for our order."

"Roger that, Rabbit," and Harper and Dr. Mercedes Lara began to head back inside the restaurant. As Harper walked past his best friend, Devereaux stood to his feet and said, "Be good here, Harp."

"You, too, Kin," Harper gave his buddy a quick pat on the back, "Keep these guys healthy. We got the regional semi-finals tomorrow against State, and we don't need any last-minute injuries."

Kinley smiled at his friend's familiar loose temperament. As he watched Harp and Mercedes head back inside the club he said, "Catch up with you in a bit." When he turned back to the table, Chase and Watkins were already on the move. He sat back down in his chair and looked at Hawk and Sloane before asking, "Does this kind of thing happen to you guys a lot?"

"Sadly, yes," answered Sloane.

"Trouble seems to find us like a cat finds its way back to its home, man. I have no doubt in my mind that we could parachute into the most remote cornfield in Kansas, and within twenty minutes someone would be shootin' at us."

Devereaux flashed a big smile. "Oh, man, I certainly remember those days. Ya wanna know why they call what I do wetwork? It's because you're always sweating. Everything. Finding where your target's going to be. Finding a hide to stowaway in until the crucial moment. Wondering if anybody saw you enough to identify you. Wondering if and when somebody is going to sell you out. I have definitely enjoyed being dead these last several months, that's for sure."

"In that case, a toast," Sloane said as he grabbed his drink and held it up in the air. "To you being dead and hoping that you won't get any more dead between now and tomorrow night."

"Hear, hear," Hawk and Dev raised their glasses. "Sa-lute."

STARTLING DISCOVERY

John walked with Laurie. "Let's head down toward the beach and circle back around front to the street. I'm hoping that van is still where it was parked when we came in."

"Okay," she agreed as she and John started walking toward the beach.

"Put your arm around me," he told her quietly. "We are just two lovers going for a stroll in the sand."

She put her arm around his waist and said, "I don't know if you were keeping score on the whole gun have and have nots back at the table, but I would be on the have not side of that particular ledger. I mean, silly me, right? What could I have possibly been thinking heading out for dinner and some drinks with my friends and leaving all my firearms at home?"

John put his arm around her shoulder. "I'd just like to point out that your friends, as you so eloquently put it, are four ex-military types, two former government wetwork guys, and one Brazilian gun runner. If I were you I think I would have brought a gun along just so I wouldn't feel left out."

"Hmm, since you put it that way, I guess you make a good point."

"And don't worry about being without a weapon," he continued.

"I have a backup piece holstered on my left ankle. Once we can stow away from unwanted onlookers I will give it to you."

"Thank you. I hope I won't need it, but thank you all the same."

"And I hope that those seven guys in the van are the extent of our troubles tonight."

"What do you mean?"

"I mean that I am hoping that these seven schlubs aren't just the scout team, and the rest of their posse will be showing up for the main event – whatever that ends up being."

"You say that as if you doubt these guys are here for a robbery after all."

"Oh, I'm pretty sure it's a robbery. It makes sense. Last night was a huge money night being New Year's Eve in Rio, and while I'm not positive of the banking practices in this town, I'm sure that most of the financial institutions around here were probably closed today. So there is a pretty good chance that the place is still sitting on its take from last night. Add to that, like you said earlier, it's less crowded. And with security measures being a lot lower then, it makes perfect sense that this is a robbery. Still, I've learned in my line of work to never assume anything."

"This looks like as good a place as any to head back up to the street – dark, but not too dark."

"Definitely looks good," Watkins said as he and Laurie turned left up a walkway that ran between two buildings. John stopped momentarily, leaned up against one of the buildings for balance, and lifted his left foot enough to remove his backup weapon from an ankle holster. He handed it to Chase. "This should do the job for you."

Laurie took the gun from John, looked it over and smiled. "Nice. A Springfield XD 40. It'll absolutely do." She checked to be sure the safety was on before she tucked it discreetly into the back of her waistband and pulled her sweater over top of it.

"Let's go then," John instructed as he started moving stealthily out of the alley. Before he stepped out of darkness and into the open light of the street, he paused to recon the area. He peered up and down the immediate vicinity and was relieved that the custom black van was still in the same spot as when he had seen it before.

"The van's still here," he said to everyone on the line with him, "and I do not see anyone in nor around it. Laurie and I will go see what we can garner as far as some kind of info, or a clue, or something that will give us just the slightest heads up to what kind of threat we're dealing with here."

"Any sign of them out on the street, Johnny?" asked Sloane.

John grabbed Laurie's hand and began skipping across the street. "Just a couple of love-drunk fools out dancin' away underneath the streetlights on New Year's night," he said to her in a hushed voice. "Seems a lot more inconspicuous than just ducking behind cars or hiding in the shadows of the night."

So while she danced merrily across the street with John Watkins, Laurie Chase continued to scan both sides of the thoroughfare and its adjoining sidewalks. Now that it was getting closer to the nine o'clock hour in Rio, more people seemed to be making their way out into the night. But even with the heavier foot traffic she did not see any sign of the would-be robbers, or bandits, or thieves, or whatever they were.

"See anything?" John asked her.

"I think we're good here."

Still sitting at the table, Sloane, Hawkins, and Devereaux were awaiting the go-ahead from John to head down toward to the beach to take care of the suspects that appeared to be eyeing up the Espetto Carioca.

Sloane pulled his Bluetooth mechanism away from his ear. "Hey, Devereaux, you're not pissy that our boss is dancing out in the street with your girl, are you?"

Devereaux laughed as he pulled his earpiece away as well. "Honestly, it's a good thing that we are keeping this question off the airwaves. Because if she heard you refer to her as 'my girl', I'm pretty sure she would be back here in about thirty seconds to punch you in the face."

Hawkins laughed out loud. "Too true," he lipped silently to Sloane.

"You'll shut your black mouth, or I'll shut it for you."

"Really?" Hawkins asked out loud.

"Really what?" asked a confused Dr. Mercedes Lara from inside the restaurant.

"Oh, nothing. Danny's just being his usual nitwit self. Showing off for our guest, I'm sure."

"What's going on?" asked the Bluetooth-less Harper.

"Oh, nothing a good kick in the rump can't fix," Mercedes frowned.

Harper gave her a baffled look.

"My two cohorts are just proving once again that they are the reincarnation of the Neanderthals."

"Ah, yes, Neanderthals. I've been there many times. I absolutely love Amsterdam," Harper joked.

Mercedes tried to hide her smile as she shook her head aporetically. She was getting ready to retort when Harper grabbed her hand and said, "I see them. Two on the far side of the bar, three right outside the glass entrance door."

Merc looked at the places Harper had brought to her attention to see a man and a woman on the far side of the bar, each dressed in similar black outfits. Just outside the front entrance doors, she saw a similarly-dressed trio that was suspiciously huddled together.

"When it comes time for shootin', do you want the couple at the bar or the three at the door?" Harper asked.

"I'll take the two at the bar," Merc smiled. "I'll leave the heavy lifting to you."

Harper nodded in agreement. "Won't be long now."

"Heads up, gang. It looks like our merry band of criminals is getting ready to make its move. We've got five of 'em in our sight. Sammy, what's going on with your guys down by the beach?"

"Looks like they might be making their way on up, but if they are – it's not in any real big hurry. Johnny, have you and Chase found anything in that van yet?"

"Sorry, everybody, it took me a few minutes to gain access into the perps' van, but we are in now, and we are combing every inch of this thing as we speak trying to find something."

"It's just about go time, fellas," Samuel Hawkins motioned to Kinley and Daniel to put their ear pieces back in. "John, we're gonna go ahead and start making our move toward the two beach-combers. We'll holla if any significant happenstances take place in the meanwhile."

"Roger that, Hawk."

"John," Laurie said. She was in the back of the van. The front of the van held two captains chairs, behind them was a bench seat that was bolted to the floor, and behind that was an open area roughly four feet wide by six feet deep that had been overlaid with carpet. "There's some sort of pamphlet or something under this carpet, but I can't seem to get to it. Give me a hand, will ya?"

John wasted no time crawling between the front seats and over the bench seat to reach Chase.

"Whatcha got?"

"There's something under here, under this corner of carpet, but I sure can't seem to get to it."

Examining the area that Chase was referring to, Watkins could see a multi-page pamphlet or tract of some sort trapped underneath the carpet in the very back corner of the driver's side. The carpet looked new, but the corner of the paperwork looked very used. John reached down, grabbed the corner of the carpet and gave it a mighty yank.

The carpet shredded away from the van floor to reveal a six-page pamphlet that was folded up like a road map. Chase picked it up and began to unfold it. The contents revealed themselves to Laurie and John simultaneously. In startled shock, the two looked at each other.

"Oh good Lord," John said out loud.

"What?" asked Merc.

"Hey, John, we're about fifty yards from our targets here on the beach head. Anything we need to know?" asked Sloane.

"Yeah," Watkins came back, "this pamphlet we just found is written in Arabic."

A momentary silence filled the gang's airwaves before John said, "I don't think we're dealing with a hold-up job here. I think these people are terrorists."

Dr. Mercedes Lara turned to Harper and said in a low voice, "John says that we may be dealing with terrorists."

And before Harper even had time to let Dr. Lara's words sink in, the trio crowding the front door of Espetto Carioca burst through, brandishing various high-powered automatic weapons and screaming, *"BISMILLAH!"*

BACK TO CROOL AND BALDWIN

Crool had left strict instructions with Agent Virginia Phelps to get any DNA that came up empty to his office. He knew that, more than likely, the DNA would have to belong to Kinley Devereaux.

For the first time in months, Crool felt like he was actually getting close to finding out where Harper Rowe really was. Knowing that Devereaux was alive, Crool suddenly had a whole new line of investigation to go down. And down it he was ready to go.

He was glad to be back in his office in D.C., and he was champing at the bit waiting for something to come across his desk from Atlanta.

Baldwin stuck his head inside the door of Crool's office. "Boss?"

"Come in, Dave. Tell me we have something."

Dave walked in uneasily. "We've got nothing."

"Is that what Phelps said?"

"It's what she said, yes."

"Then send our guys down there. Her people are a bunch of idiots. Send our guys down there, and I know they'll find something."

"Jeb, we sent our guys down already."

"How'd our guys get down there already? We just got back here ourselves."

"I called them before we left down there."

"Did you tell Phelps they were coming?"

"Of course."

"And she was good with that?"

"Absolutely. She welcomed the help. Apparently she knows that her people are a bunch of idiots, too."

"Our people found nothing?"

"Nothing that we could call evidence."

Crool looked up from his desk. "You saw the same thing I saw, right, Dave?"

"I did."

"That was Devereaux, wasn't it?"

"Nobody's saying that it wasn't, but as far as solid, dyed-in-the-wool, evidentiary evidence – there just isn't anything there."

"Fine," Crool said in disgust. "I guess I'm the idiot."

"Don't be so hard on yourself, boss. Tomorrow's a new day. There's only so many corners of the world that this guy can run to. It's just a matter of time till we get 'im. Now that we know that both of them are still out there, we'll have twice as many chances."

Crool kicked himself away from his desk. "You're a good man, Dave."

"Thank you, sir."

"Do you have a family, Dave?"

"Yes sir, but they understand that this job and getting Harper Rowe comes first, sir."

Crool spun around in his chair. "Tell me that you're kidding."

"Probably not, sir."

"Sometimes it feels like we may never get him, Dave."

"We'll get him, Jeb."

"Do me a favor, go home. Go see your family. Finding Harper Rowe and his – whatever – it always goes a lot better after you get a few hugs from your family."

"Sounds good. I'm about thirty-eight different kinds of tired anyway. You should get some rest yourself. You're lookin' about as rough as I feel."

"Ah, I'll sleep when I'm dead."

"Well, sleep while you're alive, too. You tend to get a little cranky when you don't get your beauty rest."

"Roger that, Agent Baldwin."

"I'll see ya tomorrow, boss."

"Hey, Dave, I almost forgot. Happy New Year."

Team Building Exercise

For the trio of men that burst through the front door of the Espetto Carioca, Harper Rowe made sure it was a very short-lived trip inside the club.

Before the gunmen even made their boisterous entrance into the place, the assassin had his Smith & Wesson .40 pistol in his left hand concealed behind his back. When the spokesman for the triumvirate uttered the word "*Bismillah*", Harper fired one shot right between the fellow's eyes.

For a split second the guy truly looked surprised – and why wouldn't he be? – before he fell dead to the floor. Harper's next two shots were not quite as precise, but equally effective. Three shots from his gun left all three of the terrorists lying dead in a pile.

The man and woman at the bar met a similar fate. When their nefarious Myrmidons breached the front door of the establishment, the duo stood up from their seats and pulled two handguns each.

Sadly for them, Dr. Mercedes Lara saw to it that that was all the further they got. Just about the same time Harper was gunning down his three targets, she fired two shots with the precision of a Rolex. The first went into the temple of the man and the second one through the forehead of the woman.

Lara took extra care with her shots as there were patrons on both sides of her targets. The patrons, of course, scattered as soon as the force of the gunshots sent the couple sprawling awkwardly backwards over their barstools.

Merc turned quickly to check on the status of Harper's three marks. Seeing them all lying dead on top of each other just in front of the door she said to Harp, "Nice grouping."

"Likewise," came his response as he took a quick glance at her handiwork.

The customers in the club were cowering in various spots around the place. Some hid behind the bar, some under tables, some were pressed up against walls, and some had taken refuge in the bathrooms. Harper returned his weapon to the back of his pants' waistband and pulled his shirt down over it. He put his hands up and calmly said, *"Está tudo okay, pessoal. É seguro, e a polícia está a caminho.*

"What did you say to them?"

"Just told them that everything's cool, it's safe, and that the police are on the way."

While that scene was playing inside the club, Kinley, Daniel, and Samuel were handling things outside.

As soon as the five terrorists inside had made their move, the two down by the beach began their advance on the alfresco eating area and dance floor. As they approached the lighted area, it became apparent that one was a man and one was a woman. About fifty yards shy of their targeted area, they produced high-powered automatic rifles seemingly out of thin air and raised them to fire.

Sloane and Hawkins moved toward them in a dead sprint. Seeing the suspects move their weapons into the firing position, Danny and Sammy came to a quick stop – so quick that they kicked sand up into the night breeze as they leveled their weapons to fire.

The two had been working together so long that they had no need to identify which target they were acquiring. Hawkins was on Sloane's left, so he took out the left target.

One shot. One kill.

Sloane eyed up his mark and let loose with the entire clip of bullets in his Beretta 9mm pistol.

Fifteen shots. One kill.

"Ya think ya got 'im?" Hawk asked facetiously as he and Daniel double-timed it toward the two bodies laying on the beach.

"I put a couple extra in your girl just to be sure. I don't want to be walking up on these two and surprise! – yours pops off one last round into my chest before she checks out."

"Yo, man, I don't need you double-checking my work. Besides, multiple bullet holes in a body is a sign of a sloppy marksman."

Sloane looked at his friend incredulously. "What difference does it make? Are you planning on having yours stuffed and mounted or something?"

Once they were within about ten feet of the dead terrorists, they slowed to a more cautious pace, then prudently scanned the bodies for any signs of life.

"Looks good here. I'll check the bodies for any wires or booby traps."

"Where's Devereaux?" Sam asked.

As instructed, Kinley Devereaux had stayed some distance behind Sloane and Hawkins to make sure that no unaccounted-for villains tried to flank them. Now that the moment was over and Kin felt that his two colleagues were secure, he had made his way back to the main outdoor area to help keep everyone calm. He had concealed his weapon and was walking through the maze of tables, chairs, and frantic guests.

"Okay, everybody, let's just stay calm and stay where you are. The situation is under control."

No one seemed to be listening to him. More to the point, no one seemed to understand him because Devereaux did not speak fluent Portuguese like his partner. Harper had often asked why, with all the international travel that he did, Kinley had never bothered to learn any other languages. His usual response was, "Oh, I don't know. I guess it's because when I'm somewhere trying to maintain anonymity and keep a low profile I don't go around striking up random conversations with the local townsfolk." Now, however, he was wishing just a little bit that he had.

"Does anyone here speak English?"

A handful of responses in the affirmative came back from the crowd.

"Can ya help me out then, please?" he begged. "Tell these people to stay where they are. The situation's under control and help is on the way." Then more quietly into his Bluetooth, "The situation is under control, right?"

"We're clear down here on the beach," answered Sloane, "and we're getting ready to head back up your way."

"The situation is clear inside, as well," answered John Watkins. He and Laurie had now joined the fray inside the club and were helping to restore some semblance of order to the chaos.

Big James and the club owner had emerged from the owner's office and were doing their part, too. Harper approached his friend and asked, "Are we still cool with the original plan? You got this? The owner good with giving you the security footage?"

"Absolutely. Get everybody together and get on up out of here."

"We didn't even get to talk about the weapons and the plan or anything."

"Well," Big James looked around, "this probably isn't the best time."

"Call me when you get free and clear of all this." With that Harper looked at John and Laurie and nodded toward the door. He put his arm around Merc and said, "Mom, you wanna tell Manny, Moe, and Jack to meet us around front?"

She masked a smile. "Guys, we're headed out. Meet up with us where we parked."

"Copy that, Doc. Moving that way now."

"Well, that was fun. Good work, everybody. Nice team building exercise."

Chase's Ultimate Plan

The drive back home had Laurie, Kinley, and Harper back in Chase's van. Of course Mercedes stayed with Harper and they were currently connected at the hip on the back bench seat. Once again, Chase was behind the wheel, and Devereaux was riding shotgun.

"That was crazy." said an exasperated Laurie Chase. "I'm still shaking."

Devereaux looked over to see Laurie's hands trembling on the steering wheel. He reached out and laid a comforting hand on her shoulder. "You're good here. We're all good here."

"I'm fine," she said. "At least, I will be. Honestly, I feel kind of useless for all the good I did back there."

"You? What about me? I was basically relegated to crowd control," compared Kinley. He turned in his seat and looked back at Merc and Harper. "You two, though. Right in the thick of it, weren't ya?"

Mercedes shifted uneasily in her seat. "I guess."

"You guess? Come on," Dev smiled, "you and Harper were lights out tonight."

"You may have missed this earlier on in the show, but I'm a doctor. Dr. Mercedes Alexis Lara, and I'm not a doctor of music or a doctor of physics. I'm a doctor of medicine. I took the Hippocratic

Oath which, if you know anything about common misconceptions, does not start out *Primum non nocere*, although that is generally thought to be the first concept of being a doctor: First, do no harm.

"Putting bullets into complete strangers is not my idea of being a good doctor, as I'm sure you can understand. However, when it becomes blatantly obvious to me that these complete strangers are going to do more harm to countless others unless I do some harm to them first, then I have to make a decision – not one I like to make, either."

She put her hand on Harper's knee, squeezed it gently, and leaned forward in her seat. "Hey, I get it. You all are some stone-cold killers and stuff. It's what you were trained to do, and that's your mindset. I know how it is because I, myself, work with three of the very best every day. Still, given tonight's circumstances, Laurie, sweetie, I would have much rather it had been you pulling the trigger inside that place instead of me."

"Well, Mercedes, I know that I speak for Kinley when I say thank you for doing what you did. First of all, after what you just said, I realize on many levels how difficult that was for you. So, thank you. Secondly – and without a doubt, most importantly – thank you for not letting Harper shoot all the bad guys because, Lord knows, we would never hear the end of it."

Kinley laughed, "Amen to that, sister."

Mercedes turned to Harper. "Is this true? Did I steal some of your thunder?" She leaned back into him and put her head on his chest.

"Let's not lose sight of the important part of tonight: God had us there for a reason," Harper said solemnly. "In the grand scheme of it all, the lot of us could've been a hundred different places doing countless other things, but we were where we were supposed to be, doing what we were supposed to be doing. We saved a lot of lives tonight."

For a moment the group fell silent as they appreciated what Harper was saying. Then, without lifting her head away from Rowe's chest, Merc said softly, "God."

"Ah, yes, God," Kinley smiled. "Dr. Lara, one of the many things that I got from my time with Harper over the years is that he is a man of faith, and after everything that we went through in Mexico City there is no doubt in my mind that his faith is well-placed. And this is coming from a man that had about as much need in his life for faith and religion as a one-legged man has for a pair of shoes."

"Really?" was Merc's one-word response as she slid her hand over to Harper's and laced her fingers in between his. "Well, what about you, Laurie? You were there in Mexico City. Did you find God in and amongst that craziness?"

"Kinda like Kinley, I've never been one to go in for the whole 'I found Jesus! I found Jesus!'," she said in a high, fluttering falsetto, taking her hands off the steering wheel momentarily to move them around in a mock Pentecostal gesture of enlightenment.

She began again in her regular voice. "I used to think that religion was just something that people used to help them accept the eventuality of death – their own and the death of others. Something to help them get to sleep at night. Still, I can't deny the undeniable. Sure, I could probably find ten different excuses to explain away what happened. Chance. Luck. Fate. Whatever. It's just that what happened in Mexico City, and what has been happening ever since, I have no doubt that it's all part of a greater plan. In my heart, I just can't believe that these two goofy guys coming into my world and changing my life forever is just nothing more than dumb luck. They're here for a reason. A lot of reasons, actually, and I can't – nor will I try – to deny that."

"What about you, Dr. Lara? Mercedes? You're a woman of science and medicine. Have you found any room in your world for faith or a God?" Kinley asked as he shifted his tender gaze at Chase to a more attentive and serious look toward Merc.

"Please don't be offended when I say this: I have a strong belief in God and what He can do, but the events that brought me to my belief are very personal so I would just as soon not go into it if that's okay with everyone." She squeezed Harper's hand.

Kin cleared his throat awkwardly, "Umm, yeah, absolutely. For sure."

"Faith is a personal thing," said Laurie. "Just glad to know you have it. God knows we're all going to need it going into tomorrow."

"Can I ask you guys a question?" Merc said as she sat up and away from Harper, while keeping a firm grasp on his hand.

"If it's why they made that third Karate Kid movie with Daniel-san and Mr. Miyagi, don't bother. I've been asking that one for years. Even sent a letter to the studio," Harper said.

"Seriously?" Merc poked Harper in the ribs. "How do you go from so serious to such a complete stooge in a matter of nanoseconds?"

"Oh, let me tell ya," Kinley laughed, "roller coasters get sick riding Harper's mood swings."

"Oh my gosh!" Laurie cried.

"What?" asked a worried Devereaux.

"What?" asked an equally-concerned Harper.

"Ugh, can you just let the woman ask her question, for cryin' out loud?" Chase shook her head. "I swear, you two are like a radio that controls its own volume, and you're always on ten."

Harper and Kinley silenced themselves and turned their heads like robots to Mercedes, stared at her, and in simultaneous monotone voices asked, "Question?"

It was easy to tell that Dr. Lara was used to hanging out with similar male types. She had, after all, been playing mother, doctor, coworker, and best girl friend to John Watkins, Samuel Hawkins, and Daniel Sloane for the last eight years. So without missing a beat, she flipped her long blond hair over her shoulders and asked what she had been wanting to know ever since she had realized who these three people were.

"What happened in Mexico City? And did it directly affect the assassination of the Secretary of Defense?"

Silence. And then –

"Yes," answered Kinley. He turned to face forward and said, "No more questions."

Mercedes looked around at each of them in disbelief. "Really?" Laurie was suddenly very focused on driving. Kinley was suddenly enjoying the view out the front windshield. Harper returned her glance with a reticent smile.

"Oh, come on," she pleaded. "We just fought off a terrorist attack together, and tomorrow we're going into battle together to take down a major drug lord and his drug compound, and you won't tell me even one thing about what happened with the three of you and Paul Michaels?"

"Believe me, we would love to tell you, but you have to understand that what happened with all of that – it's got all three of us on the run. It's not some secret campfire story, Mercedes. What happened is a matter of national security. It's keeping all of us from going home. Going back to the land we love. If we told you what happened then you would know what we know, and if someone found out that you knew – you'd have the same target on your back that the three of us do. I can't do that to you." Harper paused for a moment before closing his argument with, "It's not that I can't. It's just that I won't."

"He's doing you a favor," Chase said from behind the wheel. "Knowing what I know and knowing what you don't know, I know he's doing you – we're doing you a favor."

Kinley turned back around in his seat and looked good-naturedly at Mercedes. "It's not like we're keeping secrets from the person that just helped us take out some real bad guys, and the same person that will accompany us into battle tomorrow. It's just that we all really like you," he looked at Harper. "Some more than others."

Mercedes understood. "So, all right, I get that you can't answer that question. Can't blame a girl for trying, right?" and she smiled her fantastic smile. "Then maybe someone can answer this question for me. If we're going to take out Tito del Fuento and his operation tomorrow, yet he's not going to be there when we attack, then what's the plan to take him out eventually? Don't get me wrong, I know that he and his family and a bunch of his men being gone is what's giving us the opening to attack, but what's the plan for actually getting him?"

"Oh!" Laurie piped up excitedly. "I'll be more than happy to answer that one for you."

"Really?" Merc was surprised.

"Absolutely."

"Um, okay. Uh, can you hang on for a second? I feel a sneeze coming on." Lara feigned a sneezing attack to cover up her hitting the button on her Bluetooth to call John and the boys back in the jeep. She knew they would want to hear this. After all, before the craziness of the night began, this was the one assignment with which she had been charged. "Sorry about that. Stupid allergies. Anyway, you were getting ready to say, Laurie?"

"God bless you," Laurie said obligingly. "Yes, you are correct. Tito being gone is what is giving us our window of opportunity tomorrow, but tomorrow is just the first step of my plan to make him the most grief-stricken, heartbroken, and mentally-wilted person on the face of this lovely green planet. Granted, tomorrow's the biggest part of my plan, but I have no doubts that we will inflict the maximum amount of damage that can possibly be inflicted to this man's world. I'm just sorry that he and his family won't be there to witness it. Hang on everybody – we're getting to the rough part."

Kinley, Harper, and Mercedes were so enveloped in Laurie's diatribe about how she was going to dismantle Tito del Fuento's world that they misunderstood what she meant by "the rough part" until the van left the paved road and started over the unpaved section of the route back to Chase's headquarters. Once the van had jostled them about a bit, everyone was back on the same page.

Kinley spun forward in his seat, reached over his shoulder for the seat belt, and buckled up. In spite of the fact that it was an obvious gambit, Harper used the situation as an excuse to put his arms around Mercedes and bring her closer to him. She responded by putting her arms around the side of his neck. He looked at her and smiled. She moved her mouth close to his and smiled. He could practically feel her lips on his as he moved in for the kiss. But then–

"Because I would love to see the look on their faces as they watch us torch their meal ticket to the world. Doesn't matter, though. One thing that Tito will find out sooner rather than later is that the plane he and his family are on will be fine, of course, but that jet that his hundred best guys are on? Diego helped me see to it that that particular craft has some faulty landing gear. Now that I think about it, that's actually going to be the first part of my plan: Tito watching his one hundred best guys crash land in Dresden–" and she drifted off for a moment.

Harper looked up at Kinley just about the same time as he turned around and looked at him. After a quick exchange of glances, Devereaux looked at Chase. "Laurie?"

"Oh sorry," she seemed to come back to reality. "Don't worry. Our attack and that plane crashing into flames will be just moments apart. By the time Tito has any idea as to what might be going on, we'll have already torn up his compound and gone our separate ways. Then I'll let Tito digest what we did to him for a little while. Soon enough though, Diego and I will set to work on Tito's family. We'll make quick work of them. No need to make them suffer. Actually, that move is for Diego. I mean, Diego and Tito are family. Good or bad, family is family. I mean, I thank God every day for Diego. I wouldn't be where I am without him. Diego is family to me now so, yeah, we're gonna make Tito suffer the loss of his family."

"Wait," Devereaux said a bit disturbed, "doesn't Tito have little kids? Are you going to kill little kids? I mean, Judas Priest, I can understand you whackin' the guy's wife, but his kids didn't ask to be born to this monster–"

"Holy crap." Laurie interrupted. "Do you really think I am going to kill little kids?"

"Well, it kinda sounded–" Dev turned in his seat to address Harper and Mercedes. "Didn't it sound like she was – you know – saying she was–"

"Yeah, Laurs," Harper agreed. "It sounded like you were making plans to kill small children."

"Right," Chase agreed. "*Mea culpa.* Perhaps I got a little bit ahead of myself. Here's the thing. When Tito watches the plane with his best men crash and burn, and then he learns of his place being ripped to shreds, he will go into defensive mode. The first thing he's going to do is send his family away to a safe place – a place that Diego knows – and because Tito thinks Diego is dead, he won't bother changing the place where he sends his family. Diego and I will go to said place and take his wife and kids. Yeah, we'll have to get a little bit of blood from them because we will want to make it look like they really are dead, but we're not going to actually kill them. We'll hide them away for a while. Long enough to make Tito think that they're surely dead so that he will suffer their loss. Long enough that when we finally put a bullet into his bastard head we'll actually be doing him a favor."

"So, you're going to spare his wife then, too?"

"Well," Laurie shrugged, "that's kinda going to be up to her. When we take them, I'm going to give her the chance to repent of her sins. If she does – and I mean *really* confesses to her wrongdoings

– then once Diego and I am finished with Tito, we'll let her and her kids be on their merry way. However, if she keeps her allegiance to her husband and shows no remorse whatsoever for all the evil crap that she and the old man have bestowed upon the world for the last however many years – then I'm going to shoot her right in front of her own kids – just so the kids know that if they ever try to pull the same wally wally horse squish that their mother and father did, they know what's coming for them."

As soon as she was finished talking the van left the rough terrain and drove onto the smooth paved road once again.

"I hope that answered your question, Mercedes."

"Pretty sure it did," the doctor answered as she clandestinely moved her hand along her phone and turned off her Bluetooth device.

"Did you guys catch all that?" John asked Daniel and Sam.

"Sounds to me like the little lady has got herself a mother lovin' plan, fellas," Hawkins answered. "However, it do sound to me like we gonna have our work cut out for us when it come to that first step of the plan tomorrow night."

"I'll feel a little better about the whole thing once we hear from Big James later tonight," John said. "Once we know what we're working with, we can really nail down the final plan for tomorrow."

"Till then, Johnny," Sloane said, "I think we really need to hand it to Doc. You told her to get close to Rowe to find out what Laurie Chase's plan for del Fuento was, and I think she did just that." He patted Watkins on the back. "Now we know."

"Yeah," Watkins agreed, "now we know."

"Aww, you worried, aintcha, John?"

"Hey, Aunt Joe Momma's love child, he just said he'll feel a little better once he sees what Big James has for us. Leave the guy alone, will ya? We're all under a little stress here," Sloane hollered.

"Naw, naw, naw, I ain't even talkin' 'bout that. Johnny's a bit worried that our good doctor has gotten a little too close to her target. Ain't that right, boss?"

"Hawk," Sloane said in disgust, "I swear you're talking out of your ass so much right now that a two-dollar whore wouldn't kiss that mouth of yours for a hundred bucks."

"Says the king of two dollar whores," Sam smarted back.

"Knock it off, you two!" John yelled. "You make me want to pistol whip the both of ya. And if you must know, you're both right."

Sam and Daniel momentarily stopped their mini-feud as they awaited John's blessing on each other's argument.

"Normally I would be concerned with how close Mercedes has gotten to Harper. There's no denying that the guy is cool and mysterious. I guess I don't hold it against her. If we live to see another day after tomorrow, we'll be out of here anyway. Till then I would never try to tell any of you how to spend what might be your last night on earth. I just want to get back to Chase's place because, I don't know about the two of you, but I'm sleepy as can be."

"Boss, right here, right now, what do you think our chances are tomorrow?"

"The same as our chances are in every situation we go into. 50/50. We'll either live or we won't."

Sloane looked at Hawk. "He's obviously not that tired."

ONE GOOD FINAL NIGHT

By the time everyone got back to Chase's place, parked, went inside and got settled, it was almost 2 a.m.

"Oh my Lord, that ride takes just slightly less time than the long version of *Dune*," Harper griped as he plopped down in the nearest chair.

Diego came down from upstairs with a smile on his face. "Deed you guys go to thee Espetto Carioca?"

"Yeah, Diego, that is where we were. I take it that the evening's events have made the news circuit already?"

"*Sim*, Mees Laurie."

"Geez," said Kinley, "news travels fast."

"Ees everyone okay? What happened? Eet said on thee wire report that people were keelled. Ees true?"

"We're all okay, Diego," Sloane assured him. "As for the seven pieces of scum sucking cellulite that decided to rain on our parade tonight, can't really say the same for them, amigo."

"Ees *terroristas*?"

"Was *terroristas*," Harp corrected.

Diego walked up to Laurie and gave her a big hug. "*Graças a Deus está okey*, Mees Laurie." For such a diminutive guy, Diego packed a powerful hug.

"Well, everyone, I'm sorry that things went a little bit screwy tonight, and I know it's really late, but if anyone's still up for a drink, we can go chill out for a few in the rec room I have set up in the back. I know I could use a little something to calm my nerves."

"I don't often kill terrorists in the heart of Rio on the very first day of the year, but when I do – I'm down for a shot or two," smiled Hawkins.

"My adrenaline was really pumping when we first left the club, you know, back in May of '06, but I think I'm feeling okay now," Harper said. "However, Harper Rowe Protocol strictly states that it is against any and all regulations to turn down free alcohol. So, I shall also imbibe."

"I weel go get some glasses," Diego announced as he scampered out of sight.

"He sure seems handy to have around," Devereaux noted.

"It's just so odd," Laurie said in a quiet voice, "to know that Diego was the right-hand man to one of the most evil and ruthless drug lords on the planet, but ever since he and I have been working together, he's just the nicest, sweetest, most laid-back guy I've ever met. I'd swear to you and my mother that the guy was a preschool teacher or something."

"Did I hear right that he is del Fuento's cousin?" asked John.

"Yeah, that's right."

"Well, it may sound cliché," he shrugged, "but – the things we do for family."

"Not to mention the loyalty factor," added Mercedes. "He was loyal to a fault to Tito until Tito betrayed him. His life was in such a downward spiral with no hope in sight until you showed up and gave him something to live for, Laurie. Now his loyalty belongs to you. Now you're his family."

"I guess that's fair because for the last year or so he's been mine, too."

Harper, who had watched where Diego had gone, led the gang on their trek to the rec room. John Watkins brought up the rear.

"Holy crap. Is that Frogger?" Harper exclaimed as he walked into the cavernous space. "How the heck did you get Frogger up into this place?"

One by one, the rest of the team filed into the area and were astounded by the incredible collection of arcade and barroom games Chase had assembled in the warehouse-sized room. Video games, a pool table, a Wii setup, a dartboard, a shuffleboard table, pinball machines, an air hockey table, arcade-sized basketball hoops, and a video golf game were all waiting for them.

Laurie watched the lot of them suddenly turn into teenage kids as they explored the room.

"This may very well be the coolest thing that I've ever seen," laughed Hawkins as he made his way to one of the pinball games. "I haven't seen some of these since I was a teenager hanging out on Venice Beach."

"Eighteen months of watching Tito's every move," Laurie said, "I needed an escape – so I did this. Diego turned me onto a salvage company that had all these games that they were just going to junk."

"Who hauled them all the way up here? You or them?"

Chase frowned. "Do you really think I would give away my hiding spot just to have some video games hauled up here?"

"If this were to be my eternal playroom," Harper said, "I think I'd rent my soul to Hitler, dye my hair blond, and put in some blue contact lenses."

As per usual, Chase disregarded Harper's comment and said, "I brought them up here a little bit at a time. Brought them up, set them up, enjoyed them. Then I went and got some more."

Looking around, she noticed that no one was listening to her. Not even John Watkins, who had found his way over to the arcade basketball hoops. But before she had time to feel slighted, Kinley came up behind her, wrapped his arms around her waist, and whispered into her ear, "You're amazing. I never thought in a million years you could distract everybody to the point that–" Kinley paused.

Laurie looked around to see that everyone really was distracted to that point.

She giggled. "And now that I have them that distracted – what did you have in mind?"

"Maybe some of this," Kin said quietly, biting her playfully on the shoulder.

Her knees nearly buckled, but she caught herself. Dev slid his hands under both sides of her shirt and ran his fingernails ever so gently along the skin that covered her ribs. "Maybe some of that." This time her knees did buckle, and he caught her. "Yes?"

"Yes. Definitely, yes," she whispered.

Dr. Mercedes Lara was enjoying herself just as much as everyone else. She had a few drinks – courtesy of Diego – just like everyone else. She had beaten Hawkins at the video golf game – by a mile. She had beaten Danny at air hockey, 10-4, to be exact. Now she was searching for her final conquest of the night: Harper Rowe.

Looking around intently, she could not see him. Where was he? She looked left. She looked right. She did not see him. She spun around on her heels thinking he was right behind her the whole time. He was not behind her.

"Hey," she heard his voice. Seeing no one, she suddenly felt a hand on her shin. She looked down and there he was – his head between her feet.

Looking up at her, Harper said, "You do know that there are entire countries whose governments are looking for me, right? I mean, they haven't found me. I'm just wondering what made you think that you wou–"

Mercedes reached down, grabbed him by the shirt collar, and pulled him up to his feet. She was that strong.

"I'm sorry," she said, without releasing her grasp, "I didn't hear what you said, you being so far away and on the floor and everything."

Harper's eyes were as big as bowling balls and his feet were off the ground. Mercedes was waiting for a response. So he gave her one. "My high school guidance counselor, he always told me that I should reach for the stars but keep my feet on the ground," he looked into Dr. Lara's eyes and. "And you're not really helping to forward that cause right now."

She tried not to laugh as she released her clutches from his collar and lowered him to the floor. "I'll let you live if you come upstairs with me right now."

Harp shook off his momentary fear of her. "I will gladly do that, but – I am waiting on a phone call from Big James. I don't want to get too dramatic or anything, but the entire outcome of our attack tomorrow kinda depends on it. I just need your assurance that if my phone rings in an inopportune time – and I answer it – that you won't skin me alive. Okay? Can we be cool on that?"

She took his hand. "Follow me if you want to find out–" and she was off.

Harper followed right behind, although he wasn't sure she knew where she was going. "Ya know," he said, "you have a lot of upper body strength for a doctor."

They took a slow tour of the upstairs wing of Laurie Chase's hideaway. They were amazed at how finely decorated each room was, as if Chase and Diego had opened a bed and breakfast that no one would ever be able to find. They finally chose a room decorated in white and lavender with a pillow-covered canopy bed.

Mercedes led Harper into the room, closed the door, and stripped him down to his knee-length boxers. She found a plain white tee to sleep in. Once in bed, she laid her head on his shoulder and ran her long fingers through his chest hair. They had so much to ask of each other, so much to say. But–

"Good Lord, they're loud," Merc commented.

"How did we not hear that when we decided on this room?" asked a bewildered Harper.

"He's your friend. Maybe he was waiting for you so he could show off his sexual wiles with you in earshot."

"Number one, he's not that kind of friend. He'd rather out-shoot me on the firing range than out-sex me in the bedroom. Number two, I held my laughter in this time, but the next time you use the term 'sexual wiles' I will laugh like a monkey watching the banana channel. I'm just telling you now."

"Oh my goodness," Merc tried not to laugh, "they're louder than a slew of polar bears in a swimming pool."

"Is she in pain?" Harp asked.

"No," Mercedes said softly. "No, he's not hurting her." She looked up and began kissing his neck. "I don't know why I want to do this, but I do. I don't know what it is about you. I mean, you're like the dumbest person I've ever met, but – you're like a train wreck. I just can't look away."

"It's okay, Norma Rae. I know you like me. You really like me."

"So, what are you doing tomorrow after we blow up a drug compound and execute a bunch of drug lord's henchmen?"

"Oh, I don't know," Harper answered in an awe-shucks way as he moved his hands over her knees. "I guess I'll probably be waving good-bye to you and your Dragon's Men guys. I've also been needing some new shoelaces, so I might take care of that before I get on out of here tomorrow."

Mercedes lifted her hand and whacked Harper across the chest.

"Ow, ow, ow," Harper recoiled into his pillow. "Why ya gotta be hitting me all the time?"

"Awww, poor baby," she said as she kissed his chest lightly. "Better now?"

"Much."

"Let's not waste our energy on silly things like joking and hitting. I'm sure if we try real hard we can find much better things to waste our energy doing," Merc said, pressing her lips to his.

They kissed for what seemed like a lifetime – until he pulled his head back. "Where this is going, Merc – I can't," Harper confessed. "Blame it on my religion."

"What?"

"Well, it's not that I can't. It's just that I won't. It may sound dopey to you, but – I want to see you again."

It was Merc's turn to pull her head back. "What? I'm not sure I understand."

"This may be our last night on earth. So, it only makes sense that we should give in to each other, yet I was thinking – what if we waited to do all of this until we saw each other again?"

"And when would that be?" Mercedes was feeling a bit embarrassed.

"The next time we see each other," Harper repeated.

"The next time?"

"Yeah – the next time," Harper smiled. "It will definitely give me something else to fight for later on tonight."

Mercedes understood all that Harper had wrapped up into "the next time." She fell back into his arms, and he let her. They kissed for a moment, for a lifetime.

Neither one could tell who fell asleep first.

Neither one cared.

Phone Call in the Night

The phone vibrated. He felt its silent notification against his thigh, but he still turned to see if it had woken her up. She had not budged. He looked at the clock just before he picked up the phone. "Yeah?"

"I know it's late. Sorry to call at this time of night."

"What?"

"You're in bed, aren't you?"

"Mmph...mergferr," he muttered quietly as he did a Spider Man-ballerina move out of his bed.

"It's Dave, by the way," Baldwin said needlessly.

"I'm waking up, Dave. I'm not amnesiac," Crool said tersely as he moved into a more isolated part of his house. "Ya better have a real good reason as for why you're calling me at this hour."

"I wouldn't be calling you at this time of night if it wasn't of the utmost importance. Get to your computer. I've sent you a picture file."

"It better not be another cat video, Dave, or I'm putting you in for a transfer as soon as I get to work today." Jeb traipsed over to the computer in his living room office and brought it out of sleep mode.

"Seems there was an attempted terrorist attack at a club down in Rio a few hours ago. Fortunately for everyone involved – except for the terrorists themselves, mind you – there were some private citizen types there that had brought their guns with them for their night on the town."

"Any casualties? Civilian or otherwise?" Jeb's PC was up and running now. He went to his work email account and saw the email from Baldwin with the attached picture file.

"If you count the seven dead terrorist suspects then, yes, there were casualties."

"We need to find out who our heroes are. Maybe we can throw them a parade. Maybe we can give them a job."

"Well, as luck would have it, it seems that none of the security cameras at this place – The Espetto Carioca is the name of it – were working last night. So there's no video footage of this event, but some of the customers took pictures with their cell phones, and some of those pictures have already hit the net. I came across one that was particularly interesting. It's the one I sent to you."

"Yeah, my computer's taking its sweet time opening up the file. Apparently it doesn't want to be up at this hour of the night either." Jeb hummed impatiently as he waited for the image to come up on his computer monitor. "So this picture I'm going to be looking at, is it of the dead guys–" Jeb immediately stopped talking as the image revealed itself. "Holy – crap. Harper Rowe."

"I knew you'd want to see that, regardless of the time of night."

"Any idea who the blonde is that's standing next to him? Looks like they're together."

"No, but I'm working on it."

"And you say this was in Rio?"

"Yeah, and the reports that are coming in are saying that it went down about midnight or 1 a.m. our time."

"What's their time zone difference?" Crool asked.

"They're just an hour ahead of us. It's just that they're also about 4800 miles south of us, too."

"How soon can you get us on a plane to there?"

"I'm already working on it, but at this time of night trying to get clearance for an international flight, plus, finding someone to fly us there – it's taking some time. I could probably get us on a commercial flight, but that's about a nine-hour flight. Getting us something a little more private and work-friendly and faster – well, let's just say it's gonna be a few."

"Any other pictures of Rowe? Oh, and any sign of Kinley Devereaux in any of these pics?"

"No and no. I've seen a couple of other pictures, but no Devereaux and just this one of Harper Rowe."

"Where are you now, Dave? Are you in at the office?"

"No, I am still at home for the time being, but I'm getting ready to head out in just a few minutes."

"Do me a favor, will ya? Swing by here and pick me up, if you don't mind. Lisa's car has been a bit out of kilter the last couple of days, and if we're going to be out of the country for a spell, I'd just feel better if she had my car to get around in while I'm gone."

"No problem, boss. I can be there in about twenty."

"And just pull into the driveway. I'll come out," Jeb said as he subconsciously looked out his living room window at his driveway. "If you get out of your car, my dog will start barking and wake up everyone in the HOA which, in turn, will lead to me either – A, getting a letter from my Home Owner's Association – or B, getting a call from my Home Owner's Association, and since I'm not going to be here they'll end up hassling Lisa about it which will, eventually, lead to her keeping it all pent up inside until I get home from Rio at which time she will lay into me for the following fortnight about how much she despises the HOA Board – here's the thing, Dave, I am not fond of the people that make up the HOA Board in my neighborhood, but Lisa absolutely loathes them. I'm pretty sure if she could get away with it, she would systematically eliminate each and every one of them from this life as we know it. So," Jeb finally inhaled, "just do us all a favor and stay in your car."

"Absolutely. I will stay in my car. After all, I most definitely do not want the blood of an entire HOA Board on my hands or my conscience. I might have to go to therapy or something, and I don't think our insurance plan at work covers that," Agent Baldwin laughed. "See you in a few, Jeb."

*   *   *

Just about the time that the two federal agents were hanging up on their call, one time zone and roughly 4800 miles away, Harper Rowe's cell phone was resonating with the Dukes of Hazzard theme song.

He answered it before the "never meanin' no harm" line. It was Big James.

"Hey, boss, sorry it took me a bit. Things are crazy here, but I was able to keep all that security footage from earlier tonight out of the wrong hands. Still, I figured you being with your doctor friend there, you'd probably still be awake." The big man said in a sly tone, "Am I right or am I right?"

"Hit the nail right on the head, buddy." Harper shook the cobwebs out of his head as Mercedes put her head on his shoulder and wrapped her arm across his stomach.

"Oh, wait. I didn't – you know – were you guys still–"

"No, big guy, we're good. You're timing is great as always."

"Okay, Harp," Big James chuckled. "So, let's talk shop for a few minutes, and then I'll let ya get back to it."

"Alright then."

"Now you don't need to be going around worrying about that security footage. I, personally, wiped all of it clean so that even if some newshound came around offering top dollar to have a look-see, my guys couldn't give in to the temptation even if they wanted to, and I won't lie to ya, they'd probably want to. Anyways, the police showed up – I think a couple of Brazil's finest *federales* even showed up after a while – and they interviewed some of the customers, got everyone's story, cleared the place out, and shut it down."

"I'm guessing they wanted to know where we all went, right? No matter how heroic our actions were, I'm pretty sure we probably violated about half a dozen international gun laws there tonight. The cops probably wanted to ask us a few questions, I'm sure."

"Dude, the way those people were describing you guys to those investigators, you were like freakin' rock stars. What you all did there tonight was not lost on the authorities whatsoever. They had to deal with seven bodies. If y'all hadn't done what ya did, though, they'd o' been dealing with a hundred? A hundred twenty? Maybe more. Yeah, I'm sure that they would love to talk to you guys, but what they love even more is that they had a lot less bloodshed than what they could've been dealing with. A lot less."

"Well, not to get into a back patting competition, but, let's face it, without you keeping a lid on the video footage, it could have been a really sticky situation – well – for everyone, really. You came through in the clutch in a big way for us tonight, Big Time."

"Thank you, Harper. Destroying the video feed was the easy part of my day. Getting that shopping list of demolitions and weapons and a few other surprises I was able to accumulate – that was the tough part," James recalled. "Nevertheless, I got what we need, and if you guys want to give me a shout when you are all up and around later, I'll drive on up to where you guys are, I'll show yas what I got, and you filthy mongrels can show me what kind of plan you've got put together for del Fuento."

"Dude, that sounds great, but I don't really think you're going to be able to find your way up to where we are. I guarantee you that you won't find this place listed on any GPS app. The term off-road, lit'rally, applies to how you get here."

"Don't worry about me, Harp. When we met up earlier today I put a tracking device on the back of Chase's van. I know right where you guys are so even if I have to channel my inner Lewis and Clark to do it, I'll find my way to ya."

Rowe shook his head and smiled. "Big James Gray and his bottomless bag of tricks."

"Coming soon to a remote mountain hideout near you."

FINAL PREPARATIONS BEGIN

Laurie Chase was the first one to get up and head downstairs. The former DEA agent checked the clock on her computer. It read 11:47 a.m.

She was glad that she was the only one around at the moment. Humming under her breath, she punched a couple of buttons on the computer keyboard and pulled up the FAA website that showed her Tito del Fuento's flight plans. She breathed a sigh of relief when she saw that both of Tito's planes had, as scheduled, taken off at 8:15 that morning, a little over three hours earlier.

The flight from Rio to Dresden was a long one, about fifteen hours depending on airspeed, jet stream patterns, and weather conditions, and would require a refueling stop. Due to the time zone difference, Tito's planes should touch down in Dresden right around five o'clock tomorrow morning – midnight tonight, Rio time.

"Midnight tonight," Laurie said to herself, "by that time you're not even going to have a home to fly back to, ya sick prick."

"Good morning," came a voice from behind her. Laurie turned to see Dr. Mercedes Lara walking towards her. "Is it still morning?" the doctor asked. Laurie turned and took another look at the computer clock. "With just about five minutes to spare."

"Wow. Sometimes I even surprise myself."

"Did you get some decent rest? I mean – well – did you – what I'm trying to get at–"

"Did you and Devereaux keep us up way past our bedtime? Why, yes. Yes, you did." Mercedes asked and answered her own question and began to laugh.

Chase blushed, "Oh my gosh, I am so sorry. It's just that it's been awhile, ya know? I suppose I let my emotions and pretty much everything else get away from me."

"You were definitely not using your inside voice, that's for sure," Mercedes smiled, "but that's okay. We didn't mind."

"What? You mean – you and Harper?" Chase asked surprised and confused all at once.

"Yeah, me and Harper, although it's not exactly what you're thinking," Merc answered with a slightly furrowed brow. "But why?"

"I think that was going to be my next question to you, actually. Why?"

Dr. Lara found a nearby chair, dragged it closer to Chase, and sat down. Then, in a low voice, she asked, "What is it with you and him? Or am I just missing something about the guy?"

"Hmm," Chase replied. "Honestly?"

"I would hope for nothing else."

"Well, after talking to your man Hawkins, Kinley and I were under the impression that you were just charming Harp to get some information out of him about one thing or the other. So, there's that," Laurie stated flatly before moving on. "As far as me and Harper, well, you know how people will always tell you, 'just be yourself'?"

"I do. Yes."

"Well, let's just say that Harper really should try being someone else."

"His personality just rubs you the wrong way, huh?"

"Like a Brillo pad on a freshly-opened wound," Chase admitted.

"But he's here for you now," Mercedes pointed out. "That's gotta be good for something, right?"

"Don't get me wrong. I'm pretty sure he'd give me the skin off of his back if I asked him. He's loyal to a fault to anyone that he even remotely considers a friend, but I guess when it comes right down to it," and Chase took a moment to choose her next words carefully, "I guess – that whole ordeal that went down in Mexico City – I blame him. And, yes, I've had this whole thing with exacting a bit of justice on Tito del Fuento and his merry little band of pickle smacks to occupy my time since then, but if I live to see the other side of it, I'm not really sure how much of a life I'm going to have. My family, my friends – everyone thinks I'm dead. And even if I were to come back from the beyond," she said, making the air quotes motion with her fingers, "I'm going to have a pretty serious amount of explaining to do to some pretty serious people."

The two women exchanged looks of understanding. Dr. Lara reached over and put her hand on Laurie's knee. "Honey, you're going to survive tonight – we all are – and after we're all gone from here tomorrow, and you and Diego finish off del Fuento once and for all, when you get finished with all of this, you contact us. We will give you all the help you will need to get back to a good life."

"Help? Like – what kind of help?"

"We can get you any kind of new identity, put you anywhere in the world you want to be, and give you any kind of background that you desire. Oprah's got nothing on the makeovers that we give to people."

"What if I wanted you to give me the life I had up until about eighteen months ago?"

Merc drew in a deep breath, looked Chase in the eyes and said, "Well, I guess even we can't make fairy tales come true. Sorry."

"Ah, that's okay. I think the fairy tale was believing my life was all that great before I was sent to Mexico City."

When Harper walked into Laurie Chase's room, he found his buddy sprawled face down across the entire queen-sized bed. The covers were tucked tightly around him from the small of his back on down, the pillows gathered compactly under his head. Devereaux was a light sleeper, so before Harper could even say a word his eyes shot open wide as he asked, "Why are you in here?"

"Well, it would seem that both of our lady companions have left us for a better place. Man, your back is smooth. Do you use some kind of hair removal products or do you just use a razor?"

Kin lifted his head off the pillows. "What?" he asked with a scowl.

"Whoa, hey, you're drooling. C'mon, man, tighten it up a bit."

Devereaux wiped his hand across his mouth. Harper was not kidding – a wanton amount of drool strung from Kinley's mouth to his pillow. He pulled his head back even further into the air and began wiping his mouth fervently with both hands.

"Geez, Chase must've really done a number on you last night to have you slobberin' all over yourself like that. You want a towel or a rag to help you clean up? Maybe a chamois or a Swiffer perhaps?"

"Thanks. I think I got it." Kinley rolled over to the side of the bed, pulled the covers off, and swung his feet to the floor. He rubbed his eyes for a few seconds and blinked them into focus. "Can you hand me my pants from off that chair, please?" he asked of his friend.

As he waited for Harper to retrieve the requested article of clothing, he grabbed his watch from the nightstand, checked the time, slapped it across his wrist, and fastened it into place. "You get some decent rest last night?"

"I did. Yes. Good night of rest," Harper acknowledged as he handed Kinley his pants. "It sounded like you may have been up for a while last night, though. Anything you want to talk about, bud?"

Kinley exhaled a long, somewhat defeated sigh. "Go ahead and say it. Heck, you've already been saying it for the last twenty-four hours. So go ahead and say it. It's not like I have any defense at this point."

"I'm sorry. What?" Harp asked, feigning ignorance.

Kin shot him a dirty look.

"Oh, you mean the whole you and Laurie Chase thing and the two of you getting together, and there being feelings between the two of yas, right?" Harper smiled. "Eh, so what I was right. What am I gonna do? Rub your face in the fact that you got a good thing going with a real good woman? That seems a silly thing to do. I'm happy as can be for ya, buddy."

"Well, thank you then," Kin said as he lifted both feet off the floor and pulled his trousers over them and halfway up his legs, "because something else happened that I need to tell you about." Devereaux rocked back on the side of the bed, then rocked forward and vaulted himself up onto his feet so that he could pull his pants the rest of the way up.

"Something else with Laurie?"

"No, not with her. I got a phone call last night that I've been wanting to talk to you about."

"No kidding. Oddly enough, that makes two of us."

"What?"

"Not important. Tell me about your call. Who called you?"

"Right. So, I was saying that I wanted to tell you about it before, but we never got a chance to be alone till now, and it's something that I just wanted to keep between you and me." Kinley bent down and picked his shirt up off the floor, sniffed it, and made a sour face.

"Yech. That's no good," he said, dropping the shirt back onto the floor. Without another word he walked past Harper and into the room that held extra clothes for the two of them.

Harper was right on his heels. "Hey – who called you?"

A door at the end of the hall opened up and Sam Hawkins appeared. "Say hey, fellas. What's shakin'? Where's everybody else? Are we the first ones up?"

Devereaux continued his search for a clean shirt without speaking, so Harper obligingly answered, "I think the doctor and Laurie Chase are downstairs." Then he quickly followed after Kinley. "Dude, who called?"

Dev had already found a dark gray cotton tee and was pulling it over his head. Happy with the fit and comfort of the shirt, he was getting ready to answer Harper's question when Hawk entered the room.

"I'll have to tell you later, Harp."

"Aww, man," Rowe griped.

"Hey, do you two need some privacy or something? I can head on downstairs."

"Yes, that would be great," Harp agreed.

"No, we're good," Kinley opposed. "We'll come down with you."

"Ya sure?"

"Yeah," Harper gave his partner a furrowed look, "are ya sure?"

John Watkins stuck his head into the room just then. "What's going on, gang?"

"We were just getting ready to head downstairs. The doctor and Laurie are down there already," Kin replied.

"Danny still sleeping?" Hawk asked.

"He's on the phone with Jenny."

The Dragon's Men Protection Agency was a business based in the extremely prosperous city of White Pines. John Watkins, Daniel Sloane, Samuel Hawkins, and Dr. Mercedes Lara came up with the idea of opening an agency of this sort about three years before they ended their military careers. The quartet had pooled their money, obtained a rather large business loan, and purchased a five-story building on the southwest side of White Pines. They turned the first floor of the building into the offices of the agency and made the top two floors into apartments for themselves. Floors two and three had been turned into reinforced panic rooms and safe-house quarters for their clients just in case the need should ever arise.

The four had been in the protection business going on six years now. They worked together, lived together, and usually played together, too. So it was important for them to have a life outside of the agency, if for no other reason than to just not drive each other crazy. As much as they could, they tried to stay out of each other's outside activities – activities such as family, other business ventures, and love interests.

Especially love interests.

Still, background checks had to be performed occasionally because the last thing any of them needed was to be blindsided by a complication from one of the other team members' personal matters. So, things had to be checked out sometimes. Especially love interests.

But not Jenny.

Jennifer Main and Daniel Sloane had been together since they were freshmen in high school. After their high school days, when Jenny went away to college and Danny went into the military, they remained together. When she went to graduate school and he re-enlisted for another four years of military fun and frivolity, they remained together. When she got her doctorate and was offered a professorship at Harvard University and he joined his military buddies to open something called a "protection agency" in a town called White Pines, she turned down the Ivy League position and took a job teaching at a small private high school in a neighboring town so that she could move closer to Sloane. And they remained together.

She was just a shade under 5'4" and maybe 110 lbs. on a good day. She was a demure, well-spoken doctor of eighteenth century English literature that loved Pinterest, rainy days, her Miniature Schnauzer, Charlie, and – oh yeah – Daniel Sloane.

Sloane, in comparison, was a brutish, hard-nosed, somewhat bigoted ex-military type that liked beer, cigarettes, red meat, and American football.

Still, somehow when they were together none of that mattered. When Jenny and Danny were with each other, the fact that they appeared – and, indeed, were – as different as night and day went right out the window. When in each other's company, they were just the same fifteen-year-old girl and boy as they were back in their freshman year of high school. She broke down his tough-guy exterior, and he brought out the devil-may-care spirit that she kept hidden from everyone else. Simply put, they were in love.

John, Samuel, and Doc loved Jenny, too. Not in the same way as Daniel, of course, but it was definitely a strong bond that the three had formed with her over the years. On more than one occasion they had turned to her for assistance in getting Daniel under control when his unrestrained temper and impetuousness had gotten the best of him and them. The trio had all had the same thought at one point or another: if it were not for Jenny Main, the group probably would have given Sloane the boot a long time ago.

Now, thousands of miles apart, the two were locked in a rather in-depth conversation about last night's events.

"So, you're telling me that you guys – you and John and Samuel and Mercedes – you guys are responsible for breaking up the terrorist attack in Rio?"

"Yeah, babe, that's what I'm telling you. We were at that club chilling out for a bit, and next thing ya know these little retards show up, and the four of us and the people that we are here with, we had to act, so – we did."

"That's not what they're reporting on the news, my hero."

"Wait. What? It's on the news there already?"

"Is what I'm telling you. Yes."

"Well, what are those toe fungus maggots saying happened?

"They're saying that the guy that the government has been looking for over the past year and a half in connection with the shooting of the old Defense Secretary, they are saying that he did it."

"You mean Harper Rowe?" Daniel asked, bewildered.

"Yes. Yes, that's him," Jenny answered. "Someone got a picture of him with their cell phone. It's all over the news here."

"Aww, son of a bitch, that is not good. Not good at all." Sloane stood up from the foot of the bed he had been sitting on and began pacing the floor. He ran his hand nervously through his spiky short hair. "Oh-man, oh-man, oh-man, oh-man, I'm gonna have to tell him that they know he's here."

"Tell who, baby? Wait – wait. Are you with – are you with this Harper Rowe guy?" her voice took on a tone that was equal parts concern and excitement.

"Yes, sweetie pie. Harper Rowe – he's one of the people that I'm with down here."

Jenny gasped. "Oh, my dear, sweet–"

"How long ago did they start reporting that, baby?" Sloane asked with urgency in his voice. "It's important."

"Um, I don't know," she said, trying to think back. "When I got up around six this morning they weren't saying anything about it. I think it was closer to seven o'clock when I first heard them say something, when they first started showing the picture. So, about four and a half hours ago, maybe?"

Sloane let that sink in for a moment before saying, "Jenny Main, I love you lots, but I have to go right now. I promise to call you soon, okay? Will you be available after school? You have any meetings or anything?"

"It's the first day back from Christmas break. There's nothing going on until next week."

"Then I promise to try to call you around 3:30 p.m. your time, lover. Sorry that I gotta go, but I gotta go."

"Be careful, my love. That Harper Rowe guy is a really bad guy. Do whatever it is that you have to do with that man and come back to me in one piece – and, as always, know I'm with you, Danny."

"I gotcha right here in this big, dopey heart of mine," he said. He kissed the phone, and then he was gone.

Danny hustled out his bedroom door and began looking frantically for anyone he could find. "Hey!" he called out loudly. He double-timed it down the upstairs hallway, sticking his head into every bedroom. "Anybody? Anybody at all?" He got to the end of the hallway that emptied onto the walkway that overlooked the rest of the building. To the left, the walkway led to more single office rooms, and to the right were the stairs that led down to the ground floor. Sloane hurried up to the walkway railing, leaned over it, and looked around. That is when he saw Watkins approaching the bottom of the steps.

"Dan, we're down here. What's all the hub, bub?"

"We might have a big problem, John," Sloane began to make his way down the steps. "Jenny just told me that the news back in the States is reporting that Harper is the one that led the takedown of those terrorists last night. Somebody in the club – one of the customers, I guess – took a picture of him with their cell phone and must have posted it online or something. Jenny said that they started reporting it about four or five hours ago."

Sloane reached the bottom of the staircase and looked hard at John. "What are we gonna do, boss?"

John thought for a moment before saying, "I'll tell you what we are going to do. We're going to go tell the others and see what it is that they're going to do."

Sloane smiled. "Yeah, that sounds good."

The two men began walking toward the room that had Chase's diorama, Chase's computer, Chase, and everyone else in it. Watkins put his arm around Daniel's shoulder and asked, "So, how's our best girl, Jenny, doing today?"

"Okay, I guess. It's her first day back to school from Christmas break. I'm sure the kids will be in a crap mood after having been away for a week and a half. I know I always was whenever I had to go back after Christmas break."

"Yeah, well, if Jenny was my teacher – and don't take this personally – but I would've been camping out on the school steps waiting for the doors to reopen after Christmas break, if you catch my drift, brother."

"Yeah, well, they're first graders so I don't really expect them to have the same hormonal tendencies that a middle schooler – or you – might have, if ya catch my drift?" Sloane explained.

The two made their way back to the others, and both were greeted with inquisitive eyes.

"Everything okay?" Chase was the first to ask.

"Not exactly," Watkins sighed as he returned to his seat. "You want me to tell them or are you good with doing it?" he asked Sloane.

"I just got off the phone with my girlfriend back in the States," Daniel began, "and she was watching the news this morning. She told me about a news story – our news story – the story about the terrorists in Rio being taken out. It's being credited to a lone fugitive from the United States Government."

Everyone turned their heads and looked at Harper.

"Oh, come on," Harper seemed pissed.

"Sorry, dude," Sloane confirmed, "the way the story is being reported in the States is that someone in the club took a picture of you. The picture's been posted on the net. The news jerks got wind of it, and now all of a sudden – Harper, you're the hero of the day."

"Which means that whomever is looking for you now has a pretty good idea of where you are – and they'll be coming for you," John put it out there.

"It's not my call," Harper said.

"The way I see it, brother," Hawkins spoke, "it would most definitely seem to be your call. It's your face on the TV, and it's most definitely your name that's out there as the one that they're looking for. Somebody will be sending someone down here looking for your white ass."

"No, Sam, he's right," Watkins spoke up. "It's Harper who they will come looking for, but, eventually, they will ask enough questions to the point that it will lead back to all of us being here."

"I'm sorry," Chase said. "This has become so much more than what it was supposed to be. I understand that you all need to go. I can't even begin to ask any of you to stay."

Silence, anxiety, and pensiveness descended on all seven of them.

Kinley gave a long, hard look at Harper and finally got a nod of approval.

"Harper and I are going to stay."

"Doing some quick math," Watkins said, "even with the heads up that anyone in the U.S. Government may have had about this, I think we still have enough time to pull off the attack on del Fuento's place before anyone shows up looking for Harper. Regardless, if worse comes to worst, we have a guy named Latin Crimen that can put the four of us anywhere in the world but here and timestamp it to prove so."

"The guy that will be coming this way will be Special Agent Jeb Crool. He and his team of lackeys have been on my trail since S.O.D. Michaels was assassinated. He'll get here sooner rather than later, but you're right, John. It will take several hours for him to get down here even if he takes a private jet like Kinley and I did. Plus, once he and his team arrive, the first thing that they will more than likely do is head to the club to talk to them and find out what they know. From there, I'm sure their next stop will be to check in with the police and Interpol and the like."

"So?" Chase asked.

"We're in," answered Devereaux.

"We're in," answered Watkins.

Harper's phone rang, and he was quick to answer it. "Big James?"

"Are you guys stationed in an abandoned warehouse in the middle of nowhere?"

"Yeah. Why?"

"Then I apparently have the right place. So where I am I supposed to park? In Neverland or Somewhere Over the Rainbow?"

"Hang on. Let me check with the tour guide," Harper pulled the phone away from his ear and said to Laurie, "Big James is here. He wants to know where to park."

"Tell him that I'll be right out."

Putting the phone back up to his ear, Harper said to Big James in a sappy help-line operator voice, "The tour guide is on her way out to deal with your issue, personally, sir."

"Sweet. You know I'm a sucker for a woman in uniform. I'll see you in just a few minutes, boss."

Harper disconnected his phone and watched Laurie head outside.

"Anybody seen Diego this morning?" Hawk asked.

"He's back in the kitchen whipping up some breakfast for us," Mercedes answered. Sloane looked at his wristwatch to see the time was 1:22 p.m. and said, "I guess it's breakfast o'clock somewhere."

"Breakfast, lunch, supper, whatever – I'm definitely ready for something," Kin admitted.

"Ya don't say," Danny smirked. "Burn a lot of carbs in your sleep last night, chief?"

"Well, I'm just not one to go into battle on an empty stomach. I don't want to run out of gas when I'm out there trying to rid the world of a couple hundred scum-sucking dirt bags."

"Indeed," agreed Watkins, "I am ready for the pre-game meal, myself."

"Sounds good. We'll fire down some grub, go over the plan with Big James, ask and answer any questions and concerns, load up, and get ready to head back to the airfield."

"Ya know, I'm thinkin' about Chase's plan," Devereaux brought up, "and it seems like you might have a bit of trouble, Harp. Not that you're not used to that, getting pigeonholed and everything."

"How bad am I getting pigeonholed here?"

"Well, if you're going to be driving that truck through the front gate, you're not going to be able to be all geared up with whatever weapons you'll be wanting to use tonight. I'm thinking if you're trying to convince whoever meets that truck that you're a legit replacement driver, then sitting behind the wheel with grenades, knives, and guns strapped all over your person probably isn't going to be the way to go on that one."

"Hmm, I see your point," Harper acknowledged. "Well, I'm just going to throw this out there to everyone. Any takers on spotting me once the shooting starts until I can get properly attired for this blood bath?"

"I'll take that action," Kinley nodded to his partner.

"Tell ya what, my brother," spoke up Hawkins, "we've got some real cutting edge stuff as far as the latest in Kevlar wear you can use. No more of those big bulky flak jackets, the cumbersome helmets with those stupid Plexiglas shields, and those heavy, burdensome pants. No sir, those are soon to be fossils from an eagerly-forgotten past."

"Okay, well, what do you guys have then?"

"It's basically Kevlar long johns. You can wear them under pretty much anything, and nobody can tell a thing. Believe it or not, I'm actually wearing some right now, and I ain't even breakin' a sweat. It's like that stay-dri material. Kinda like Under Armour and Kevlar got together and designed the product."

"Now that there sounds like something that's just a little too good to be true," came a doubtful Devereaux. "I mean, if it's so thin then it doesn't sound like there's very much there to absorb the impact of the bullets when they hit. What keeps the force of the bullet from just breaking the bones in whatever part of the body it strikes?"

"Science, baby. Science."

Kin looked at John for some sort of confirmation. "Is he for real?"

"He is," Watkins verified. "He's for real, and it's for real."

"Wait. If it's a legitimate product then how come I've never heard of it?"

"Because it was developed by a small weapons tech company out of New Hampshire. Sadly, when they went to sell it to the U.S. military, the higher-ups decided that, in the end, it wasn't cost effective so they turned it down."

"Then how did you guys get your hands on it?" Harper asked.

"Well, unlike the United States military, we found it extremely cost effective, and we got some," Sloane answered.

"Hold on a stupid second," Dev shook his head in disbelief. "You're telling me that the U.S. military couldn't afford the bullet-proof underwear, but you guys could?"

"Sure," Watkins responded quickly, "but keep in mind that the military would've been buying over a million units just for its four major branches alone, and that's not even counting the reserves or the paramilitary. We bought, like, ten."

"Slightly smaller scale," Merc said holding her forefinger and thumb slightly apart.

"And it really doesn't hurt when you get hit?"

"Hey, it don't feel like getting kissed by a tall cool brunette or anything like that. It'll leave ya with a bit of a contusion, perhaps, but that's a far sight better than the alternative," Sam smiled.

"Ya got any that'll fit me?" came a familiar voice from behind the group. No one had noticed that Big James and Laurie had made their way back into the building. "I wear an extra mondo – unless it's cut small. Then I wear a 2X mondo."

"Big James is in the house!" Harper hollered.

"What's going on, crew?"

"Just shootin' the breeze. Waitin' on some chow."

"You hungry, Big Time?" Harper asked.

James Gray smiled. "I never met a meal I didn't like."

And right on cue, Diego came from the kitchen area and announced that food was ready for anyone and everyone.

The Plan One Last Time

If Diego was half as good at fighting as he was at cooking, then no one had a thing to worry about. For as much talking as had been going on leading up to the "pre-game meal", as John Watkins had put it, hardly a word was being said now as the squad of nine men and women shoveled forkful after forkful of delicious cuisine into their mouths.

Hardly a word. But there were several grunts and groans of enjoyment in appreciation for the masterful meal that Diego had put together for them.

"Ees good, no?" Diego smiled his big Portuguese smile.

"Is good, yes," Dr. Lara said, smacking her lips.

"Good golly, Diego, this is marvelous work," Harper looked at Laurie and said, "If I had been living with this guy for the last year or so, geez – how is it you don't weigh 300 pounds?"

"I'm not sure if you've noticed or not, but it's really hot down here. Sometimes I even sweat when I'm taking a shower."

Harper looked at Big James and joked, "Yet somehow you've managed to maintain your girlish figure."

"You know how this food tastes really good to you? All food tastes this good to me. Plus, I travel a lot, so I don't sweat year 'round like if I lived here all 365."

And that was it for the talking. Everyone resumed eating for the next twenty minutes, until every plate was clean.

Once they had finished eating, they made their way back to the main room of the warehouse where the diorama of Tito del Fuento's compound was set up. Big James was highly impressed with Chase's work. "How long did it take you to put all this together?"

"All told, a few months. I did it little by little to make sure that all the scales were correct."

"Are you ready to go over the plan then, Big James?" Harper asked.

"I'm ready when you guys are."

"Super. Then let's get to it," Harper looked at Laurie. "You have the floor, madam."

"Thank you, Harper," Laurie smiled, then started in on the plan. "It all starts right here," she said to James Gray as she pointed to the truck positioned at the front of the diorama, "with this truck."

"What are we going to be doing with that truck?"

"Well, in your case, you will be doing nothing with the truck. You and Diego will be over here," and she pointed to the west side of the scaled-down plantation. "At the appropriate time, the two of you are going to enter through here. Diego will be able to guide you through an opening that is a dead spot in the security. You'll need to set up the ground-to-air launcher as quickly as possible to take out the two overhead planes. You were able to get one of those, right?"

"Absolutely. I've already taken an entire horse trailer of arms and munitions over to the hangar where their plane is and dropped it off before I came here."

"I don't want to put any undue pressure on the two of you," Chase stated with complete seriousness, "but if we're going to have a snowball's chance at pulling this off it's going to completely hinge on the two of you taking those planes out of the sky and fast."

"Okay. So, that's me and Diego, when the time is right, but what about that truck? How does that play into things?"

"The rest of us will be lying in wait for this truck once it leaves the main highway and heads back toward the compound. There will be a window of opportunity for us to take it while it's in a blind spot before it gets in range of the compound's radar. We're going to hijack it, and we're going to use it to gain entrance into the place. It's a supply truck that they will be expecting. What they won't be expecting is for us to be in it. Since he speaks the best Portuguese out of any of us, Harper will be driving and will get us past whoever's there to meet the truck."

"Well, it's wonderful that he speaks great Portuguese, but how will he know what to say? They're going to notice that he's not the regular driver, and when they do they're going to start grilling the guy about what's going on. How's he going to know what to say without giving himself away?"

"Diego will be able to cue him in to what to say," she answered.

"Yeah, but you said that Diego was going to be with Big James on the other side of the compound," Harper pointed out.

"With the coms that we will be using, Diego will be able to hear everything that is going on, and he will be able to tell you just what to say." She looked at Diego. "Right?"

"Absolutely, Mees Laurie. I weel be able to hear what ees being said through thee coms, and I weel tell Mees'er Harper exactly what to say to those guys. Eet weel be no problem. No problem at all, Mees Laurie." Diego seemed to believe what he was saying, which was good because no one else in the room had even the foggiest idea as to what he was saying. They all just nodded at him and grinned.

"Okay, then," Chase smiled. "So, we will drive the truck onto the compound, Harper and Diego will get us past the guards at the gate, we will get to where we need to be, and that's when John will set off the EMP device."

"EMP device?" Big James asked incredulously, "Those things

aren't even real. They're just the figment of the imaginations of people who write movies. EMP device – that's a riot."

"It might be a riot, but it's also a big part of our plan. Other than you and Diego knocking those birds out of the sky, it's probably the most important part of our plan."

James looked around at everyone else in the room waiting for someone to let him in on the joke, but no one was laughing. "If you all are seriously thinking that an EMP device is going to be a legitimate part of this plan, then you're all crazier than I ever imagined. They do not exist, people."

"We have one, and I'm quite confident it will work," John said pragmatically. "Regardless, there's no need to get into a squabble over its mere existence. At this point, we are rather pressed for time. So let's get back to the plan."

Chase gave a nod of appreciation toward John and set back in on the plan. "I guess the question is this: how are we going to get the EMP device into place so that we can utilize it?"

"It just needs to be in the relative vicinity. Say, maybe a quarter of a mile. Here's the issue we're going to run into with that: the device is big, but it will fit into the back of your van, Laurie, so transporting it and positioning it shouldn't be much of a problem. What is going to be a problem is that while Hawk, Doc, Danny, and I can ride in our jeep, and the three of you can fit into the front of your van, with the amount of weapons and firepower that we're going to need to take with us," John paused and looked at Big James, "we're going to need another transport vehicle. A truck or a van, preferably. Is that doable?"

"Sure," answered the ever-confident big man, "I just need someone to ride with me on our way back to the airfield. We can swing by my place and pick up my Astro van."

"I'm good for that," Harper raised his hand.

"Good night, James," Sloane laughed, "how many soccer mom vehicles do you have?"

"I have an entire fleet of them, actually, and I find that they're just as useful at hauling around weapon payloads as they are at hauling around prepubescent footballers. Plus, they're as inconspicuous as it gets."

"Problem solved then," John said. He looked back at Chase. "We'll load the EMP device into your van, our weapons into the second van, and we'll drive them and our jeep to right about here somewhere." Watkins pointed to the area on the diorama that Laurie Chase had designated to commandeer the supply truck.

"We'll take the truck and unload the weapons out of the van and into the back of it. Everyone will get on the truck, and I'll stay back with the van and the EMP. When I hear that the time is right, I'll pull the van up close enough for the device to be effective and set it off. From there, I will be along rightly."

"Once the EMP device has been employed, that will be our cue to go." Chase looked at Gray. "Big James, you and Diego move as fast as you can to wherever you need to get to in order to start firing at those planes." She pointed at a specific spot on the diorama. "My best guess is that the two of you will need to get right here. That's going to be about 150 yards from your starting point outside the perimeter."

"Hey, Diego, are we going to be able to drive to there? Or are we going to have to go on foot?"

"Eets an area that ees out of range of veedeo cameras an' any guards, but eet ees steell area that ees fenced een. Eef we can drive through thee fence, we can drive thee rest of thee way."

"What's the fence made out of?"

"Ees chain leenk. About five meters high."

James did some quick calculations in his head.

"Your soccer mom van gonna be able to bust through a chain link fence, Carol Brady?" Hawkins joked. "Ya know, ya might wanna call the Beaver's mom. See if she can loan ya her station wagon as a backup plan."

Big James looked at Sloane and Hawkins. "Ya know, fellas, I have a couple of baseball bats out in my ride. Maybe y'all could grab 'em, go dig up Barbaro, and beat that dead horse for a while."

Harper burst out in laughter. "Big Time shoots and scores with a zinger from the blue line!"

Mercedes was laughing, too. "If it's true that laughter is the best medicine then I think Big James just cured the common cold with that one."

"Yeah, ha ha ha, laugh it up," came Sloane's sour grapes response. "Let's get back to the matter at hand. If that's okay with everybody else?"

"Absolutely," Laurie answered. "So, Big Ja–"

"No, not yet," Harper interrupted as he raised his hand and continued to laugh. Finally, he inhaled a deep breath, collected himself, and nodded to Laurie. "Okay. I'm good."

"Ya sure?" Chase asked, somewhat perturbed. "Because I wouldn't want to cut short the good time that you're having over there."

"Yeah, he's good," Devereaux answered before his friend had a chance to exacerbate the situation any further.

"So, like I was saying," Laurie began again quite curtly, "Big James and Diego start doing their part to take out the overhead planes. Harper – if he hasn't laughed himself to death – Kinley, and I will find proper cover to start laying down serious gunfire–" While Kinley, Harper, John, Danny, Hawk, Merc, and Diego stood around listening, Chase only seemed to be talking to Big James.

"–firing at anyone that might be coming out of these garrisons here," and again Laurie pointed to a particular spot on the diorama. "Diego says that when the boss is away, this is the spot where Tito's troops that get left behind congregate to defile themselves." She looked at James and asked, "Are you with me so far?"

Without waiting for an answer, she proceeded to go over the

rest of the plan, describing how the Dragon's Men were going to be moving on the helicopter pilots' barracks and taking them out.

Next she explained their hope that Hawkins could get one of the Black Hawks up in the air and dispatch its payload to destroy the cocaine and marijuana fields while everyone was finishing off what was left of del Fuento's men.

Then she told Big James about the money, and how much there was going to be, and the plan for how they were going to procure it, load it, and take it with them when they made their getaway.

Finally, Chase described the getaway plan. She told Big James how they would make their exit out of Tito's compound, how the meetup point would be back at the airfield if any of them were to get separated from the pack. Once everyone was back at the hangar, the money would be split between the parties. From there it would be quick goodbyes and going their separate ways.

"What? We won't be hanging out for a victory party?" Big James asked, somewhat disappointed. "I mean, if we survive these odds and pull off a successful raid, I'd say that's a pretty darn good reason for cuttin' loose one good time, ya know?"

The rest of the crew suddenly realized that they had not yet informed James Gray that Harper had been recognized back in the States – and, by now, probably everywhere else, too – and the extreme likelihood that agents had already been dispatched to Rio.

"Here's the thing," Chase explained. "Somebody at the club last night snapped a picture of Harper and put it up on the internet. It hit the U.S. newswires about five or six hours ago, which means that the feds probably caught wind of it about eight hours ago. Harper said that he's not only sure that they are sending agents, but he even knows who they're sending. We contemplated if we should even go on with the plan to take out del Fuento's place or not, but we all came up with the same math that told us we should have enough time to still pull this job off. But it's going to make for some quick departure times after the show's over. Hopefully, once this all blows over and the ash dies down, we can all get together somewhere and celebrate properly. For now, though, we're on a bit of a time crunch."

The big guy nodded his red-hair-covered head understandingly. "What about you and Diego? You two splittin' for greener pastures, as well?"

"No, Diego and I will be staying here. We will still have some unfinished business to tend to once Tito and the rest of his family come back to the mess that will be waiting for them."

"I'd like to get in on that action, if I can," Gray volunteered. "I'm going to assume that you will be wrapping up the remainder of this project sooner rather than later, right?"

"If everything goes well, and we aren't dead later on tonight, then our plan is to meet up with everyone at the hangar, divvy up the money, and Diego and I will be making our way back here to track del Fuento's return flight. We'll also have to make sure that the second plane that is flying over to Dresden with him – the one with all of his guys on it – has taken a header on the runway like we are planning."

"All right, all right, all right," Sloane said as he gave a halting motion, "that's a different plan for a different time. Let's stay focused on the task at hand here. Who's got questions?"

"I do," Big James answered. "You said something about Tito del Fuento's family, and I realize that's for later, but what about tonight? What about the women and children of the soldiers that we are going to encounter tonight? What's our plan for them?"

"Not going to be an issue tonight, buddy," Harper said. "We already covered this earlier so I will catch you up to speed when we are headed over to your place once we leave here."

"I have a question." This time it was Kinley. "How are we going to divvy up the money? Are we all going to get equal cuts, or will we get paid by squad? A certain amount for me and Harp, a little more for Dragon's Men because there's more of them and we're using some of their equipment, another amount for Big James to reimburse him for the money he's put out and for his time and for the use of his fleet of soccer mom vehicles?"

"Once we see how much we're dealing with we can figure all that out. Diego assures me that we should have more than enough to take care of everyone financially," Laurie paused pensively. "Let's get the job done and get everyone out on the clean side of this."

"She's right," concurred Watkins. "We start getting distracted by dollar signs, and who's getting how much, someone's going to take a bullet unnecessarily, and in a job like this with a crew this size – if one of us goes down, the domino effect may be too much for the rest of us to handle."

"Also," Harper chirped, "I know that it would be ideal if you could get yourself into one of those Black Hawks and tear up some soil with it, Sam, but don't go letting your heart out-kick your mind's coverage. Safety first. I know with the grand scheme of this whole mission and the depths of danger which we will be encountering here that saying, 'safety first' seems a bit out of place, but, seriously, an ounce of precaution when available is better than a pound of cure."

"Hey, you can count on me on that one, brother," Hawk agreed. "I often find that the only good mission is the mission that I get to come home from. Far as I'm concerned, even if the mission's objective is reached, but I end up dead? Bad mission."

"That goes for the rest of us, too," Mercedes put in.

"Look," Laurie shrugged, "I think we all know that there are a lot of things that have to go perfectly right for this whole thing to work. The main thing here is to try to stick to the plan as best we can, stay alive, and keep everyone else alive as best we can."

She looked at her watch. "It's getting close to time for us to hit the road. We're under three hours until it's time to take the truck, and I wouldn't mind being there a bit early just in case. So? Any last questions before we take off?"

"Yes," John Watkins inserted, "I have one last question." He looked at Harper, then at Kinley, and then to Laurie before he went on, "You three seem like the real deal, and you don't have to admit to any sort of guilt or culpability about any of this, but," and Johnny looked at his other team members, "before any of my unit can totally commit to this whole thing, we just need to know – did Paul Michaels have to die?"

Laurie Chase and Kinley Devereaux hesitated for a moment, but Harper Rowe did not. "Oh, boy, did he ever. That guy was the third cousin to evil and the brother-in-law to bad news. He killed, lied, manipulated, and I'm sure, sold his own mother down the river over what happened a year and a half ago."

"And those family reunions won't ever be what they once were," Kin finally answered. "Yeah, that guy had to go. If not, a lot of other good people would've ended up going instead." Devereaux took a moment, and that's when Chase chimed in, "Once again, as you said, John – not admitting any sort of guilt or culpability – Paul Michaels had to die."

The members of Dragon's Men looked at each other.

"I'm good with that," said Sloane.

"Yeah," nodded Hawkins, "same."

"I'm ready to roll," Merc said.

"Well, let's roll, then," Watkins conceded.

Harper looked at Kin and Laurie, shrugged, looked at Merc and then to James. "Let's go help Laurie Chase get her revenge and rid this planet of one of its stinkier armpits."

"Most of us probably aren't coming back here – live or die – so grab whatever you came with and don't want to leave behind."

For one last moment, everyone looked around at each other. No doubt, there was an unspoken love and kinship between the group. The nine of them had only known each other for a short time, but in that short time they had already fused an unbreakable bond of trust.

Tonight – they would need every bit of it.

Two Flights into Rio

It was a one hour, fifty-minute jaunt from Prague to DeGaulle Airport in Paris. After a ninety-minute layover, the Air France flight from Prague to *Galeão* International Airport in Rio de Janeiro was about twelve hours. A long flight, but not nearly long enough as far as she was concerned.

She sat on the plane and waited for takeoff, catching her reflection in the glass next to her window seat. She looked tired. She was tired. Really tired and really nervous.

She was nervous because she had not seen him in such a long time. Now she was flying all these hours to ask for what was probably the biggest favor of her life. Not just ask him for his help to rescue someone that he had never met and would probably never see again once the job was over, but also to ask him for the help of his closest friend – a man of whom she had very little knowledge. And she knew that if he were going to assist her in her quandary, it would be due completely to his loyalty to his friend and have absolutely nothing to do with her. Still, without him, the job would most likely be a complete loss.

The job? Getting an innocent mother and daughter out of a city that was suddenly dead-set on not letting either one of them leave. Getting them out and someplace safe where they would not be found or threatened by people who were, apparently, very powerful and very evil.

She had thought she could do it by herself – at least, the getting them out of the city part. She had changed their look to the point that they could barely recognize themselves. She had arranged temporary shelter until she could get them new identification and a permanent place to live, with the help of him and his friend.

However, she was unable to accomplish even the first part of her plan. Once she had satisfactorily changed their appearance, packed a few things, and double-checked the interim staying arrangements, she and her best friend, Eliska Lukasik, were getting ready to usher them to her car when she saw the TV news report.

The entire city of Prague was on high alert to find Anezka and Jana. Bus depots, train stations, airports, even car rental places were being monitored and heavily manned with extra security personnel to make sure that the on-the-run mother and daughter team did not have a prayer of leaving the city. Suddenly this was no longer a few sexual deviants trying to keep their dirty little secret under wraps. No. Now, this was the Czech Republic's largest city having an invisible net cast over it in an attempt to catch two people who had, seemingly, overnight, gone from nobodies to "persons wanted in connection with a capital murder investigation." Some news outlets had even gone as far as labeling them "armed and dangerous".

Whatever it was – or whoever it was – that they had seen inside that orphanage was, without a doubt, some kind of major player in something big. It was not just anybody that could get an entire city of this size to pool all of its resources to put together a manhunt of this nature.

Seeing the news report, she realized two things: number one, getting Anezka and Jana out of Prague and to a safe place was going to take nothing short of a miracle, and number two, if caught, anyone that was going to get involved with helping her on this undertaking would not just be risking their freedom but, more than likely, their very existence.

* * *

It had taken a few hours to get everything together, but finally Special Agent Jeb Crool, Special Agent David Baldwin, and about a dozen other agents from Homeland Security were winging their way toward Rio de Janeiro.

While they had been waiting on the government jet to be readied, both Crool and Baldwin had been on the phone with the authorities in Rio trying to get the local police jumpstarted on the search for Harper Rowe and Kinley Devereaux. After a flight of this length, the last thing they wanted to do when they landed was to stand around waiting for red tape to be cut before any real searching could get underway.

For now, though, Jeb and Dave were seated next to each other in a section of the jet that was separated from the other agents. Both men were busying themselves on their respective laptops – Baldwin was getting caught up on delinquent paperwork while Jeb Crool was frantically searching the web for a specific news story.

Without looking away from his computer, Jeb said, "The Rio police have Rowe and Devereaux's pictures splashed all over every media source in the city. Local and federal authorities are already coordinating a manhunt as we speak. They'll be there to meet us as soon as we touch down to loop us into everything."

"Are they going to be putting up roadblocks and checking all access points out of the city? Airports, trains, and so on?"

"They've got everyone on high alert, but it's been such an extensive amount of time that if they were going to leave Rio, they'd already be in the wind." He continued to peck feverishly at his laptop's keyboard. "However, I don't think that they've left Rio."

"Oh? Why not?" Agent Baldwin furrowed his brow.

"Well, if you can hang on just a minute," Crool continued his search, "I think I can show you why not."

Dave stopped his own task and leaned back, waiting for Jeb to find whatever it was that he was looking for.

He waited. And he waited. And he waited. And then –

"Yes," exclaimed Jeb, "here it is. Look at this, Dave."

Jeb angled his laptop toward Special Agent Baldwin. "This is an article that I came across a few months ago. I didn't really make the connection to it and everything that's happened in the last few hours until just a little bit ago. If Laurie Chase is still alive, and she's still hanging with Rowe and Devereaux, then this piece could very well explain why they're in Rio."

David leaned forward in his seat and began reading the story on Crool's laptop. It was a story about a United States DEA team that had been wiped out during an ill-fated drug raid in Mexico City two summers ago. Baldwin was not real sure of the significance of the story until he got to the part about the raid being on a shipment that allegedly belonged to a Brazilian drug lord named Tito del Fuento.

"So, the DEA team in this story," he looked at his boss, "that was Chase's team?"

"Sure was. She was the sole survivor of it all."

"And this del Fuento guy? I'm going to assume he's based in or around Rio?"

"Two for two, Dave."

"You're thinking she's brought in two former government assassins to exact a little revenge and take the guy out? Is that it?"

"Well, let's break down what's happened in the last twenty-four to thirty-six hours or so, shall we? Ever since the assassination of Paul Michaels, Harper Rowe has shown his face in a lot of different places all over the world, but never once has he shown up in the U.S. until two nights ago. Two nights ago he shows up – and in fine form, might I add – and now we know it was to help Devereaux procure his assassin's rifle that somehow ended up in an Atlanta police evidence locker. I'm sure they wanted to get that gun because it probably has several professional hits linked to it, but I'm also guessing that Kinley Devereaux wanted it to do one more hit for his old friend, Laurel Elizabeth Chase. A hit on the man responsible for killing all of her team members and friends."

"That all does seem to add up, circumstantially speaking, but aren't you forgetting about the whole reason we even know that Harper Rowe is in Rio in the first place? The terrorist attack that he and his friends thwarted. How do we know that he didn't somehow get wind of the attack, and that's the reason he was there?"

"I don't know. I'm still trying to factor that in."

Baldwin looked at Jeb incredulously. "Really? Because if we go with your drug lord assassination theory, why would he have totally given away his position by making such a grand move as killing seven terrorists? It just wouldn't make any sense, boss."

"I get that, I do. But let's not forget that this is Harper Rowe we're talking about here. The guy plays from a completely different deck of cards than anybody else, which is why when everybody else is holding a royal flush in their hands, he's throwing down a 'Draw Four' and changing the color on us. So, please, don't sit there and think you can make sense out of anything he does."

Agent Baldwin slumped back into his seat. "Right. You're right. But, hey, has anybody even checked on the well-being of the drug lord? I mean, for all we know, they may have cut the power to this guy and then went and nabbed the terrorists for a few extra points in the bonus round."

"Actually, when I remembered this article about the DEA team and started to connect a few dots I made a call to do just that – check the status of Tito del Fuento," Jeb asserted.

"And?"

"And I got a call just before we got on the plane giving me the information that has led me to believe that our targets are still in Rio as we speak."

"Well, come on, man. Spit it out. What's going on?"

"Del Fuento, his family, and a rather large contingent of his men took off around eight a.m. this morning – alive and well – for Dresden, Germany. They're due to arrive back tomorrow night, and my gut feeling tells me that they'll be coming home to a rather rude welcoming committee."

"You think Chase, Rowe, and Devereaux are still in Rio because they are waiting on their target to get back home?"

"Yes, I do," Crool answered without hesitation.

"Seriously? I mean, if we know that Rowe's in Rio then ya gotta know that Rowe knows that we know he's in Rio. You really think he's just going to stay put and wait for us to show up? That's crazy."

"And you've got some kind of short term memory problem, man. In the last eighteen months how many times have we said, 'This is absurd.' Or 'Rowe must've lost his mind.' Or 'This tactic is just plain foolish'? Geez, buddy, we just admitted three minutes ago that Rowe's actions rarely make sense. Did you forget that already, too?" Jeb Crool's shaved head was beginning to turn red with frustration as he drew in a deep breath. "My heart and my head both say that the three of them are in Rio, laying low, waiting on del Fuento to fly back home from Germany.

"Look around, agent. We're in a million-dollar government jet with twelve other federal agents headed to Rio. We're getting ready to be working together with international agents from South America on a manhunt the size of Texas. If I thought for even a second that they were already gone, do you think I would be doing any of this?" Jeb made a point to keep his voice down. The last thing he wanted was to have the other agents on board think that there was dissension in the ranks when this operation was just getting off the ground.

"They're still in Rio, and we're going to catch them. Of this, I have no doubt. And if you do then ya might just want to stay on the plane when we land."

Baldwin cocked his head and then shook it from side to side and smiled. "Now that is a really dopey thing for you to say to me, boss. I may not have started my career with you, but for the last year and a half, who's the one guy that's been with you every step of the way? Sometimes we've butted heads; sometimes we've been frustrated to the point of nervous breakdowns. Still, when the next day comes around, it's been me and you right back at it again.

"You need me to question your methods and ideas because it's the only way to make sure you're steadfast and don't have any doubts about what you're doing. And let's face it, the only way I can believe that you're making the right call is to know that you believe you're making the right call. Now I know. So yeah, I'll be getting off this jet when we touch down in Rio."

Jeb smiled apologetically and patted Special Agent Baldwin on the shoulder. "And that's why you're my number-one guy."

The two men breathed a long sigh of relief. Then Jeb started to laugh, at first just a chuckle, then a real laugh. Moments later Jeb was in a full-on cackle.

"What the heck, boss?" questioned a baffled Baldwin. "What's got you so tickled?"

Jeb took a minute to compose himself before answering. "Those terrorists – that whole thing. What if it really was dumb luck that Rowe was there. It's like those idiot robbers that didn't do their homework before a hold-up job, and the bar they chose to rob was a cop bar. They practically walked right into the lion's den wearing a three-piece suit made out of red meat. Except those robbers had it one better than those terrorists," and Jeb started laughing again. "The cops just arrested them. I'm pretty sure Harper Rowe and his group of cronies were shooting first, and the only question they were asking–" Crool had to stop for a second to gather himself again, "is whether or not they should re-load. I mean, who knows how long those terrorist bastards had planned to wipe that place out and make their big religious or political statement, and – and due to the worst luck in the history of bad luck, those little jerks were done before they even got started."

Crool burst into laughter again, and, by now, Dave was laughing even if for no other reason than the hilarity of his boss' own outrageous cachinnations. It felt good to laugh though. It meant that the tension that had filled the space between them earlier was now over and done.

Crisis averted, David Baldwin set back to task on his overdue paperwork.

"So, how long are we looking at until we touch down in Rio, Dave?"

"A while, boss. Probably between twelve and thirteen hours."

"Geez," Crool sighed. "This is one of those times I wish I had a time machine that we could jump into and wormhole our way into the future about half a day."

"I have a time machine, Jeb," Dave stated.

"What?"

"Yeah. It's called a clock," Baldwin smiled without looking away from his work.

Jeb looked out the window at the multitude of white clouds that the jet seemed to be riding on.

"Well, since we've got some time to kill, think I'm gonna blow off some steam and play a few rounds of 'Whack the Penguin'."

This did make Baldwin look away from his work. "I'm sorry – you're going to play a few rounds of what?"

"Whack the Penguin," Jeb repeated. "Don't tell me you've never played before."

"I – may have," Baldwin answered cautiously. "What exactly

are you referring to when you say "Whack the Penguin"? Is that a real game?"

"Dude! Yes." Crool reacted as if Agent Baldwin was telling him that he had never heard of the wheel. "It's very much my number-one stress reliever of all time. Here, let me show you."

Baldwin recoiled uneasily in his seat. "That – that's not necessary, Jeb."

"No, come on, buddy. It's fun." And with the exuberance of a small child on Christmas morning, Crool moved the cursor around on his computer screen, clicking on links and prompts until the words "Whack the Penguin" appeared in cartoon script. A few seconds later they were replaced by a cartoon screen that consisted of a snow-covered cliff with a cartoon polar bear that would drop a single cartoon penguin to the bottom of the cliff, where a second cartoon polar bear would swing a wooden club like a baseball bat and "whack" the cartoon penguin as far as it could.

"The challenge of the game is to see how far you can whack the penguin," Jeb explained, "and you click on the polar bear to make him swing the club. The strategy is to time your swing just right. If you swing too soon, you'll just hit a little dinky penguin pop-up. If you swing too late, you'll end up hitting nothing but penguin grounders. Time it just right, and that penguin will go a-flying."

"That's it? That's the whole game?"

"That's it, yes. Now, I'm sure you're probably wondering what I was thinking the first time someone showed me this game. You're thinking that it seems kinda juvenile and inane–"

"Actually," Baldwin smiled a relieved smile, "I'm just glad it *is* a game."

"Yes, it's a game. Of course it's a game. What did you think it was?" Crool asked in confusion.

"Well, c'mon, Jeb," David laughed nervously. "I mean, whack the penguin? Stress reliever? It just kinda sounded like–"

"Just wait. Once you start playing – you'll see. You'll see."

"Okay. Okay. Send me the link."

"I'm sending you the link." Jeb copied and pasted the link into an email and sent it on. "It's coming your way now. Check your mail." While David waited for the email to show up, Jeb said, "One last thing."

"What's that?"

"You can never, ever, ever tell my wife about this. She loves penguins. If she ever found out that I was playing a game called 'Whack the Penguin', I know beyond a shadow of a doubt that I'd be the one getting whacked and she wouldn't be asking any questions first."

"I understand. Mum's the word, Jeb. Okay, I got the link."

"Well then, by God, let's whack some penguins."

And in the early afternoon of January second, as they jetted their way to the most important assignment of their careers, two of America's most highly-trained special agents began passing the time by playing "Whack the Penguin". And just as Jeb predicted, it was not long before any remaining tension that either man may have felt was quickly alleviated.

Soccer Mom Vans

They left in three different vehicles. Laurie, Diego, and Kinley jumped in Chase's white cargo van. John, Daniel, and Hawk rode in their black jeep. Dr. Mercedes Lara had hopped a ride with Big James and Harper. The first two vehicles were headed back to the old Santa Cruz Air Force Base while Big James and crew were headed to his place.

Harper was filling Big James in on why the women and children would not be at the compound tonight when the attack began. "–so with the womenfolk away, as well as the boss man, then the men are gonna play, and, hopefully, they will be playing right into our hands."

"Just for safe measure, we should've shipped an extra case of tequila to those daffy flamers. Make sure that they were good and soused for our arrival tonight."

Harp laughed, looked at his friend, and joked, "You know your body may look like a human tub of butter, but your brain is still one streamlined and sexy beast."

"Thank ya, brother. I do what I can to keep in shape." Gray looked in his rearview mirror at Dr. Lara. "You doin' alright back there, Doc?" Big James and Harper were up front in the bucket seats while Merc lounged in the captain's chair behind Harper.

"Absolutely. I've gotta say that this is one of the most

comfortable seats I have ever ridden in when it comes to this type of vehicle. Did these captain's chairs come standard?"

"Sure didn't. I got them in a trade I conducted a few years back. I installed them a long time ago, but I'm pretty sure that you're, like, maybe the third person to ever ride back there, and if you asked me who the first two were, I'm quite sure I couldn't tell you. Hey, before we get to talking about whatever," Big James changed the subject, "I just need to know. Do you guys really have a working EMP device?"

"Yes, we really have one, and, in theory, it really should work."

"In theory?" came back a doubting James Gray.

"Yes, in theory, meaning that we had three in stock. Danny built them all three exactly the same. We tried out one a few months back, and it worked. Since all three of them are exactly alike, in theory, the one that we have here – the one that we'll be using tonight – should absolutely work."

"Well, it better, or our gaggle of geese is cooked."

Harper spun a quarter turn in his seat so he could see both Big James and Merc. "So, tell us about you, Dr. Lara. Which came first? You becoming a doctor, or you becoming a soldier?"

"I became a doctor first, actually. Right after high school I attended the University of Florida Medical School. I studied there for four years, and then I finished up my doctorate at Johns Hopkins University in Baltimore. My specific field of study was trauma and ER procedures."

"So what took you into the military?"

"Same as a lot of people: 9-11."

"How long were you in medical school?"

"Seven years."

"Holy crap!" Big James interjected. "That makes you – you're *forty*?"

Mercedes smiled a pearly white smile. "I will be this year. December baby, baby."

"That's – wow. I really thought you were 26 or 27. I really truly did."

"Dude–" Harper gave a look of skepticism.

"What?"

"Don't exaggerate."

"I'm not!" the big man protested. "Okay, fine. I won't exaggerate if you don't lie. Tell the truth. How old did you think she was when you first saw her?"

"Yeah," Mercedes leaned forward and gave Harper a good poke in his shoulder, "how old did you think I was?"

"Thirty-three."

Merc leaned back in her chair and stroked her chin in contemplation. "Hmm, well, that's also a very acceptable answer, but not as good as our big fluffy buddy's answer, so – he wins the prize."

"What's the prize?" Harp asked apprehensively.

"Yeah, what's the prize?" Big James was beaming.

"Just this." Lara got up from her seat and made her way up to Big James. She put her arms around his neck and planted a series of sweet smooches on his right cheek.

"Whoa, whoa, whoa!" objected Rowe. "You're gonna make the guy wreck."

"No, I'm good," James spoke up quickly. "Quite fine, good, and exceptional."

Mercedes pulled back from the driver and turned to the passenger. "Don't worry, big boy, if we live through tonight I've got plenty left in my reserve tank just for you."

As she moved back to her seat, James smiled and said, "Dang, Harp, I have really missed hanging out with you, *meu irmão*."

Harper picked back up where he had left off before he had been derailed onto the subject of Dr. Mercedes Lara's age. "You joined the military after 9-11. What is the path that you were set upon that led you to being with your current crew?"

"Well, they sent me to Saudi as soon as I finished up my six-week orientation. Once I got there they told me that I would be traveling out into the field on a relatively regular basis to fix up soldiers that had been wounded to the point that they wouldn't survive a transport back to the base. Since I would be traveling out and about in the field like that, I was put through a pretty intense crash course in munitions and recognizing and disarming IEDs and other explosive devices that I would encounter on a daily basis. I did that for about two years.

"Then one day I was transferred to Kabul in Afghanistan where I was told that I would be the medic and munitions specialist for an elite Delta Force team that would be performing a series of black ops missions in and around the capital city. I really thought it was just a short-term assignment. There were eight of us when we started. About three months in, we were doing a job, and one of our team was KIA. We thought they would replace him, but, alas, they did not. We got back from that assignment and twelve hours later we were sent out on our next stint a man down.

"They never did send a replacement, and when the next member on our team went down, there was no replacement sent for her, either. It didn't seem to matter though. Every assignment we were sent on got accomplished. Not to mention, it wasn't too long after we got started that the missions were just about anywhere: Berlin, Nice, Vienna, Barcelona.

"Once it got down to just the four of us, we did three or four jobs, and then they did send us some replacements. That was tough." Mercedes stopped her story for a moment as she got lost in thought. She made a subtle shake of her head before continuing on. "It was almost like we had gotten too good working together – just the four of us – and when the newbies showed up it was more like a chore than a help trying to get them acclimated to our team. I remember almost getting killed in several missions because one or more of the newbies had dropped the ball in one aspect or another.

"It got to the point where we were running missions *and* playing babysitter to these people. Three of them got killed, two couldn't get along and were pulled out, and ultimately, John called HQ and told them to stop sending replacements. From there on out it was just the four of us. I thought, eventually, that we would get sick of each other, but we never did, never have. No doubt, we have John to thank for that. The dude is like the foremost peacekeeper I've ever met. When he gets mad though – good Lord, watch out."

"That's why they're called Dragon's Men," Big James reminded Harper, "because when Johnny gets mad, it's like you can see the fire shootin' out of his nostrils, and the guy will just go pillaging whatever is in his path."

"I gotta say," Harper ridged his brow, "I haven't seen any signs at all of him being that guy. If anything, he comes across as being too laid back."

"He's like one of those oxymorons," Gray noted.

"Yes," agreed Lara, "that's exactly what he is."

"Was he the CO of your team when you guys were military?"

"That he was."

"And now? Is he still the head of your contingent, or how does that work?"

"When we left the military and started our venture in the civilian world, he let it be known to us that he was no longer our CO, and that this was everybody being equal; no one greater than the other. Still, whether it's out of habit or out of necessity, we look to him when things get tight and we need a quick decision. Everybody knows what's going on. We call him 'boss' a lot, and at first he put up a bit of a squawk about it. But over time, he just went with it."

"In all the times that you've gone to him for those quick decisions, has he ever been wrong?"

"Sure, but in all the time that I've worked with him, and the thousand or so decisions that he's made over all those years, I could probably count the wrong ones on all of my fingers and still have enough fingers left over to roll a bowling ball."

"Sounds like a heckuva guy." Harper looked out the front windshield. He hadn't realized that they were almost back to the city already. He looked at his watch. 4:15 p.m. local time. Then he remembered another thing he had wanted to ask Mercedes. "Hey, I heard John say something about a guy named 'Latin Crimen' back there. Who's that? Is he part of your team?"

"Latin? No – well – kinda maybe. Depends on what your take on the word *part* is. He's got an interesting look to him. Always wears a fedora and suspenders. Looks like he stepped right out of a 1940s edition of *GQ*. Kinda looks like Edward G. Robinson and Salma Hayek had a love child. And when it comes to Latin, he's not part of the criminal element. He *is* the criminal element. He has been the source of contention between the four of us on several occasions."

"Because he's just that kind of bad?"

"Let's just say that when it comes to getting what he wants, Latin doesn't have a lot of scruples as to how he gets it, and sometimes it can be a little hard to look past that, if ya know what I mean."

"Then why stay in cahoots with him?" Big James questioned as he realized that the criminal element description Mercedes had given of Latin Crimen sounded an awful lot like his own self.

"Two reasons. Number one, his results are unparalleled by anything or anyone else. Number two, John Watkins – the weathervane for all that is good and holy in this world – thinks the world of the guy. You'd think the two of them were long-lost frat brothers the way they carry on with each other sometimes."

"Hmm, yeah," Harper started and then stopped for a second. "I guess if the results are fruitful, though, you really have to take the bad with the good."

"Yeah," she sighed, "and that's pretty much what we do. Use him as a means to an end."

"Heads up, gang," Big James alerted, "we're approaching 'Casa Grande James', as the locals call it, in just about T-minus ten seconds."

Mercedes and Harper saw that they were riding up a ridge that overlooked the north side of the city. On their left were mostly tree-filled lots with a few dilapidated dwellings set far back from the road.

"This view of the city is spectacular," Merc said in awe.

"Don't I know it," Big James acknowledged. "It's like I'm always telling people, if I can just get the ladies to make it this far with me, the rest of the night is a piece of cake." He laughed at his own joke as he turned right into his driveway, a long gravel path that inclined uphill through a dense cluster of trees. After kicking up stone and dirt for about a quarter of a mile, the group came to an opening in the forest that, to the left, revealed a handsome two-story home with a paved circular drive. To the right of the lane was an acre-sized clearing upon which sat the mother lode of all soccer mom minivans and SUVs.

"Great day, son!" Harper exclaimed. "Are these all yours?"

"Bought and paid for, yes sir." He pulled the vehicle to a stop on the circular drive and the trio exited the minivan. "Go ahead on over and check them out if you want to. I'm gonna run in and get a set of keys. I'll be right back."

"Oh, hey," Mercedes said as she turned to face the house. "Is it cool to use your bathroom? About five minutes after we left Chase's place, the urge hit me, and I don't need to tell ya that the roads around here don't necessarily make that situation easily tenable."

"Absolutely, as long as you don't mind the mess. If you *do* mind the mess, please feel free to clean it up until you no longer mind the mess, and then go about your business."

Big James lumbered up the three steps that led to his front

porch. By the time he unlocked the front door, Mercedes was right behind him. He opened the door, stepped aside, and allowed the doctor to gain entrance first.

"Down the hall, first door on the left," he instructed as he watched her move briskly out of sight. He walked into his kitchen and towards the refrigerator. On the wall to the left of the fridge hung an enormous key rack, two feet wide by four feet long. He scanned the twenty-some sets of keys until he spotted the ones for the Astro van. He grabbed them, but then hesitated.

"Eh, better safe than sorry," Big James said to himself as he put the Astro van keys back and grabbed the set marked "box truck".

Upon his return outside, he saw his buddy Harper Rowe walking around the collection of soccer mom vehicles, peering into, literally, every one.

"See anything you like, Harp?"

Harper straightened up to look at his friend, then sidestepped to his right to get a better view of the house. "Yeah, I do – and she's walking down the steps of your front porch as we speak."

Big James did not have to turn around to know what Harper was talking about. "She's a real nice girl, buddy. I don't think you could do any better than her, like, ever."

"Smart, gorgeous, and dangerous. She's like the s'mores of beautiful women."

About that time Mercedes approached the two men and said, "I'd love a grand tour of the grounds, but I'm afraid that will have to wait for the next visit." She pointed to her watch. "Time waits for no man."

"Either of you two ever drive a box truck before?"

"Yeah," they answered simultaneously. Harper added, "I thought we were taking the Astro van, though."

"I was going to, but I'd sure feel like a useless fart if we got it down there to the airfield and that EMP device didn't fit in it. With the box truck, I know we'll have ample room. That's it directly behind you." He tossed the keys to Harper. "I'll let you two fight it out over who gets to drive. I'm gonna go lock up. You need to use the bathroom, Harp?"

"No, I think I'm good here. Thanks, though."

"Ima go lock up, and you two can follow me to the airfield."

"How long of a drive is that from here?" Mercedes asked.

"Fifteen to twenty minutes. Depends on how many traffic lights we catch in town."

Mercedes walked up to Harper with her hand held out, palm up. "Do you mind if I drive? Back home, Danny does almost all of the driving, and when he's not driving it's because we've probably found ourselves in a situation in which we didn't want be in the first place. Who wants to be driving then?"

Without the slightest hesitation, Harper flipped her the keys. "Have at it, my dear. Besides, I haven't had a valid driver's license in years. Not with *my* name on it, at least."

They turned and headed quickly toward the box truck. Merc came up on Harper's right side and smacked him on the butt.

"Do me a favor tonight, sweet cheeks."

"What's that, my lover?" he asked as he put his arm around her shoulder.

"Don't die tonight. I still have so many things that I want to show you."

Gearing Up for the Finale

When they arrived at the hangar, both vehicles pulled to a stop outside the giant opening. Walking out of the bright Rio sunlight into the dim interior, it took their eyes a few seconds to adjust. Soon enough they could see Kinley and Laurie, just to their right, enjoying a passionate kiss.

"Yo, I got next," Big James hollered at them playfully.

John, Sam, and Diego had found the trailer full of weapons and ammo that Gray had dropped off earlier, and they were working in earnest unloading and packing it carefully into the back of Chase's cargo van.

Sloane was driving a forklift, carrying what looked like a space-age engine to a UFO down the rear hatch ramp of the plane that Dragon's Men had flown in.

"Is that the EMP, Doc?" James asked.

"It sure is."

James sauntered his big frame over to Sloane and the forklift. "You ready to load that up, or do you have to do some last minute tinkering with it?"

"Ready to load it, my man. Did you bring your Astro van?"

"No, I thought the better of it. Brought a box truck instead. It's roomier, and it's got a lot better shocks on it than that van does, so when we go off-road it won't jostle your machine around so much."

"Let's do that then."

James Gray broke into full-on run toward the box truck. As he passed Laurie and Kinley on his way out, he yelled without looking at them, "I still got next!"

James made it to the truck, opened the driver's side door, and casually pulled his three-hundred-plus pound body up into the driver's seat. Much to his delight, Mercedes had left the keys in it. After taking a few seconds to catch his breath, he put the truck in gear, backed it into the building, and stopped just a few feet from where Daniel had the forklift readied.

While Danny and Big James loaded the EMP device, Mercedes led Harper up the hatch ramp and into the plane's mid-section. The middle of the plane was definitely the "lounging" section of the aircraft. It was set up like a huge living room complete with multiple couches, recliners, tables, and a big 60" flat-screen television hitched upon the front wall.

"Whoa. Nice set-up you guys got here. This is better than flying Delta Airlines."

"Yeah, we use it for multiple purposes. But, ya know, there's one purpose that I, personally, have never used it for, but always wanted to."

"And what exactly might that be?" Harper encouraged.

"Maybe a little taste of things to come?"

Not needing a second invitation, Harper moved in for a follow-up appointment with the good doctor.

John and Hawk were poring over the inventory of the trailer that they were currently relocating to the back of Chase's van. "I guess this must be what it looks like under the tree on Christmas morning at militia houses all around the world. We got rockets, rocket launchers, grenades, grenade launchers, some C-4, a ground-to-air missile launching kit, assault rifles, handguns, and – a buttload of knives?"

Watkins looked at Hawk and shrugged. "I don't know."

"They're for Harper," Big James said. John and Hawk were so engrossed in combing through the contents of the trailer that they had failed to notice the presence of Big James Gray in their midst.

"Harper?" Hawk asked a bit befuddled. "Awww, don't tell me that dope is bringing a knife to a gunfight."

"Well, if it makes you feel any better, he's bringing guns to a gunfight as well. It's just that outside of his deadly chemical friend, TINA, he prefers knives and daggers to the loudness, and oft times inaccuracy, of a loaded firearm."

"Tina? Whozzat? He got 'imself another woman on the side somewhere?"

"No, no, no. TINA's not a woman. TINA's a deadly chemical combination that Harper uses quite frequently to take down his targets – well, back when he was in the taking down targets business."

Still not having a clear idea as to what James was talking about, Hawk just nodded knowingly. "Well, that's a good thing then because I think our girl might have a thing for your boy.

"Yeah, they seem to have taken quite a shine to each other." And since Big James was pretty sure he was the only one that saw Harper and Mercedes sneak away onto the big plane, he took it upon himself to change the subject before anyone else noticed that they were gone.

"Let me give you a hand with that GTA launching kit. We can just set it off to the side here, and I will load it into my van when we're ready to move out. Also, be careful with those two boxes back there."

Hawkins turned around to see two cardboard boxes marked "FRAGILE" which were stacked on top of each other toward the back of the trailer. He climbed in to retrieve them. As he delicately picked up the top box he queried, "What's in this? More explosives?"

"Night vision goggles. Very expensive ones, at that."

"We've got night vision gogs on the plane there."

"Yeah, but not like these," Gray countered. "These are state of the art, buddy. They'll automatically adjust to your eyes. It's like you're wearing prescription glasses with night vision."

"What? No way," said a disbelieving Hawkins.

"Oh, yeah. Try a pair on, and tell me I'm lying."

John and Sam carefully pulled open the top of the box. They each retrieved a set of goggles and handed a third to Diego. Meanwhile, Big James described another unique feature that these night specs offered.

"You know how with night vision goggles, when somebody shines a bright light in your direction, it momentarily blinds you?"

"Yeah," the trio answered as they pulled the apparatus over their heads and down onto their eyes.

"These adjust instantaneously to any sudden lights that may appear in your immediate vicinity."

The three men hit the power buttons located on the side of the goggles and watched as the dimly-lit hangar took on a facade of green and then, just like their big buddy had predicted, their vision turned crystal clear.

"What the–" Hawk started.

"*Puta merda*," Diego exclaimed with his usual big smile.

"Whoa, dude, beefcake wasn't lyin'. This is like opium clear." Hawkins pushed the night vision specs onto his forehead and yelled at Sloane to come over and check them out. "This is unreal. Most night vision mechs always have that weird green fog going on when you're looking through them."

"Not these, huh?" Danny carefully pulled the night vision goggles into place and tapped the power button on the side. As advertised, he could see everything 20/20. "So, Big James, let me ask you a question. If we survive the night, do we get to keep these?"

"For the type of cabbage that we might have coming our way,

yes, you can." Gray paused for a moment and then said, "I'll tell ya what, if you do get killed in battle tonight, you can also keep them because, I don't know about your squad, but I, for one, don't intend on going around post-siege and looting corpses for these things."

"I guess it's about time to get suited up and run through things one more time," came a female voice from behind them. The five men turned to see that Kinley and Laurie had joined them from the corner of the building.

"We've got a few more things to haul out of here and onto your van. Then we'll get Big James here loaded up, and we should be ready to suit up and get going. In the meantime, you two gotta try these on for size. Easily the coolest thing I've seen in a while." John handed his pair to Kinley, and Sloane gave his to Laurie.

"Anybody seen my partner bee-boppin' around here?" Kinley asked.

Sam looked around. "Yeah, and anybody seen the Doc?"

"Um, yeah, I did," spoke up Big James. "I saw them go up into the plane a few minutes ago. I think she was just going to show him around."

"Yeah, show him around alright," Sloane said under his breath.

Merc was lost in the moment of Harper's kiss until, for some inexplicable reason, she decided to peek to see if he was just as lost in the moment as she was. A second after she opened her eyes – he opened his. Despite the fact that they were still in mid-smooch, they burst into laugher.

"Sweet doin's," said Harper. "Hang on. We must do something about your hair. You have a bit of a hairdo going on." He reached up and started messing around with her golden mane.

While he was getting her hair back to some semblance of normal, she pulled him in tight and pressed her forehead against his. "Please don't die tonight, Harper Rowe. I cannot remember the last time I have had a connection like this with anybody, let alone an attractive man anybody."

"You know what the crazy thing is, babe?"

"What's that, lover?"

"It would seem like tonight would be a big hurdle for us to clear in our new-found relationship. But in reality," Harper could not resist the proximity of his eyes to hers. He gave her butterfly kisses and finished his thought, "if we get through tonight, it's just a gateway to a hundred other hurdles that we'll have to clear if we want to pursue this down the road."

"Did I tell you that I ran track in high school?"

"Not yet."

"I did. I did indeed. Care to venture a guess as to what my specialty was?"

"Well, now, I will venture my guess to be–" and for theatrics he rubbed his chin and looked up at the ceiling, "the hurdles?"

"You got it, big boy."

Suddenly they heard footsteps coming toward them from the back of the plane.

"To be continued. Now, come with me," and she led him forward by the hand to yet another part of the plane. The personal storage section held multiple walk-in closets along with five different sets of dressers and bureaus. She took him to one of the smaller dressers and opened the top drawer. Inside of it were what looked like twenty or thirty small metal pill containers.

Just as she reached in and grabbed a handful, Hawkins stuck his head through the open doorway. "Whatchoo two up to?"

"Just showing Harper around. Figured I'd grab a handful of these while we were up here," Mercedes held up several of the small metal containers.

"And what are these again?" Harper asked quietly.

"Those," Hawk took the liberty of answering, "are what's going to protect our coms from being turned into toast when John sets off that EMP device later on tonight. Those little things are gonna be what help give us a leg up in this evening's competition."

"Cool."

"Hey, Merc, the boss sent me up here to get the bulletproof long johns for the rest of everybody. You know where they at? I thought they's in the back, but I'll be dumb if I can find 'em."

"Right next to you in that closet," she pointed to Hawk's right.

He cracked open the door to a big walk-in closet and glanced inside.

"There y'are, ya little turkeys." He flipped on the light switch, stepped into the closet and out of sight. Merc took this fleeting moment alone with Harper to steal one last kiss.

"Hey, Doc, you got your jammies on, or do you need me to grab a set for you?"

She pulled her lips back slowly from Rowe's, savoring the moment for all that it was worth.

"Doc? You still out there?"

"Yes, and yes, I need some."

A few seconds later, Sam emerged from the closet carrying several sets of the "bullet-proof long johns".

"I guess it's time to get ready for the show, y'all."

Go Time

Hawkins hung a pair of the long johns up against one of the hangar walls as he prepared to demonstrate their effectiveness to the others. He took four steps back from his target, got behind a makeshift protective barrier and proceeded to empty a clip from an AK-47 into the garb.

The bullets bounced off harmlessly. When Hawkins had finished firing the rounds, he waved everyone up to take a look at the results. He pulled the outfit off the wall and held it up to reveal absolutely no bullet holes in it.

"Now to see what kind of damage the wall incurred." He motioned to Diego to come check it out. "Tell the good people whatcha see, or should I say, whatcha don't see."

The short Portuguese man walked up to the wall, examined it, ran his fingers across it, and reported, "Ees fine. Thee wall ees fine."

"As advertised, gang. And I can give you several testimonials myself about how well this stuff works. It's saved my beautiful black butt more times than I care to admit."

"How the science of it all works is far beyond the comprehension of my mind," John admitted, "but it works, it doesn't chafe, and it's machine washable. The price was steep, but as far as I'm concerned, it was well worth it."

Laurie Chase looked around at everyone. If any of them were not ready for the upcoming battle ahead, they sure did not look like it. Except for Harper and Mercedes, everyone was strapped to the nines with various sorts of weapons. The group really looked like a small army.

"Okay, gather 'round, everyone. Let's go over this one last time," Chase instructed. "Big James, you and Diego will be set up in your van about two miles prior to where the supply truck will exit off the main road. Diego, you know what that truck looks like, so as soon as you see it pass, give us the word. From that point the two of you will take off to your station on the fence perimeter. Clear?"

"Clear as a bell."

"John, you'll be in the box truck with the EMP. I think it's going to be too hard to hide that thing off the side of the road. You'll need to hang back even further than Big James and Diego. Once Diego gives the sign that the truck is en route, you come on in. Keep your distance, obviously, until you see us taking the truck."

"Totally understood."

"The rest of us will be in my van or the black jeep. We'll hide my van off the road, and all of us will lay in wait. Mercedes, you'll have the black jeep pulled off the side of the road with the hood up. It'll be up to you to flag that truck down to a stop. You're a hot chick," Laurie winked at her. "I don't think you'll have too much of a problem."

"Diego, my man," Harper piped up, "is the driver by himself in the cab? Or is someone riding in the passenger's seat?"

"Driver rides alone. Usually four or five helpers in thee back of thee truck. They weell be armed," Diego looked around at his cohorts and smiled, "but not like thees."

"As soon as the truck stops, we move on it. Mercedes, you'll take the driver. The rest of us will come up from behind and take the men in the back. Now, I cannot overemphasize how utterly important it is that we don't go shooting the truck all to pieces when we commandeer it. It's going to be hard enough to get Harper past the guards as it is. If the truck is all riddled with bullet holes, that's probably going to be more than we will be able to explain away."

The team nodded in understanding.

"Once we take the truck, I'll bring my van up, we'll transfer everything we can out of it and onto the back of the truck. We've got two minutes to do this. Whatever's not loaded after two minutes gets left behind."

"Why two minutes, Laurs?" Big James asked.

"Again, it comes down to appearances. With Harper driving, I don't want to raise any suspicions by the truck showing up fifteen minutes late."

"Roger that, boss."

"Does everybody have one of these?" Watkins held up the little metal box that would insulate everyone's coms from the EMP blast. Everyone held theirs up in the air as affirmation.

"As soon as Harper gets us past the initial guards, John, that's your cue to get the EMP device into position. Give us a ten-second countdown so we will have time to get our coms out and protected. Once that EMP goes off and the lights go out, we put on the night vision goggles, re-insert our coms, and we attack."

"I'll hop in your van, Laurie, and drive it in. So make sure you leave the keys in it," John reminded her.

"During the attack, let's keep the chatter going so we know who needs help and how far we've advanced. Other than that," Chase sighed, "we're ready to go."

"It's go time, people," Sloane yelled. "Let's kick it!"

They loaded up. The familiar trio of Chase, Devereaux, and Rowe hopped into Chase's cargo van. Mercedes, Daniel, and Samuel were in the black jeep which, despite the incredible heat, had to be driven all closed up because three people strapped with varying degrees of weapons riding down the road in an open jeep would draw too much unwanted attention. John Watkins scrambled into the box truck. Diego and Big James climbed into his minivan.

The four-vehicle caravan pulled out of the hangar, and started their trek to their destination.

Bad Landing

The flight from Rio de Janeiro to Dresden, Germany was a long one – about sixteen hours total. Fortunately, the trip was on Tito del Fuento's private jet so there was plenty to keep him, his wife, and their three kids occupied.

They had flown a little over eleven hours so far, and all five of them, as well as a handful of security guards, were more than happy to hear the pilot's voice come over the intercom to inform them that they were starting their descent to refuel at Amsterdam Airport Schiphol. Everyone was ready to stretch their legs and get some air, and an hour in Amsterdam was always a good time.

All souls were buckled in. Sitting next to a window, Tito looked out to see if he could catch a view of the accompanying plane that was carrying his hundred best men. He did not spot it right off, as it was flying below his jet and was momentarily lost in a cloud bank until it emerged into his line of sight. He breathed a small sigh of relief as he saw the blinking lights of the craft cut through the night sky, then he leaned back into his seat, took his wife's hand, and waited for the landing.

Soon the pilot's voice came over the loudspeaker to inform everyone that they were circling around to runway 11. The second plane would be coming in right next to them on runway 12.

The drug lord was feeling good. And really, what was there not to feel good about? He was getting ready to make a deal with some very influential people in the drug world, and he was going to make a lot of money doing it. He daydreamed about the power he would be wielding in South America very soon. It was going to be a great day.

Tito had gotten plenty of rest during the flight, so he was ready to go get this done and get back home to celebrate with the rest of his men. He checked the clocks on the wall of his jet: local time in Amsterdam was 12:23 a.m.; local time in Rio was 7:23 p.m.

He watched as the lights from the ground came up quickly. "Just a few more minutes," he assured his family in his native tongue. He looked out the window and saw his second plane descending rapidly toward its runway.

Tito gave a peculiar look; he thought for a moment that he did not see the landing gear come down. But then the plane banked to the right for its approach run and he lost sight of what had caught his eye. No worries. All of his mechanics, whether they were for his planes or his vehicles, were the best that South America had to offer. He was sure it was just the darkness playing tricks on his eyes.

Still, he kept staring out the window to be sure he saw the landing gear deploy on the second plane. It was just about thirty seconds until touchdown, and del Fuento was searching for his cell phone to confirm with the pilot that everything was okay. He was sure he had put it in his pocket, but he could not seem to feel it there. Now the second plane was twenty seconds from touchdown.

Turning to his wife, Mitra, he asked her, "*Cadê meu celular, Mitra?*"

Mitra shrugged; she did not know where his phone was. Looking around at her children buckled in the seat beside her, she saw it. "*Ah, as crianças têm isso, Tito!*"

Del Fuento snatched the phone out of his youngest son's hand

and frantically dialed the other plane's pilot. Just seconds from landing, Tito was sure he did not see any landing gear. The co-pilot answered on the first ring, "*Ei, Tito, vamos aterrar.*"

"*Levante-se! Levante-se!*" he yelled at them to pull up. "*Seu trem de pouso não está funcionando!*" Tito screamed into the phone trying to tell the co-pilot that the landing gear was not working. But it was for naught. The plane touched down onto runway 12 and skidded on its belly for a hundred yards before bursting into flames.

"*Não!*" Tito screamed as he watched helplessly from his own jet.

Then it hit him. Was his own plane going to suffer the same fate? He saw the ground coming up fast. He clutched his wife and said a quick prayer, "*Jesus, salve-nos!*" He nearly wet himself with fear; when he felt the landing gear of his own plane hit the runway safely, he began crying like a baby.

Moments later his jet taxied to a stop. Fire and rescue were on the scene in no time and they took Mitra and his boys off the plane first. Del Fuento's security team was already making phone calls, trying to find out what had happened.

Tito sat in his seat, his face was as pale as a ghost. Over and over he repeated, "*O que aconteceu? O que aconteceu?*" What happened? What happened?

What happened was Diego del Fuento and Laurie Chase.

What happened was that Tito del Fuento's hundred best men had just been turned into charcoal briquettes. That is what happened.

When Laurie and Diego had sabotaged the landing gear, they made sure that, to the pilot and co-pilot in the cockpit, everything looked just fine. The instrument landing system showed no warning signs. No one on that plane had any idea that there was a problem until it was too late.

It was, indeed, a job well done.

The Sunset Before the Storm

For Laurie Chase, the last eighteen months had been a test of her will, fortitude, mental acuity, and heart. Eighteen months of researching, investigating, experimenting, verifying, planning, and preparing would soon rise to crescendo. Seeking justice or exacting revenge, call it what you like, Laurie Chase was going to get herself some tonight.

Everyone was in place for the first part of the plan: taking the delivery truck that would help them gain access into Tito del Fuento's drug plantation.

John Watkins and the box truck were nestled discreetly amongst several hundred other vehicles of varying shapes and sizes in a shopping center parking lot.

Approximately a mile down the same road, Big James Gray and Diego del Fuento were sitting in Gray's Dodge Caravan at a roadside service station. The constant traffic pulling in and out was the perfect cover for the two of them to sit there, unnoticed, while keeping a watchful eye out for the delivery truck.

About three miles down from the lookout duo was a wide gravel and dirt road that branched off to the right of the main thoroughfare. Just before the turnoff, in the parking lot of a dilapidated old chapel, a white cargo van and a black jeep sat side by side with their driver's sides adjacent to each other. Since they were the only two that were not armed to the teeth like walking military depots, Mercedes and Harper stood outside of the vehicles while the other four stayed inside, trying not to attract undue attention.

"I don't want to rush things," said Sloane out the open driver's side window of the jeep, "but I wish the delivery truck would hurry up because I am about to spontaneously combust from this heat."

"Don't you have AC in that thing?" Chase asked.

"AC!" Hawkins screeched from the passenger's seat. "We in a black jeep that's closed up and sittin' still, and we wearin' about twenty pounds of ordnance in temperatures that are what uppity white folk refer to as," and he changed his voice to sound like a British aristocrat, "a bit sweltering, old chap." Then back to normal Hawkins, "So, we could have Siberia's finest blowin' inside this mutha, and we'd still be meltin' like the Wicked Witch o' the West in a wet tee shirt contest."

"Eloquently put, my good man," Devereaux replied from his respective passenger's seat.

"Well, instead of just sitting around and thinking about it," said Harper, "why don't we go over the plan for the truck one more time."

"That's a good idea, Harper," Watkins' voice crackled through their coms.

"Okay. I'll start," Big James began. "Very soon the delivery truck is going to come past where we are. Diego is going to identify it, and, once he does, the plan will be set in motion. He and I will leave here and make our way to the perimeter fence on the west side of the compound."

"Right," Laurie went next, "and once we get the heads up that the truck is on its way here, the six of us will head down the road to the attack point. We'll hide my van out of sight. We'll position the black jeep on the side of the road, hood up, Mercedes next to it as the damsel in distress. The other five of us will be lying in wait.

"When the truck comes by, Mercedes will flag it down. Once it stops, Mercedes will take out the driver, and the rest of us will take out the other members of the unit that are holed up in the back of the ride. Remember, guys and girls, use your silencers and make this vehicle seizure as clean as possible."

"While that's going on," interjected Watkins, "I'm going be exiting my location and heading to the attack point. I'm hoping to time my arrival so that I can give you any extra support you might need in commandeering the truck. I'll also be there to assist you in moving the weapons and ammo from Laurie's van into the back of the truck which will, hopefully, be enough to get you guys out of there in the two-minute time frame we're working with."

"And that, boys and girls, is the plan."

"I have a question," said Harper.

"Okay."

"What if the truck doesn't stop?"

No one said anything for a few seconds, but then Mercedes said reassuringly, "Don't worry, baby. That truck's gonna stop."

"Hey. Hey, you guys," Diego spoke up excitedly. "Be quiet."

Everyone was quiet in anticipation, as they all assumed that Diego had spotted the truck. Big James was scanning the highway trying to see the rig for himself, but saw nothing resembling a big supply truck. He looked over at Diego, who was not even looking at the highway. He was looking at the radio.

"What?" he asked his partner.

"Leesten."

Big James had the radio on, but it was turned down so low that he could barely hear it. Between the com in his ears and talking to the others, he was completely oblivious to the sound.

"Turn eet up?"

"Yeah, yeah," Big James reached down and adjusted the volume button. It was a Portuguese news broadcast that was interrupting the usual programming. Both men listened intently to the breaking news story out of Amsterdam about an airplane that had crashed upon landing at the Amsterdam-Schiphol Airport just minutes ago.

"Hey, does somebody mind telling the rest of us what's going on there?" John asked from his location in the shopping center parking lot.

Nothing but silence filled the coms for the next few moments, and then Diego said excitedly, "Meess Laurie, turn on the 1440 AM station. Eet's Tito's plane weeth hees other men."

"What? Already?" She turned on the radio in her van and tuned it to the designated station. Daniel Sloane did the same thing in the jeep. He and Hawkins started listening to the announcer, but of course neither of them understood a word of what he was saying.

"You know any Portuguese, Danny?"

"No, but I do know someone that does." Sloane leaned out the window of the jeep. "Hey, Harper, come over here and tell us what this guy's saying."

Harper shuffled over to the jeep and stuck his head inside to hear the radio a little better. "Turn it up a bit?"

At this point, everyone except for John Watkins was listening to the broadcast. He did not bother tuning in his radio because he did not know Portuguese, and he figured it was just a matter of time before the others clued him in as to what was going on. He was right.

One by one, the other team members began to reveal the news report. Big James was first. He looked at Diego and slapped him on the back. "You did it, little man! Your former amigo's done gone bye-bye, buddy."

Chase was not far behind. "Yes, yes, yes!" She exchanged an exaggerated high five with Devereaux.

Dr. Mercedes Lara leaned in through the driver's side window of the van and wrapped her arms around Chase's neck and hugged her joyfully, "Ya did it, girlfriend. Chalk one up for the good guys."

"The first of many tonight, to be sure," Kinley reached over and squeezed Chase's hand.

"What's everyone celebrating again?" Sloane looked to Harper.

"Del Fuento's plane – the one with all his stooge henchmen on it – the one that Laurie and Diego sabotaged – it crashed and burned in Amsterdam. The report is saying that there do not appear to be any survivors."

"Amsterdam?" questioned Hawk. "I thought it was supposed to be in Dresden."

"Ees my fault, guys. I forgot to factor een the refueling stop," Diego laughed.

"Tell ya what," Harper said as he stood up from leaning against the black jeep, "hearing this gives me hope that our plan for tonight might work out after all."

"What? You don't think my plan is going to work?"

Harper shrugged. "Let's just say that I've been doing a lot of praying about it."

"You are such a jackass!" Laurie Chase retorted.

"Arguably, yes, but I think it says a lot about my character that I've been on board with this whole thing from its genesis in spite of my belief regarding its validity."

"Truth," Hawkins recognized.

"Well, then, that just goes to show you that you're not just a jackass, but you're a stupid jackass, at that."

"Also truth," Hawk observed.

"Come on, gang," urged Watkins, "a win's a win. Del Fuento is reeling right now, and after we raid his compound tonight, destroy everything he has, and make off with his money, that guy's going to be ripe for the picking when he gets back to town. Now let's stay focused on the task at hand and get out of here with a win of our own."

"Absolutely right," agreed Big James. He and Diego were still listening to the radio broadcast, but their eyes were back on the road as they scanned diligently for the approaching delivery truck.

Harper walked up to Mercedes. He switched off his com and motioned for her to do the same. When she did, Harper held out his hand to her and asked, "May I?"

She was not sure what he was asking her permission to do, but she smiled obligingly and took his hand. He led her away from the vehicles to a more secluded part of the church parking lot. "What are we doing?" she finally asked.

"Well," he began in earnest, "after tonight I have no idea when I'm going to see you again so I thought that maybe we could share a sunset together." She blushed slightly at the gesture, but letting go of his hand, she slid into his arms as they turned to look at the horizon and watch the sun set slowly out of sight.

In a soft voice, she said, "You know, I've developed a certain set of feelings for you that I'm not used to having for someone so quickly. And of course I don't know what the future holds, and I do know that after tonight we will be going in different directions. But I can promise you this: from the moment we part, I will be doing everything I can to get back with you again as soon as humanly possible."

He reached up and touched her cheek. She turned her head and looked him in the eyes. He smiled and asked her, "These feelings that you've developed for me – could they be love feelings?"

"Well," she smiled back, "I'm not sure about all the particulars involved in the entire love process with a guy like you, but I would have to say yes, for as much as it is realistically possible to love someone that you met twenty-four hours ago, my feelings for you are definitely on an avalanche-like course toward the love spectrum."

"Good. That's good, and I'll tell ya why."

"I think I might already know why it's good, but okay."

"No, you know why it's good for you. I'm going to tell you why it's good for me. See, I'm thirty-five years old, and I have never really been in love before. Now, there are people that I love, to be sure, – like Kinley, Big James, and yes, even Laurie – but as far as being *in* love with someone, no ma'am. So, I think I had gotten to a point where I wasn't even really sure that I would be able to recognize the actual symptoms of being in love with someone, or if I would be able to tell if someone was in love with me back. I have good news, though. Just now, when we were looking at the sunset together, I thought to myself, 'I think this is how it feels to be in love with someone,' or at least the beginning part of the process."

"Really?"

"Yes, really. So, I can say to you without any hesitation or misgiving, my feelings for you are on an avalanche-like course toward the love spectrum, as well. Still, I guess I have to ask, how good are you at long distance relationships, and – do you like to travel?"

"We're both resourceful adults. I'm sure we will find new and creative ways to get together. Besides, don't you ever think that you'll be able to clear your name in the whole Paul Michaels fiasco?"

Harper pursed his lips and shook his head in uncertainty. "I don't think so. In order for me to do that, I would have to be able to find someone that knew what Paul Michaels was doing and could vouch for the actions we took. I just don't think such a person exists. The only other way to clear my name is to tell them the truth, and that would mean that Kinley would be the one that would be going away for some hard time. Plus, they'd probably throw me in the cell next to him as an accomplice. Not to mention all the money that they've spent in their efforts to try to capture me over the last year and a half. Pretty sure that would come up at some point."

"It doesn't matter," Mercedes said. "If I had to fly to the North Pole every month just to meet you in a snow tunnel for thirty minutes, I would do that."

"Oh gosh. Don't say that. Can you imagine the field day that the environmental folk would have with that story? They'd be on every news show in America saying, 'The polar ice caps are melting at an even more alarming rate than they were before! By this time next week we will all be dead because the Greenhouse Effect – which is something we totally made up in one of our club meetings, but now we have apparently lied it into existence – has gotten out of control, and we can't stop it!' Of course, you and I would go our separate ways, and nothing would happen, and the environmentalists would look even kookier than usual, but then the following month when we got back together in our little North Pole snow tunnel, the whole bat-daffy scene would play out all over again."

A mischievous grin crept across Dr. Lara's lips. "I don't know if I could help myself, doll. A chance to be with you *and* make the environmentalists look like lame brained apes? That might be more than this girl can resist."

They shared a laugh, then that was the end of their secluded session. Sloane hollered out his window at them, "Doc, Harper, it's time to roll, kids. Truck's on its way."

"Here we go." The two of them sprinted back toward their vehicles.

Just as Dr. Lara was climbing into the jeep, Harper yelled, "See ya 'round downtown, gang!" He turned his com back on and scrambled into the back of Chase's van.

TAKING THE TRUCK

As planned, Chase had driven her van far enough off the dirt and gravel road so that it was out of sight. Along with Kinley and Harper, she made her way back to within about twenty yards of the road where the trio found Sloane and Hawkins already holed up in a secluded ditch.

The Rio sky was nearly consumed with darkness, so it would be more than just a little difficult for the truck driver to spot the quintet in their current position. All five of them had their weapons at the ready: handguns drawn, silencers on, safeties off.

As for the sixth member of the troop, Mercedes was standing in front of the jeep with her hood up and hazard lights flashing. She had positioned it toward the right side of the road, making sure that it blocked enough of the road to make it very difficult for the big delivery truck to just roll on past her.

Her nine mil was tucked into the back of her pants waistband. Her flashlight was in her right hand. She was ready.

"Okay, Doc, here we go. I see the headlights coming your way now."

"I see it. Just tell me what to say when it's time, Harper."

"Don't worry about that. I won't leave ya hangin', Merc. Just focus on getting the truck to stop."

The truck was close enough now for her to start trying to flag it down. She stepped out from behind the jeep and started waving her hands frantically. "What's the word for 'hey'?"

"*Ei*," Harper said.

"*Ei!*" she started screaming. The truck kept up its speed, causing Mercedes' screams to become louder and her arm waving more frantic. She added jumping up and down to the mix.

"Wow," commented Hawk, "I don't know what the truck driver can see, but from here that is a nice look. Her jumping up and down, the tight black tee shirt. That's a real nice look."

"Yeah, it is," Harper agreed. "I just hope the driver's not gay."

Either the jumping did the trick, or the truck driver finally got close enough to see just how beautiful the panicked woman before him really was. Whatever the case, he was persuaded to hit his brakes and bring the truck to a halt.

Mercedes wasted no time moving to the truck to approach the driver.

On her way there, Harper said over the com, "The words for 'can you help me, please' are '*Você pode ajudar-me, por favor*'."

The doctor did her best to parrot the words to the truck driver. Sticking his head out the window of the cab, he asked, "*Como chegaste aqui?*"

"He just asked you what you're doing out here. Let's see if, perchance, this guy speaks English. Say, '*Eu sou uma turista americana perdido. Você fala inglês?*' and see what happens."

Merc had no idea what she was saying, but she did her best to repeat Harper's words. The truck driver's response was just what they wanted to hear.

"Ha! I thought I detected an American accent in your voice." It seemed that his English was rather polished.

"Oh, thank God," Mercedes feigned gratitude incredibly well. "My Portuguese is just slightly better than awful."

"Is okay," he assured. "How did you get out here? This road is private property."

"I don't even know where I am," Mercedes laughed foolishly. "My GPS doesn't know where I am either, apparently. It told me to turn onto this road, and then it told me to turn around. I was looking for someplace to do that, and that's when the motor shut off. I have no idea what to do with a jeep that doesn't run. Do you think you could look at it for me?"

"Well, I'm on a delivery schedule–"

Merc did not give him a chance to finish with his excuse. She put out her lower lip, flipped her hair just so, shined the flashlight to illuminate her pouty face, and said in the most seductive voice she could muster, "Please?"

She could tell that he was thinking about it, and she knew just the right thing to say to convince him to step out of the truck and come with her. She ran her hands seductively up the black tee shirt she was wearing, winked at the driver, and salaciously said, "I can definitely make it worth your while. A girl in a situation like I find myself in can be very appreciative, if you understand what I'm saying."

It was more than the dumb sucker could resist. "Okay," he agreed as he opened the cab door and climbed down out of the rig. It was not until then that she realized just how big the man really was. He towered over her by a good ten inches and appeared to outweigh her by eighty to a hundred pounds. He also appeared to be in decent shape, with a flat stomach, toned arms, and broad shoulders. He could have been attractive in an insanely different situation. But then he opened his mouth.

"Hey, I've got five guys riding in the back of my truck. Them, too?"

"Five guys? You don't say." She wanted to be sure that the other members of her team knew just how many baddies they were going to have to deal with in the back of the truck.

"Oh, the more, the merrier," Mercedes sounded extremely convincing. She took the flashlight and shined it into the engine.

"Now, when the engine cut out on me, I got out and lifted the hood, and there was some smoke coming off the engine back there. I'm afraid that I'm just so small I couldn't really get a good look at it. Can you look back there for me? See if you can see anything that might be wrong?" She took her hand that was not holding the flashlight and began running her nails up and down his back. "Such a big, strong man."

He was so mesmerized by Mercedes that when he leaned into the engine to look for the problem, he had not a clue of what was about to befall him.

"May I see your flashlight?" he asked.

"Absolutely," she answered. With a single, swift motion, she bashed her big metal flashlight against the base of his skull. She was surprised at how little damage it seemed to do.

He grunted slightly and grabbed the back of his head. "What the he–"

Merc grabbed the hood and slammed it down on him as hard as she could, to much greater effect. He cried out in pain, and she thought she heard some ribs crack. She lifted the hood and slammed it down a second time across his back, thinking that this would slow him down enough to allow her to put a bullet into his brain without much resistance.

However, when she lifted the hood up after the second slam, the goon used all of his remaining strength to make a wild lunge at her. His big arm wound around her waist, but Mercedes was able to fend him off by slamming her flashlight across the top of his head. He fell to the ground, face first. His last-gasp attempt had little impact on Mercedes, but it did knock the gun out of her waistband and across the road somewhere.

"Oh, are you serious?" she said in complete frustration. She turned to look for her gun, but discovered that she had broken the flashlight's bulb in the fray. Now she could see nothing outside the scope of the jeep's headlights.

What she could see, though, was that the truck driver with the great English skills was not giving up without an effort. He was still moaning down on the ground and attempting to get on his hands and knees.

"You have got to be kidding me," Mercedes muttered. Without her gun she could not put this poor mook out of his – or her – misery by putting a bullet into his skull. So she took the only course of action that she could think of on the spot.

Dropping the flashlight onto the road, she stepped around to the left side of the driver, reached down and grabbed the back of his collar with her left hand and the back of his waistband with her right hand. After making sure she had a firm grasp on both places, she lifted the near-motionless man with all her might, took a three-step start, and used his head as a battering ram, smashing it crown-first into the jeep's chrome bumper. It hit with so much force that it knocked the body out of her clutches.

"Hey," she said completely breathless, "are you still awake down there?"

No response.

Mercedes leaned over with her hands on her knees. She pushed the motionless frame with her foot, at which point she saw blood coming from his ears. If he was not dead yet, it would not be long until he was.

"Tough break, perv." Still trying to catch her breath, she said, "Driver's down. Where are you guys?"

Suddenly Merc heard a small smattering of applause coming from some ten feet away. Still breathing heavily, she stood up see her five associates standing there and giving mock cheers for her successful drubbing of the truck driver.

"What the–? How long have you guys been standing there? What did you do with the five people in the back of the truck?"

"When the truck stopped," Sloane answered, "those five morons got out to see what was going on, so we shot them. Took about ten seconds. Then we heard all the commotion coming from up here and came up to see just what it was you had gotten yourself into."

"That was quite impressive," Kin commented.

"Really, we would have stepped in to help, but it looked like you had things pretty much going your way," Harper said. "You've really got quite a bit of aggression pent up in that little body of yours. I was amazed and intimidated by the whole scene, truth be told."

"Why didn't you just shoot the guy?" Chase asked.

"Well," Mercedes shrugged, "you said that you didn't want us shooting up the truck. Just figured I'd get him over here and then do it, but–" and she inhaled deeply to finally catch her breath, "when he asked me about his five friends in the back of the truck – I don't know – I just wanted to hurt him. I guess I got a little careless because he did knock my gun away from me during our fracas.

"Speaking of which–" The doctor walked over to Harper to borrow his flashlight and started looking around for her weapon.

"All right, people, we've got plenty of work to do here in a very short time, so let's get to it."

GETTING PAST THE GATE

Chase left the scene to fetch her van while the others took the bodies of the truck workers and carried them off the road and out of sight. Harper hopped up into the cab of the delivery truck and started looking for some sort of paperwork that would tell him just what was being delivered.

"Hey, Diego, I'm looking at the delivery manifest. When I get to the main gate, what am I going to need to do with this?"

"Show eet to the guard, he weell sign eet, and geeve eet back to you."

"That's it?"

"That's eet. Believe me, I know. I used to be thee guy that met thee trucks for years. I know thee dreell. Eet's why I'm going to walk you through eet weeth no pro'lems."

"Then we're golden."

"Like a globe," Kinley chimed in.

Watkins drove the box truck up to the scene just as Chase pulled her van back onto the road.

"Good timing, boss," Sloane said as he moved into position to help guide Laurie as she backed the van up to the truck. Once the van was in place, all seven members of the team began removing the hoard of weapons from the rear of the van and into the back of the delivery truck's trailer. The trailer was only about two-thirds full with supplies that were being delivered to del Fuento's compound, so there was plenty of room for the stockpile of munitions. Due to phenomenal teamwork, the total transfer time was less than two minutes.

Once the task was completed, Laurie, Kinley, Daniel, Mercedes, and Samuel hopped up into the back of the trailer.

"I'll try to drive gently," Harper said to the troop just before he shut the trailer doors and locked them in. He then turned to John, who was standing about three feet behind him, and said, "I guess this is it."

"Good luck, Harper," Watkins said as he shook Harper's hand.

"Luck is for people who don't know what they're doing, John." Harper released from the handshake and patted Watkins on the shoulder. "Besides, I have Diego to walk me through this whole process. I'm practically having to fight off being over-confident. Still," and he began making his way to the front of the rig, "don't hang back too long with that blackout bomb. The sooner you set that thing off, the sooner we can get this party started."

Harper waved a temporary goodbye to John and then climbed into the truck. A Marlboro ball cap was on the front seat, so he picked it up and put it on. He slid his gun into a small pocket in the driver's side door, started up the truck, hit the lights, and started the remainder of the drive toward del Fuento's place.

Meanwhile, John Watkins moved the black jeep out of sight. Knowing that he would be coming back for Chase's van after the deployment of the EMP bomb, he then pulled it off the road just slightly. From there, he hopped back behind the wheel of the box truck and waited for the moment when it would be his turn to move into action.

"Nervous, kid?" Kinley asked from the back of the truck.

"I do know that there are a lot of key elements to this plan of attack," Harper answered, "but if I can't get us past the security gate and onto the property, then none of that will really matter. So, yes, I do realize that the pressure is on Diego and me to pull this off."

"You're gonna do great, Harp. I wouldn't want anyone else up there in that cab doing this job. You're the coolest cucumber in the entire produce section, buddy. You do have a gun, though, right? You know – just in case."

"Roger that, Kin," Harper answered his buddy and then asked, "Hey, Big Time, where are you and Diego?"

"We are in position at our pre-appointed area of attack."

"Hey, those surface-to-air launchers are pretty heavy, aren't they? How are you two going to be able to move that and the missiles at the same time? Are you going to have to make two trips or what?"

"I have two makeshift sleds in the back of the van. I have the launcher tied to one and four missiles tied to the other one, and we will transport them that way. If I can't hit those birds with four missiles then my window of opportunity for a clean strike will be gone, and more than likely, Diego and I will be dead because I'm sure that our targets will have dropped some sort of payload on us by that point."

"Just remember, big guy, failure is not an option, and since that's the case then thinking about failure is also not an option."

"I'm just going to sit here and think about pie. Which kind of pie – I will not be telling you."

Harper knew that it was time to start getting to the task at hand. "Diego, let's do this."

"We weell do thees, Meester Harper," came the little man's response.

"When I get up here, will the gates be open? Or will I be expected to know a code or show some ID?"

"They are expecting the truck so the front gates weell be open. You weell see a secureety checkpoint just a few yards down the main drive. Thees ees where you weell show your paperwork. Seence you are a deeferent driver, the guy might ask you a few questions."

"Like what?"

"Oh, like, where ees the regular driver," Diego replied. "Meester Harper, do not worry. I weell get you through eet."

"Well, I hope so because I just drove through the front gate, and I'm closing in on that security checkpoint right now."

Instinctively, all five passengers in the back of the truck became tense. Even from his seat in the box truck, John Watkins became a little nervous.

This was it. This was the real deal.

Harper took a deep breath as he pulled the delivery truck to a stop at the security booth. He pulled the Marlboro cap down a little lower as he double checked with Diego, "Hand him the paperwork, right?"

"Hand heem the paperwork."

Harper handed the guy the paperwork. "*Olá, mi amigo.*"

"Tell heem that Tito and Mr. Cruz talked earlier today, and that you have been approved to deleever thees load."

"*Tito e Mister Cruz conversaram hoje cedo,*" Harper said in perfect dialect. "*Foram aprovado para entregar essa carga.*"

"*Você conhece o Senhor Cruz?*"

"He just asked you eef you know Meester Cruz. Tell him you do. Meester Cruz is a tall man weeth a short temper."

"*Sim, senhor Cruz é um homem alto com um pavio curto,*" Harper said as he looked at the guard's face, trying to get a read on how things were going.

He felt a little more at ease when the guard smiled and said, "*Que ele é. Onde está o Hector hoje?*"

"He just asked you where Hector ees," Diego came back. "I know thees Hector. Hector has a wife named Camilla. Tell thee guard that Hector's wife, Camilla, was een a car acceedent today. He ees at thee hospeetal weeth her right now. Ees why you are driving tonight."

Following Diego's lead, Harper said, "*Eu estou dirigindo esta noite porque a mulher do Hector foi em um acidente de carro. Aconteceu esta tarde. Ela provavelmente vai morrer. Hector está com ela agora. É por isso que eu estou dirigindo esta noite.*"

The guard looked at Harper and then back down at the paperwork and then back at Harper.

"*Papelada está em ordem. Diga ao Hector que vou rezar por ele e sua esposa. Pare o caminhão para aquele prédio à sua esquerda.*"

"You are good, Meester Harper. Take your copy of the paperwork from heem, thank heem and pull away to thee beelding to your left. Thees beelding weell have three loading docks coming off of thee front."

Harper looked up ahead and immediately saw the building that Diego was describing.

The security guard handed a copy of the paperwork back to Harper and asked him if he knew where to go to unload, "*Você sabe onde ir para descarregar?*"

"*Eu acho que sim. Aquele prédio ali?*" Harp answered as he pointed to the designated building.

The guard nodded in affirmation. "*Tenha uma boa noite. Por favor diga ao Hector que vamos orar por sua esposa.*" He told Harper to let Hector know that they would be praying for his wife.

"*Obrigado, amigo,*" he thanked the security guard and slowly accelerated toward the appointed area. Once they felt the truck moving forward, everyone in the back of the truck breathed a huge sigh of relief.

"Diego, you were great." Harper exclaimed. "Although, just for the record, I knew what the guy was saying to me. I just needed you to tell me what to say back," and Harp laughed to let Diego that he was just giving him a hard time.

"Alright, everybody, I am on my way up," Watkins said.

"While I'm pulling this rig into position, somebody put together a weapons jacket for me," Harper requested. "Once the lights go out, and I'm back there opening the doors, I'll expect to be heavily armed within ten seconds. For now," Harper emphasized, "off to my left – gosh – I'm looking at anywhere from eighty to a hundred guys that are drinking and dancing and standing around completely oblivious that anything is getting ready to happen. We got some music playing. We got some food cooking on grills. Seriously, if we weren't getting ready to kill these little pricks, I wouldn't mind joining their party."

"Off to your right, you should see a two-story building. It's painted a pale green. Do you see it?" asked Laurie.

"I think so. It's dark, and the lights that are on kind of skew the real-life colors of things, but, yeah, I'm pretty sure that's the building I'm looking at."

"That is the munitions building. It's the one with all the stuff that goes 'BOOM' without too much of an effort. With the lights going out and the five of us back here not having any real sense of bearing where that building is, it's going to be up to you to keep track of its location. When we get out of here, that's the building that we're going to want to light up first. They'll be disoriented and confused from the blackout, so once we hit that building and light up the sky, it's going to be our best opportunity to take out a slew of them. No pressure, but all of this will be up to you."

"Good to know. You'll also be excited to know that I am – here?"

"Me, too," Watkins said as he pulled the box truck into position. "You guys ready?"

"Yes," answered Sloane, "I don't mind telling ya, I'm a little claustrophobic and being shut in this trailer with no lights on is not helping with that at all."

"Yeah, let's go already." Chase instructed.

John Watkins made a quick exit out of the box truck and ran like crazy away from it. After sprinting some two hundred yards, he pulled the detonator for the EMP apparatus from his pocket and said loudly, "Ten seconds, everyone!"

10 –

Everyone began reaching for their protective cases.

9 –

They fished them out of their pockets.

8 –

They opened them up.

7 –

They reached up and removed their coms.

6 –

They nervously fumbled with them for a second.

5 –

They put them in the protective cases.

4 –

They shut the cases.

3 –

Harper pulled his gun out of the driver's side door pocket.

2 –

He looked around one more time to get his geographical bearings.

1 –

Complete darkness.

Checking in with Big James and Diego

While Diego was giving Harper instructions as to what to say to the guard at the security checkpoint, Big James had gotten out of the minivan and unpacked the two sleds. The first sled held the surface-to-air missile launcher, and the second one held the surface-to-air missiles.

Once Harper was past the guard and on his way onto the property, Diego had jumped out of the minivan and joined Big James. They each had hooked a sled up to their shoulders: Big James with the launcher, Diego with the rockets.

While Harper was driving the delivery truck to the specified building, Big James and Diego had started their trek to where they needed to be to set up the missile launcher. The duo moved as quickly as they could. Even at this time of night, the heat was getting to them. They were dripping in sweat. It was stinging their eyes.

"Come on, buddy," Big James said in the most upbeat voice he could muster, "just a little bit further."

To their credit, the only time they stopped was when they heard John Watkins start the countdown to the detonation of the EMP device. They paused just long enough to put their coms in the small protective cases that they had been given, then they were back on the move again.

Big James and Diego did not stop again until they had reached the spot that Laurie Chase had designated on the diorama.

Exhausted and out of breath, the two men put their coms back into their ears.

A few more heavy breaths and Big James informed the others, "Diego and I are setting up the missile launcher."

Total Annihilation

Besides everything going dark, everything also went quiet. The music that had been playing up to the point of the EMP device firing was gone. The yelling, whooping, and loud partying – also gone.

Harper took pains to make as little noise as possible when he opened the driver's side door of the cab. Once his feet hit the ground and he had steadied himself, he put his com back in his ear just in time to hear Big James announce that he and Diego were already in place. Harper hustled back to the doors of the trailer.

"I read ya, Big Boy. Is everybody else back on, too?"

No answer from anyone.

Harper tried to be as quiet as he could while he unlocked the trailer doors, but once he did, he wasted no time in saying, "Hey, put your coms back in, ya mopes. Big James and Diego are in place, and somebody arm me up already! Oh, and the munitions building you're looking for is that way."

Laurie Chase, Kinley Devereaux, Samuel Hawkins, and Daniel Sloane jumped out of the back of the trailer. Each was heavily armed, adorned with night vision goggles, and held an RPG in either hand.

"Merc has your armed outfit. We thought you'd like it best coming from her," Sloane informed him, as he was the last of the quartet out of the back of the truck. Before Harper could speak, object, or form any sort of question, the four of them were gone into the darkness in the direction of the munitions building.

Mercedes climbed out of the trailer about ten seconds later. She put an ordnance jacket equipped with knives, grenades, smoke bombs, ammunition, flash grenades, and a few other deadly novelties across Harper's shoulders and helped him get his arms through the bunglesome attire.

Merc handed him a set of night vision goggles and kissed him quickly. "Gotta go, sweets," and then she was gone, too.

"Big James, Diego, get ready. If those birds in the sky haven't already headed your way because of the blackout, they'll definitely be on the move once–"

And before Rowe could finish his sentence, the munitions building erupted like a small nuclear explosion.

"Aim high, Big Time," Harper said. He climbed into the back of the truck, used the night vision gogs to help him find two armed AK-47s, bounded back onto the ground and began making his way across the two hundred-some yards that separated him from the large throng of confused and disoriented soldiers.

Harp figured he had about thirty to forty seconds of free-firing before he would encounter any return fire and would have to take cover. He secured one AK across his right shoulder and raised the other one up to his left shoulder and prepared to begin his offensive.

"Greetings and salutations, ya cheese ball retards! My name is Harper Rowe!" Harper began firing impartially into the large crowd of del Fuento's men. "Some people believe that there is a reason for everything, well, I'm here to tell ya – I'm that reason!"

Harper did not bother aiming his shots because with a target audience of this size, it did not matter. "Oh, man, this is, like, the easiest video game I've ever played. Ever." Rowe emptied the contents of the first assault rifle, tossed it aside, grabbed the second one off his right shoulder, and continued his incursion.

Before he knew it, Harper had the backing of Laurie Chase and Kinley Devereaux firing at the large throng of drunken soldiers. With the night vision goggles on, the trio could see the effectiveness of their onslaught. The three of them were having such early success that they were actually running out of targets to shoot at. Up to this point, the attack on del Fuento's compound was a complete annihilation.

That, however, was getting ready to change.

The three of them had gotten so caught up in the early success of the attack that they had forgotten about the outer perimeter guards, and now roughly seven of them were flanking the trio and had them well within their sites. In a matter of seconds, Laurie, Kin, and Harper were getting ready to be shot dead.

Suddenly, John Watkins came barrelling onto the scene in Chase's cargo van. He immediately recognized the peril of the situation, gunned the engine, and drove through the band of gunmen like a bowling ball through duck pins. He blindsided the band of shooters at an incredibly high rate of speed and sent them all to an unforeseen and premature death.

In a moment of lucidity, John laughed, "And Watkins picks up the spare!" and then, immediately, back to business with his comment, "Hey, Laurie, don't forget to check your six," he began to drive toward the other members of Dragon's Men.

John looked up into the night sky. He could see the overhead Lockheeds approaching and, presumably, locking onto the threat below.

"How ya doin', Big James?" Johnny asked.

"The launcher's been anchored, loaded, and we are just seconds away from firing missile number one!" Gray yelled.

Big James had brought with him two sets of noise-cancelling military-issued earmuffs. He was wearing a pair, and he had given the second pair to Diego. James looked at his partner, motioned to the earmuffs, motioned to the ground, and as both men took a knee away from the surface-to-air rocket launcher, Big James yelled, "Hit it, now!"

The projectile fired and snaked its way toward its target.

For a moment, those that were not near to the launching sight took a quick second to look up and watch the results.

Due to the brunt of the blast from the launch of the surface-to-air missile, Big James and Diego had been sent rolling onto the ground like dice from a Yahtzee cup. Now, with crucial seconds on the line, the two men did not even bother to look up into the Rio night sky to admire their results. Instead, they shook out the cobwebs, regained their composure, scrambled back to their feet, grabbed another missile and prepared it for launch.

Once the missile was readied for firing, both men nodded to each other, ran in opposite directions, and dived to the ground as they covered their heads.

Being so close to the launch area, the two men unfortunately did not realize the concussive effect that the first blast had taken on them, nor had they heard the cheers of their cohorts due to the results of said blast. By the time Big James and Diego hit the ground from their second defensive dives, neither one would remember the second launching.

Nor would they remember hearing the members of the team screaming like wild banshees into their coms about how the duo had gone two-for-two with their surface-to-air missile strikes. The group expected to hear some sort of reply from the two men in response to all the whooping and hollering.

"Big James? Diego? Are you guys there?"

Nothing.

"The blast from the launch may have disabled their coms," Harper pointed out. "I'm sure they'll be along rightly."

With the two direct hits on the Lockheed Scorpions, everything had turned in the favor of the good guys, but the battle was not yet over. A third wave of the battle, that was just as important as the first two waves, had yet to be waged.

"Looks like they are already on the move," Mercedes said calmly as she pointed toward the collection of buildings that held the barracks for the pilots of the Black Hawk choppers, as well as the bunk rooms of their accompanying guards. "I guess some of them weren't drinking as much as we had hoped."

She, Hawk, and Sloane were on a dead sprint to make sure none of those pilots made it to the Black Hawk choppers. Still, at this point, the troupe was too far away to make any significant damage on the enemy with the small arms weapons that they had been firing.

"Johnny, where you at?" Hawk asked. "Pick us up!"

"Keep moving," Watkins said calmly, "I'm right on your six. I'm not picking you up, though. Just follow me in. Stay on me and strike hard."

Just as he had finished his sentence, Danny, Hawk, and Merc felt the momentum of Chase's van practically knock them down as Watkins raced past them at an amazing speed.

"The boss is torchin' the trail!" yelled Sloane. "Reload and follow him in!"

Daniel Sloane, Samuel Hawkins, and Dr. Mercedes Lara each stopped, focused, and quickly reloaded everything they had in their arsenal. By the time they looked up, they realized that John was about fifty yards ahead of them.

They also saw the blades from one of the four Black Hawk helicopters start to slowly rotate.

"John, it looks like the effects of that EMP bomb are wearing off already. Do you see–"

"I see it, and I'm getting ready to fire that bird up like it was Thanksgiving Day!" Watkins yelled as he carefully steered, aimed, and floored the accelerator of the van in the direction of the attack helicopter. He held true until the last possible second, then he opened up and dived out of the driver's side door of the van.

Watkins violently shoulder-rolled some twenty yards before he could gain his bearings. When he finally came to a stop on all fours, he heard what he thought were the other three members of his team running up to him.

Watkins knew they were stopping for one of two reasons. Reason one, to admire his marksmanship, as the van struck a direct blow into the undercarriage of the Black Hawk, turning it and its pilot into a ball of billowing flame. Or reason two, to get him on his feet so that he could help them continue the onslaught. As it turned out, it was both.

"Hey, man, nice shot," somebody said just as he blacked out completely. His body was hoisted off the ground and to a nearby cover zone.

"You okay?" he heard someone ask as he felt a hand across his cheek. "Come on, boss. Ya still alive?"

"How are we doing?" he asked as he shook his head from side to side like a wet dog emerging from the ocean. "How long was I out?"

"Not long. We're covered for now." It was Hawkins talking. "The bad guys are shootin' like a bunch o' scared chickens and scramblin' like eggs. Getcha self t'gether, and put on ya night goggles. I think now's the time for me to make a run at one o' those Black Hawks. Stuff's startin' to power back up. By the time I git to one o' them copters, we should be ready-da-roll."

Realizing the boss was temporarily unable to put two thoughts together, Sloane stepped up with a plan. "Johnny, come on, babe," and Daniel reached down and lifted Watkins to his feet. "Any way possible you can get up on top of this building that we're next to?"

Still trying to clear the bats from his proverbial belfry, John woozily surveyed the two-story building that he was standing next to. "I can do that."

"Doc and I will position ourselves on top of those two buildings over there. Thanks to Big James and Diego – God rest their souls if they're really dead – there's no longer a threat from overhead. The three of us should be able to give Sammy enough cover to get to one of those copters."

John Watkins nodded in agreement. "That's a good plan, Dan. I'm up here. You two over there." He looked at Hawkins and gave an approving smile. "Hawk – time to shine, brother."

Timing is everything, and the time that Laurie Chase had chosen to strike Tito del Fuento's compound could not have been better. From bringing down Tito's mighty hundred, to taking the delivery truck, to getting past the guard at the gate, to the first offensive strike, things could not have gone better.

Still, as with any plan, resistance was bound to happen.

The three of them, Kin, Harp, and Laurie, had made major strides to take out most of del Fuento's troops, but – just as they had anticipated – there were soldiers guarding the outer perimeters of the property that were now making a move toward the main foreground of the skirmish.

They were small in number, but they were coming from all directions.

If del Fuento's plantation were to survive, it would be because of these battle-tested, battle-readied soldiers.

Chase, Devereaux, and Rowe separated like a bad marriage, each taking cover to where they could interpret, decide, and fire upon the opposition's incoming attack.

Because Kinley Devereaux had developed such intense feelings for Laurie Chase, he had actually been hanging on every word she said. He was even listening in the meetings where she was using her diorama to point out important things to her surrounding audience. Due to this advantage, he had remembered when she said that the vacated migrant workers' quarters located on the east side of Tito del Fuento's property would be a good place to take cover once the battle started to intensify. And that is exactly what he did.

Kinley ran as fast as he could to the closest of those buildings while simultaneously ripping off his night vision specs. He did not break stride as he lowered his shoulder and plowed through the front door. Once inside the vacant building, he put the goggles back on so that he could navigate his way inside. He quickly spotted a set of stairs leading up to the second floor. Like a gazelle, he took the staircase three steps at a time up to the next level. He scoured the area for the perfect vantage point facing the conflict.

Bingo. Within a few seconds, Devereaux found the perfect spot. And he had the perfect weapon for the occasion. Amidst all the variations of arms and ammo that he had access to when he was readying himself for this particular fight, the one thing he made sure to have on his person was the very rifle that he and Harper had rescued from the evidence locker of APD-5 some forty-eight hours ago. He made short work of smashing the glass in the window and finding a comfortable position from which to fire. He removed the goggles and tossed them aside, turned on the infrared scope that sat atop his gun, and he was ready to go. He found his first mark, exhaled slowly, and fired.

The bullet entered the upper part of the soldier's left ribcage, ripped through his pulmonary artery and both lungs before exiting out the other side of his body.

Kinley quickly reloaded before finding his next victim and repeating the process.

Same procedure. Same result.

Kinley reloaded for the third time and began surveying for his next mark. However, upon looking through his hi-tech scope, he quickly realized that the next casualty was set up to be his best buddy. Harper and Laurie had stayed closer to the fray and were each having major success deleting del Fuento's soldiers from existence.

Still, with the incredible numbers that were against them, Harp and Laurie – for as well as they were positioned – remained vulnerable from their blindsides.

"Harp! Behind you!" Kin yelled.

Instead of turning to look for his attacker, Harper simply ducked down and let his best friend put a sniper's shot into the skull of the would-be assailant.

"Much obliged, brother," Harp remarked, and lifted his head to see two targets running blindly in his direction. Harper rolled to elude them, and with each hand grabbed a dagger from his armored jacket and flipped them forcefully at his attackers.

Two separate blades into two separate carotid arteries.

"See ya 'round downtown, boys," he rolled over and watched them land, lifelessly, next to him. "If synchronized killing were an Olympic sport, I'd be golden."

"Like a medal," Kinley said from his second story perch. "Laurs, you still with us, baby?"

"Am I ever," she replied.

Laurie Chase had found a perfect place to take out the leftover henchmen. The soldiers that had survived the initial onslaught of the attack knew just where to go to arm themselves and come out firing. Unfortunately, for them, anyone that had done their homework on the men's routine was also very familiar with this place of retreat and gathering.

The remainder of the troops armed themselves with equal parts weapons, armor, and delusions of making a difference in the battle. Tragically, when they emerged from the bunker ready to be heroes, Chase ended their short-lived dreams by putting them down like ducks at a carnival booth.

Bing! Bang! Boom!

For the swearing impaired, it was "Lights Out, Mother Fluffers!"

Sam Hawkins was a member of the Big Brothers Big Sisters

program, and he had a particular favorite little brother that was named Nicholas Sehrklug. Nicholas was constantly doing Arnie impersonations, of which Hawkins' favorite was, "Get to the choppa!". So as Hawkins was running like a madman, firing off handguns from both his left and right hands, and hoping that John, Merc, and Danny had his six from wherever they were up on high, "Get to the choppa!" was rattling around in his head.

"Hawk! On your 12!" he heard and he reacted.

"Hawk! On your 4!" he heard and he reacted.

For every gunman that showed up, he was being instructed from either John, Daniel, or Merc where to look and where to shoot, like a cheat sheet to a video game. After what seemed like an eternity, Sam Hawkins and his three confederates had shot his way clear to one of the Black Hawk attack helicopters.

He knew what to do, and–

He knew how to do it.

Like leaving a message on an answering machine, Hawkins took control of the Black Hawk and rose high above del Fuento's property. He began firing away, ripping to shreds the future of next year's crop, next year's hope, and next year's dream. With this fully-equipped Black Hawk, it took Hawkins less than ten minutes to turn del Fuento's entire lifetime of work into nothing more than wreckage and ruin.

For the first and only time ever, Sammy was able to fly a helicopter of this nature without anyone telling him what to do, or anything firing back at him. So he was determined to enjoy it while it lasted. In the midst of his demolition and destruction of del Fuento's compound, he began singing Jeffrey Osborne's "On the Wings of Love" at the top of his lungs.

"Um, Earth to Hawkins," Mercedes cut in, "can you *please* shut your com down for the four minutes it will take you to get through the entirety of that song?"

Skipping not a beat in either the eradication of his targets or his song lyrics, Hawk reached up and slapped his com. He was on a natural high, and he planned on taking full advantage of it as long as he could. The last thing he wanted was to be hearing comments from the peanut gallery.

"I'm not dead!" Big James suddenly blurted into everyone's headsets from out of nowhere. "Diego, either. Please, please, please tell me that y'all are okay."

"Raid's over," Harper spoke up first. "I'm the only one left, but I somehow managed to kill all the bad guys, rescue a beautiful maiden, and now we're heading to the money."

"I see a helicopter overhead," Big James came back. "Is that you or the beautiful maiden flying that thing?"

After a round of laughter subsided, Chase set the record straight. "Big James, we're all okay. That is Hawkins in the helicopter that you're seeing. I'm sorry that you missed the festivities, but things went – for lack of a better term – perfectly perfect. While Hawkins is up in the sky, the rest of us are headed to the money building. Can you find your way to us?"

"I'm gonna do you one better than that," Big James said urgently. "From where we are we can hear sirens from all directions. You need to get what ya want, and get the heck out of there within the next three to five minutes."

"In that case, we're going to get what we can. We'll see you and Diego back at the hangar in less than an hour."

"See you then," Big James acquiesced. "The little man and I are outta here."

MONEY GRAB

Number one, everyone was glad to be alive.

Number two, upon entering the building that Diego had told them held the bulk of Tito's money, they found themselves really glad to be alive.

"Holy – simoleons."

"Good Lord."

"Tighten it up, gang," Harp smacked his hands together. "We're on a schedule."

"What are we going to put all this money in?" Chase asked, in shock at just how much money there was sitting before them. "What about that truck we came in on? How damaged is that?"

"The truck is in good shape," Harper offered.

"I feel like I want to give you a hug," Mercedes said to Laurie. "I feel bad for you."

"What? Why? Why would you feel bad for me?" Chase sounded confused.

"Well, because you spent the last year and a half on this mission, and from the time we hijacked that delivery truck up to this moment in time, we have wrapped this entire job up, put a bow on it, and shipped it off UPS in just about twenty-two minutes."

"Ah, too true. Too true," said Hawkins as he entered the building, seemingly from out of nowhere. "But let's not sell ourselves short, boys and girls. Mizz Chase had no idea of the talent level with which she would be working with. I can assure you of that."

"Good golly, it's Hawk." Devereaux said loudly. "What's it look like outside now that you're done?"

"Ain't gonna lie to ya, my brutha. It looks a bit like Armageddon out there, but," and Hawkins raised his arms up high and did "praise hands", "If ya on the side of Jesus then Armageddon is a joyous day of revelation and salvation!"

"Somebody give that guy an amen." But before anyone could follow through on the request, a loud smashing sound interrupted the proceedings.

Some ducked for cover and covered their heads. Those that remained upright immediately realized that somewhere in the commotion, they had lost track of Harper Rowe.

The same Harper Rowe who was now backing the tractor and trailer that he had driven into the compound less than an hour ago through the side of the money building and causing an unbelievable ruckus.

"I do believe that's our cue to start loading the money," Chase said with a smile as wide as the Grand Canyon.

"Yeah, but how?" asked Merc. "There's, literally, tons of cash sitting here, and we have just a few short minutes to get it loaded by hand. We'll be lucky if we can throw a million dollars into the back of the truck in the time we're working with."

"No, I think we're good," Sloane said in a rare moment of calm. "I see the answer to our problems right over there." He pointed to the corner of the building where sat a heavy-duty forklift.

"You know how to drive one of those?" Devereaux asked.

"Yeah, he does," confirmed Harper Rowe. "Maybe if you hadn't been playing kissy face in the corner with Laurie the whole time the rest of us were busy loading everything up – you might've avoided asking such an embarrassing question."

Sloane gave Kin a sullen look. "If I learned three things during my time in the military it was how to kill, how to eat fast and not get sick, and how to drive a stinkin' forklift, so, yeah, I know how to drive one of those."

"Awesome," Dev said without making a scene. "I'm over here – out of the way."

The team watched with deep respect as Sloane climbed aboard the fork truck and lifted several pallets of money into the trailer. Seven, in all.

Then it was time to go.

They had no idea how much money Sloane had loaded onto the truck.

61

Crool Touches Down in Rio

"Wake up, Shemp. The plane has touched down. It's time to rise and shine." Crool nudged Baldwin.

David raised a tired head. "How long was I out?"

"It's still dark out, if that helps."

Baldwin sat upright and lifted the shade on the closest window.

It was, indeed, still dark out.

"How ya feelin', Dave?" Crool asked.

"Good. Feelin' good. Got some rest."

"That's fantastic. That means you get to deal with the press, the local authorities, and all the other bull crap."

"I thought that's why we brought the other agents," Baldwin protested.

"Good. I like the way you're thinking. You handle the other agents, and whatever else there is to handle. I'm gonna go find Harper Rowe."

"Really? You're gonna go just like that?"

"C'mon, Dave. This is why I hired you," Crool explained. "We're Americans on foreign soil. This situation needs to be handled with care. You know me. I'm a boxer inside a house of cats. You do this stuff well. So – go do this stuff well."

"Text me if you learn something," Baldwin requested.

"Absolutely," Jeb got up and began to exit the plane. He turned around to Baldwin, "You, too. Text me. Only if you find something though. Text me. And thank you." Crool got off the plane.

If there really was such a thing as Spidey sense, Crool felt his going off, and it was because Harper Rowe was close.

Payday

"Do we have any volunteers to count these massive amounts of cabbage?" Hawk asked. "I feel like Howard Hughes, just without the insanity – and the really pasty skin."

Harper had backed the big rig into the airplane hangar where the Dragon's Men plane was currently hidden. He hopped out and opened up the back.

"So – who wants what?"

"I would like a million dollars," Big James said.

"Um," Hawk stammered, "you do realize that there's about a quarter of a billion dollars sitting there. You sure that a million is all you want?"

"When I came into this thing, I was hoping for a million dollars. Now that it's over, I'm alive, the mission is accomplished, I've made some new friends – a million dollars seems very good to me. You guys can fight over the rest. Besides, I have a five-star headache, and if I didn't have my name written on the inside of my drawers, I'm not real sure I could tell you what it is."

Big James walked over to the minivan in which he and Diego had been riding. He opened the hatch and pulled out a J.W. Hulme classic leather briefcase that probably cost more than the minivan he was driving it in. He took the case, climbed into the back of the truck, and began packing the stacks of cash.

"What about the rest of us?" Watkins asked.

"You guys came all the way down here," Chase pointed out the obvious, "so I think it's only fair that you take all of it, John. Take it, and steadily siphon it into an account. When the smoke clears, you can cut us some checks and make it right."

"Are you serious?" Sloane asked, almost choking on his own tongue. "You're going to trust us with a quarter of a billion dollars?"

"Hey, good news, sailor: a few hours ago you bet your life on me. And now I'm willing to bet a quarter of a billion – or whatever is there – on you. Only seems fair. You lived. You win," Chase said bluntly.

Sloane looked at Devereaux. "Besides the hot body and good looks, I now see what you see in her. She's the coolest chick – other than the Doc – that I've ever met."

"Is everyone else here cool with that?" Watkins asked.

"I'm cool. You cool, Harp?" Devereaux asked his friend.

Harper exhaled a heavy sigh. "I guess so."

"Hey, if you're not good with–"

"No," Harper cut off John Watkins. "No, it's not that at all." Harper hesitated. "It's just that once we settle on this, you guys fly away to your next adventure. Big James – don't forget to hug me before you leave, buddy – goes on to his next gig, we'll all go our–"

"Hey, Harp," Sloane interrupted the interrupter, "life gets tough, but as far outside the boundaries as this whole thing was, you came through. Everyone here showed up and did what was necessary. This ain't a goodbye, brother. This is just the beginning." Sloane looked over at Mercedes. "Gotta feeling we'll be hearing from you sooner rather than later, Harper Rowe."

Harper smiled.

"Besides, Harp," Dev brought up, "now that this is over, I've got some things I need to talk to you about. Kind of important."

"Is it about that phone call you were going to tell me about earlier?"

"Yep."

Harper walked up to Sloane, "You don't seem like the hugging type, but, nonetheless–" the two men hugged long enough to pat each other on the back twice.

From there, it was hugs all around – some longer than others – as everyone said their goodbyes, their adieus, their toodle-oos, their see ya 'round downtowns.

The adventure was over, but the relationships would last a lifetime – especially with the amount of money that was owed between the parties involved.

WHO'S CALLING?

Once the raid was wrapped, Sloane had circled back around and picked up the black jeep. Back at the hangar, Dragon's Men packed up their gear, minus the EMP bomb. Then they took off back to the States loaded with money – lots of money.

Harper had said his goodbyes with Merc, and they promised to talk soon once the dust had settled.

Big James, Diego, and Laurie Chase reminded Kin and Harp that there were United States agents coming into town to find them. They needed to be on the move.

Hugs. Tears. Laughs.

"Wait," Harper brought up, "we didn't actually drive here. Can someone give us a ride into town?"

"No, we're good," Kin said confidently. "We're only two miles from the airfield that we'll be using to fly out of here. We'll just have to keep our heads down when we walk through town. It'll be a nice trip."

"Give you boys some time to talk?" Chase asked.

"Most definitely," Kin answered.

"You don't really have to go so soon, ya know?" Chase tried to say convincingly.

"Eh, you've got your del Fuento attack to tend to. He will be back soon, and you will be taking that guy out. If not – this was all for naught."

"I know," Chase admitted. "I just hate to leave you here like this."

"We're the heroes," Harper laughed. "We get to walk off into the sunset. Haven't you ever watched movies before?"

"I have," Laurie smiled, "but the sun set about two hours ago."

Harper took a hard look at his best friend. "Well, I guess we have some catching up to do then."

Goodbyes were said. Ways were parted.

Kinley and Harper watched their cohorts drive away.

"Well, this is just about daggone depressing," Harper said in a dour note.

"It's been a pretty good adventure, and like you said – we didn't die."

"True. By the way, where are we headed?"

"There's a café near the airfield we'll be taking off from."

"Aww, just like the last time we parted ways. A café. Neat."

"Yeah, but unlike last time, I don't think we will be parting ways."

His phone went off.

"Hang tight," he said.

"Who's calling you?"

He put his hand up, walked away for a moment, and said something unintelligible into his phone. Then he clearly said, "We'll be there in about fifteen minutes," and hung up.

"Who did you just tell that we would be somewhere in fifteen minutes?"

Final Scene at a Café . . . Again.

Seventeen minutes later, Kinley and Harper were sitting in a quaint little twenty-four-hour café called Boteco Cabidinho.

Both men were unsure why they were there, but one of them was laying the Sipowicz on the other.

"So, what did she say? Kelly. You've been more secretive about this phone call from her than the Masons have been about their role in 9-11."

"The Masons? 9-11?" Dev arched an eyebrow. "What do you know that you aren't telling me?"

"Which is precisely my question to you," Harper came back. You – Kelly Campbell – phone call – and here I am having to practically pull your teeth just to get you to acknowledge that you even said anything to me about it. I mean, did she even tell you what took her so ridiculously long to let you know she was even alive?"

"Of course she did."

"And?"

"After surviving the car bomb at her house, she went into hiding and waited for things to blow over. Once they did, she – much like everyone else – thought I was dead. It took her some time to put the pieces together to realize that I really wasn't. As soon as she figured out I was alive, she started working on a way to try to clear our names."

"And you're just now telling me this?" asked an exasperated Harper Rowe.

"I just wanted to wait for the right time, is all," Devereaux took his time answering.

"The time seems right," Harper seemed a bit tense. "What has she come up with?"

"Kelly thinks she can clear our names."

Harper dropped his spoon.

"You okay?" Dev asked.

"Yes. I'm fine. I drop stuff all the time."

"She said it will take a few days. She has to look into some things, and she will get back with me. She asked me to keep it under wraps in the meantime. That's why I've been a bit secretive until I could actually be alone with you."

"It's cool. I'm cool. You're cool, right? Cool?"

"Absolutely. I just figured we could hang out until we hear more. Obviously, not here," Kin continued. "The last thing you want to have happen is to get caught just before you get a shot at clearing your name."

"Yes. That would be awkward." Harper agreed. "Wanna know what else is awkward?"

"Not really, but I'm sure you're going to tell me anyway."

"Do me a small favor. You don't even have to get up from your seat to do it. That's how small of a favor it is that I'm asking of you." Harper tried his best to not give a silly smile, but, despite his best efforts – he gave a silly smile.

"This is going to suck for me, isn't it?" Kin asked.

Harper did not deny it. "Yes. Maybe. Probably. Yes."

"Spill it, Goober."

"Two tables away there is a woman sitting by herself. Go ahead.

You can look, but try not to make it obvious."

Kinley did his best to be discreet with his glance toward the woman that was two tables away.

"Okay," he said afterward, "who is she, and why does she look familiar?"

"A friend – sort of. You've met her."

"I may have, but it's just not coming to me," Kinley said. Kin looked over at her again. "Definitely looks familiar, though."

"She looks familiar because, well, that's – she's–"

"Holy crap that's – that's–" Kinley closed his eyes in deep thought and snapped his fingers. "That's the flight attendant. That's Taralyn Tharp, isn't it?" Kinley asked as the recognition flickered through his memory bank.

"Yes, it is," Harper smiled.

Devereaux shot an unfriendly glare at his partner. "Are you out of your ever-lovin' mind, Harper?"

"Well, I think we both know the answer to that."

Kinley reached across the table and grabbed Harper's wrist in anger. "You better get serious real quick and in a hurry, ya little jackass, or I will kick you so hard under this table that your grand-kids will be singing soprano." Kin said in a harsh but controlled voice. "You do remember that her employer is the Government of the United States of America, don't you?"

"Yes, I do, but calm down and let go of my wrist. Or do you really want the people that are in here to start looking at us a little longer than they should and suddenly realize that we look familiar, too?"

Kin released his grasp on Rowe and sat back in his seat. He did not, however, calm down. "Judas Priest, man, she could be leading the authorities right to us."

"Calm down. She's cool, man."

"Is she?" Dev's glare continued. "How can you be so sure?"

"Because she's known that you and Laurie have been alive for, pretty much, the whole time. If she was looking to do some damage to us, I'm quite confident that she would have gone to her bosses with that little nugget by now."

"Then why is she here? Seems like a rather random place for her to be."

"Well, her being here isn't exactly random."

"Oh?"

"You know how you gave me that cell phone to keep on me just in case you should ever need me, or I should ever need you?"

"Right."

"And I'm sure you remember how she and I hit it off on the plane ride into Mexico City, yeah?"

"Seems to ring a bell."

"Well, after Mexico City," Harp began to explain, "I was worried that she might still be in danger for whatever reasons, and I wanted to ensure her safety, so I tracked her down."

"Right," Devereaux grinned, "to ensure her safety. I hear ya."

Harper smiled sheepishly. "Anyhow, when she and I eventually parted ways, I did your little cell phone idea with her."

"Yeah?"

"Yeah, which means if she wanted to turn me in, she could've done that a hundred times by now."

"I see." Devereaux was starting to calm down.

"She needs our help."

"To kill somebody?"

"No," answered Harper. "From what I gather, pretty much the exact opposite."

"From what you gather?"

"Don't really have a lot of intel on the whole thing yet, which is why she is here. To fill us in on the details."

"How committed to this whole thing do you have us at this point?"

"Dude," Harper said, almost sounding disappointed in Dev's question, "what's my Rule Number Three?"

Devereaux cast a thoughtful glance down at the table before answering, "Never agree to do a favor for someone until you know what said favor is."

"Exactly."

"So, we're just up to the listening stage at this point?"

"That's right. Just gonna listen."

"And what, so far, have you gathered about what she wants? Also, are you sure she wants both of us and not just you?"

"Yeah, I'm sure. She needs us," Harp confirmed, "and she needs us to help her with an extraction."

"An extraction? From where to where?"

"From Prague to – parts unknown, at this point."

"Czechia?"

"Yeppers."

"Bit of a hop, skip, and a jump from here, isn't it?" Kin seemed concerned by this, which in turn concerned Harper.

"Yeah, cab fare might be a little steep."

"Any idea on the danger factor?"

"Somewhere between a little more dangerous than crossing the road, and slightly less dangerous than urinating on an electric fence."

"I don't know, man," Kinley said with some trepidation. He began to look around the place anxiously. "Where the heck is the help staff around this joint anyway?"

"We're just gonna listen, bud," Harper reminded him. "That's it. If either one of us doesn't like what she has going on, we're Donesville on the whole thing, buddy."

"I get that. I do."

"So, what's the hang up, chief?"

"It's just – I mean, you do understand that Kelly Campbell is trying to clear your – our – name, and you bring me a woman that I don't really know, and she's looking to put us in play with a situation that we don't really know that much about in a place that certainly doesn't give us any sort of a home field advantage either."

"A girl that looks like that and has the job that she does and has the connections that she has – come on, bud – she could have had her pick of people to assist her on this, but she came to us. I figure I want to at least hear what she has to say. Don't you?"

At that moment, the waitress came by and set two glasses of ice water in front of the two men. In her native tongue she asked, "May I take your order?"

"You speak Portuguese. Tell this waitress that I want the greasiest, fattiest, worstest for your heart cheese burger they've got in stock." Dev was still apprehensive. "And then tell your little heathen friend that – I'll listen."

A WORD FROM DOC

Thank you for reading *Chasing Revenge*.
I hope you enjoyed it.

Please read on, because I've included
an excerpt of the trio's continuing story in
Chasing Liberation, book three of the
Boom!!...Killers. series.

I occasionally send newsletters with details on
new releases, special offers, and other bits of
news relating to my characters. If you would like
to sign up to the mailing list, please go to:

www.docephraimbates.com or
www.goldenalleypress.com/boom-killers-series

You can make a difference . . .

Reviews are the most powerful weapon I have
when it comes to getting my books noticed.
Honest reviews help bring them to the attention
of other readers.

If you've enjoyed this book, please consider
leaving a review on Amazon.com.

Doc

If you enjoyed *Chasing Revenge*,
please keep reading for an exciting preview of

CHASING LIBERATION

Boom!!...Killers.

SERIES BOOK #3

Doc Ephraim Bates

Available in print and ebook
from Golden Alley Press

Damsel in Distress

```
RIO DE JANEIRO - THE BOTECO
                   CABIDINHO
                 JANUARY 3RD
             1:55 A.M. BRST
```

Not terribly long ago – just about eighteen months or so – Kinley Devereaux and Harper Rowe were highly-esteemed and highly-requested government wetwork agents. The two men had carried out copious assignments that had either directly or indirectly stopped potential coups, possible wars, and likely terrorist attacks. The results of their efforts were as immeasurable as a mother's love for her children. Nonetheless, due to the nature of their work, their heroics remained as anonymous as the assassins themselves. Still, to the select few that were "in the know," Harper and Kinley were like rock stars.

But that was some six seasons ago.

Six seasons that, at times, seemed more like six years.

For Kinley Devereaux, the last eighteen months of his life had become an infinitesimal struggle for some semblance of existence. Presumed dead by most, he lived underground and off the grid as he bounced from city to city, country to country, and continent to continent while working as a shadow assassin to whoever could contract his services through the necessary channels. When he was not doing wetwork jobs, he was busy tracking and keeping a watchful eye on his friend, Harper Rowe.

Harper Rowe, who for the last year and a half had also been keeping his movements frequent and unpredictable as he traversed the globe performing various acts of assassination and kindness to whoever might find their way into his always welcoming world. However, unlike Kinley Devereaux, Harper was not presumed dead by anyone. Harper Rowe was just a wanted man.

And not just any wanted man.

No. He was the *most* wanted man. At least, that's what it said on most of the "WANTED" lists that hung in almost every state and federal building throughout the United States of America.

Harper Rowe was wanted for questioning in connection with the assassination of the former United States Secretary of Defense, Paul Michaels. A high-ranking government official had been shot dead in a very public forum, and someone needed to be held accountable. Since Harper Rowe was the one that every eyewitness had identified as the man talking to the Defense Secretary at the time of the shooting, that meant Harper Rowe was the closest thing they had to a suspect or, at least, a person of interest.

Seemingly endless government officials in innumerable interviews had consistently said, "Harper Rowe is not a suspect. We just need to ask him about the events of that day. But with his constant avoidance of cooperation with this investigation, it does make him look more and more culpable for having had some kind of hand in the shooting death of Secretary Michaels."

Harper was not stupid. He knew the game, and he knew all too well the nature of the interrogation that he would be given even if he were to voluntarily turn himself in. It would not be pretty, and it would not end until he told them what he knew, or there was just nothing left of him to interrogate – or torture – anymore.

With that being the case, it would seem that the wanted man would have been keeping an extremely low profile all this time – out of sight, out of trouble. Yet such was not always the case with Harper Rowe. From time to time and in very random yet very public spots around the globe, he would make almost farcical appearances. He wanted to get the attention of his pursuers. As he liked to put it, "I don't show my face so that they'll know where I am. I show my face so I'll know where they are."

So, for the last eighteen months this was the life for Harper Rowe and Kinley Devereaux: cloak and dagger, hide and seek, living in obscurity, and no place to call home. Oddly enough, though, it was not the assassination of the U.S. Secretary of Defense that had actually set in motion the downward spiral that had taken over these two men's lives. In fact, the assassination of Paul Michaels was more like the exclamation point at the end of a very loud, forty-eight hour-long exclamatory sentence.

The true genesis of Kinley and Harper's extended dilemma lay with one person and one person alone: Tara Madison.

Alias: Black Ice.

Some might argue that the official beginning to the duo's tribulations was when Harper went snooping around the cordoned off area of Doug Hopkins' mansion when it was clear that the area was not to be snooped around.

That's a bit of a technicality.

If Black Ice had not been burglarizing the upstairs safe of the Hopkins' residence, then Kinley and Harper would never have caught her in the act, chased her, accidently killed a bunch of government agents, let her get away, tracked her down in Mexico City, met the amazing and ebullient Laurie Chase, got shot at, lied to, double crossed, used, betrayed, shot at some more...none of that would have ever happened. Harper would eventually try to explain it to Kinley by comparing the situation to when Eve went to the Tree of Knowledge in the Garden of Eden. Of course she had been warned not to eat from it, but she would have been fine – if not for that snake.

From the moment that Tara Madison – Kinley and Harper's personal Garden of Eden serpent – had entered their lives, nothing had been the same.

However, one of the bright spots that came out of that whole fiasco was the flight that the two men had taken from D.C.to Mexico City. On it, Harper Rowe had begun a relationship with the woman that had served as their flight attendant, Taralyn Tharp. It was the first time that Harper Rowe had ever met her, and as far as Kinley Devereaux knew, it was also the last. For as much as the elder of the duo had tried to keep tabs on his sometimes-partner, always-friend, he was finding out that Harper had been able to sneak a few things past him – one of which was his continued relationship with Taralyn Tharp.

It was an abrupt revelation. Kinley was taken aback, not so much by the news that Harper had, indeed, had further contact with the beautiful Taralyn. No, the real shock to Devereaux's system was that, now, a year and a half later, he found himself sitting just two tables away from her at a nondescript café in Rio de Janeiro in the wee morning hours of January 3rd, listening to Harper Rowe telling him that Taralyn needed their help.

The two men went back and forth at each other about this particular situation for some time. Harper tried to get Kin to calm down. Naturally, Kin was concerned by the fact that Taralyn was employed by the United States government – the same United States government that currently had Harper at the top of its "Most Wanted" list, and the same United States government that had dispatched a faction of agents to the Rio area that very night in hopes of apprehending the fugitive.

"And what, so far, have you gathered about what she wants? Also, are you sure she wants both of us and not just you?" Devereaux asked curtly.

"Yeah, I'm sure. She needs us," Harp confirmed, "and she needs us to help her with an extraction."

"An extraction? From where to where?"

"From Prague to...parts unknown, at this point."

"Czechia?"

"Yeppers."

"Bit of a hop, skip, and a jump from here, isn't it?" Kin seemed concerned by this, which, in turn, concerned Harper.

"Yeah, cab fare might be a little steep."

"Any idea on the danger factor?"

"Somewhere between a little more dangerous than crossing the road and slightly less dangerous than peeing on an electric fence."

"I don't know, man," Kinley said with some trepidation. He began to look around the place anxiously. "Where the heck is the help staff around this joint, anyway?"

"We're just gonna listen, bud," Harper reminded him. "That's it. If either one of us doesn't like what she has going on, we're Donesville on the whole thing."

"I get that. I do."

"So, what's the hang-up, chief?"

"It's just...I mean, you do understand that Kelly Campbell is trying to clear your – our – name, and you bring me a woman that I don't really know, and she's looking to put us in play with a situation that we don't really know that much about, and in a place that certainly doesn't give us any sort of a home field advantage either."

"A girl that looks like that and has the job that she does and has the connections that she has – come on, bud – she could have had her pick of people to assist her on this, but she came to us. I figure I want to at least hear what she has to say. Don't you?"

At that moment, the waitress came by and set two glasses of ice water in front of the men and asked in her native tongue, "May I take your order?"

"You speak Portuguese. Tell this waitress that I want the greasiest, fattiest, worstest for your heart cheeseburger they've got in stock." Dev was still apprehensive. "And then tell your little heathen friend that...I'll listen."

Harper smiled up at the waitress and said, "*Um hambúrguer de queijo grande para meu amigo.*"

"*Muito bom e para o senhor?*"

"*Tenho a feijoada, por favor,*" Harper responded, ordering a traditional Brazilian dish of beef, black beans and rice, and a coentro sauce.

The waitress nodded, smiled, and walked away as she jotted down Harper's order on her little waitress notebook.

"Did you get me the burger?"

"No, I got you the cheeseburger with extra fat and extra grease."

"What did you order?" Kinley asked.

"The house special."

"So...what are you thinking?"

"I'm hoping that they don't get chintzy with the sauce. It's good stuff."

"No, not that," Kinley said, a bit irritated. "You want to invite your friend over here while we eat, or do you want to take our food over to where she is? I mean, it seems kinda rude to make her sit over there by herself while we eat."

"Might be kinda rude to eat in front of her, though, don't ya think?"

Kinley shrugged. "Look, I don't care what you do. I'm just tellin' ya right now that when my food gets here, I'm going to eat it. I'm dangerously hungry, and sometimes when I get this way my royal manners take a hike, and my primal instincts for red meat take over. That's my position on the matter. The ball's in your court now."

"I'll go get her," Harper informed his friend, then stood up and retrieved Taralyn back to the table. She gave a strained smile as she timidly approached and extended her hand toward Kinley. He could see about six different signs that told him this woman was scared to death. He courteously stood and shook her hand. "Taralyn," he greeted her as congenially as he could.

"Mr. Devereaux," she responded, some of the tension leaving her face.

Harper pulled a third chair up to the café table, and the slender woman took a seat. He resumed his position across the table from his partner, to Taralyn's right. "How was your flight in?" he asked her.

"Oh gosh, so very long. I took a sedative to help me sleep, but it didn't really seem to kick in until I landed here in Rio."

"So, you're a little sleepy?"

"Oh, I'm fine. I'm sure it's helping to keep my nerves from —" She stopped in mid-sentence as if she was catching herself before she let out some deep, dark secret. The tension suddenly returned to her face and swept over her entire body. Harper put his hand on her shoulder in an attempt to assuage her fears. Even Kinley – who was never the touchy/feely type – felt the need to reach out and grab her hand reassuringly.

"You're among friends here," he said. "You don't have to be so afraid."

"But I am," she replied, her gaze fixed firmly on the table in front of her. "And I've seen and done a lot of things before and never got scared, but this —."

"Then tell us why we're here, sweetheart, and let us help you," Devereaux said in a comforting voice.

"Because we can help you," Harper assured.

The shaken women took a few seconds to gather herself. Kinley produced a handkerchief and handed it to her. She dabbed around her eyes, made a quick pass under her nose, took a few deep breaths, and handed the satin cloth back to Kin.

"Thank you," she said. She started telling the story of how her best friend in the whole world, Eliska Lukasik, had suddenly called her from Prague about two weeks ago. She said that she needed help, and she did not know who else to go to because she was afraid. Taralyn told Kinley and Harper how she dropped everything and flew straight to her friend to find out what was wrong, and how upon arriving in Prague, Eliska told her about a young mother and her little daughter, Anezka and Jana Bucek, that had seen way too much of a horrible situation.

According to Eliska Lukasik, the mother and daughter had both been privy to a sex trafficking operation that was going on at a local children's home. Taralyn thought at first that she could handle the situation. Take the mother and daughter, give them a makeover to change their appearance, and then get them out of town to someplace safe.

However, something was not as it seemed. What should have been a simple snatch-and-grab relocation had turned into something much more dangerous. Seemingly, somebody that was involved in the sex ring had some major stroke in the Prague community because the city went from its typical distinction of being open and friendly to going on complete shutdown in just a matter of hours.

"They initiated a manhunt like they were going after some sort of savage serial killer who had been on the loose for weeks, when in reality it's just some innocent, helpless, scared woman and her precious, little daughter. I'm telling you right now," Taralyn looked back and forth between the two men as her voice hit a serious tone that equaled that of a nun under oath, "I don't know what they will do to them if they catch them. That's why I came to you two."

Harper could see the intense angst on Taralyn's face. He then looked at Kinley, only to see that his head was buried in his cell phone.

"What are you doing?"

Kin looked up from his phone. "I'm checking to see how bad we're screwed," and immediately looked back down at his phone.

"He's looking to see how badly we're screwed," Harper repeated. He looked at Taralyn and explained, "We use this scale. It goes from 'Couldn't possibly ever die ever' to 'No pulse. Crapped your pants. Peed yourself.' And I think that we are somewhere around 'We found out that Ronald Reagan was our surrogate father' at this point."

Taralyn looked at Harper with a totally confused looked.

He squeezed her hand and smiled. "We're going to help you."

Kinley grunted.

Harp looked at him. "How bad is it?"

"We're probably going to need a change of underwear." Kin passed his cell phone over to Harper as he said, "I was sort of hoping that maybe she was exaggerating a little bit, or perhaps had misread the situation somehow. But that does not seem to be the case...at all."

Harper took possession of Kinley's phone and began reading the news story that he had pulled up. The story backed up everything that Taralyn had said. It also instilled in Harper and Kinley a great deal of uneasiness about the entire situation.

"Taralyn, do you mind giving me and my young comrade here a few minutes to discuss a couple of things?" Devereaux asked the woman.

"Yes, of course," she answered. As she stood up from the table, she gave Harper a worried look, but he was quick to return it with a reassuring look of his own.

Devereaux waited until Taralyn was out of earshot before saying to his friend, "When did she contact you about this?"

"Yesterday afternoon," Rowe replied. "When we had gotten back from picking up John Watkins and his crew at the old airport hangar."

"Did she tell you that this is what was going on? That an entire Eastern European city was looking for this woman and her child, and that she needed us to help her get them to some sort of safe haven?"

"No, she did not."

"So, this really is the first time you're hearing about what she wants from us?"

"Yes, I told you it was."

"And you haven't given her any sort of false promises about us definitely helping her with this mess, right?"

"What are you getting at, dude?"

"Well," Kinley said, bobbing his head slightly, "I don't think this is a job for us to be getting into, ya know?"

"Why wouldn't we?"

"It's just too dangerous. It's little side jobs like these that can get us sidetracked from the big picture and end up landing us in some serious – if not perilous – situations."

"And what exactly is the big picture again?"

"What I told you earlier about Kelly Campbell having a seem-ingly very legitimate way for you and Chase and me to clear our names so that we can finally go home again."

"You said that it was going to be a couple of days before that happened, though," Harper pointed out.

"Well...yeah."

"So, let's kill some time by doing this then."

Harper handed Devereaux's phone back to him.

"I just don't think we should, Harp. I mean, this is some real danger here."

Harper shook his head in disbelief at his buddy's comment.

"Real danger? What would you call what we just walked away from about three hours ago? We just took on about two hundred soldiers of one of the world's biggest bad guys. And you suddenly think that helping a woman and her child flee a city of millions to someplace – anyplace – safer is more dangerous than that?"

"That is a situation that is one hundred and eighty degrees different from this situation. Taking out del Fuento's goons and his compound is something that had been planned out far, far in advance. Not to mention, we had some serious back-up and a lot of weapons to assist us in all of that. That was us doing what we do best: killing bad guys. This is not what we do. We aren't Harriet Tubman and William Still or any of the heroes of the Underground Railroad. We don't just go to people who are looking to escape a bad spot and usher them to safety. It's not like we just show up to a tenuous situation, and everything, magically, turns out okay."

"Well," Harper started to say as his gaze drifted off into deep thought for a moment.

"Well, what?"

"Well...it kinda does."

"What?"

"When we're together, bad situations seem to turn out okay... no matter how screwed up it tends to get, stuff always – and I don't mean to insinuate that we have magical powers – seems to work out okay. Mexico City, that little stunt we pulled in Atlanta a few nights ago, those terrorists at the nightclub, taking out—"

"Harper, I see where you're going with this, but—"

"But nothing, Kinley. You heard what Taralyn said. You read that story on your cell phone. That woman and child, they, lit'rally, have nowhere to go, and if we don't help them their goose is as good as cooked. Yeah, with our help it's going to be difficult, no doubt, but without our help it is just going to be downright impossible for those two to survive this."

Kinley looked at Harper with disgust because he knew he was right.

"Yeah," Devereaux sighed, "I don't suppose there's much of a point in you and me being able to go back home if we have to live with the guilt of those two on our conscience the rest of our lives."

"Not unless we're looking to while away the hours of our remaining days drinking bad memories off of our minds...which I, for one, do not intend to do." Harper drew in a deep breath, looked at his friend, and said excitedly, "C'mon, man. Let's go save some lives and have a good time doing it. What do you say?"

This time Kinley shook his head in disgust at himself for being so easily swayed.

Before he could answer, Harper cut in, "I can tell by that look on your face that you're disappointed in yourself. Don't be. I have come to accept that this is what you and I do now. We help people."

Devereaux reached across the table and grabbed Harper by the wrist. He gave him a hard look and said, "No. This is not who we are, and this is not what we do. I really, really, really need you to wake up from this little fairy tale world that you seem to have embraced, and please join me back here in reality." He let go of Harper's wrist but held his intense look before asking, "Can you do that for me?"

"And you need to stop denying the fact that you and I are natural born heroes. Sometimes people need our specific set of attributes, and we show up and deliver. Just like we did with Chase, just like we've been doing to stay afloat for the last year and a half, either separately or together."

"You know what you have? An apparent attraction to dying young. Let me tell you who wants to die young, Harp. Nobody...ten seconds after they're dead."

Suddenly, the two men heard a throat being cleared next to them.

"Did I come back at a bad time?" Taralyn asked.

Devereaux looked up at her and smiled. "Absolutely not. Harper and I were just discussing how we're going to help you and your mother-daughter friends." He looked at his buddy. "Weren't we, Harper?"

Harper looked up at Kinley, a bit caught off guard by his friend's statement. Then he looked up at the beautiful Taralyn. "If the man says we're working on a plan, then you can bet your sweet cheeks that is exactly what we're doing."

She pulled a chair out, sat down, and smiled as she asked, "So, what are you guys coming up with so far?"

"Gonna need to make a few phone calls," Dev admitted. "How long is the flight to Prague?"

LAURIE CHASE, BIG JAMES, AND DIEGO

Laurie Chase drove her van through the weed-infested, broken pavement surrounding the abandoned warehouse that she had been calling home for the last year and a half. She pulled into the hidden parking area inside the structure, placing her vehicle out of sight from any unwanted observers that might be flying overhead or, for some inexplicable reason, trespassing on her property.

The night could not have gone better. Laurie was all smiles as she entered the warehouse. For the most part it was dark, but she saw lights on in a distant room and saw Diego sitting in one of the chairs, waiting for her return. Making her way back, she said to Diego, "We kicked some ass tonight, didn't we?"

Hearing a voice behind her, she practically jumped out of her skin.

"Got that right, we did." It was Big James.

"Holy—" Laurie spun around to face the big man.

"Ease up there, Hawaiian noises. Don't go bangin' on the bongos like a chimpanzee."

"You scared the crap out of me. Why are you here?"

"Eh, I had to drop off the little man, plus I had to use the facilities. So I just decided to stick around and wait for you. Besides, did you think I was going to let you and Diego have all the fun of putting del Fuento in his grave when he returns home?" Big James smiled.

"Really? You think that I am going to have fun killing another human being? I think you must have me confused with some sort of psychopath from another one of—"

Laurie broke out into uncontrollable laughter.

"Sorry, I tried. Heck to the yeahs I am going to love bringing this piece of butt mud all the way to his knees before I watch him breathe his last breath...and I will be pleased as punch if you can help us out with that."

Big James threw his beefy arms around Laurie and gave her a friendly squeeze. Looking at Diego, he said, "C'mon, li'l man, get on in here and get some of this."

Jeb Crool and the Close Call

3:15 A.M. BRST

United States Special Agent Jeb Crool walked down the Rua Visconde de Pirajá in Ipanema, the main drag that ran through the busiest part of Rio de Janeiro. He was headed toward the Espeto Carioca, a night club that had fallen prey to a probable terrorist just two nights prior.

The attack had been a complete failure. The only lives that had been lost were those of the terrorists themselves, due to a supposedly small group of men and women that had caught on to the strike and headed it off. Lives were saved and some bad people were taken down and out of this world.

Some of the club's patrons had filmed the brief incursion with their cell phones. One of these videos had been posted online, catching the attention of Special Agent David Baldwin, sidekick to Special Agent Jeb Crool. The video clearly showed Harper Rowe as one of the heroes that had thwarted the gunmen. That is what had set in motion the events that had Jeb and his team in Rio at the moment.

Jeb did not have any real directions to the club, but he figured that he would know it when he got there. Until then he was more than content to take in Rio's warm winter air and see what the city's wee morning hours had to offer.

And he was hungry.

Crool told himself that at the first decent-looking open restaurant that he came to, he would get something to tide him over for the next few hours. He hated working on an empty stomach. True to his word, the first place he came to – even though he could not pronounce the name of it – was decent enough and open enough for his liking. Inside he went.

He would never know that, had he only walked another two hundred feet, he would have found a quaint little 24-hour café named Boteco Cabidinho. Inside he would have found a friendly atmosphere, reasonable prices, great food...and Harper Rowe and Kinley Devereaux at the genesis of their next great adventure.

ACKNOWLEDGEMENTS

I would like to thank *you*, the reader. Knowing that you take time out of your life to give me the opportunity to entertain you is truly humbling. I hope that I have held up my end of the deal by bringing you some smiles and enjoyment.

In the process of writing this book there has been a small group of people that helped me out of some jams, did me some favors, and gave me support in times of distress. I would now like to officially thank them for their support and contributions.

Thank you to Robin Browning, Nancy & Michael Sayre, Liz Wade, Regina Dowden Rickenbach, Debbie & Casey Tytlandsvik, PJ Steelman, Michael J. Hoffman, Alene Fast, and Laurie Shen.

Finally, an extraordinarily fabulous thank you to the two people to whom I owe an immeasurable amount of love and gratitude, Dr. Cyril Jenkins and the amazing Sally Anne Martin.

ABOUT THE AUTHOR

Doc Ephraim Bates is the author of the popular *Boom!!...Killers.* series.

He has been writing comedic action thrillers since age fourteen. The youngest of seven sons, Doc mastered the three skills most valuable to his assassin characters: maintaining a sense of humor, learning how to take a beating, and the art of not getting caught.

Doc makes his online home at www.docephraimbates.com.

You can connect with him on Facebook at www.facebook.com/DocEphraimBates.

If the mood strikes you, send him an email at doc@docephraimbates.com.

www.ingramcontent.com/pod-product-compliance
Lightning Source LLC
Chambersburg PA
CBHW070757120726
47910CB00001B/200